Shadow Conflict

SHADOW CONFLICT

WILL JORDAN

CANELO

First published in the United Kingdom in 2017 by Canelo

This edition published in Great Britain in 2019 by

Canelo Digital Publishing Limited
57 Shepherds Lane
Beaconsfield, Bucks HP9 2DU
United Kingdom

A CIP catalogue record for this book is available from the British Library.

Print ISBN 978 1 78863 462 5
Ebook ISBN 978 1 910859 72 8

Look for more great books at www.canelo.co

For Maureen and Wilma,
my thanks for their encouragement and support.

Prologue

Berlin, 2 April 2010

Anya coughed, pain lancing through her body with the effort. Her eyes were streaming, the smoke-filled air searing her throat with every breath. All around her was fire and ruin and destruction, the building devastated by the recent explosion.

She had to leave while there was still time.

She tried to move, but the smashed remnants of a table were pinning her down. Gripping the splintered wood, she gritted her teeth and pushed with all the strength she could summon. But as she fought to escape, a figure emerged from the drifting smoke and sparks, appearing like a demon come to claim her.

A tall, powerful figure who moved with slow, deliberate strides. His clothes were torn and darkened with dust and soot, his face bloodied by shrapnel, but his eyes were fixed on her as he approached.

'You planned all of this,' he said, his voice rasping through the smoke. 'Everything you did, every person you killed, all of it brought you here to this moment.'

Anya turned away, looking desperately around for the carry bag she had brought with her, seeking the compact UMP-45 submachine gun that was inside.

There!

It had been moved by the blast, but lay just feet away from her now, the bag partly ripped open to reveal the weapon's collapsible stock. Still trying to free herself from the wooden wreckage, she stretched out her arm towards the weapon.

Cain watched her as he approached, knowing now he had the advantage. Knowing he could take his time.

'You said you would rather die for something than live for nothing,' he said, drawing the automatic holstered inside his jacket. 'Is this what you're ready to die for, Anya?'

She was almost there. Her fingers brushed against the canvas bag, almost enough to pull it towards her, agonisingly close but infuriatingly far.

'You were right,' Cain said as she kicked frantically at the table, managing to shift it a little, gaining a few meagre inches in which to move. Straining towards the weapon. 'In the end, it did come down to the two of us.'

He raised the gun, taking aim with slow, deliberate precision. Anya's eyes turned on him then, knowing she had lost. The eyes of a hunted animal now cornered, awaiting its fate.

'It was always between us,' Cain said, staring down the sights at the woman he'd once risked his life for.

The woman he would have died for.

'The things we could have done together,' he whispered.

Part I

Repercussion

'Truly, it is in darkness that one finds the light, so when we are in sorrow, then this light is nearest of all to us.'
— Meister Eckhart

Chapter 1

Five days earlier

The cold was insidious.

Like a living, devious enemy constantly seeking new ways to overcome him. It crept into his body through every inch of bare skin that rested on the rough stone floor, or leaned against the damp, uneven brick walls. Slow at first, barely noticeable, but relentless, like a glacier inexorably grinding its way down a valley and devouring everything before it.

He'd tried to fight it for the longest time – keeping his body moving, exercising as much as possible, minimizing his contact with the ground, even trying to turn the aching grief into anger that he could use to fuel his efforts.

For a time he'd occupied himself with ideas of escape, instinctively falling back on his years of training to divert himself from his own dark thoughts. He had spent hours groping and feeling his way around every inch of his six-by-eight cell, searching for hidden crevices in the walls or floor that could yield something useful, fallen objects he might turn into weapons or tools, weaknesses around the hinges or frame of the solid wooden door that barred the only exit.

But his captors were nothing if not methodical, sweeping the floor clean of anything that might have been useful, and ensuring the walls yielded up not a single loose brick or sliver of mortar. At last, frustrated by his fruitless efforts, he'd given in to his mounting anger and hammered his fists against the door until his skin split and bled, screamed until his throat was left raw with the effort.

It changed nothing.

And always the cold was with him, and it was a patient enemy. It had all the time in the world to wear him down, and after two days and nights without sleep or food, that was exactly what it was doing.

Ryan Drake lay curled in a foetal position on the floor of his windowless cell, shivering violently, the sheer and absolute darkness concealing the cuts and bruises that marked his naked body. The chill air around him smelled of damp, mould and stale urine. He was too weary to stand up. What was the point anyway? Eventually his meagre strength would wane and he'd slump back down again.

How long he'd been here he could no longer say. With no windows there was no way of marking the passage of day and night. In any case, time had begun to lose all meaning as fatigue and malnutrition took their toll. He couldn't sleep. Sleep in conditions like these would bring death by hypothermia.

Everything had fallen apart in Pakistan two days earlier. He had gambled with the lives of his friends, staking everything on one last chance to take down Marcus Cain, the corrupt deputy director of the CIA. And he had lost, completely and utterly.

His companions were all gone now. Cole Mason, his loyal second in command, had been executed right in front of his eyes. Drake had chosen him for death, been made to choose him, hoping it would spare the life of another. He would never forget the look in Mason's eyes just before the gun went off.

Keira Frost, the fiery young technical specialist who had stood by him more times than Drake could count, was separated from him, perhaps dead herself. Another little game by his captors to hammer home how completely he had failed.

Worse was to come. Samantha McKnight, the woman he'd placed so much faith in, had been working against them all along. She had given away their plans, compromised their operation, crippled the entire scheme before it even began. That betrayal had cut particularly deep, because he'd trusted her most of all.

And as for Anya, the woman who had started it all: she too was gone. Maybe she had somehow managed to escape the disastrous battle, or maybe her enemies had finally caught up with her and ended it. Drake would likely never know.

He closed his eyes as a fresh wave of shivering rocked his depleted body, clenching his fists so hard that it hurt. Good – he wanted to feel the pain. Pain was something he could use.

The sound of footsteps in the corridor drew his thoughts back to the present. Someone was coming for him. This was the first sign of activity since he'd been brought here, and straightaway he felt his heart start to pound fast and hard, adrenaline rushing through his veins as his body reacted to the primordial instinct for fight or flight.

He had no means or desire to attempt the latter. That only left one option.

He was already resigned to the fact he wasn't getting out of here alive. What was the point in deluding himself with false hope? No, hope was something he'd abandoned in Pakistan. When you accept that you're doing to die, you can do and endure things you'd never have the courage or desperation to attempt otherwise.

That was what he needed now, as he clawed at the freezing concrete and heaved himself to his feet, sucking in gulps of air to try to get more oxygen into his bloodstream. He was naked and unarmed, but that didn't matter now. He could kill a man with his bare hands if it came down to it.

It wouldn't be the first time, and he'd rather go down fighting than spend what remained of his life in this cell. Maybe he'd even take one or two of the bastards with him.

A slow and lingering death, whether by hypothermia, starvation or torture, was his starting point. Anything up from that was an improvement.

The steps had halted outside the door. There was a sudden metallic scraping, and Drake found himself squinting into a sliver of harsh light that had appeared at eye level. After two days of darkness it was like staring into the core of the sun.

'Stand facing the rear wall with your hands on top of your head!' A loud, commanding voice echoed through the small cell. 'Do it now!'

They wouldn't open the door until he complied; Drake knew that much. Standard procedure for dealing with dangerous prisoners.

'Stand facing the rear wall now!' the voice repeated. Drake didn't recognize it as belonging to any of the men who had captured him in Pakistan, not that that meant much. Cain commanded a large pool of manpower.

Drake turned and shuffled towards the rear of the cell, limping noticeably so that they could see the poor condition he was in. A pathetic, wretched form worn down by injury and hunger, no more of a threat to them than a bent old man in the street.

'P-please, don't hurt me again,' Drake mumbled through the shivering as he stared at the wall and placed his hands on the back of his head.

'No talking! Eyes front!'

The light shining in through the viewing port at last afforded a proper look at his surroundings, and he immediately drank in as much detail as possible. Despite everything, he found himself oddly surprised that the bricks facing him were darkly coloured, almost black, and gleaming faintly with moisture. The wear around the edges and their slightly irregular shape suggested they were pre-industrial, carved by hand in an earlier era.

Wherever he was being held, it wasn't a new building, which meant it was unlikely to be a purpose-built prison. A building not originally designed to hold prisoners was inherently less secure, less easy to patrol and guard. He made sure to file that piece of information away for later. For now, he had more important matters to attend to.

He heard the gritty hiss as a rusted bolt was withdrawn from the door, and took another deep breath to psych himself up. He couldn't say what would happen in the next few seconds, but it was likely to be very fast, very violent and very painful. After two days spent shivering in the dark, he was ready for all three.

A moment later he heard the creak of old hinges as the door swung inwards, and knew the time had come.

Don't think about what might happen. Just act.

Spinning around, he turned and launched himself across the cell with every ounce of speed and aggression at his command. The close confines of his prison worked in his favour now, cutting down the distance he needed to cover. He knew he'd have a second or so of surprise on his side, but no more. They'd recover quickly, and act to stop him.

His first priority was to wedge himself between the door and the frame, preventing them from closing it. That was likely to cost him a lot of hurt, as he was quite certain they'd do everything in their power to batter and shove him backwards into the cell, but it had to be done. Men he could fight, but a locked wooden door braced with metal would bar his way for ever.

Once this was done, he would turn his attention to the guards beyond. He'd only heard one voice, but there were almost certainly more waiting. No way would a lone man enter the cell of someone like Drake without backup.

Still, the first man in the door was his priority – putting him out of action was Drake's goal. In lieu of weapons, fists, kicks and teeth would have to suffice. There was no finesse or honour in moments like this, no prizes awarded for fair play or mercy. You used every tool at your disposal, hurt or killed your enemy in any way you could.

You won, or you died. It was that simple.

Despite his weakened state, Drake was still fast off the mark. In barely a second he had almost covered the distance from the far wall to the door, and was already lowering his shoulder to ram his way through whoever happened to be standing in his path. He'd never been much of a rugby player, but he had nearly two hundred pounds of solid muscle, and knew how to utilize that weight to its fullest effect.

Any fucker unlucky enough to be caught by that impact was going down hard.

He could see them in the doorway now, silhouetted against the light filtering in from whatever room or corridor lay beyond. The door was fully open, and they were making no attempt to close it, as if they'd already realized such an effort would be futile.

Smart of them, but it made no difference. He was almost on them.

Then he saw something. A blur of movement, something short and stubby pointed at him…

Bang!

Drake's first impression was that a firework had just gone off right in his face. The muzzle flash and sudden discharge of sparks and smoke reminded him more of a stage pyrotechnic than any kind of firearm. This spectacular piece of illumination was accompanied by a dull boom that reverberated around the small room like the inside of a drum.

Then its purpose became all too obvious.

Something slammed into Drake's left shoulder like a concrete fist, jerking it backwards so hard he felt sure his arm had been wrenched from its socket, and spinning him around with the sheer power of the impact. Twisting in agony, he immediately fell backwards and collapsed, hitting the stone flagstones with bruising force.

Through a fog of pain and disorientation, Drake was vaguely aware of voices shouting at him.

'Stay down on the ground! Do not move or we *will* fire again!'

Fire again. He'd been shot – that much was obvious. But by what?

Reaching up with his good arm, he felt around the impact site, expecting to find torn flesh seeping blood. Instead his fingers brushed heavily bruised skin, and in that moment the pieces came together.

He'd been hit with a non-lethal projectile, either a rubber baton or more likely a 'beanbag round' – a shotgun shell loaded with rubber buckshot inside a high tensile bag, designed to flatten against anything it hit and spread the force of the impact. They were popular with riot police for crowd control, because they packed a comparable force to a rubber bullet but were generally less dangerous. He'd never used one himself but the effect was, as he'd discovered, akin to being punched with a giant fist, particularly when fired at close range.

That explained the pyrotechnic display as well. Such rounds employed a more primitive, less powerful form of gunpowder not dissimilar to the kind used by musketeers two centuries earlier. Big on flash and bang, small on killing power. That being said, if he'd taken the round in the face or chest rather than the meat of his shoulder, it almost certainly would have broken ribs or fractured his skull.

Which meant they didn't want to kill him. They needed him alive.

He watched as one of his captors moved into the cell, looming over him like a vast black shadow. The man was getting ready to restrain him, and temporarily blocking the shotgunner's line of sight with his sheer size. In a show of defiance, Drake twisted around, forcing aside the pain in his shoulder, and slammed a fist straight into the man's midsection, expecting to double him over so he could grab for a weapon.

He knew from experience that a good body shot to the base of the ribs could knock the wind right out of a man's lungs, incapacitating him and buying valuable seconds to do some serious damage. Such was his hope.

Instead his fist met solid, unyielding muscle, barely eliciting a grunt from his intended victim. It was like trying to punch his way through a brick wall. The man must have been a quarterback or a bodybuilder in another life, because his neck was as thick as Drake's thigh, his arms and shoulders rippling with huge corded muscles.

No way was Drake taking down a man of that size in his condition.

The answering fist, when it swung at him out of the darkness, snapped Drake's head around and came close to knocking him out altogether. With his vision blurring and his senses dulled, Drake was unable to offer further resistance as the giant jerked his hands in front of him and secured a pair of plasticuffs around his wrists.

Drake could see nothing of his opponent's face. He was wearing a black balaclava that left only his eyes exposed, but Drake could hear the rasp as the man's lungs sucked air in greedily through the fabric, and smell the coffee and tobacco on his breath.

Once bound, the giant hauled Drake out of the cell, his knees and feet dragging behind as he was too disoriented to walk properly. He saw a second man stand aside to make way for them, his shotgun no doubt loaded with more beanbag rounds in case Drake was foolish enough to try anything.

The room beyond seemed cavernous compared to the claustrophobic confines of his cell, perhaps 30 feet square, and lit by a couple of bare light bulbs crudely wired into the ceiling in opposite corners. There was no furniture, and no windows that he could see, no source of natural light. The room was clearly underground: a basement or cellar of some sort, and extremely old. The walls were made up of large, crudely hewn blocks of stone, with thick, primitive support columns running down both sides and connected by a series of vaulted archways overhead. A simple flight of stone steps set into the wall opposite led to the level above, all worn down by long centuries of use. The place reminded him of some medieval dungeon.

Coming to a stop in the middle of the room, Drake suddenly found himself hauled up from the floor, the giant picking him up as easily as a child would lift a doll. His arms were raised above him, and suddenly the support was withdrawn, gravity pulling him downwards until he was jerked to an agonising stop.

Grimacing in pain, he looked up to see his plasticuffs looped into a metal hook protruding from the ceiling. It looked like the kind of thing one might string carcasses from in a slaughterhouse, and with his feet dangling at least 12 inches off the floor, Drake was suddenly very aware of how vulnerable he now was. The cuffs dug painfully into his wrists, warm blood trickling down his forearms.

Another injury to add to the list.

'That was brave, Ryan. Not very smart, but brave all the same,' a voice said from the top of the stairs. 'Then again, I guess that pretty much sums you up.'

Drake watched as a new figure descended the stairs in a careful, unhurried fashion, taking the worn and uneven steps with caution. It was a man Drake knew all too well.

Tall and broad-shouldered, well dressed in suit trousers, expensive-looking shoes and a dark woollen overcoat, Marcus Cain looked little different from the first time Drake had met him in a plush briefing room at Langley three years ago. His neatly combed hair was greying a little more at the temples now, but his face still possessed the same chiselled, movie-star good looks. His pale blue eyes were bright and alert behind a slender-framed pair of glasses, and they were regarding Drake now with a look that might have been pity.

Marcus Cain: the man Drake had travelled halfway around the world to confront in Pakistan, and risked everything to defeat. The man who had cost him everything he held dear.

'You fucking—' Drake snarled, struggling against his cuffs. The sharp plastic bit deeper into his wrists, straining joints and sinew.

'Do yourself a favour and quit whatever you're thinking,' Cain advised, indicating the two armed men flanking him. Both now had shotguns trained on Drake, a plainly needless precaution since he had no means of unhooking himself. 'I'm sure a man in your position can appreciate there are worse places to get shot than the shoulder.'

It didn't take a genius to see what he had in mind. Drake was suddenly very conscious of the fact that he was hanging naked and exposed, but resisted the impulse to try to cover himself up. He wouldn't give the bastard the satisfaction.

'That's better,' Cain said, taking Drake's inaction for acceptance. 'I'd hate to think I came all this way for nothing.'

Drake wanted to tackle him to the ground, tear those expensive clothes apart, pound that movie-star face into bloody pulp and shattered bone. But even in the red mist of his hatred, he knew he couldn't come close to laying a finger on the deputy director of the CIA. Even if he could somehow find the strength to unlatch his cuffs from the meat hook, Cain's bodyguards could put half a dozen more rounds into him before he made it two paces.

'Wouldn't want to disappoint you, Marcus,' he spat instead. 'Come to gloat, you piece of shit?'

He saw a flicker of a smile. 'Actually, I'm here for two reasons. First, I wanted to commend you on that job in Pakistan. Not many guys would have had the balls to try something like that, and even fewer could have pulled it off. You came close, Ryan. Closer than most others ever have. You deserve respect for that at least.'

'And you deserve a hollow-point round in the back of the head,' Drake fired back at him. 'But I suppose we don't always get what we deserve, do we?'

Cain shook his head, looking almost regretful as he surveyed the starving, defeated man hanging before him. 'What a waste. So much time and energy spent fighting for a lost cause, and where did it get you?' he asked quietly. 'You could have done something meaningful with your life.'

'Like work for you?' Drake snorted. 'I've seen how that plays out. Keep your enemies close, right?'

'You were never my enemy, Ryan,' Cain said then, and Drake had a hard time deciding whether he was telling the truth or not. 'At worst you were an irritating distraction, at best you were a useful asset. More useful than you could imagine.'

Drake frowned. Had such words come from another man, he would have taken them for hyperbole, but not from Cain.

'Useful for what?' he asked, unable to help himself. Fuck it, if he was going to die here anyway, he at least deserved some answers first.

Removing his glasses, Cain reached into his breast pocket for a cloth, then set about carefully wiping the lenses.

'I'd imagine you've had a lot of time lately to reflect on your situation, and ask yourself a few questions. Like if I had Samantha spying on you all this time, why didn't I move against you sooner? Why let you get so close when there was no need?'

Drake said nothing. In truth, he had asked himself that same question, and many more, alone in the cold and darkness with only his thoughts for company.

'You were bait, Ryan,' Cain went on, his tone that of a sharp-tempered teacher dealing with a particularly dim student. 'Anya was the real prize, and you were my link to her. You were her only real weakness.'

Drake couldn't have been sure, but he thought he detected an under-current of resentment in the older man's voice. Cain was looking at Drake self-reflectively, trying to work out what separated the two of them, why Anya was drawn to one and repelled by the other.

'She had her uses too, of course,' Cain went on. 'She always did. The trick was to make her believe she was acting of her own free will. Do that, and you can make her do almost anything, kill almost anyone. And I had a lot of people that needed killing.'

Drake's mind flashed through the events of the past few years, firstly to Afghanistan, where he and his team had become embroiled in a dirty war fought by a rogue private military contractor, headed by a retired army colonel named Carpenter. Anya had made sure Carpenter paid for his crimes, old and new, with his life.

Months later, in Russia, she had infiltrated a terrorist group to get her hands on the corrupt head of the Russian Federal Security Bureau, who had once done everything in his power to destroy her. Again, her vengeance had been long in the making, but swift and merciless in its execution.

Cain had done nothing to interfere in either case.

'So you used Anya to kill off a few of your rivals,' Drake scoffed, refusing to see his actions as anything but the work of a manipulative coward who let others fight his battles for him. 'That makes you no better than them.'

That seemed to amuse Cain. 'Not exactly – they're dead and I'm alive. That makes us quite different. But for what it's worth, they deserved it. They got what was coming to them.'

Drake looked right at him. 'And you? What have you got coming to you, Marcus?'

The deputy director didn't answer that. Instead, having finished cleaning his glasses, he placed them back on the bridge of his nose and carefully folded the handkerchief back into his pocket.

'I told you I came here for two reasons,' he continued. 'The first, like I said, was to pay my respects.'

'And the second?'

'I'm here to offer you a deal. It's the only one you're going to get and it's a one-time offer, so I suggest you think carefully before deciding. More than just your life depends on it,' he warned. 'Give me Anya, or at least solid intel that leads me to her, and I let you and Frost go free. No conditions, no strings attached. I'll never come after you, your family or any of your friends again for as long as you live, provided you don't come after me. You can have whatever you need to start a new life. Passports, new identities, even money. Enough to live comfortably for the rest of your days.'

Drake barely managed to hide the sudden spark of hope that Cain's words had inadvertently kindled in him. Not only was his teammate Frost still alive, but so was Anya. Somehow she must have escaped the ambush in Pakistan and evaded her pursuers, which meant she remained a threat. Whatever victory Cain might have won that night, the ultimate prize had eluded him.

'One way or another your war's over, Ryan,' Cain finished. 'The only question is how you want it to end – as a free man with the rest of his life to live, or... in this place.'

'How do I know you'll keep your word?' he asked.

'Like I said, you were never my enemy. I don't blame you for the things you've done; you're just the wrong guy in the wrong place, caught up in something he doesn't understand. You're compelled to protect the people close to you, and I respect that. But take a moment to consider where it's gotten you.' He glanced around, taking in the dimly lit underground space. 'This doesn't have to be how it ends. You can still have a life, go home and put all of this behind you. All you have to do is help me.'

He could have been telling the truth, Drake knew. For a brief moment he found himself considering Cain's offer, taken in by his softly persuasive voice. He thought of himself and Frost far away from this dark and terrible place, standing in the sunlight once more. He thought of his sister Jessica no longer living with the looming threat of abduction that had haunted her for the past three years. He thought of a life free from fear and danger.

It could all be his. But it all came at a terrible price.

'And in return, Anya dies.'

Cain's expression darkened, but he didn't look away. 'I'm not a monster, despite what she might have told you. I don't want to hurt Anya. I want to help her.'

Drake couldn't help it. He started laughing then. The harsh, bitter laugh of a man with nothing left. In light of all the things he'd done, all the lives he'd sacrificed and destroyed, such a claim could only be met with derision.

'Help her?' he repeated. 'You destroyed her, and even now you still can't see it.'

'Don't presume to lecture me about things you couldn't possibly understand. We were changing the world while you were still in goddamn high school,' Cain snapped, his voice betraying real anger for the first time. He shook his head, taking a breath to calm himself. 'Anya was different back then. We both were. We were going to do incredible things together, before she was taken away from me.'

Drake knew what Cain was referring to. Anya, serving as a young CIA operative in Afghanistan two decades ago, had been caught in an ambush and captured by the Soviets. She'd never said much about the imprisonment and torture that had followed, but her scars told their own story. The ordeal had been a defining moment in her life.

Judging by the haunted look in his eyes, Cain was reflecting on the same thing, though from a very different perspective. He'd lived through it and Drake hadn't. Worse, he'd seen its terrible aftermath.

'When I finally got a call from a hospital in Pakistan saying she'd been found, I thought all my prayers had been answered. Somehow she'd come back, back from the dead,' he went on. 'I couldn't get out there fast enough. I even tried to kid myself that things could go back to the way they were, but I was wrong.'

He sighed the weary sigh of a man old beyond his years, beaten down by too many compromises and disappointments and failures.

'After a while, I began to realize that Anya never really came back. The woman I found in that hospital was something else. She was broken, deep inside, and I couldn't fix her.'

He blinked, then seemed to come back to himself, and looked at Drake again.

'I can't rewrite history, Drake. I can't change the things that were done, or the mistakes that were made. All I can do is try to make amends for them, and that starts with finding her. I want Anya in a safe place – a place she can't hurt herself or anyone else, and where no one can hurt her. Because if there's even a chance that a piece of the Anya I knew is still in there, I have to try to bring it back. Maybe then she can find some kind of peace. Maybe we both can.'

Whatever Drake's thoughts on Marcus Cain, the sheer force of conviction in his voice was undeniable. For perhaps the first time, Drake perceived him not as a distant and menacing figure of authority, not as a master manipulator, but simply as a man. A man looking back on a life of regrets, desperate to undo some of the wrongs he'd inflicted while there was still time.

A man looking for redemption.

But not everyone seeking redemption deserved it.

'I can't help you,' Drake said at last. 'I *won't* help you.'

Cain stared back at him, saying nothing.

'You had your chance to help Anya 20 years ago,' he went on, relishing the old pain and guilt his words evoked as every ounce of his hatred and disgust for this man came pouring forth in a final, bitter act of defiance. 'She told me everything, Marcus. She told me you knew where she was being held, what they were doing to her. She told me how she stayed strong, how she kept telling herself you would come for her, but you never did. You could have gotten her out, but you chose to stand back and do nothing. You showed her exactly what kind of man you were. You're a cowardly, selfish piece of shit, and everything that's happening now is your fault. If Anya's a monster, then you created her, and you deserve everything that's coming to you. I'll never help you.'

Cain backed away a pace then, staring at Drake with disappointment and resignation, as if this were an argument he'd been through many times before and no longer had the energy to engage in.

He made a faint gesture, a slight nod of the head, as if acknowledging that his errand had failed. A harder road lay ahead for both men. Harder, and far more unpleasant for one of them.

'It's your call, Ryan. I'd hoped you would see things differently now.' He turned away, heading for the stairs leading to the building's upper level, but paused at the bottom step, regarding Drake with the same mixture of pity and disdain as before. 'For what it's worth, *when* I find Anya, I'll tell her you refused to give her up.'

As Cain ascended the stairs, returning to the world of light above, one of the guards moved forward and lifted Drake down from the hook, hauling him back to the darkness of his cell.

Chapter 2

Krakow, Poland

Anya was running out of time.

Every hour that passed increased the chance that Drake and his team would be killed or compromised, yet she knew she had to play her hand carefully. The man whose help she needed owed her nothing, and in fact had lost a great deal by assisting her previously. He might well choose to stay out of this fight, and she wouldn't blame him if he did.

Emerging from the basement club where she'd finally tracked him down, into the chill night air of early spring, Anya had to admit that he'd chosen his new home well. One of the best-preserved medieval cities in eastern Europe, Krakow had emerged relatively unscathed from the Second World War, its splendid Renaissance and Baroque architecture spared the destructive air and artillery bombing that had laid waste to much of eastern Europe.

Even the five decades of Communist rule that had followed had done little to diminish its beauty, and with the fall of the Iron Curtain, the city had wisely turned its eyes westwards. Property and goods were cheap here, and foreign investment welcome.

All of these factors had combined to make Krakow one of the most popular cities in Europe for tourists, with hundreds of thousands of them flocking there every year. An easy place for an outsider to blend in amongst the mass of Americans, Germans, Russians, and most of all, Brits.

They seemed to be everywhere, mostly groups of young men in their early twenties, and almost universally intoxicated. It wasn't surprising given the late hour and the number of bars and nightclubs in the area, waiting to soak up foreign beer money, but even Anya was surprised by their prevalence.

She watched in distaste as one young man with bleached blonde hair calmly staggered out of a nearby bar, doubled over and loudly emptied the contents of his stomach into the doorway of an apartment block, much to the amusement of his fellow drinkers. This done, he wiped his mouth with the garish football shirt he was wearing and followed his companions in search of more drink, laughing and chanting a song she wasn't familiar with.

'What's the matter? Never seen a stag do before?' Alex Yates asked, noticing that she'd stopped to watch the unruly spectacle.

Anya looked at him. 'A stag what?'

He made a dismissive gesture. 'Never mind. Follow me.'

'How far is it?' she asked, eager to get down to business. She hadn't travelled 6,000 miles to go on a night tour of the city.

'Not far,' he promised.

Crossing a modern road bridge that spanned the Vistula river, beneath the floodlit walls of Wawel castle, they soon found themselves in the network of narrow side streets that made up the city's old town. Alex guided her with speed and confidence, never stopping to check his location or direction.

Doubtless he knew this area better than she, and Anya was content to let him lead. She did, however, notice that he wasn't following a direct route, instead cutting left and right seemingly at random, and at one point almost doubling back on himself.

The part of Anya's mind devoted to tradecraft and situational aware-ness recognized this basic anti-surveillance routine straightaway, having employed it countless times herself. She was however surprised that an untrained civilian like Alex should be so inclined.

'Relax, Alex,' she advised. When it came to potential tails, he was in safe hands as long as she was around. 'No one is going to find you.'

'You did,' he pointed out with an edge of irritation.

She decided to let that one slide. In fairness, she couldn't blame him for being nervous. When she'd caught up with him at an underground gambling den a short while earlier, he'd just fleeced nearly a thousand euros from a Russian thug at a game of poker. If the man's body language had been anything to go by, he wasn't the sort to let such a humiliation stand.

The street soon opened out onto a much larger square, ringed by more bars and restaurants, and dominated on its western side by a massive clock tower. Groups of tourists were pausing to take selfies in the city's central square as they passed. Anya instinctively turned her face away from the camera phones, cursing the march of technology that had given virtually every civilian an easy means of capturing her image.

Approaching a small but busy café-bar just off the main square, Alex seemed to have found what he was looking for. He led her inside, found a free table near the back and dumped his coat over a chair.

'Have a seat,' he said, gesturing to the chair opposite. He'd already made himself comfortable, and had caught the eye of one of the waitresses.

Anya frowned. 'You said we were going to your apartment.'

'No, I said we'd go somewhere we could talk,' Alex corrected her. 'Trust me, I've got a pretty good memory for these things. We can talk here. It's busy, so no one's going to overhear us. Our table has a good field of view, so no one can come in without being seen, and there's a back door that leads to an alleyway if we need to bail in a hurry.'

Anya's look of surprise must have been obvious even to him. 'I've been reading a lot of spy fiction lately,' he said by way of explanation. 'And frankly,

I'd rather you didn't know where I live. So take a seat and have a drink with me.'

Anya compared the man before her to the weak, indecisive and down-trodden individual she'd parted company with nearly a year ago. He was different now, more confident, tougher. She supposed anyone would have been altered by what he'd been through, seeing his life fall down around him, becoming a wanted criminal. She knew it was largely her own actions that had wrought this change.

He was smirking at her, perhaps enjoying the slight but perceptible shift in the dynamics of their relationship. She'd come here in search of his help, and it was within his power to refuse her. For now at least, he could call the shots.

'Fine,' she said unhappily, slipping into the chair opposite and reposi-tioning it slightly to afford her a better view of the bar. She'd been doing her best to watch for possible tails on the way here and found nothing suspicious, though the throngs of tourists and late-night revellers made it impossible to watch everyone.

It was one of the reasons Anya had always found busy cities unnerving.

'You told me I should look you up if I ever needed help,' she began, struggling for the right words. She was used to people trying to pry infor-mation out of her, not the other way around. 'Here I am.'

Alex cocked an eyebrow. 'That's it? That's all I get?'

'What would you like?'

'I don't know. What about, "How have you been doing for the past year, Alex?" Or maybe, "Sorry for fucking up your life and cutting you loose once you did my dirty work?" You know, something along those lines. Surprise me, get creative.'

Anya had sensed something like this was coming, but it didn't make it any easier to listen to. 'Nobody is proud of what happened to you, Alex. But I can't spend my life dwelling on it. Neither should you,' she added with a meaningful look.

Alex met her gaze evenly, as if to test himself against her. The young man she'd first met would have backed down at a moment like this, but not now. For a moment, the tension between them seemed to hang heavy in the air.

At this moment however, the pretty young waitress working the tables caught sight of them, and wove her way skilfully through the bar to take their order.

Normally Anya might have been irritated by such an interruption, but this time she welcomed it. Alex, speaking fluent Polish that surpassed Anya's grasp of the language, greeted her and ordered a bottle of Żywiec beer.

Not for the first time, she caught herself envying the photographic memory of her younger companion. She could commit important infor-mation to memory, and had learned to speak a number of languages in the course of her long career, but it required great effort and mental discipline. For Alex, it simply happened. And it was a talent he'd clearly put to good use in his new life.

The waitress returned shortly with a beer for Alex and a mineral water for Anya. She was here to talk, not to get drunk. Alex, however, didn't look impressed with her choice.

'Least you can do is humour me with a proper drink,' he said, tipping his beer back and downing half the bottle in one gulp.

Anya gave him a look of disapproval. 'Would you like to hear me out, or are you planning on starting your own... "stag do" tonight?'

This prompted a snort of amusement. 'Not unless you make me a proposal. Anyway, I've got a feeling I'm not going to like what you're about to ask.' Sensing his humour had fallen on an unappreciative audience, he put down his beer and leaned forward. 'All right, Anya. Say what you came here to say.'

'I need your help finding someone. This person has been carefully hidden and protected, and my usual contacts won't be enough to get the job done. But as we both know, you have certain... skills that could be useful.'

Alex was, or had been, a gifted computer hacker when she first met him. His years of coding experience had enabled him to hack into the CIA's secure network and steal a highly classified file known as the Black List for her. The endeavour had nearly cost both their lives, but his abilities were undeniable.

'Aw, now I feel like Liam Neeson, only younger and better looking,' he remarked sarcastically. 'So you want me to run a digital trace on this mystery person. Why? What are you caught up in this time?'

Anya took a sip of her water. 'Better that you don't know.'

'No, I think it's better that I do,' he countered. 'I got into that whole Black List bollocks last year without even knowing what I was dealing with, or why people were trying to kill me. Yourself included. No, this time I want to know what's at stake, then I'll decide if I want to help you.'

Anya was silent for a few moments, weighing up how much to tell him. It went against her nature to give out information that wasn't necessary to an operation, but she was beginning to understand that such an approach didn't exactly foster a sense of trust or loyalty in others. Alex's ultimatum was proof of that, and forcing his cooperation would take more time than she had.

'It's about Marcus Cain,' she said at length.

That was enough to darken Alex's mood. 'The guy who sent all those black ops arseholes to kill us in Istanbul?'

She nodded. 'Myself and a few others staged an operation to take him out in Pakistan. It did not work as we'd hoped.'

She shifted position, her jaw clenched tight. A stray round had slammed into the left side of her chest, partially penetrating her body armour and cracking two ribs. Painkillers had kept it under control for the past couple of days, but it was clear she needed time to heal up.

'The rest of my group were taken prisoner,' she went on. 'Only I made it out.'

The pieces seemed to come together in Alex's mind then. 'So you want me to find your missing friends?'

Anya shook her head. 'No. They will be completely off the grid. And even if you could find them, he will have them well guarded. Cain will take no chances this time. I would not be able to get to them alone.'

He frowned, confused. 'So who *do* you want me to find?'

So Anya told him. She told him everything she knew about her target, why they were so important, and what she was planning to do once she got her hands on them.

Although he wasn't normally lost for words, Alex remained silent once she'd finished. She watched as he raised the beer to his lips and drained the remainder of the bottle, putting it down carefully on the table. Spotting his empty drink, the waitress came over to ask if he wanted another, but he waved her off.

'Jesus,' he said at last. 'I mean, going after Cain I can understand. But this—'

'This is the world we live in, Alex,' Anya cut in, pain and urgency undermining her patience. Every minute that passed increased the chance of Drake or one of the others breaking. 'He would do the same if the situation were reversed.'

'What does that say about the two of you?'

Anya could feel her throat tightening, not just because of what he'd said, but the way he looked at her. It was as if she had diminished in his estimation somehow, as if she had exposed an aspect of her life she would rather he hadn't seen. But there it was.

As she'd said, that was the world they lived in.

'I am not proud of this,' she assured him.

'So you keep saying.'

'But lives are at stake, and I am running out of options,' she pressed. 'Good people risked their lives to help me.'

'Lot of that going around.'

She ignored his biting remark with difficulty, just as she ignored the pain in her ribs. 'And they *will* die if we don't do something.'

'Hate to say this, but what makes you think they're not dead already?'

Alex jumped as Anya slammed her fist down on the table hard enough to rattle the empty bottle, pain and mounting frustration finally getting the better of her. The chatter seemed to die down then, several customers casting curious or anxious glances their way as they waited to see what would happen next.

Anya said nothing. She was prepared to endure a frosty reception if it meant recruiting his help, but there were lines even she wasn't willing to cross.

'No offence intended,' he mumbled, realizing he'd gone too far.

As it became obvious that a raging argument wasn't about to flare up, the conversation in the bar began to pick up again and Anya felt secure enough to speak.

'Cain will keep them alive for now, because he thinks they can lead him to me,' she explained, fervently hoping it was true. 'But if their lives mean nothing to you, think of this as a chance to take down the man who made you a wanted fugitive.'

'Well, technically *you* did that.'

Anya sighed, sensing any potential justification she tried to give him would be similarly rebuffed. 'I can't do this without you, Alex,' she said, deciding simply to be honest with him. She leaned closer, finally allowing herself to show some of the guilt and fear that had wracked her since leaving Pakistan. 'I'm asking for your help, because there is no one else I can turn to. Please.'

Alex looked down, saying nothing, but she could sense her words had struck a chord. The only question was whether it was enough to change his mind.

When he looked up again, his expression was difficult to read, even for Anya, and she felt herself tense up.

'All right,' he conceded. 'I'll need as much information as you've got on her.'

That wouldn't take long, Anya thought. Most of her information was at least 15 years old; the rest would have to come from conjecture and assumption.

'You will have it.'

'And a guarantee we won't hurt her.'

That wasn't so easy given what they were about to attempt. 'I promise I have no intention of harming her,' she said, formulating a compromise of sorts.

It was enough. Nodding, Alex rose from his chair and grabbed his coat. 'Well then, we'd better get started. I'm guessing you'd rather not wait until morning.' He gave her a wry smile. 'Looks like you *will* get to see my apartment after all, but only if you promise not to fuck the place up.'

Somehow Anya doubted that would be the honour he was making it out to be. Still, at least he'd agreed to help her.

She stood up, letting out a sharp breath as her ribs protested. Alex spotted it, and took a step towards her. 'You all right?'

'I'm fine,' she replied, shaking her head. 'Come on, let's get to work.'

Finding Marcus Cain's daughter was going to be difficult enough, abducting and taking her hostage even more so. And as for trading her life in exchange for Drake and the others... well, that was a bridge she would cross once she got to it.

For now, they had a starting point. That was enough.

Chapter 3

Drake was dying. He knew the symptoms of hypothermia well enough, and in some part of his groggy mind he was aware that they were taking hold. Sluggish movements, slowed heart rate and respiration, impaired concentration. If it hadn't been pitch black in his cell, he imagined his vision would be growing hazy as he slowly lost consciousness.

Physical sensations were fading away, replaced by a dreamlike state where memories and thoughts intermingled with the world around him, taunting him with images of battles already lost and companions already dead.

One moment he was here in this freezing cell, the next he was storming into a conference room in a Pakistani safe house, expecting to catch his most dangerous enemy unawares, but instead finding himself fighting for his life. In another flash, he saw himself speeding away from the scene, injured and furious at his failure, then there was an explosion of noise and sickening weightlessness, and the vision faded as darkness encroached on him.

Drake's eyes were growing heavy as his exhausted body pleaded with him for sleep. He could almost feel himself surrendering to it, his mind relinquishing the iron grip it had retained on his consciousness these past couple of days.

Accepting the inevitable.

Another vision came to him then. He was strapped to a chair in some dingy basement, surrounded by armed enemies, forced to choose between his two friends tied up in front of him. Choose one, or they both die. He saw the pistol being raised, saw the look of acceptance in Mason's eyes, and jumped violently at the harsh crack of a gunshot.

Drake snapped as shock and grief exploded from his lungs, his mind returning to itself at least temporarily as the terrible vision lingered.

But it wasn't a gunshot that he'd heard. It was the clang of his cell door being unbolted.

Harsh light flooded in from the room beyond, blinding him. Too weak to resist, Drake could do nothing but watch as the giant's enormous silhouette bent over him, grasping the plasticuffs that still secured his wrists, and hauling him to his feet. At least, he would have been on his feet if he had been capable of walking.

Instead he was dragged through to the main room, his body as limp as a rag doll. As his vision slowly returned he saw the meat hook suspended from the ceiling again, and braced himself for the inevitable wave of pain as he was hoisted up onto it. It didn't hurt as much this time, perhaps because hypothermia had reduced the blood flow to his extremities, numbing them to the damage.

At least it had some advantages, then.

Trying to focus what remained of his senses, Drake looked around. There wasn't much to see: the same illumination coming from a couple of bare bulbs wired into the ceiling, the same rough paved floor and dark brick walls. The only new addition was the sturdy wooden table placed near the centre of the room, directly in front of him. About six feet in length and three in width, it looked like the kind of rustic, hard-wearing kitchen table one might find in a farmhouse.

He almost expected to find drills, saws and other torture implements laid out to give him a good look at what was in store, but to Drake's surprise the table was entirely bare. Still, he knew it had been placed there for a reason, and he had a feeling he'd find out what it was soon enough.

'Well, well,' a familiar voice spoke from somewhere behind him. 'How's it hanging, Ryan?'

Drake watched as its owner sauntered into view. Tall and powerfully built, he cut an imposing figure that was down to more than just physical size. There was a presence, a confidence in his movements, an unhurried ease that spoke of a man used to doing whatever he wants, in whatever way he sees fit.

His face, rugged and strong-featured, might have been called handsome but for the long snaking scar that bisected the left side, running from the jawline to just above the eye, and leaving his mouth permanently contorted into a faintly sneering smile. The effect was to render an already intimidating visage truly frightening.

The smile broadened as he regarded Drake. 'Sorry. Just couldn't help myself. I mean, how often does a man find himself in a situation like this?'

Quite often, if Drake's memory of Jason Hawkins served. Torture and interrogation might have been a necessary evil for some people in their profession, but for Hawkins it was something else: a chance to indulge his baser appetites and apply some of his terrible creativity to the infliction of pain. It was something he took great pleasure in.

Hawkins took a sip from the cup of coffee he was carrying. Drake could see the steam rising from the cup, curling into tantalising wisps. He could only imagine what it would be like to gulp down that hot liquid, or to be clothed in the heavy jacket and woollen jumper that Hawkins was wearing.

'I've got to admit, buddy, you're not looking too good,' he decided after surveying Drake's battered body. He leaned in closer, lowering his voice conspiratorially. 'Between you and me, I don't think the accommodation here is up to much. The guys here haven't been looking after you too well, have they? It's cool, man, you can tell me.'

Drake could hear a few sniggers from behind, but said nothing. He refused to give Hawkins the satisfaction.

'Oh, I get it,' Hawkins went on. 'You're still steamed up about what happened in Pakistan, right? Look, I don't blame you. It was a tough day for everybody, but I think we should both try to move past it. I mean, is it really worth jeopardising a friendship over something like that?' Soulless blue eyes stared at Drake, probing and searching for a reaction. 'And in the spirit of friendship, I thought we'd have ourselves a little reunion.'

The sudden thump of footsteps on the stairs announced the arrival of another of Hawkins' men: a stocky man with a shaved head and long, bushy beard that was turning to grey around the chin. He was hauling a bound and hooded figure beside him. Drake could feel his heart beating faster at the sight of the torn and bloodied clothes, the short stature and petite frame, and felt his empty stomach churn at the stream of curses and threats pouring out from beneath the hood.

'You fucking prick!' a muffled female voice yelled. 'Take your goddamn hands off me, you piece of shit! Too fucking scared to fight a woman, huh?'

A booted foot shot out, catching her captor hard across the shin. Far from taking him down, however, the stinging blow only raised his ire.

As the operative yanked and fought with her, Hawkins turned to Drake and grinned in amusement. 'Got a mouth on her, that one,' he observed. 'Kinda makes you wonder what else she can do with it, huh?'

'This is between us,' Drake said then, his voice rasping through a parched throat that hadn't seen water in days. 'Leave her out of it.'

Hawkins' sneer was still there, but his eyes told a different story. 'Relax, Ryan. Jesus, you're so uptight these days,' the older man chided. 'We're just going to have ourselves a little talk. What happens after that… Well, that's up to you.'

Finally manhandling the diminutive young woman into the middle of the room, the operative whipped her hood off to reveal a tangle of short dark hair and a bruised, cut and furious face.

Keira Frost possessed perhaps the fiercest temper and the foulest mouth Drake had ever encountered in the military or CIA – a combination that had immediately endeared her to him. Standing only a couple of inches over five feet and weighing barely a hundred pounds, she was hardly a dominant physical presence, but she made up for her lack of stature with grit, determination and unbridled physical aggression.

As soon as she caught Drake's eye, however, that aggression melted away, replaced by fear, concern and, worst of all, pity.

'Ryan,' she gasped.

'Good of you to join us, Keira,' Hawkins said, seemingly enjoying the look on her face. 'Ryan and I were just catching up on old times. Weren't we, Ryan?'

In that instant, hearing Hawkins' voice, the shock and compassion vanished from her and she launched herself straight at him. Armed with nothing but her bare hands, she was willing to take anything, endure any injury or torment to get at the man who had killed her friend right in front of her.

But it wasn't to be. For all her frenzied rage, Keira couldn't break the hold of her far larger and stronger captor. A kick to the back of the leg dropped her to her knees, and a painful armlock applied with little restraint was enough to elicit a groan of pain.

'Well, I can tell you're going to be the life and soul of this party,' Hawkins remarked, both impressed and amused by her attempt to attack him. 'And thank God, because Ryan's not exactly setting the room alight just now.'

'Want me to break her arm, boss?' the bearded operative asked, clearly eager to hear an affirmative after the abuse he'd taken from her.

Hawkins fixed him with a sharp look that suggested his presence was wanted here, but his opinions were not. 'We're not savages, Hoffmann. Let's not act like it.'

'Cut him down from there, you sick fuck,' Frost demanded, struggling vainly against her captor's hold. 'Can't you see he's freezing to death?'

Hawkins shrugged, apparently unconcerned with the possibility that another prisoner might die under his charge. 'Ryan's a tough guy. In fact, between you and me, he used to scare the shit out of me.'

Frost looked from Hawkins to Drake. 'What the fuck are you talking about?'

'You mean he never told you?' Hawkins glanced over at Drake, feigning shock. 'Seriously, man? You never told her how far you and I go back?'

Drake said nothing. He didn't trust himself to speak.

'Ryan, I am hurt and offended by that, my friend. Guess I'll just have to fill her in myself.' Sighing as if resigning himself to a difficult task, Hawkins hunkered down so that he was at eye level with the young woman. 'How long have you known Ryan? Four, five years? Bet he's a nice guy to work for, huh? Fair, decent, always doing the right thing. Boring as shit.'

Frost looked from Hawkins to Drake, trying to work out what was coming.

'But he wasn't always like that,' Hawkins went on. 'Old Ryan used to be a stone-cold killer. We were in the same unit in Afghanistan. Kind of a... special group of like-minded individuals, doing jobs other soldiers would find... difficult to live with. But not us. They gave us everything we needed, turned us loose, and we made all their dreams come true. Afghanistan was our canvas, and we painted masterpieces all over it. Of course, we only worked in red.' He grinned in amusement, then rose and walked towards Drake. 'And Ryan was one of my best artists. You know why? It's not skill or experience, it's *passion* that makes the difference. Ryan loved what he did. Watching him at work… well, it was a thing of beauty. You should have seen him in his prime. *Then* you'd know him like I do.'

'I *do* know him, asshole,' Frost hissed through gritted teeth. 'Ryan's a good man. I don't give a shit what he did before. Doesn't change who he is now.'

'Really? Because I'm wondering just who, exactly, Ryan Drake is right now,' Hawkins said. 'From what I've seen over the past few days, he's a guy willing to pass up the chance to kill Osama bin fucking Laden himself, just to settle a personal score. He's a guy willing to endanger innocent civilians who get in his way. He's also a guy willing to trade one friend's life over another. Is that who Ryan Drake is to you, Keira?'

'Fuck you,' she replied. 'You put him in that position.'

Drake was focussed less on their argument than on the memories Hawkins' accusation had stirred up. For a long time now, he had sensed there were two people within him, locked in an eternal battle for dominance. One was the man his friends and comrades had come to know over the past few years, a man who was compassionate, logical, understanding and loyal.

Then there was the other side of him. The Ryan Drake who had been created and unleashed in Afghanistan. A man who was violent and sadistic and filled with animalistic rage, driven by a lust for killing, who revelled in death and destruction.

A man Hawkins had instantly felt a kinship with.

Even since then, that darker side of Drake had lain dormant – a monster hiding in the shadows waiting for its chance to rise again. But over the past couple of years, it had begun to reassert itself at times of great danger and desperation, clouding his behaviour and darkening his thoughts. Drake had had to work harder and harder to force the monster back into the shadows. But this time every ounce of that monster's hatred, rage and malice was directed at Hawkins.

Hawkins saw it too, and his smile was triumphant. 'There he is,' he said quietly, looking like a man reunited with a long-lost friend. 'There's the Ryan I used to know. So he's still in there after all.'

'Don't listen to this fucking asshole, Ryan,' Frost implored, wincing as her captor increased the pressure on her arm. 'He doesn't know you, and he doesn't control you.'

'You know, it's a shame we had to part ways like we did,' Hawkins went on, ignoring her pleas. 'I always thought the best was still to come. It's a pity Operation Hydra had to fuck everything up.'

Drake felt his stomach twist at the name. Hydra – the operation that had changed everything. A disaster that had caused him to be court-martialled in secret and ejected from the military with the threat of dire repercussions if he so much as spoke of it to anyone.

Once again, he was assailed by the same horror he'd experienced that day. A blur of confused and disjointed images appeared in his mind. Smoke and fire, charred bodies and the cries of his dying comrades. Silent figures stalking through the black haze with drawn weapons, while the sun shone like blood. Drake fleeing the scene, and gunfire ringing out behind him.

'Because I stopped being one of your killers that day?' Drake rasped, his look of utter hatred making up for the weakness of his voice. 'Or because I didn't turn into *you*? I wonder which one hurts the most.'

Hawkins' smile turned into a chuckle of amusement. 'That really how you remember it?' he asked, looking genuinely interested. 'Maybe you ought to think about it some more, Ryan. Go ahead, see how much you can really remember about that day.'

Drake frowned, trying to focus his thoughts, to gather the images and scenes into a coherent narrative. Drake was running, stinging smoke and heat rasping his throat. The sun casting a crimson glow on everything. Silent, faceless men with drawn weapons.

A blood-red sun, growing stronger and darker. Becoming black, absorbing everything, until the world was swallowed up around him.

Screams in the darkness.

Drake came back to himself with a gasp, trembling visibly, a sheen of sweat coating his brow.

Hawkins stood watching him. 'Didn't work, did it? Let me guess, the black sun?' he taunted. 'They're nothing if not consistent.'

'What... what did they do to me?' Drake whispered, shocked by the feelings stirred up by his attempt to remember. He felt physically sick and utterly terrified. It was the kind of primal, irrational terror that visited children in nightmares.

'Insurance,' Hawkins said by way of explanation. 'Can't have you going out into the world knowing what you knew. Even if you promised not to talk, there was always a chance you'd change your mind. And they don't deal in chances. To be honest, I'm surprised they didn't just kill you.' He shrugged. 'Must be what happens when you have friends in high places.'

'Who are *they*?' he asked.

Hawkins held Drake's eye. 'Who do you think? Same people you pissed off in Libya.'

Another piece of the puzzle fell into place. 'The Circle,' Drake said slowly.

The Circle. The shadowy organization of shifting allegiances, unknown motives and virtually unlimited resources that Drake and his team had encountered in Libya almost a year prior. Men with the power and influence to start wars, topple governments, cripple economies and snuff out individual lives like they were nothing.

He couldn't believe what he was hearing. The men who were now Drake's enemies had once been his employers.

'Are you really that surprised? They've been running the show since before you were born, Ryan, and they'll be around long after you're gone. Anyway, they're not your concern any more,' he said, backing away. 'Right now, I want to talk about something a little closer to home. Well, actually some*one*.'

Drake could already guess who he was referring to. Anya. She was the reason he and Frost were still alive. Somehow she'd escaped the failed mission in Pakistan, and was still at large. As Drake had already learned, Cain was determined to get his hands on her, and had almost certainly tasked Hawkins with forcing the information from Drake.

'You might think, given our respective situations, that I'm in control here,' Hawkins continued, setting his cup of coffee on the table. 'But you'd be wrong, Ryan. I don't want you to think that way. Because the truth is, *you're* in control. You make the decisions. What happens from this point on is entirely up to you. Whether you and Frost leave this place alive or dead depends on how you answer one simple question. Where's Anya?'

Drake said and did nothing. He just hung there suspended from the cuffs, while the frantic beating of his heart filled his ears.

'No answer is still an answer, Ryan,' Hawkins warned him. 'Are you sure you want to test me like this?'

Drake saw Frost giving a barely discernible shake of the head. He understood her sentiment – don't give the bastard anything. I can take whatever he dishes out.

'I don't know,' Drake said, speaking honestly. 'I lost her in Pakistan. She could be anywhere by now.'

Hawkins, glancing at the guard holding Frost, let out a sigh of disappointment. 'I had a feeling you'd say that.'

Whirling around, he drew back a clenched fist and slammed it into Drake's midsection. Restrained and hanging as he was, Drake could do nothing to protect himself, and groaned as the impact rippled through his already bruised body. Had there been anything left in his stomach, he was quite certain he would have thrown up at that point.

'You know, I'm trying to work with you here, buddy,' Hawkins said, placing a hand on Drake's shoulder and leaning in close. 'I'm trying to steer you on the right course, give you a chance to help us out. But you are making it real difficult for both of us.'

Drake spotted movement behind Hawkins. Frost had jerked her foot backwards, landing a solid blow to the guard's groin. As he bent double, his grip on her arm slackened and she was able to wrench free, launching herself at Hawkins.

She never got the chance to strike. Whirling around to face her as if he'd been expecting the attack all along, Hawkins backhanded her with a blow powerful enough to snap her head around.

'No!' Drake cried out as Hawkins grabbed the young woman by the neck, lifted her off the ground and slammed her down on the heavy wooden table, which shuddered under the impact.

Drake heard the distinctive metallic rasp as a blade was unsheathed, saw a flash of steel in the harsh electric lights, and suddenly the room was filled with Frost's screams. Drake could only stare in horror at the knife protruding from Frost's right hand, its point deeply embedded in the table's scarred surface as bright red blood began to pool beneath it. She was now trapped on the table, literally skewered to its surface.

'Now that has *got* to hurt,' Hawkins exclaimed, rolling his shoulders to loosen them up. 'I mean I'm no doctor, but shit, all the way through? Goddamn, guess you won't be using any computers for a while, huh?'

It was then that Drake understood Hawkins' act of self-defence hadn't just been a quick reaction. He'd planned the exact moment Frost would escape from her guard, just as he'd planned to have that table in here.

Frost's attempt to yank the blade free was a wasted effort. She couldn't hope to equal the brute strength that had driven it into the table, and even if she could, her position afforded her no leverage.

Frost, her teeth bared, her face tight with pain, nonetheless managed a show of defiant rage. 'Fuck you!' she screamed, spitting at him.

Hawkins shook his head. 'Not exactly what I had in mind, but the boys here will be happy to oblige you.'

At a nod, the two guards began to approach the injured woman from different directions. Frost lashed out at them with her feet and her free hand, but she was incapable of fending them off for long.

'What the fuck are you doing?' Drake demanded. 'Stop this!'

Hawkins folded his arms, keeping his eyes on the spectacle unfolding before them. 'Like I said, Ryan, everything that happens here is down to you. We can stop right now if you want. Or... we can watch while the boys have some fun.'

One of the guards had succeeded in pinning Frost's other hand to the table, while the second, dodging several vicious kicks, managed to get in close and spread her legs apart.

'You fucking sick bastard,' Drake growled, still struggling to get air into his lungs after Hawkins' punch.

'Been a while since they had any action, so I'm guessing they can go two, maybe three times each.' Hawkins shrugged, making it clear he would do nothing to intervene either way. 'And I *will* make you watch every single one of them, Ryan. Believe that.'

The harsh rip of tearing fabric, and Frost's shirt was ripped aside to expose her breasts. She was bucking and thrashing wildly, but it was clear she was fighting a losing battle.

'I could just have them taser her, but it's more interesting when they make a fight of it, know what I mean?' Hawkins remarked conversationally. 'How much longer do you think she'll last anyway? A minute? Two?'

'Tell them to stop!' Drake shouted.

'Give me Anya. Then we'll see.'

'Don't you do it!' Frost snarled. 'Don't give him shit!'

'I told you, I don't know where she is!' Drake pleaded. 'She cut us loose after Pakistan. Even you must know she would have had to go dark so we couldn't compromise her.'

'There must be a way to contact her,' Hawkins pressed, as the bearded guard started working at Frost's trousers. 'Think, Ryan.'

Drake shook his head, refusing to watch. 'We used burner email accounts. No phone number, nothing that could be tracked.'

'What about places? You must have had a safe house or a fallback location.' When Drake hesitated, Hawkins realized he was on to something. 'It's going to be a very long night for all of us unless you speak up.'

Drake saw the fear and defiance in Frost's eyes, and the determination not to be used as a pawn against him. She knew what he was thinking, knew he was close to breaking, and every atom of her being rebelled against it.

'Don't,' she hissed at Drake as her captor yanked her trousers down. She was already bracing herself for what was coming, willing to endure it rather than betray another of their team.

'I'll tell you,' Drake said, unable to watch any more.

Hawkins leaned in closer. 'Sorry, you'll have to say that again.'

The bastard was going to make him go through every motion. 'Call them off! I'll tell you what you want to know.'

Glancing at the would-be rapists, Hawkins raised a hand. 'Hold up, boys. Let's hear what Ryan has to say.' He turned his attention back to Drake, prepared to have them resume their horrific task if he didn't get the answer he wanted. 'I'm all ears.'

'The *Alamo*,' Drake mumbled, head hung low in defeat, unable to look at either Frost or Hawkins. 'That was our fallback location.'

'You'll have to enlighten me. What is the *Alamo*? A place?'

'A ship,' Drake explained. 'An old fishing trawler, moored off the coast of Marseille. That was our safe house before we left for Pakistan. All our mission planning, our equipment, everything came from there.'

Hawkins cocked his head and nodded thoughtfully. 'A mobile safe house. Very enterprising of you, Ryan.'

His expression was cold and assessing as he stared at Drake, looking for any hint of deception. The seconds seemed to stretch out into eternity as he hung there in silence, awaiting Hawkins' decision.

'All right,' Hawkins said at last, apparently deciding the intel was worth acting on. 'That wasn't such a chore now, was it?'

Drake said nothing. He had no words for what had just happened.

'Don't worry, I'm not going to fuck you over now,' he promised. 'I'm a man of my word. You helped me, so I'll help you.'

Approaching Frost, Hawkins leered at her appreciatively. She glared back at him, breathing hard, making no attempt to cover herself, before Hawkins leaned in and grasped the knife.

'For what it's worth, I'm glad we didn't have to go through with that,' he whispered to her. 'Never did appreciate having rapists on my team.'

Frost opened her mouth to respond, but at that moment Hawkins pulled the knife free with a single hard yank, and her burgeoning insult turned into a cry of pain. Hawkins allowed her to slide off the table onto the ground, clutching her maimed and bleeding hand.

'Clean her up, dress that wound,' he instructed the guards. 'Nobody touches her without my permission. Clear?'

None of them was foolish enough to argue.

'And get my buddy here some clothes and food,' he added. 'I'd say he's earned it.'

Hawkins was about to leave when a final thought occurred to him. 'Oh, and Ryan?'

Drake could barely bring himself to look at the man who had taken everything from him, but somehow he forced himself.

'Be a real shame if I was to travel all that way for nothing,' he said with a smile. 'Let's just hope your tip pans out. For all our sakes.'

Chapter 4

Krakow, Poland

Given its distinctly undomesticated owner, Anya had expected Alex's apartment to be a cluttered, disorganized space filled with unwashed clothes, dirty dishes and takeaway food containers.

What she found instead was a small but neat one-bedroom flat situated about half a mile east of the Vistula, overlooking a confluence of several roads and tram lines.

Furniture and decorations were minimal, the living room containing no more than a plain leather couch and a TV. The walls were a neutral beige colour, the floors covered by cheap laminate wood. The kitchen unit and breakfast bar overlooking the living area were equally clean, bland and functional.

There were no paintings or photographs, no unopened mail by the door, no unusual foods or condiments in the kitchen, not even any magazines or books. She was willing to bet the other rooms were similarly furnished, and equally devoid of character.

This lack of personalization might have struck the average visitor as odd, but to Anya it made perfect sense. This was a drop-and-go kind of place, the sort of living arrangement that she'd become all too accustomed to over the past few years. If Alex encountered trouble and had to leave Krakow in a hurry, he could do so knowing he was leaving nothing of financial or personal value behind. More importantly, there was nothing here that could help potential enemies track him.

She should have felt a measure of professional approval at the very practical measures he'd taken to protect his own safety, yet strangely Alex's flat left her with a lingering sense of disappointment. She knew all too well the loneliness and isolation that this kind of life entailed, and felt a momentary pang of guilt for inflicting it on him.

'I know,' Alex said, perhaps seeing her thoughts reflected in her expression. 'You're blown away by the decor, aren't you...?' He shrugged, trying to break the uneasy stand-off. 'This isn't exactly a long-term arrangement. And it's not like I've had the money to—'

'It's all right, Alex,' she reassured him, holding up a hand to forestall further explanation. 'I understand.'

'Right, well,' he said, clearing his throat. 'We'd better get started.'

Making for the kitchen, he opened the fridge and fished out a can of Red Bull. Anya noticed there were several more in there, and recalled that people in his profession had a fondness for such beverages that bordered on addiction – not that she could blame them. Staring at a computer screen until late into the night was, she imagined, a laborious job that taxed one's mental stamina in the extreme.

Downing a gulp of the energy drink, Alex settled himself at the only other piece of furniture in the room – a small, efficient writing desk on which rested a laptop computer, plugged in and standing by.

'Do you always leave that in plain view?' she asked as she removed her coat, surprised that he'd be so careless with such a goldmine of personal information when he appeared otherwise fastidious about keeping his apartment sterile.

Alex grinned and opened the desk drawer, revealing a simple portable keyboard nestled within.

'The laptop's rigged with an anti-tamper device – a little trick I learned back in the old days. Anyone hits a button on the inbuilt keyboard, it automatically formats and overwrites the entire drive. Even if someone had a gun to my head, I couldn't recover the contents,' he explained, plugging the spare keyboard into the side of the computer. 'The only way to use it is through a USB port.'

Anya nodded, impressed by this simple but very effective trick. As Alex logged into the system, she laid a hand on his shoulder and leaned over to get a look at the screen. She would rather not admit that her ribs were paining her, and that it was an effort to stand up straight.

'So how does this work?' she asked.

'First you need to tell me everything you know about Cain's daughter. Full name, date of birth, physical description, schools attended, any medical conditions. Every piece of information helps.'

Anya closed her eyes for a moment, thinking of the young woman that Cain had helped bring into this world. A life born of his. She wondered then just how much of him was in his daughter, how much she knew of her father's work, whether or not she agreed with his methods.

'She was born... 22 September 1990,' she said, searching back through her memory. 'Her full name was Lauren Louise Cain, but she will probably be living under a different identity now. I know nothing of her medical history or the schools she went to.'

Alex lowered his head. 'So that's it? We've got a date of birth and a possibly useless name. Not a lot to go on, Anya.'

'I didn't say this would be easy. Why do you think I asked for your help?'

'For my handsome features and charming wit,' he replied sarcastically. 'But even I need data to work with.' He thought for a few moments. 'Maybe I can trace her through other family members. What's her mother's name?'

When Anya didn't respond, Alex spun around, a look of dawning comprehension on his face.

'No fucking way,' he said in disbelief. 'Tell me it isn't you.'

In that regard at least, Anya could afford to be completely honest. 'I have never had children, Alex. Never,' she replied firmly, much to his disappointment. 'And as for her mother, I know little about her except that she's dead.'

That wasn't strictly true, but her mother's true name and identity had been well hidden throughout Anya's life. What little information Anya knew about her would likely lead to a dead end. Anyway, there were some things she was still unwilling to reveal.

'Okay...' Alex said, drawing the word out. 'Well, we know who her dad is at least. Where were they when Lauren was born? Was he serving overseas?'

Anya shook her head. 'No, he was based out of Langley.'

'Right, so presumably Cain lived somewhere within the DC area. That'll have to do as a starting point. Tell me, were they close?'

Anya blinked, jolted from her thoughts. 'Close?'

'Yes, *close*,' he repeated, vexed by her passivity. 'Did he love and care about her? Was he the sort of guy to play an active part in her childhood, or pack her off to boarding schools and forget about her?'

Anya thought about it for a moment. Marcus Cain was many things, but a natural father wasn't one of them. Even during the time she'd known him, he had spoken little of his daughter or the brief relationship that had brought her into the world, preferring to devote himself slavishly to his work. She certainly couldn't imagine him caring for an infant, changing soiled diapers or doing any of the other things most parents did for their children.

Part of Anya had always wondered why he'd maintained any ties to the child at all, when it would have been easier simply to put her up for adoption or find some other arrangement. Instead he had paid others to raise her, care for her, school her. Keeping her close but distant at the same time.

Something to be observed from a distance, but never truly made part of his life. Protected, but not loved.

'He wasn't close to her,' Anya said at length. 'Not at first anyway. But he took his responsibilities as a father seriously.'

'Fair enough,' Alex conceded. 'Well, the first thing to do is find where she was born.'

Anya frowned. 'Why?'

'The secret to finding someone is to start at the beginning and work your way forward. Unless her mum gave birth in a cave somewhere, young Lauren has to have a birth certificate, hospital records, social security information, all the rest. That's my starting point. Once I've got something more concrete to work with, I can put the pieces together and figure out where the hell she ended up.'

'Cain will have hidden or destroyed her records.'

Alex's grin was that of a master dealing with an overconfident student. 'Nobody's that well hidden, especially from me. One way or another I'll find her.'

She admired his optimism. She just hoped it wasn't misplaced.

'Do you need anything else from me?' Anya asked, finding it hard to keep her fatigue from showing. She had barely stopped or eaten, never mind slept, since fleeing Pakistan two days ago. Pain, constant tension and simple exhaustion were three factors that even she couldn't withstand for ever.

'Not right now.'

'Good. Then you won't mind if I rest for a while.' It went against Anya's better judgement to let her guard down, even amongst relative allies like Alex, but there wasn't much choice.

'Bed's yours if you want it. I'd be lying if I said the sheets were freshly laundered, though,' he added with a wry grin.

'Thank you, but the couch will do fine.' She was actually more accustomed to sleeping on the floor, after spending much of her life living rough in the field, but with cracked ribs it was simply too painful. Rising from the edge of the couch, she added, 'Make sure you—'

She caught her breath, pressing a hand against her injured side.

'Shit, I knew you were hurt,' Alex said, with a mixture of alarm and anger. He jumped up from his computer. 'What the hell have you done to yourself?'

He was already crossing the room, concern overriding his other emotions, but Anya waved him away. 'It's not serious.'

'You're in pain and you look like shit,' he countered. 'What happened? You get shot?'

'I don't need a nursemaid,' Anya snapped, pushing him away. 'Just focus on your work – that's all that matters for now.'

Alex backed off, looking almost hurt.

Realizing she'd allowed emotion to get the better of her, Anya lowered her voice and forced herself to be calm. 'I appreciate the concern, but I can look after myself. Where's your bathroom?'

Hesitating, Alex nodded down the short corridor that led off the living room. 'First door on the right.'

Anya straightened up and walked away, leaving him to get on with his daunting but vital task. Only when she was safely inside the apartment's cramped bathroom and had locked the door behind her did she double over, taking small, shallow breaths and clutching at the sink for support.

She reached down and pulled up her dark sweater. A surgical dressing was wrapped around her torso, just below her breasts, and pulled tight to help stabilize the cracked ribs. As she'd suspected, a few spots of bright red blood were showing through the bandages.

Sniffing and wiping her nose, Anya allowed the sweater to fall back into place and looked up at her reflection in the mirror. Alex's earlier assessment of her appearance might have been harsh, but it wasn't entirely inaccurate. Her face was pale and haggard, her eyes hollow and ringed by dark circles of fatigue, her blonde hair limp and tangled. She'd been through a lot over the past couple of days, and it showed.

But she couldn't allow herself to give in now. If she was to have any chance of getting Drake and the others back, she had to stay the course. She had to see her plan through, find a way to make it work and undo some of the damage she'd caused.

It wouldn't change anything, but it might make it a little easier to sleep at night.

With that thought lingering in her mind, she fished a tab of painkillers from her pocket and swallowed a couple.

Chapter 5

CIA headquarters, Langley

'Goddamn it,' Dan Franklin cursed, listening to his contact's report from Pakistan with astonishment and disbelief.

Everything had fallen apart. The plan that Drake had hatched, and Franklin had facilitated, had ended in disaster. Cain had escaped unscathed, and Drake and the survivors had been taken into custody.

'ISI are already working to cover this thing up,' his contact went on. 'Their agents are all over the ambush site.'

The Inter-Services Intelligence agency – Pakistan's fearsome and secretive intelligence organization, which was widely believed to have been covertly supporting al-Qaeda for years.

'So Cain's working with them?'

Had he been capable, Franklin would likely have been pacing his office. But he could manage little more than a fast shuffle, leaning heavily on his stick for support. Recent spinal surgery had cured him of debilitating pain, but his recovery had been arduous.

'Seems so, or at least elements within their organization,' the station chief in Islamabad – Hayden Quinn – confirmed. He had first tipped them off about Cain's secretive mission several days ago. 'Nothing can be proven, of course. He was too careful for that.'

'Of course he was,' Franklin said, standing in the centre of his office. 'What about Drake and the others? Where are they now?'

'Unknown. If they weren't executed on the spot, my guess is they were bundled onto a black flight out of the country. Totally off the books, even for us. They could be anywhere.'

'That's not good enough.'

'It's all I've got,' Quinn protested. 'I'm not in the loop any more. Cain's shut me out.'

'Fuck,' Franklin growled.

He glanced over at a photograph of himself, dressed in military fatigues with the snow-capped mountains of Afghanistan in the background. When he'd still been a soldier. Before an IED had blown his Humvee apart and left him with a career-ending injury.

And standing beside him, glowing with youthful confidence, was the man who had pulled him out of the wreck: Ryan Drake.

'We've got to find him,' he said quietly.

'Then I wish you luck, but there's nothing more I can do,' Quinn replied, a tremor in his voice now. 'This thing's out of control. I must have been out of my mind to get involved. I'm sorry, Dan, but I'm done. I'm out.'

'Wait, I can—' Franklin started to protest, but it was too late.

Quinn had hung up.

–

Marseille, France

Off the southern coast of France the night was mild and calm, with only a gentle breeze and a light swell. The warm waters of the Mediterranean shone in the moonlight and the glow of the distant city of Marseille.

And in the midst of this peace, anchored about half a mile offshore, sat a bluff-bowed, wide-beamed fishing boat. It was a vessel neither graceful nor elegant in design, built for sturdy handling in rough weather, designed for strength and reliability rather than speed or aesthetics. Sea beams shimmered across its wooden hull, while its old timbers creaked and groaned comfortingly as it rode the swell. The masts and rigging overhead that had once accommodated fishing nets now sat unused, the square wheelhouse near the stern unlit, the engines quiet.

A seagull that had stopped to roost on board for the night stirred in its makeshift nest, alerted by the low hum of an approaching engine. Peeking its head up, keenly scanning the surrounding seas, the bird suddenly took flight and disappeared into the night sky with an angry squawk and a flutter of wings.

Hawkins paid the bird no heed as his fast patrol boat closed in on the silent hull of the *Alamo*, flanked by a similar vessel 30 yards off their starboard beam. Both craft were running with high-powered electric outboard motors, reducing the usual roar of such engines to a throb that was barely louder than the crash of waves against their hulls as they sped through the water.

'Thirty seconds,' he called out over the radio net, scanning the ship through his infrared goggles. There were no lights burning aboard, no thermal blooms that indicated running engines. The *Alamo* appeared to be dead in the water.

And yet, she was here, just as Drake had said she would be. Whether or not there was anyone on board remained to be seen, though Hawkins doubted an operative of Anya's experience would be foolish enough to allow herself to be boxed in like this.

Still, if Drake was telling the truth, and this ship had been the centre of their planning phase for Pakistan, there could be a wealth of intel that could lead them to Anya.

One thing was certain — that old tub couldn't outrun them if this turned into a pursuit. They could make 60 knots if they pushed the electric motors to maximum. By the looks of her, the *Alamo* would struggle to hit 15.

'Twenty seconds. Alpha Team, stand by.'

In the second boat, weapons were checked for the last time, radios tested and equipment secured for deployment. Hawkins would have preferred to come in by chopper, but retrieving the intel on board could take time, and a helicopter hovering over a ship so close to shore would have attracted immediate and unwanted attention from the French authorities.

The *Alamo* was visible even without night-vision now, the high-bowed vessel silhouetted against the moonlit horizon.

'Ten seconds. Look sharp, boys,' Hawkins advised.

As they came within 50 yards, Hawkins' own craft peeled off to port, the pilot slowing the engine to bring them into a holding pattern to cover the assault team. Although accustomed to leading from the front, he was content to sit back and allow the more junior members of his team handle this one.

The second inflatable went straight for the stern, where the hull was lowest and the deck scuppers afforded easy access. Hawkins watched as the pilot cut power at the last moment, allowing the bow to drift into the side of the fishing trawler. A single grappling line was thrown onto the deck, pulling them close, and moments later a cluster of four men scurried aboard.

'Deck clear,' he heard one of them report over the radio net, his voice hushed.

'Moving forward. Bow clear.'

'Check the wheelhouse.'

He heard the thump of a door being kicked in, followed by a terse confirmation. 'Wheelhouse clear. Nobody's home.'

'Got a deck hatch here,' another voice reported. 'It's secured and locked.'

'Copy that, Alpha Team,' Hawkins acknowledged. 'Proceed below, and watch for booby traps.'

'We're on it. Telford, hydraulic cutters.'

The high-powered cutting tool made short work of the simple steel padlock. Removing the lock, one operative gently raised the hatch half an inch while two of his comrades covered him, ready to open fire on anything or anyone that looked like it might be a threat.

It took only a moment or two for their flashlight beams to pick out a tiny sliver of fishing wire, stretched taut by the hatch.

'Got a tripwire here.' A pause. 'It's not electrified. I'm cutting it now.'

Hawkins tensed up. If the wire itself were some kind of conductor rather than just a tripwire, cutting it would interrupt whatever circuit it was rigged to maintain and likely trigger an explosive device. In which case, he could say goodbye to the assault team and any chance of retrieving whatever intel was aboard that ship.

Anxious moments passed, broken only by the gentle lap of the waves against the inflatable hull of his boat.

'Tripwire's removed,' the operative reported, his relief obvious. 'I'm proceeding below deck.'

Hawkins frowned, struck by the sudden thought that this was all playing out a little too easy. Drake was many things, but careless wasn't one of them. Would he really have entrusted a place like this to so obvious a safeguard?

'Hold up, Alpha Team,' he commanded as the first operative ventured down through the open hatch, failing to notice the second tripwire attached to the ladder he was descending. 'Check for secondary—'

The bright flash of a detonation within the vessel was followed half a second later by a concussive boom that seemed to flatten the waves around them. Hawkins instinctively ducked as pieces of the wooden hull peeled backwards from the point of the explosion in a sudden blossom of fire and smoke.

The effect on the deck was even worse, as the vessel's midsection disintegrated in a storm of shattered wood and twisted metal. Both masts were shattered like matchsticks and thrown aside by the force of the explosion, taking with them the complex network of rigging suspended between them. Even the wheelhouse was partially caved in, as if struck by a giant fist.

Picking himself up as fragments of burning wreckage rained down all around them, Hawkins watched as the crippled trawler appeared to collapse in on itself, the hull torn into two pieces by the devastating explosion amidships. Shattered decks tilted towards the waves, causing loose gear and the shredded corpse of one of his operatives to bump down their rapidly listing surfaces.

The stern, weighed down by the heavy engines and steering gear, went first, quickly disappearing from view amidst a sea of churning foam as the few remaining pockets of air collapsed. The forward section lingered stubbornly for a moment or two, the bow pointing defiantly skywards, before finally succumbing and sliding beneath the waves.

As the gurgling and rumbling of the sinking vessel receded and the fires burning on the surface began to flicker out, Hawkins let out a sigh and rolled his neck to loosen the taut muscles. The casualties on the assault team meant little to him; they were grunts, of little value and easily replaceable. But one thing he couldn't recover was the time he'd wasted on this operation.

'Nice move, Ryan,' he said under his breath, impressed by his former comrade's audacity, if nothing else. 'But you *will* pay for it.'

It was becoming clear to him that Drake wasn't going to give in easily. Breaking him was still perfectly possible, of course – every man could be broken, given enough time and pressure – but doing so might take longer than he had. Perhaps there was an easier way to get what he needed.

'We've wasted enough time,' he said, turning to the patrol boat's pilot. 'Get us out of here before the police show up.'

The explosion would have been audible for miles around, and the distinctive orange flash visible to anyone who cared to look.

'One of Alpha team might still be alive in the water, sir,' the pilot protested weakly, nodding towards the floating debris field. 'Shouldn't we...'

He trailed off, a look from Hawkins silencing further protests. He swung the wheel over and throttled the engine up to full power.

Chapter 6

Anya sighed as she stared up at a vast, uninterrupted afternoon sky that seemed to stretch out for ever. Only a single thin white line, as straight as an arrow, marred its pale-blue perfection. An aircraft contrail, moving slowly from east to west as if a child were drawing a careful, deliberate line across a chalkboard. And for a moment, she caught the glint of sunlight off the wings of the aircraft. Too high to make out the details, but bright and distinct all the same, reminding her of a shooting star.

As a child, lying on the grassy slope overlooking her parents' home, she had often enjoyed being amidst the gently swaying stalks and watching high-flying aircraft, wondering where they were heading, who they were carrying. In some part of her childish mind she even imagined them transporting her off to some distant new land. A land of far horizons and endless skies, where she could finally do something worthy of the life she'd been given.

'Not interrupting, am I?'

Glancing at the young man standing over her with an ice cream cone in each hand, Anya smiled and sat up, shaking loose sand from her hair.

'Not when you come bearing gifts,' she said.

Grinning, Marcus Cain sat down beside her and handed her one of the cones. 'Enjoy. The asshole running the stall wouldn't break a twenty for me. Had to walk two blocks to get change.' He shrugged. 'Just saying, is all.'

'My hero.' She tilted her head in acknowledgement before taking a bite, savouring the taste that was at once pleasing yet strangely unfamiliar to her. Such simple things as this would have been considered a luxury during her own childhood.

'Well, I guess you earned it,' he acknowledged with mock reluctance, leaning back a little on the sand. Dressed in jeans and a casual short-sleeved shirt, he was a far cry from the formally suited intelligence operative who prowled the corridors at Langley.

And yet somehow this more relaxed look suited him, she thought, knowing in that moment that Cain's professional life was little more than a veneer covering the real man beneath. For the first time in a long while, Marcus Cain looked at ease with himself. And in a way, Anya knew some of that was because of her. She felt a blush of warmth rise within her at the thought.

It had been nearly three years since her unit first set foot on the war-torn soil of Afghanistan. Three years of fighting and killing, clawing for survival, trying to stay one step ahead of an enemy that was growing increasingly ruthless and desperate as the tide of battle turned against them. Three years of war. But now it seemed their war was ending.

Weakened and drained by nearly ten years of constant fighting, the Soviets were preparing to withdraw their demoralized forces from Afghanistan, just as the British had done a century earlier. And as for Anya and the unit she had been part of, they too had been withdrawn from the field to await further orders. Given the secret nature of their work, she doubted history would ever record their names or deeds, but it would be nice to know that someone beyond their small circle of CIA handlers was aware of them.

Still, she had to admit the orders to return home hadn't been entirely unwelcome. Anya and her comrades had acquitted themselves admirably on the battlefield, exceeding the CIA's wildest expectations, but the war had been almost as draining for them as it had been for their enemies.

And none more so than for their youngest member. Her time in Afghanistan had changed her. The fire and lust for revenge that had driven Anya in the early days had cooled. She was older, perhaps a little wiser and more mature than she'd been back then, able to see the world from a different perspective. She'd even found herself pondering what she might do with her life once this was over, whether she could be more useful in peacetime than she'd been in war.

Much of that still lay in the hands of the CIA, of course. There had been a great deal of discussion about what to do with her now, countless debriefings and interviews with intelligence experts eager to learn from her experiences against the Soviet military, and her thoughts on which of their Mujahedeen allies might be best suited to help form a post-war government. Her head was spinning from all the questions, but finally Cain had wrestled her from their clutches so that she could enjoy some proper downtime.

And here she was, sitting on the opposite side of the country, staring out across a sandy beach to the shimmering, endless blue waters of the Pacific. It was the first time in her life that she'd seen it, and it was beautiful. It was a world away from Washington, from the Agency, from global politics and the all concerns that had defined her life for the past three years. Cain had seen to it that their journey here had gone unmarked, that there was no Agency escort or surveillance of any kind.

No one on this beach had a clue who either of them were, and no one cared. In short, they were free.

Shouts and laughter momentarily drew Anya's attention to an impromptu football game unfolding off to their left, played by a big group that looked to be of college age. The beach was a popular location for sports of all kinds, but the American passion for football seemed to take precedent over everything else.

Anya watched as one young man, catching a long, sailing pass with effortless ease, slipped his way past one of his opponents before suddenly changing direction and pushing aside a second who tried to tackle him. Flushed with his success, he turned to gloat at the two young men he'd just beaten, only for a third to barrel straight into him, knocking him flat into the soft sand, much to the amusement of the others.

Anya couldn't help but laugh, both at their antics and the strange, unfamiliar but wonderfully liberating situation in which she now found herself. For the first time in her adult life, she was free. Free to go where she would, eat and drink whatever she wanted, indulge whatever whim occurred to her.

'Kids. A lot of testosterone, not a lot of brains,' Cain remarked with a good-natured smile, following her gaze. 'Not yet, at least.'

Kids, she thought. In reality they were probably only a year or so younger than her, even if their lives were drastically different. But here they both were on the same beach, beneath the same afternoon sky. Two worlds briefly overlapping but, she sensed, never fated to join.

'Believe it or not, I was like that once.'

Pushing aside these thoughts, Anya grinned mischievously at Cain. 'What do you mean "once"? I think you would join in if you had half a chance,' she teased, though she soon turned a little more serious. 'Anyway, I was just thinking.'

'About what?'

'About how it feels, being here. Sitting on this beach eating ice cream, watching people playing games. Doing normal things.'

'And?' Cain asked.

'I don't know.' She shook her head, struggling to make sense of the conflicting emotions within her. 'There were times... out there, when I almost forgot what it could be like.'

She didn't say it out loud, on the unlikely chance that someone might overhear their conversation, but he knew what she meant. Afghanistan, the place where she'd spent the better part of three years — fighting, killing, risking her life on an almost daily basis, enduring hardships that the kids playing games around her could barely imagine.

Only the man sitting beside her had some inkling.

She felt a warm hand on her arm, and looked around at Cain. 'Then maybe it's a good thing you came home,' he said gently. 'For what it's worth, I'm glad you did.'

'Home,' she repeated, as if unfamiliar with the word. She'd had little cause to use it in her life. The home and the life she'd once known had been torn away from her as a child, replaced first with years of imprisonment in one form or another, then later by harsh and unrelenting battles to survive, to escape, and to wreak revenge on those who had taken so much from her.

No, it had been a long time since Anya had called anywhere home.

'Why not?' Cain asked, turning more serious now. 'This is your home now, Anya. This is where you belong. If you want it, that is,' he added.

He was waiting for her reply, waiting to hear her decision. She could practically feel the tension radiating from him as the moments crawled by. The choice was hers. She was free — free to choose her own path now.

A home, a life, a future. If she wanted this place. If she wanted him.

She didn't think she'd ever wanted anything more.

'Marcus,' she whispered, her lips parting slightly as her breathing came faster.

He leaned in closer, sensing her need and responding in kind. 'Yeah?'

Giggling, Anya reached up and touched her ice cream against his nose, leaving a smear of melted cream behind.

'Hey!' he sputtered as he wiped it away, both amused and surprised by the trick she'd played. 'That's gonna cost you.'

'You have to catch me first,' Anya teased, springing to her feet. 'Come on, you said you were like those kids once. Show me, old man.'

She felt alive, emboldened, bristling with energy she needed to expend. For the first time in a long time, she felt young. She felt like the future was a great open adventure stretching before her, as vast and perfect as the blue sky above. And it was because of him.

As she took off down the beach, laughing with unrestrained excitement, Cain scrambled to his feet and sprinted after her.

'Old man, my ass! Wait until I catch you!' he called out.

—

Anya was awoken with a start by an exclamation from the other side of the room. 'Yes! Get in there, my son!' Alex called out, punching the air in triumph.

Anya blinked and shook her head, trying to rouse her mind from the dream that still lingered, leaving her feeling uncharacteristically disoriented and confused. She had no idea how long she'd been asleep. Rubbing her eyes, she looked at her wrist watch, the iridium dial glowing faintly in the gloom.

6.12 a.m. Alex had been working for nearly seven hours straight.

'Have you found something?' Anya asked, rising from the couch with difficulty. Her body, contorted into an unnatural sleeping position by the need to keep pressure off her ribs, ached as she stretched out her muscles.

'Something? I've found everything on young Miss Cain,' Alex explained hurriedly. 'Only she's going by the name Shaw these days. I knew she couldn't hide from me for ever.'

His eyes were wide and bloodshot, the pupils fully dilated, his words tumbling out so fast they seemed to blend together into a mass of sound. Anya caught herself wondering if he'd taken to using something stronger to keep his energy up while she was asleep, but the three crumpled cans of Red Bull lying on the floor by his computer desk offered some explanation.

'Show me,' Anya said, shaking off the last vestiges of sleep and hurrying over to review his findings.

Grinning, he spun around to face his laptop. 'Cain was clever, very clever. He'd wiped all digital records of her birth, medical reports, the whole lot. And that was his first fuck-up.'

Anya frowned. 'I don't understand.'

'I knew you wouldn't. But like Sun Tzu said, don't fight the enemy where they are; fight them where they aren't.'

46

Anya folded her arms. Being well versed with *The Art of War*, his attempted quotation cut little ice with her. 'Sun Tzu said nothing of the sort. Now where are you going with this?'

'Well, he should have,' Alex said with a shrug. 'Anyway, my point is that instead of altering his daughter's birth records, Cain just had them deleted outright. It's brutal but lacking in subtlety. And it's the key, you see. All I had to do was run a null-value error search for hospitals in the continental United States on that particular date, and suddenly the playing field narrows considerably.' Bringing up a website, he pointed to the screen like a game show host touting a prize. 'The Pinewood Hills medical centre – lovely little private clinic for the rich and famous to push mini-humans out of their—'

'All right, I understand,' Anya interrupted. 'So we have a deleted birth record. Where does that get us?'

'It proves she was born near Cain's home, which is pretty lucky for us because this search would have been a nightmare if she'd been born outside the US. It also proves that he didn't want it happening in just any old hospital. He wanted somewhere discreet, out of the way. And I'm guessing the rest of her childhood followed a similar pattern, so I started hacking the databases for private schools in the same area, looking for where my enemy wasn't. Again, same story. Deleted records, but then I delved into their accounting history.'

Opening up a new window, he showed her a spreadsheet with what looked like ledgers dating back decades. However, Alex had highlighted one line in particular.

'See that?' he prompted. 'Monthly payments from M. Cain.'

Anya looked closer, and sure enough there was his name.

'I had a school, and after a fair bit of trawling, I found a picture of a yearbook posted online by a former student. Took a while, but I was able to cross-reference each of the female students against archived records, until I found the one little girl without a name.'

His last window brought up a picture of a girl, perhaps 10 years old and dressed in the school's uniform, all dimpled smiles and bushy dark hair. But beneath the soft, youthful features, she saw a faint resemblance to Cain himself.

The name beneath her picture read – Lauren Louise Shaw.

'It's her,' Anya whispered, recognizing the face instantly. It was a face she'd seen only once, but which was for ever imprinted on her memory.

'Not bad for a bloke who got a B− in computer studies, eh?' Alex said, looking immeasurably pleased with himself.

Anya blinked, her mind returning to their present dilemma. 'So where is she now?'

'That's where I ran into a bit of a snag,' he said. 'The trail went cold after that. And I mean stone cold. Every trace of her had been wiped off the internet. Even the Deep Web seemed to have nothing on her, which scares the shit out of me, to be honest.'

'Why?' she asked.

Alex suddenly had the impatient teacher look she'd been seeing a lot of in the past few minutes. 'Okay, imagine all the data on the web as a pint of beer. The little frothy bit on top is the part that normal people can find through search engines like Google or whatever, but there's a huge quantity of data lurking beneath the surface that never even gets touched. Hundreds of times bigger. That's the Deep Web, and if you know how to navigate it, you can find just about anyone or anything. It's entirely unpoliced and uncontrolled. At least, that's what I thought.'

'So what are you saying?'

'If someone has the ability to control the entire pint of beer, imagine what they could do to the little frothy bit on top. The bit most of us rely on for pretty much all our information. You could change public opinions overnight, rewrite history, make people believe anything you wanted. Knowledge is power, as they say. Well, control of worldwide data would be the ultimate weapon of power.'

Anya was struck by his look of genuine concern, made all the worse because she already sensed who was behind it. So did he. The same shadowy group who had almost brought about their deaths the previous year.

Alex allowed that thought to hang in the air before continuing. 'Anyway, that's a question I don't have nearly enough time to answer right now. The point is that whoever did this did a pretty thorough job of wiping away all digital record of Lauren Cain. But fucking Twitter was their undoing.'

Anya's frown deepened. 'Twitter?'

'Yeah, you know? Your life in 140 characters or less—'

'I know what it is,' she snapped. 'But why would she be using social media?'

Alex looked at her like she'd just sprouted a second head. 'She's a 19-year-old American girl. Why *wouldn't* she be on social media?'

Anya said nothing to that. When she'd been Lauren's age, the internet hadn't even existed in a meaningful form, never mind social media. Not to mention that sharing her daily activities at that point in her life would have compromised national security and landed her in prison.

'Anyway, it didn't take me long to track down her account, even if she's using a pseudonym. It was easy once I referenced it against some of her high school yearbook mates. Young Lauren's been posting like crazy over the past few months. Look,' he said, bringing up a new tab showing Lauren's account.

The sight of the little girl suddenly ten years older was a shock to the system, but sure enough she could still make out the resemblance in the considerably more mature face smiling back from the pictures.

Judging by the cityscape in the background, one had been taken in New York, showing Lauren on the observation deck of a high rise looking out over Central Park. Another had been taken in a bar that could have been anywhere, showing Lauren with her arms around two other girls in the midst of a night out.

'The most recent one,' she prompted, having neither the time nor the inclination to see the young woman's life unfold in pictures. 'Show me.'

Scrolling to the top, Alex brought up a picture dated only two days ago: a selfie of Lauren standing in the midst of a wide courtyard before a grand, Baroque building. And in the centre of the courtyard, directly behind her, a huge glass pyramid rose up from the ground.

Anya recognized the location immediately. It was the Louvre.

'Paris,' she said, hardly believing their luck. 'She's in Paris.'

'Very good. Studying history and classical philosophy at Paris-Sorbonne University, as it happens,' Alex added. 'I checked.'

Anya turned away, her heart pounding as plans and possibilities whirled through her mind. It wouldn't be easy, and she was quite certain Cain wouldn't have left his daughter unprotected, no matter how well hidden her identity was, but she had a target to aim for.

And it was all because of the man seated behind her.

'Thank you, Alex,' she whispered. 'I don't know what else to say.'

'Then don't say anything. Just keep the noise down, because I badly need some sleep,' he said, rising from his chair. Sniffing his underarms, he added, 'And a shower. Shower first, then—'

He was silenced as Anya suddenly reached out and hugged him. Her injured ribs blazed with pain but she didn't care. He'd been as good as his word, and done what few others could have done.

When she let go and Alex stepped back, his face was flushed with colour. He stood there for a moment or two, not sure what to say or do.

'I'm going to, erm...' He pointed towards the bathroom. 'Yep.'

Saying nothing else, he brushed past her, gratefully retreating from the room. Anya allowed herself a smile of amusement before reaching for her cell phone. She needed to get to Paris, and time was not on her side.

She could only hope it wasn't too late for Drake.

Chapter 7

Islamabad, Pakistan

'It was just... the sound of that explosion, the sight of the car flipping over, knowing there were people inside it. It was horrible,' the old woman said, wringing her hands in an exaggerated expression of anguish as she related her tale for the third time to the two Pakistani intelligence operatives. 'This is a peaceful neighbourhood. No troublemakers, no outsiders from across the border. It is a place for academics and decent people. We have never seen anything like this here. I still can't believe it happened.'

Senior field operative Sajid Gondal forced himself to show his most sympathetic expression. After questioning her for nearly half an hour, he had the distinct notion that this woman was more concerned about the potential impact on property prices in the area than the fact that several people had apparently been killed in an armed confrontation in the street right outside her home.

A confrontation that was rapidly being swept under the rug.

'It was a terrible tragedy, Mrs Awan,' he agreed. 'And I regret asking you to relive it, but if you could answer my question about the origin of the fighters, it would be of great help.'

The woman fixed him with a shrewd look, sensing his patience was running thin. Old women seemed to have a disconcerting way of knowing what people were thinking. More than once he'd wondered why the ISI didn't recruit a few of them.

'They were American,' she said flatly.

Gondal frowned. 'You are certain?'

She nodded. 'I have heard enough of them to know what they sound like, and they were doing a lot of shouting. And the people they hauled out of the wrecked car were definitely Westerners. Two of them were even women. Can you imagine? Women fighting alongside men? It's disgusting!' she said, scandalized.

'And you heard no Afghan during the exchange?' Gondal pressed on. 'No Pashto?'

Again she shook her head. 'All English. Americans stirring up trouble again, trying to turn this country into the next Afghanistan.'

Gondal sighed but nodded. 'Thank you very much for your time, Mrs Awan,' he said, rising with difficulty from the worn, floral-patterned chair he'd been sitting in for the past half-hour. 'You have been very helpful.'

Returning outside into the humid heat of mid-afternoon, Gondal glanced left at the shattered, fire-scarred building further up the street. The building had been sealed off, and already engineers were preparing it for demolition. Erasing all the evidence.

The question was, what were they trying to hide?

A car was waiting for him nearby, his partner Mahsud squeezed behind the wheel. Gondal hurried over and slipped into the passenger seat, turning up the air conditioner and loosening his collar.

'Anything?' Mahsud asked, his unusually deep voice perfectly complementing his heavy, unsmiling features.

'Same story,' Gondal said as they eased away from their parking space, merging with the traffic. 'One group of Americans ambushing and battling another as they tried to escape.'

'The same group we questioned at that warehouse?' Mahsud asked, referring to the small band of Americans posing as a delivery company they'd spoken to mere hours before the deadly battle had erupted.

Gondal glanced at his partner. 'Was there ever any doubt?' he asked rhetorically. 'What I want to know is who the other side were, and why they were fighting each other.'

'You know this isn't our investigation. We've already been warned off it.'

'Exactly. That's what makes me uneasy,' Gondal said, leaning back in his seat. 'Americans fighting each other on the streets of Islamabad, and our own agency trying to cover it up. It doesn't sit well with me.'

'Nor me,' Mahsud agreed. 'But what do you propose we do?'

Gondal thought about it for a moment. He wasn't a maverick by any means, and in fact had developed a reputation for respecting the chain of command and playing by the rules, but he was also a man who trusted his instincts. And they told him something was very wrong. That the battle a couple of days earlier was just the beginning of something larger and more deadly.

Something in which elements of the ISI were complicit.

'We keep looking,' he decided. 'Start with that building and who owns it. I want to know who was involved in this. And I want to know what else they are planning.'

Chapter 8

Hawkins' men grudgingly obeyed his command to feed and clothe Drake. However, they had clearly resolved to follow the letter rather than the intent of his orders. A pair of mud-streaked trousers that were too big for him, and a torn shirt were about as far as their generosity extended. He was given no shoes or socks to cover his feet.

Still, even this meagre covering had gone some way to improving his condition. Within minutes of pulling on the clothes, fumbling with numb hands that struggled to obey his commands, the feeling had begun to return to his limbs. His core temperature had begun to rise, he'd started shivering again as his body worked to generate more heat, then finally this too settled down as he found some kind of equilibrium. He was still damp and cold, and likely to stay that way as long as he remained here, but at least the danger of hypothermia was abating.

There were still plenty of other ways to die, however, starting with the man who put him here. His false tip to Hawkins had been a desperate ploy to buy some time, and to save Frost from something he couldn't bear to watch. There was a chance he'd get lucky and Hawkins would be killed trying to make entry to the *Alamo*, but luck hadn't been on his side much lately. As soon as he realized he'd been duped, Hawkins would be back, and Drake couldn't fool him a second time.

He had to find a way out of here, but how? He was in a locked cell, guarded by men with riot guns and the will to use them with brutal efficiency. As he'd already discovered, there was no obvious way to break out, whether by strength or cunning, and even if he did, he had no means to defend himself. He could think of few faster ways to die than taking on two armed men with his bare hands.

As if in response to his thoughts, he heard footsteps in the room outside, and scrambled to his feet just as the viewing port was opened with a shuddering clank, bright light flooding in.

'Food,' a voice grunted from the other side. When Drake didn't move, he added, 'Come get it, asshole. Unless you want to go without?'

Drake moved forward, wary in case it was some kind of trick. But to his surprise, a hand appeared in the narrow port, holding something. Drake reached out and took it without speaking, feeling something coarse and yielding in his hand.

He was more than a little tempted to grab the man's arm, yank it through the port and break it. With a nice hard metal edge like that to brace it against and plenty of weight on his side, he was pretty confident he could snap the humerus like an old twig.

Then again, taking petty vengeance would almost certainly lead to brutal reprisals. These guys didn't seem like the forgive-and-forget types.

'Water. Take it,' the voice barked, thrusting a cup through the gap.

Drake grasped at it immediately. Food he could forgo for a time, but without water he would surely die.

Before he could mutter any kind of reply, the viewing port snapped shut. Sliding down the wall, Drake raised the metal cup to his lips and forced himself to take only a small, experimental sip. The water was cold, and tasted slightly brackish and unpleasant, but at that moment he couldn't have cared less. It was potable, and that was good enough.

He drained the entire can within seconds. He briefly toyed with the idea of rationing but immediately decided against it, wary his captors might take it away just to fuck with his head. Better to get it down while he could.

The food was next. Though it was impossible to see in the dark confines of his cell, touch and smell confirmed that it was a hunk of bread and some kind of processed meat. The bread was stale and the meat had an odd taste he wasn't familiar with. Not rotten or spoiled, but an unusual flavour that suggested foreign origin. Nonetheless, he'd wolfed down all of it in under a minute, eating as only a starving man could.

The brief interlude had provided a distraction from his overriding problem, but with the last of the food gone the issue settled back on him: How to get the hell out of here before Hawkins returned?

Yet again he had no answers. His mind had attacked the problem from every angle and come up with nothing.

'Fuck,' he mumbled. Resting the back of his head against the wall, he closed his eyes and tried to clear his mind. He was deathly tired: of fighting, of losing, of wasting his time trying to find solutions to impossible problems.

In that moment he wanted nothing more than to rest.

Just for a short while...

'So what's the plan, Ryan?'

Opening his eyes, Drake glanced around, seeing nothing but darkness. The acoustics of the cell had scattered the voice, making it seem to come from every direction at once.

'Who's there?' he demanded, backing into a corner, his heart rate doubling in a matter of seconds. Having never been afraid of the dark before, he was suddenly very much aware that anyone or anything could be in the cell with him.

'Come on, buddy. You know who it is,' the voice chided him. A man's voice, American accent, the tone one of warmth and familiarity. 'We've been friends a long time. Haven't forgotten me already, have you?'

Drake felt his heart sink. And with that came a crushing feeling of guilt and grief. 'Cole,' he whispered, struggling to say the name.

In an instant, he saw his friend, bound and kneeling in front of him, saw a pistol raised to his head, heard the thunderclap of the shot.

'You can't be here,' Drake said, willing the voice to leave him. 'It's not… not possible. You're not real.'

'*You're* talking to me, aren't you?' Mason asked, his voice reaching Drake as clearly as ever, despite his attempts to block it. 'Isn't that enough?'

Was this some fresh torment? Had Mason somehow returned to punish Drake for failing him? For choosing Frost's life over his?

'What do you want?'

He heard a gentle chuckle of amusement. 'You're asking all the wrong questions, buddy. *You* brought me here, after all. I guess I should be the one asking what *you* want.'

'I don't want anything from you!' he shouted, not caring whether the guards heard him. He was furious, brimming with rage and frustration that was desperate to find an outlet. 'Fuck off and leave me alone! You hear me? *Leave me alone!*'

When the echo of his scream had died down, he heard a faint sigh of disappointment. 'If you wanted me to go, I wouldn't still be talking to you. You brought me here for a reason. Because you *do* want something, Ryan.'

Mason was right. He did want something.

'I do.'

'What do you want?'

'I want… I suppose… I want to be forgiven.'

'Why?'

Drake's voice was strained when he spoke again. 'Because you died and I didn't. Because you trusted me, and I let you down, Cole. You didn't want to go, but you followed me anyway. I wanted you to forgive me, but you shouldn't. I don't deserve it.'

It all came pouring out before he could stop it. All of his guilt, the crushing grief at what he and his friends had lost. All of it came out. Tears ran down his face, unseen in the darkness.

'You're right, Ryan,' Mason said. 'You don't deserve to be forgiven. Because you haven't earned it. You haven't made this right.'

'Made it right,' Drake repeated mockingly, his laugh brittle and cold. 'There's no making this right.'

'Which brings me back to my first question. What's the plan, Ryan?' Mason's voice had taken on a harder, more demanding edge now. 'Are you going to curl up and cry like a little bitch? Are you going to quit because you're down and out? Because you gambled and lost? Is Ryan Drake really that much of a goddamn pussy?'

Drake shook his head, refusing to acknowledge it. 'You're a fucking voice in my head…'

'I'm the only voice you need to listen to now!' Mason shouted back. 'Because the Ryan Drake I know wouldn't be sitting in a corner feeling sorry for himself and crying like a fucking baby! So you took a beating? Grow the fuck up. You lost people you care about? Put it behind you and move on, because *that's the way it is!*'

Drake gritted his teeth. He wasn't trying to block Mason's words out now. They were everywhere, all around him and within him all at once. And at last, he was listening.

'The Ryan Drake I know wouldn't give up. He'd keep pushing, keep fighting back, take everything they threw at him, and no matter what it took he'd find a way to make it out the other side, because *that's who you are*, Ryan! That's who you've always been. And that's who you need to be right now. Who are you going to be, Ryan? *Who are you going to be?*'

Drake awoke with a jolt, his brow damp with sweat. He looked around, struggling to pierce the darkness that enveloped him.

It had been a dream, he realized, the rational part of his mind trying to reassert itself. Of course it had been a dream. He must have given in to his exhaustion for a few moments, not realizing how quickly sleep would close in.

He shook his head and tensed his muscles, trying to quell the shivering that had started up again. He needed to move around, get some blood flowing through his veins again and generate a little warmth, in case hypothermia started to…

The bang of a door opening deeper in the building alerted him to movement. His captors. He could hear footsteps in the larger room beyond his cell, the soft thump of boots on old flagstones. They were coming for him!

Drake's heartbeat, which had only just started to calm down, suddenly kicked into high gear once more. He planted his hands on the ground to heave himself up, only for his fingers to brush against something that rattled across the concrete floor. It was the metal cup he'd been given.

He reached down and picked it up, using touch alone to determine its shape and dimensions. He hadn't noticed it before because he'd been too eager to consume its contents, but he quickly discovered that it wasn't a cup at all: it was a simple tin can, possibly the same one that had contained the processed meat he'd eaten earlier. The rim was still sharp from where it had been opened.

That was when an idea came to him.

Feeling around the bottom of the can, he found a distinctive ridge of metal that told him this was a three-piece construction. The bottom and top were joined mechanically to the cylinder to form a sealed container, held in place by little more than friction. That meant the bottom could be removed.

The steps were almost at the bottom of the stairs now.

Setting the can upright on the rough concrete floor, Drake gripped it in both hands and began to move it back and forward in a sawing motion, applying as much downward force as possible the whole time. The underside of the rim scraped and scratched across the surface, taking off a layer of metal in the process and weakening the join between the two sections.

After a few seconds, he lifted the container up, gripped it tight and squeezed with every ounce of strength he could summon. The can creaked, gave slightly under the pressure, but held firm.

He increased the pressure, adrenaline lending extra strength to his effort, and with a sudden pop the circular bottom section sprang free. Setting down the open metal cylinder, Drake snatched up the bottom piece and bent it quickly between his hands, forming a semi-circle of metal with a smooth flat edge on one side, and a ragged, wickedly sharp curve on the other.

They were outside the door now. In a second or two they would open it and come for him. With no other place to conceal his improvised weapon, Drake had little choice but to shove it into the back pocket of his trousers.

Scrambling to his feet, he turned towards the door just as the viewing port snapped open.

Chapter 9

'Back up and face the rear wall,' Jacob Moore commanded, shining his flashlight straight into the eyes of the blinking, filthy prisoner who stood hunched and cowering in the cell. 'Hands on your head. Move!'

There was no hesitation this time. Drake flinched like a startled animal, backed away and turned to face the wall with his fingers interlocked behind his head. Compliant, just as he'd been when they brought him food earlier.

Moore glanced at his fellow guard Aaron Parker, who held his riot shotgun at the ready. The normally rugged and intimidating weapon looked like a toy in Parker's massive hands. The big man gave Moore a nod, letting him know he was ready.

Taking a breath, Moore undid the bolt and shoved the door inwards. Parker went first, his considerable frame nearly filling the doorway as he advanced, keeping the prisoner covered at all times. They'd been well warned about Drake and what he was capable of, and however cowed and beaten he might appear now, they were taking no chances.

Moore went in next, a pair of plastic handcuffs clutched in his left hand. His flashlight beam briefly scanned the floor, spotting the tin can they'd given him to drink from sitting upright and empty.

Satisfied that nothing was out of place, he returned his attention to the prisoner. Parker's under-barrel flashlight was pointed straight at Drake, keeping him illuminated the whole time.

'Not gonna give us any trouble, are you, tough guy?' Moore asked as he yanked Drake's left arm downwards and slipped the plastic cuff over it, tightening it without concern for the prisoner's comfort or safety. The right hand went next, similarly locked in place so that his hands were trapped behind his back.

Drake said nothing throughout the process.

'Didn't think so,' Moore went on, feeling more secure now that their prisoner was properly restrained. 'Come on, let's go for a walk.'

Taking him by the arm, Moore led Drake back through to the main room. The table was still laid out in the centre where they'd left it after the last interrogation session, though a pair of wooden blocks had been wedged beneath the legs at one end, leaving it inclined at an angle. Moore had had a feeling they might need it again, and he was about to be proven all too right.

57

'Take a seat, man. Make yourself comfortable,' he said, forcing Drake to sit on the edge of the table. This done, he stepped back a pace and just looked at the prisoner for a long moment, taking the measure of the man.

Drake looked back at him in silence.

'Sorry, I didn't mean to stare,' Moore said at last. 'It's just, this is the first time I've really looked at you, face to face. We were guarding you before, had ourselves a good laugh when the boss was interrogating you, but I guess I never really saw you. And I *wanted* to see you – the guy everyone's talking about, everyone's afraid of. But here's the thing – I don't think you're such a tough guy underneath all that bullshit and reputation, Drake.'

Parker snorted in amusement, having set his shotgun down against the wall so that he could prepare for what was coming next. 'Nobody really is once they get to a place like this.'

Moore's smile was malicious. He was going to enjoy this. 'That's true. You know, I've seen Taliban leaders crying like babies. I've seen ISIS warlords down on their knees begging for mercy. All it takes is a little patience and hard work.' He leaned closer to Drake. 'And I want you to know I'm a patient man.'

Approaching from behind, Parker threw a black fabric hood over Drake's head, yanking him backwards so that he fell onto the table, and applying enough force to the hood that it was impossible for him to rise again.

'See, we just got word from the boss,' Moore went on, watching as Drake thrashed and kicked, trying to free himself from the hood's claustrophobic hold. 'About the little surprise you left for him in France. Three men dead – not bad work for a helpless prisoner in a cell.'

Unfastening a pocket in his jacket, Moore pulled out a plastic device little bigger than a TV remote, with a pair of electrical conductors mounted on the end. Pressing it against Drake's leg, he flicked the safety guard aside and depressed the trigger.

Drake jerked and cried out as the taser discharged, overloading his neuro-muscular system and setting every nerve of his body on fire. Moore kept the button held down for a good ten seconds, relishing the pain elicited.

Drake went limp, but the steady rise and fall of the hood's fabric told Moore he was still alive.

'Just so you know, one of my good buddies was on that assault team,' Moore went on, calmly replacing the taser in his pocket. 'Knew the guy for ten years, fought alongside him in Africa and Iraq. We were like brothers. And now he's dead.'

Moore knew Hawkins was on his way back, but he intended to have some fun with Drake first. The kind that wouldn't leave any permanent marks. Anyway, Hoffmann was upstairs, ensuring they weren't disturbed while they went about their work.

Moore reached for the bucket of cold water he'd placed beside the table and picked it up, positioning it over Drake's head.

'The boss told us not to hurt you, and we're men of our word.' He smiled. 'Not a scratch.'

The moment the icy water hit the hood and began to seep through the fabric, Drake started to fight back weakly, his body still partially paralysed by the effect of the taser.

There was nothing quite like a waterboarding to get a prisoner squirming. The relentless flow of water created the immediate sensation of drowning. Panic set in quickly, no matter how disciplined the victim. And if the torture carried on long enough, drowning was exactly what would happen.

'You like it, champ?' Moore taunted. 'Makes things a little more exciting when you can't fight against it, huh? Parker and I both went through this before we deployed to Iraq, part of our survival training. We used to call it the shock and drop. The average candidate lasted 14 seconds.' He grinned. 'I made it to 22. Wonder if you can do better, huh?'

He intended to find out. Not a mark on him – that was what they'd promised Hawkins. But they could do this all night without fear of causing permanent injury. The trick was knowing when to stop, but he figured Drake would let them know.

'That's ten seconds,' Parker said, as he held the struggling man down. 'You know they tried to make us stop doing this to terror suspects? Said the intel was unreliable, that guys will say just about anything. Lucky for us, we don't want intel from you.'

Drake was choking as the water filled his nose and mouth, his limbs flailing. Moore kept on pouring the water, a steady stream, perfectly happy to use the entire bucket before relenting.

'Once we're done with you, we'll bring the little bitch with the big mouth down and work on her for a while,' Moore mused thoughtfully. 'Might take her clothes off first, of course. No sense them getting wet.'

Then, suddenly, the struggling stopped. Drake lay still, his chest no longer rising and falling. Moore carried on applying the water for a few more seconds, convinced that Drake was faking it.

'Christ, quit it, will you? He's had enough,' Parker growled, releasing his grip and yanking the hood from Drake's head. His face was pale, eyes staring blankly at the ceiling. 'Ah, fuck! I think he's stopped breathing.'

Moore felt a well of fear rise up inside him. Having their fun with Drake was one thing, but killing him was something Hawkins would not tolerate. His order had been specific – Drake was to be kept alive until his return. And Hawkins was a man whose orders you didn't want to disobey.

'Check his pulse,' he said, dropping the bucket, which landed on the concrete floor with a clatter.

Tossing the soaking hood aside, Parker moved in to feel the pulse at Drake's neck. Moore considered whether to summon Hoffmann and have him bring down the kit with adrenaline syringes. They might need it if Drake had gone into cardiac arrest.

His thoughts were interrupted as the apparently unconscious man abruptly sprang from the table, whipping his right hand towards Parker's face. Moore caught a momentary gleam of something metallic in the harsh electric lights, and an instant later Parker was lurching backwards, screaming in pain and clutching at his face. Blood spurted from between his fingers.

'Oh shit!' Moore gasped, seeing the single plastic cuff around Drake's wrist, its end hanging limp and frayed where it had been sawn through.

It had been a ploy, he realized. Drake had faked unconsciousness to get them to remove the hood to check his condition. Now Parker was injured, their prisoner was no longer restrained, and his life was in danger if he didn't act fast.

'Hoffmann! Get down here!' he yelled.

Even as Drake rolled off the table and landed on the floor, Moore whipped back his jacket and yanked the Glock 17 pistol from the holster at the small of his back. Injuring Drake was now unavoidable, but it was the only way to put him down.

Drake had other ideas. Snatching up the metal bucket that Moore had dropped on the ground moments earlier, he charged straight at his captor with frightening speed, swinging the heavy utensil just as Moore drew down on him.

The room echoed with the twin sound of metal impacting metal as the bucket struck the side of the weapon, instantly followed by an ear-splitting crack as a round discharged, sailing over Drake's shoulder to impact the far wall.

Drake wasn't about to let him fire again. Dropping the improvised weapon, he charged straight at Moore, driving his shoulder into his chest with all the aggression and energy he could find. The force of the collision caught Moore off guard and he stumbled several paces before his back met the brick wall with bruising force, momentarily stunning him.

The sound of footsteps on the stairs announced Hoffmann, who had responded to his comrade's urgent summons, not to mention the sound of gunfire and screaming. He was armed with a weapon like Moore's, and immediately brought it to bear on the prisoner.

Drake was faster. Seizing Moore's arm, he spun towards the stairway, managed to get his finger around the Glock's trigger, and opened fire on Hoffmann, the room echoing with the weapon's thunderous report. The first two shots missed, but three more tore through his chest, painting the wall with a spray of dark blood.

As the stocky man collapsed down the last few stairs, Drake laid into Moore with everything he had, a blur of savage fists and kicks. The gun was knocked from his grip and clattered to the stone floor.

Drake was in his own world now, consumed by vengeance and rage and fury that finally had an outlet. Grabbing his former captor by the hair, he yanked his head forward into his knee, feeling the satisfying crunch as cartilage broke, accompanied by a gush of warm blood. His enemy cried out, and Drake knew he was out of the fight for now. With his nose broken, his eyes would water profusely, tears and blood combining to temporarily blind him.

That should have been enough, but it wasn't. Seizing the collar of his jacket, Drake lifted him up and drove his fist into his bleeding face. He couldn't stop himself, nor did he want to. The monster had risen from the shadows and taken command. Adrenaline was surging through his veins. The pain of his own injuries barely registered as his entire being focussed on inflicting as much damage as possible.

He was drawing his arm back for another strike when a shadow fell across them both, accompanied by growls of pain and heavy, laboured breathing.

Drake reacted instinctively, throwing himself aside just as an explosive resounded throughout the underground room, and something slammed into the wall less than a foot away.

Drake's head snapped around to see the giant standing not 10 yards away, the riot shotgun clutched in his huge grip. Drake had been so focussed on finishing off Moore he'd almost forgotten about his comrade, who had recovered sufficiently to retrieve his weapon and had barely missed with his first shot.

He was unlikely to miss a second time. The weapon might have been loaded with non-lethal rounds, but anything that took Drake out of the fight now was as good as killing him later anyway. One way or another, he had to do something.

Drake made his decision, releasing his grip on the first man and charging at the giant. He had no idea what he was going to do against a guy of that size and strength, but now was no time to question the finer points of strategy. If you're up against an armed opponent and retreating or taking cover isn't an option, the only priority is to close the range as fast as possible. At least then the odds are even.

The pump-action shotgun was devastating at close range, but it was big and cumbersome, and poorly suited to hand-to-hand fighting. If Drake could get inside the weapon's firing arc before the giant could reload, he might have a chance.

For a moment, his mind flicked back to the grim thoughts he'd entertained in his cell before being dragged out for interrogation. Dying a slow death was his starting point; anything beyond that was an improvement.

Almost there.

All his attention was centred on the gun now as the world seemed to go into slow motion around him, each ponderous step bringing him closer to his enemy. He saw the barrel rise up as the giant worked the pump action, saw the brightly coloured shell casing ejected from the breech, gunpowder smoke still trailing. He could almost picture the fresh round being drawn in as the pump handle slid forward once more.

A few more paces.

Another step, and the weapon barrel began to drop as his opponent took aim, finger already tightening on the trigger. For a moment Drake had a hideous vision of the blinding flash of the weapon discharging right into his face, followed by the bone-breaking impact as the round hit home.

He ducked down to buy himself a fraction of a second, the giant forced to adjust his aim.

Now.

Rising from his near-crouching position, Drake snatched the shotgun by the barrel and jerked it upwards. The vibration as the round blasted outwards jarred Drake's arm to the bone, but somehow he maintained his grip, knowing he couldn't afford to let the giant bring the weapon to bear on him again.

It was only then, locked in a desperate struggle for survival inches from his enemy, that Drake got his first proper look at the man's face. Cast into sharp relief by the electric lights behind them, it was like something from a horror movie. A ragged vertical slice ran from the corner of his mouth up to his forehead, his right eye socket a mass of torn tissue that would never function again.

It wasn't fast reactions that had saved Drake from being shot: his opponent's partial blindness had affected his aim. The improvised weapon that allowed Drake to saw through his restraints had proven gruesomely effective.

He felt not a twinge of pity or regret for what he'd done. There were no awards for fair play in fights like this. It was kill or be killed, and Drake wasn't done killing yet.

Neither was his enemy. Injured and bleeding he might have been, but he was still very much in the fight. His remaining eye was on Drake, his mouth a snarl of fury as he yanked the weapon so hard Drake was practically lifted off his feet. Unable to maintain his hold, he dropped to the ground just as the giant rounded on him again, ducking as the bigger man swung the shotgun like a club, barely missing his head.

He couldn't dodge or block the next blow however, a rock-solid punch that slammed into his side, almost knocking him over. Pain blazed outwards from the point of impact, muscles and joints flexing to their limits as they tried to absorb the blow.

The devastating punch was followed by a headbutt that would have taken Drake out of the game immediately if he hadn't turned his head away at the last moment. As it was, he felt like someone had struck his skull with a hammer, and for a moment darkness encroached on his vision and blood roared in his ears. His body threatened to quit on him.

Dazed, Drake felt a giant hand clamp around his neck, lift him off the ground and hurl him onto the table like a rag doll. Straightaway he knew what the giant had in mind – put some distance between them so he could finish Drake off with the shotgun.

Landing hard on the table's scored wooden surface, Drake threw out a hand and gripped the edge as he slid across it. The transfer of momentum caused the table to tip over, just as the giant worked the pump on his shotgun and levelled the weapon.

With a violent crash, Drake landed on the other side of the now over-turned table. An instant later, the bark of the shotgun was followed by a powerful thump and the crunch of splintering wood less than a foot from his head, and Drake turned to look at the fist-sized dent that suddenly appeared in the thick wooden surface beside him.

'You're fucked now, you little son of a bitch,' the giant snarled, his deep voice echoing off the cold brick walls. 'Nowhere left to run.'

Drake had been a fighter once upon a time, used to taking body and head shots, but this guy was in a different league. He was simply a monster, far stronger than any opponent Drake had faced inside or outside the ring. Going toe to toe against a man like that was suicide, even if he'd been in peak condition. Drake knew the only option was to end this fight quickly.

For that he would need a weapon.

He reached up for the nearest table leg, now protruding horizontally from the overturned table, and pulled on it with savage force. Wood splintered and cracked, and the nails holding it in place slipped free with a creaking groan. He was now armed, after a fashion. The only question was how best to use his new weapon.

'If you thought it was bad before, wait 'til you see what's coming,' his enemy taunted him. 'Before I kill you, I'm gonna carve you into pieces.'

He heard the distinctive double click as the shotgun was reloaded, followed by the heavy tread and scuff of boots on the stone floor. The giant was keeping his distance as he circled around the table to get a clean shot at Drake, but by doing so he was allowing himself to be backed into a corner.

Bracing his shoulder against the overturned table, Drake began to push it forward, digging his feet into the gaps between the worn flagstones. He barely noticed the pain as the table edge bumped onwards, picking up speed and momentum as he put more force into it.

With nowhere to retreat to, the giant was left with only one option. The table shuddered as a round slammed into it, punching another dent in its surface, but failing to break through. Then, a second or so later, Drake's moving shield came to a sudden halt as a massive boot jammed against it.

Drake looked up as the shotgun appeared over the edge of the table. Unable to advance, Drake was now a sitting duck as the giant simply leaned over the top of his cover, ready to fire at point-blank range.

There was only one thing he hadn't counted on.

Playing his final card, Drake seized the table leg and swung upwards, aiming for anything that looked unprotected. A soft, wet thump was followed by a roar, as the nails still sticking from the leg's upper section embedded themselves deep in the giant's forearm, severing nerves and tendons.

Tearing the improvised weapon free, Drake jumped up and launched himself at his ailing enemy. Just get in and do as much damage as humanly possible; that was what he'd been taught when it came to unarmed combat. Technique and strategy was useful up to a point, but when you're fighting for your life against long odds, sometimes there's no substitute for sheer, raw aggression.

He swung again, landing a second crippling blow on a heavily muscled shoulder, before finally bringing the weapon around against his head like a baseball player swinging for a home run. He felt the vicious impact as wood slammed into his opponent's skull and nails penetrated through to the vital organ within, heard a confused grunt as the blow registered, then watched as the damage took effect.

There was no dramatic fall; the giant just seemed to go limp and stop fighting back. He staggered once with the nails and table leg still embedded in the side of his head, reached up half-heartedly as if to pull it out, then let out a mumbled groan as his legs gave way and he slumped onto the floor. And there he lay, twitching and jerking spasmodically, a mountain of flesh at last laid low.

Then, for a few unbelievable seconds, silence descended, broken only by the sound of Drake's strained breathing.

Only then did he hear movement on the other side of the room, Moore crawling slowly towards the weapon that had been knocked from his grasp at the start of the fight.

Drake wasn't about to let him get to it. Taking the shotgun from the giant's dead hand, he rose to his feet, calmly took aim, and fired.

As the bean bag round hit Moore in the abdomen, he immediately doubled over and vomited across the floor, steam rising from the acrid-smelling liquid.

Working the pump action, Drake advanced on his target and knelt down beside him. He reached for the man's jacket, lifting his head so they had eye contact.

'Where's Frost?' Drake demanded.

'Fuck you!' he spat back.

That was all the excuse Drake needed. Jamming the shotgun barrel against the man's groin, he pulled the trigger.

The blast of the weapon discharge was muted this time by fabric and flesh, but the sound of the man's screams were almost as loud. Drake watched with a curiously satisfied feeling as his former tormentor curled up into a foetal position, hands clutched against what was left of his genitals.

'Don't make me ask again,' he advised, cocking the shotgun. 'Where's Frost? Where have you taken her?'

The man looked at him, blood from his nose mixing with the vomit still trailing from his mouth. 'Don't... know,' he managed. 'They... moved her. Another location. Didn't... tell us where.'

He wasn't going to get much else from this guy. Bean bag rounds might have been designed as non-lethal, but Drake was pretty certain a strike to the head from this range would still do the trick.

He took aim and pulled the trigger.

Click.

Of course, Drake thought. Four rounds fired during his battle with the giant, another two used on this man. The shotgun was empty.

'Must be your lucky day,' Drake said, tossing the useless shotgun aside.

Rising to his feet, he walked calmly over to where the Glock 17 had fallen during their struggle, picked the automatic up and took aim. The old Ryan Drake might have spared this man's life, might have seen it as unfair to kill an enemy who was no longer a threat, but that Ryan Drake was gone.

This was a new kind of war. One that took no prisoners, and left no survivors.

'Say hello to your colleagues when you see them,' Drake advised as his finger tightened on the trigger. He saw his enemy's blank terror. 'Tell them there's more coming.'

One last gunshot echoed through the room.

Chapter 10

Anya was waiting for Alex as he emerged from the steaming bathroom, a towel wrapped around his waist, his damp hair sticking up at all angles. The young man paused, looking confused by her presence.

'Anya. I thought you'd be long gone,' he remarked suspiciously. 'Isn't that your style? Kind of like the Milk Tray Man in reverse.'

'I wanted to thank you for helping me.' She gestured to the kitchen counter, where she'd laid out a breakfast of toast, scrambled eggs, coffee and orange juice. There hadn't been much to work with in his fridge, and she hardly considered herself a gifted cook at the best of times, but it was the best she could conjure up while he was showering. 'I thought you could use some breakfast after working all night.'

She saw the realization dawn on him as her uncharacteristically altruistic act was revealed for what it was.

'No,' he said, pointing a finger accusingly. 'I'm not doing it.'

'Doing what?' she asked, feigning innocence.

'Whatever horrible and probably life-threatening thing you're about to ask me to do,' he said, snatching up yesterday's dirty clothes from the bathroom floor. 'I know your game – you made breakfast to butter me up. Well, it's not happening. I got you the information you need, so we're all square now.'

'I need your help to get close to her,' Anya persisted, following him across the room as he dumped the clothes in the laundry basket.

'You mean, you need me to help kidnap her,' Alex fired back. 'Isn't that your area of expertise?'

'It is, but I can't do it alone. Lauren is a university student, Alex. I need someone who can blend in, move around the campus without arousing suspicion.'

What she was telling him was certainly true, but it wasn't the entire truth. Anya sensed he would refuse outright if she told him why he was really needed. At least this way she had a fighting chance.

Alex rounded on her. 'Jesus, isn't it enough that I'm wanted for stealing top-secret information by everyone from the NSA to the CIA to fucking AC/DC? Want to add kidnapping to the list?'

Anya decided not to mention that if he was captured by the authorities, he'd quickly find himself handed over to a CIA black ops team for interrogation and probably execution. One more crime wasn't going to change his prospects.

'You would not be directly involved. All I need is for you to be my eyes and ears. The rest I will handle myself,' she promised.

Alex hesitated. 'That wasn't our deal.'

Clearly he was going to need a little extra motivation. 'Then we make a new deal.'

His brows narrowed in a frown. 'What do you mean?'

'Fifty thousand euros,' she said simply. 'Paid into a bank account of your choice, once we have her secured.'

There was no need to ask whether he had the necessary savvy to open a secure numbered bank account. She was quite certain he had that covered already. The question was whether he would bite.

Alex's face went blank, betraying his surprise that she could toss such a figure around. The look was quickly masked, replaced by one of shrewd calculation, but Anya had seen enough already. She knew she had him.

'I'd want sixty,' he said.

'Fifty-five,' she countered, mostly because she wanted him to believe it was a tough sell and he was being a slick negotiator. 'That should be enough to sustain your life here for some time, without having to get on the wrong side of Russian gangsters. It's also my final offer. You can take it, or I can find someone more willing.'

'But less trustworthy,' he remarked, articulating her fundamental dilemma. Having made his point, he walked over to the breakfast bar, picked up a fork and helped himself to a mouthful of scrambled eggs.

'Damn, they're good,' he said, sounding almost annoyed that she hadn't messed them up. 'Why do mine never work out like this?'

Anya followed, sliding onto a stool beside him. She watched as he poured himself a cup of coffee from the pot, neglecting to offer her one.

'One way or another, I'm leaving within the hour,' she said gently. She had to persuade him; she couldn't force his cooperation this time. 'Am I leaving alone, Alex?'

Alex sighed before he'd even taken a sip of coffee. The sigh of a man preparing himself for a difficult and likely unpleasant task.

She could sense his hardening resolve.

'You know you're not,' he said.

Chapter 11

It took Drake less than two minutes to search both of his former captors and strip them of anything useful, particularly the jacket and boots belonging to the smaller of the two. The boots were a tight fit, but beggars couldn't be choosers. And it was a hell of a lot better than going barefoot.

The adrenaline and lust for vengeance that helped overpower his guards had certainly been useful, but now he needed to calm down and play it smart if he was to make use of his new-found freedom. As he'd expected, neither man was carrying any form of identification. Standard protocol was to go into jobs like this sterile in case they were caught or killed, and both men had adhered to it rigidly. He did, however, find a spare magazine for the Glock in a concealed carry pouch strapped to the smaller man's back, along with about two hundred euros in mixed notes that he wasn't too proud to help himself to.

Both men had burner phones, though the giant's device had been smashed and rendered inoperable during their fight. The other was still up and running, but there were no numbers saved in the directory and the call logs had been deleted. Again, nothing that could compromise the operation if the phone fell into the wrong hands. After muting the ring tone, Drake slipped the phone into his jacket pocket.

The other item lurking in the pocket of the giant's jeans would likely prove far more useful, however.

'I'll be taking these, mate,' Drake whispered, turning over the set of car keys in his hand. They were stamped with the Toyota symbol, and looked fairly new.

He had no idea what model they'd used to get here, but Drake guessed it must have been both big and sturdy to accommodate a man of his size. Either way, Drake would have no problem putting it to use as a getaway car.

But before he went anywhere, his priority was to confirm they had been lying about Frost. It was possible she was still on site somewhere and they'd simply been discouraging Drake from searching. If so, there was no way Drake was leaving without her.

A quick survey revealed more cells like the one he'd been held in, all of which were empty and showed no sign of recent use. It appeared he was alone, whatever and wherever this place was.

He would learn nothing further here, and had no desire to spend a second longer in such a gloomy shithole. More importantly, he knew that each passing minute increased the chance of his escape being discovered.

Clutching the Glock tight, he crept up the stairs, watching his footing on the worn stone steps as he picked his way past Hoffmann's slumped corpse. A quick check of the artery at his neck confirmed he was dead. That was just fine with Drake – one less arsehole in the world.

The familiar faint green glow of the weapon's tritium sights was oddly comforting as he resumed his ascent, the weapons training so deeply ingrained it was almost second nature.

The Glock was a good weapon to have in a tight spot like this. Accurate up to 50 metres, and with seventeen 9mm rounds in the magazine, it was a popular weapon with everyone from police to FBI agents, even Marine special forces, and had become a standard sidearm for most NATO units. The frame used a lot of polymers and composite materials, making it unusually light and easy to handle. If it came to a firefight, Drake knew he could do a fair amount of damage with the Glock.

Something was staining the wooden steps by his foot, gleaming black in the glow of electric lights. Stooping down, he touched his finger to it and held it up to get a better look. It was blood, most probably Frost's blood from her maimed hand as they carried her upstairs. It prompted a shudder, and a deep sense of foreboding and urgency.

It was difficult for Drake to plan his next move until he knew more about his environment and situation. In the unlikely event there were more armed operatives waiting upstairs, he'd react very much as he had previously: go at them with maximum speed and aggression, and use the resulting confusion to fight his way out.

It wasn't much as far as plans went, but improvisation would have to suffice.

A plain wooden door stood at the top of the stairs, its frame warped by time and exposure. Taking a moment to compose himself, Drake reached out, turned the handle and gently pushed the door open, moving quickly through the gap and sweeping his weapon left and right.

As he adjusted to the poor light, it became clear that this building wasn't part of any organized military set-up. A large, cavernous space stretched off into the darkness, the bare expanse of stone floor lacking any fixtures or fittings. Ancient walls rose up to a high vaulted ceiling, interspersed with long tapered windows that had likely once held stained glass.

Drake was in a church.

A disused church, judging by the water dripping from the failing roof, but a church all the same. This revelation confirmed his theory that this makeshift prison and interrogation centre had been set up in a hurry.

Drake tensed as he felt the cell phone buzz in his pocket. Digging it out, he quickly scanned the caller display, but the number came up as withheld.

Almost certainly it was the team's commander calling for an update. He debated what to do, whether to answer in the hope of learning something useful, or simply ignore it.

He soon decided against the former. If his adversaries were smart and organized – and he had no reason to suspect otherwise – they would have agreed password systems and duress codes in advance. Attempting to bluff through would only alert them that he had escaped. Instead he hit the reject call icon, hoping to stall them.

He needed to finish his sweep and pull out of here quickly.

Drake's attention turned to the floor, where more spots of blood marked the bare stone, leading towards the far end where the pulpit had once stood. Frost had been dragged this way. Drake crept forward, following the blood trail, his eyes flitting constantly in search of anything hostile.

The original wooden pulpit from which generations of priests had no doubt rained fire and brimstone on their congregation had long since been removed, but the main altar remained intact, accessed via a short flight of steps. Ascending these, Drake faced a small, low door set into the wall. Old wood set within a rusted metal frame. It was hanging ajar.

Drake closed his eyes and took a breath, steeling himself for what he might find. He had no doubt that Hawkins would kill Frost if she was no longer useful, and knew there was a real chance he might find her lying cold and dead within.

The thought of losing another of his friends was more than he could bear. His only hope was that Hawkins still saw her as valuable leverage.

With a well-practised movement, he shoved open the door and advanced inside, staring down the Glock's glowing night sight as he swept.

His first reaction was one of relief that the small, low-ceilinged room beyond – likely a vestry where the priest prepared before a service – was empty. However, he did see several large bloodstains on the floor, presumably where the young woman had lain. Venturing closer, he found a bloodied dressing and several wads of used surgical gauze lying beside them. They must have cleaned and dressed her wounds here before moving her.

As his friend downstairs had confirmed, Frost was gone.

That was when something within him, held taut since his escape, finally snapped. Anguished, he turned and slammed his boot into the door, kicking it so hard that the old wood broke and splintered.

He might have won freedom for himself – for now at least – but he couldn't bring her back. That realization seemed to sap the last of his energy. He felt his legs weaken and give way as he slumped down the cold, damp wall, until he was on the floor, battered, bruised and exhausted.

His hands were trembling, and for once it had nothing to do with the cold. He'd been able to push past it all until now, but there was no ignoring the fact he was in shit condition. The pain from his various injuries was putting his body in a state not unlike shock. It was common in soldiers

70

after battle, when they were no longer fighting for their lives and could start to process what they'd seen and done.

No, a voice within him said at that moment, hard and insistent and resolute. You're not going to fall apart now. Not when you've come this far. A few hours ago you were naked and freezing to death in a cell; now you're out and free, and you've got a chance. *Don't waste it.*

Drake snapped back into awareness then, reassessing what he'd found. As much as it pained him to have lost contact with Frost, the grisly discovery in here at least kindled a flicker of hope. They wouldn't have gone to the trouble of patching Frost's wounds if they intended to kill her. Wherever they'd taken her, he had to believe Frost was alive.

But she wouldn't be if he lingered here much longer. It was time to go.

He was just straightening up when he felt his phone buzzing again. Whoever was trying to get through wasn't taking no for an answer, and the lack of response was only going to arouse more suspicion.

Deciding he had little to lose, Drake hit receive call and held the phone to his ear.

–

Seated in the back of the Land Rover Discovery as it bumped and jolted down the lonely forest track, Hawkins watched as the windscreen wipers battled vainly against formidable rain and sleet. It was only a few hours earlier he'd been roaring across the warm waters of the Mediterranean.

'Moore, what's your sitrep?' he asked as soon as the line connected. 'And why weren't you answering your phone?'

'He can't hear you.' The voice that answered wasn't that of the operative he'd left to supervise Drake. Hawkins was silent as it sank in – Drake was no longer captive.

'Ryan, well goddamn if it isn't you!' he said at last, recovering his poise. 'I guess you're more resourceful than I gave you credit for.'

His acknowledgement was met with a brooding silence.

'Nice little trick you played with the *Alamo*, by the way. At this rate, I'm going to need to hire more help.' The operatives seated in the vehicle with him exchanged a few nervous glances. 'Tell me the boys there at least put up a decent fight? Hate to think we were paying them for nothing.'

That was enough to provoke a response. 'What I did to them is nothing compared to what you've got coming.'

There was no anger or emotion in Drake's voice; it was as if he were speaking of some preordained, immutable fact.

Such a threat might have chilled another man to the bone, but in Hawkins it prompted a different reaction. Drake had chosen to fight back, and Hawkins always liked it when they fought back. It made it all the more satisfying to break them down.

'Buddy, I really hope you're not wasting time shooting the breeze when you could be running for your life,' Hawkins advised. Craning his neck, he followed the long curve of the road into the distance, where the derelict church lay less than two miles away. 'If I get there and find you trying to turn that church into your own personal Alamo, I'll be very disappointed.'

Silence greeted him for a second or two, and he began to wonder whether Drake had abandoned the phone and fled. However, his adversary had one last message for him.

'Remember what you said to me in that basement, about wanting the old Ryan Drake back?'

'I do,' Hawkins acknowledged.

'You got what you wanted, Jason.'

With that, the call cut out.

Calmly replacing the phone in his pocket, Hawkins leaned back in his seat and stared thoughtfully out of the window at the darkened forest rushing past. Without prompting, the driver stomped on the accelerator, increasing speed.

It took about 90 seconds for the two-vehicle convoy to cover the remaining mile of rough, unpaved road. Screeching to a halt about 20 yards from the church, armed operatives piled out of both cars, quickly spreading to form a perimeter. Aside from the rattle of wind and the constant patter of rain, the place was ominously quiet.

Hawkins exited at a more leisurely pace, seeing little sense in rushing. He noted that the Toyota 4 x 4 belonging to his three-man team was sitting where they'd left it. Drake must have been smart enough to realize there was only one road in or out, and trying to steal the car would have resulted in a head-on confrontation with an armed tactical team.

Around him, operatives glanced his way, awaiting orders. 'Move in,' Hawkins instructed, amused by their trepidation. 'Secure the building.'

Nervily holding FN P90 submachine guns, four men ventured through the main entrance, the red dots from their under-barrel laser sights piercing the darkness. The remainder of the team waited in anxious silence, the rain slowly soaking through their clothes.

'Building secure,' came the radio call about 30 seconds later. The tone of the man's voice told Hawkins the news wasn't good. 'We've found our men. They're in the basement.'

'Dead?'

'You'd better see for yourself, sir.'

This ought to be good, Hawkins thought. 'On my way.'

Making his way inside, Hawkins descended the stairs to what had once been the crypt. He knew nothing of the building's history, but he liked to imagine this was where the heretics and sinners of centuries gone by had been held until they found the light of God – willingly or unwillingly.

He could almost picture the medieval torture devices breaking bones and tearing flesh.

Reaching the bottom, Hawkins let out an appreciative whistle as he took in the scene, picked out by the probing beams of the assault team's flashlights.

Hoffmann was lying sprawled at the base of the stairs in a pool of blood, his body perforated by several gunshots to the chest and abdomen. The electric lights gleamed across the bald dome of his head.

Parker was lying beside the overturned table, his massive body in an ungainly heap, with one of the wooden table legs embedded against the side of his maimed head. An inventive enough way to take someone out, he supposed, but that wasn't what really caught his attention.

Drake had found a use for the hook mounted in the ceiling. Moore was hanging from it, his hands bound by the same plastic cuffs they'd used on Drake, stripped to the waist and with blood dripping from what was left of his head. And across his exposed chest, carved in crude lettering with some kind of ragged bladed instrument, was a simple but chilling message.

YOU'RE NEXT

'Oh, Ryan, you weren't kidding,' Hawkins said, folding his arms and taking it in like an artist critiquing another man's work. He shook his head in regret. 'The things we could have done together...'

'Sir, what are your orders?' the assault team leader asked, visibly shaken. He and his team were nothing but piss-ant security contractors, easily demoralized, not the hardened soldiers Hawkins was used to leading.

Hawkins touched the blood dripping from the lettering carved into Moore's chest.

'Blood's still warm; he can't have gotten far. Get some teams out into the woods and track him down. And bring in our air assets.' The team stood rooted to the spot, still staring at the dead man hanging from the ceiling. 'Anyone got a problem with that?'

They couldn't leave fast enough. As the team hurried back upstairs, the assault leader paused beside Hawkins and gestured to the two bodies. 'What about them, sir?'

Hawkins shrugged, unconcerned. 'What about them? They're not going anywhere.'

Part II

Evasion

'It is necessary to have wished for death in order to know how good it is to live.'

– Alexandre Dumas

Chapter 12

Drake was running, pounding through the woods as fast as his legs would carry him. His boots splashed through sodden ground – muddy earth and last season's leaves sucking him down, branches and tangled thorns ripping at his clothes. And all the while, freezing rain lashed down.

For the first few minutes he'd headed directly away from the church, wanting to gain maximum distance, before turning 45 degrees right and resuming his run, his course carrying him downhill into a shallow valley lined with leafless trees. When Hawkins inevitably sent men out to track him, Drake needed to put in some unpredictable changes of direction to make their job difficult.

He was under no illusions that he could run or hide in these woods for ever, particularly if Hawkins was able to call on air assets armed with thermal imaging cameras, but he needed to be as far away as possible before the sun came up. Assuming the clock on the burner phone had been accurate before Drake discarded it, the local time was somewhere around six thirty in the morning. That meant he had less than an hour before sunrise.

Not much time to make an escape.

Redoubling his efforts, he pushed on, following the slope of the ground, partly because it allowed him to move faster but mostly because he was already too tired to climb. Two days of no sleep, beatings and virtual starvation, not to mention the fight to free himself, had taken a toll that was not easily fixed.

He was cold despite his exertions. Movement was helping to keep his core temperature up, but the wet terrain had infiltrated his boots, numbing his feet.

All in all, he was reminded very much of the escape and evasion phase he'd endured during selection for the SAS. Trekking for miles through the snow-covered Brecon Beacons in mid-January, armed with little more than an outdated map, a moth-eaten greatcoat that smelled like it had been lying in a storage depot since WW1, and a pair of boots that didn't fit. And all the while, a larger and far better equipped hunter force had been pursuing him.

Except this time around, there would be no fake interrogations, stern lectures and piss-taking if he was caught. Only a bullet to the head or a return to his cell. Drake couldn't make up his mind which was worse, but he was determined to avoid both.

He managed to cover another mile or so before his strength began to fail him. He backed up against a tree, struggling to draw breath that wouldn't come. His lungs strained against his ribs as if the bony cage was too small to contain them. His shoulder blazed with pain from where he'd been hit by the riot gun, not to mention the countless other cuts and bruises that marked his body.

He couldn't keep this up much longer. Already the overcast sky was marginally brighter in the east as the sun crept up, rendering the bleak, muddy woodland in a sombre predawn light.

That was when he heard it – the distinctive *whup, whup, whup* of rotor blades. Turning southwards, he caught the flashing navigation lights of a chopper about a mile distant, partially obscured by low cloud. It was moving slowly and deliberately, orbiting in concentric circles outwards from the church.

Drake recognized a search pattern when he saw one. Given the poor visibility it was safe to assume Hawkins wouldn't have requested air support unless the chopper was armed with infrared navigation equipment. It also meant that Drake's warm body would stand out easily against the cold background.

It wouldn't take them long to find him, and hiding wasn't an option. He could take cover and obscure himself from the air temporarily, but Hawkins would have these woods crawling with men and probably tracker dogs within hours. Sooner or later they would pick up his trail and follow it straight to him.

The only option was to flee.

Pushing himself off the tree, he hurried onwards, pounding down the muddy slope and almost losing his footing several times as the loose earth gave way. And all the while the chopper circled ever closer.

Gradually he became aware of another noise: the steady, muted roar of water cascading over rocks. A river was flowing nearby, likely following the line of the valley.

Pausing to lean against a moss-covered boulder and catch his breath, Drake spotted the white churning foam of a fast-flowing stream, no doubt swollen by the incessant rain. And, winding beside it, the distinctive black hardtop of a paved road.

No sooner had he caught sight of this roadway than a pair of headlight beams rounded a bend in the valley off to the west, heading in his direction. But was it a civilian car, or an Agency transport filled with armed operatives? He couldn't tell from this distance, particularly with the lights shining more or less straight at him. But whatever its purpose, the vehicle was moving at a steady 40 or 50 miles an hour by his reckoning – fast enough to be driving with a destination in mind, but slow enough to avoid undue risk on the wet and treacherous road.

A local on their way home, perhaps?

The chopper was circling around to the north again, its spiralling course carrying it away from Drake's position for the time being. If Drake was going to act, it would have to be now.

He went for it, pushing towards the road even as the vehicle headed towards him. He could hear the rattling chug of an old, poorly maintained engine approaching, which gave him more hope of civilian origin.

It was getting close. He needed to hurry if he was going to—

The muddy ground suddenly caved beneath him and Drake slid down a steep section, unable to slow or even control his descent with nothing to hold on to. All he could do was try to balance and prevent his weight from pitching him forward, where it would be all too easy to crack his skull on a rock or tree root.

He landed with a bump amid a pile of old branches, mud and rotting leaves. Thorns snagged his wet clothes as he fought to extricate himself, the vehicle headlights now less than a hundred yards away.

Tearing fabric and skin, he staggered out and sprinted the last few yards to the roadway, feeling his boots make contact with solid ground.

Drake drew the Glock and stepped out into the middle of the road, levelling his weapon at a spot slightly above the twin headlights. Brakes screeched and the vehicle swerved sideways, tyres skidding on the road. For a heart-stopping moment Drake wondered if the car might mow him down.

The vehicle shuddered to a stop barely 10 yards from him. He saw a young, frightened face behind the wheel as he rushed towards it, weapon up and ready.

'Don't move! Hands where I can see them!' Drake yelled, advancing.

One look was enough to confirm this wasn't anything to do with Hawkins' operation. Rather than a sleek, black, intimidating SUV, he found himself facing a compact two-door coupé, its once-white paintwork patched with rust. It was a Skoda Rapid, he realized, recognizing the angular lines of its 1980s bodywork from his childhood. Made long before Skoda went all upmarket, the name Rapid was, he assumed, applied tongue-in-cheek to the clunky, unreliable cars.

Still, a shit car it might have been, but it was a car nonetheless.

He tugged open the door on the passenger side and peered inside, brandishing the Glock. There was just the driver – a young woman in ripped jeans and a black vest top, who let out a squeal at the sight of the weapon and tried to press herself against her door. Too terrified to remove her seatbelt and make a run for it.

Drake couldn't blame her for being frightened. If a bloody, mud-covered man with a gun had hijacked his car on a lonely road like this, he'd have been worried too. Still, this was no time for gentle reassurances. Right now he needed cooperation, not friendship.

'Stay where you are!' he yelled, jumping into the passenger seat. The car rocked noticeably on worn-out shock absorbers. 'Get us out of here!'

She was pleading with him in a language he didn't recognize, her eyes wet with tears. Most probably she was politely suggesting he take the car and fuck off without her, but Drake had already decided that wasn't going to happen. The next car that passed would be sure to stop for her, and it wouldn't be long before the local police were mobilized. Even worse, if Hawkins' men picked her up first, they would soon learn how he'd escaped.

He would ditch her along with the car later when he was well clear of the area, but for now he needed them both.

'Shut up and drive!' he shouted, levelling the pistol at her forehead. 'Drive now!'

He couldn't tell if she understood what he was saying, but an automatic handgun was enough to overcome most language barriers.

She fumbled for the gearstick, crunching the gearbox a couple of times before finding first and stamping on the accelerator. Tyres skidding, the old car fishtailed left and right before eventually finding purchase and rocketing off down the darkened road.

Chapter 13

'No, sir,' Marcus Cain said firmly, having to fight the growing urge to bang his fist on the table in frustration at what he was hearing. 'We can't do that.'

He'd been called into one of the plush high-security conference rooms at Langley for a special briefing on the clandestine group he'd helped create, now informally known within closed circles as Task Force Black. Straightaway he'd known something big was up. The chairman of the meeting was Bradley Simmons, the head of the Agency's Special Activities Division.

In his late fifties, gaunt, balding and bespectacled, Simmons' unsmiling countenance had always put Cain in mind of a frustrated accountant or perhaps an overworked math teacher. Someone who had spent their life locked away in a cubicle office beneath cheap strip lighting.

But appearances aside, Simmons was definitely not a man to fuck with. As head of the Agency's clandestine operations arm, he was privy to some of the deepest secrets within the US intelligence world.

With him was Colonel Richard Carpenter, the man who had overseen the training and deployment of the task force, and acted as their military liaison for the past two years. If the field reports were accurate, Carpenter was becoming increasingly disconnected from their activities as operational command passed to the leaders of the group itself. That hadn't stopped him riding the wave of their stunning military successes in Afghanistan however, or ingratiating himself with the Agency's higher echelons.

'Task Force Black has done four tours in Afghanistan already,' Cain went on, forcing calm into his voice. 'They've had more time in the field than any other clandestine group since Vietnam.'

The truth was, Task Force Black had succeeded far beyond anyone's expectations, including Cain's. What had once been viewed as a risky, unpredictable experiment was now being touted as one of the Agency's biggest victories in clandestine warfare for the past two decades. But with such victories had come increased expectation, and demands for them to be redeployed to other hard-pressed areas of the conflict. They had, in effect, become victims of their own success.

'Which is exactly why we need them now more than ever,' said Simmons. 'Nobody knows that country like they do. More importantly, nobody knows the Mujahedeen like they do — they're trusted, respected even. That's not an easy commodity to come by.'

Commodity – that was how men like Simmons thought of conflicts like Afghanistan, and the people caught up in them. Just dry numbers and resources to be used up or redistributed as necessary. They didn't see casualty figures and kill ratios in terms of coffins coming home, or families robbed of sons and fathers; all they saw were variables in the great equation of war. And it was their job to balance the books.

'The fact is, we've got the Soviets on the ropes,' Carpenter interrupted, bullish as always. The bright and ambitious colonel with his eyes on a general's star, always so eager to say what the top brass wanted to hear. 'Our Stinger missiles have negated their air advantage, their logistics network is getting raided night and day, and they're even losing the big set-piece battles they used to be so desperate to fight. All we need is the knockout blow.'

Simmons nodded thoughtfully on this, showing neither enthusiasm nor disdain for Carpenter's assessment of the situation there. They might have been united by a common purpose, but Cain always had the impression Simmons tolerated rather than respected Carpenter. In which case, the feeling was mutual.

'Mr Qalat, what's your read on this?' he asked, turning to the third member of the group that Cain was up against. Small, efficient and neatly groomed, Vizur Qalat was an officer with Pakistani military intelligence – a vital ally in the region since much of Task Force Black's operations were staged out of Pakistani territory.

Qalat had been their liaison with the CIA since the group went into the field, supplying them with useful intel about Soviet movements and plans, but this was the first time Cain had met the man face to face. He spoke rarely of his own accord, volunteering little but listening a great deal. Cain was left with the distinct impression that beneath his undistinguished visage was an intelligence both shrewd and calculating.

'Sir, I would be inclined to agree with the colonel's summary,' he said. 'Our debriefings with Soviet defectors tell us their morale is at breaking point. Most just want to go home. Many regions have already ceded operational responsibility to the Afghan military.'

Trying to get the Afghans to do their fighting for them, Cain knew. The Americans had done the same thing in the closing stages of Vietnam. Hadn't worked out too well for them either.

'Then we don't need further intervention,' Cain reasoned. 'If what you say is true, the Soviets will be out of there within a year anyway. What's the point in kicking them when they're already down? We'd be provoking them into escalating all over again.'

This was a waste of time and energy, Cain knew. They should have been concentrating their efforts on preparing a moderate, pro-Western government for when the puppet regime in Kabul was overthrown. They should have been planning aid shipments and reconstruction programmes for the devastated country. Instead they were talking about prolonging a war that was all but won.

'An orderly withdrawal can still be spun as a victory by Moscow, especially given their state propaganda,' Qalat pointed out. 'But a chaotic retreat would be an outright humiliation that even they couldn't hide.'

Cain wasn't convinced by their optimistic assessments. Though it was true the Soviets had their eyes firmly on an exit from Afghanistan, they were by no means a broken force. Worse, they'd started hearing rumours that the KGB had deployed elements of their most feared special forces unit, the Alpha Group, to hunt down Task Force Black. The group's success and fearsome reputation was now becoming a liability.

As skilled as Anya and her comrades were at guerrilla warfare, a confrontation with a highly trained, more numerous and battle-hardened enemy was one fight they couldn't hope to win. It was part of the reason he'd petitioned the Agency to bring the task force home ahead of schedule.

'Marcus, you're not seeing the bigger picture here,' Carpenter chided him in his most patronising tone. 'This isn't just about Afghanistan now; this is about going after the big prize. Gorbachev's losing control of the Eastern Bloc, and pretty much all the Islamic republics are looking to break away. The only thing he has left is the threat of military force, but a major defeat for the Red Army... well, we'd be taking away his trump card just when he needs it most. Then there's nothing left to hold the Soviet Union together. What do you think will happen then?'

'Times are changing,' Simmons concluded. 'We're standing at a crossroads, and it falls to us to steer the world down the right path. This is the way to do it. Task Force Black helped us change the course of this war. Now we need them to go in one more time, help change the course of history.'

Cain let out a frustrated breath. If Simmons expected him to be swayed by such histrionics, he was sorely mistaken.

'And isn't that what we all want, buddy? Peace in our time?' Carpenter asked.

Cain looked at him, knowing full well that the last thing a man like him ever desired was peace. For Carpenter, there would always be more wars to fight, more glory to chase, more young lives to sacrifice.

'I need to think about this,' Cain said, stalling for time. 'I can't send them anywhere until I've had a chance to think it through.'

Simmons' brows rose, but nonetheless he closed his briefing folders. 'All right. You have until the end of the day, then I want a decision.'

Five minutes later, Cain was in a restroom just down the corridor from the conference suite where the fate of his task force, of Anya, had just been decided. Splashing cold water on his face, he looked up at his reflection.

Marcus Cain, the young rising star within the Agency. Ambitious, focussed, willing to do what it took to get results. He knew he could push back, could outright refuse to obey Simmons' directive and have the task force stand down. It would hurt his career badly, perhaps irreparably, but he could do it.

Suddenly Cain slammed his fist down on the counter so hard that the entire unit rattled loudly, leaving his hand aching.

'Careful, buddy. You're going to hurt yourself.'

Turning around, Cain glared at Carpenter who was standing over by the door, preventing anyone else from entering.

'What do you want?' he asked, drying his face with some paper towels. 'I told you I haven't made my decision yet.'

He saw a faint smile flicker on the colonel's face. 'Don't make it personal, Marcus. We're both professionals here. That being the case, you can think of this as a professional courtesy.'

Cain frowned. 'For what?'

'For not telling Simmons what I know.' The smile had broadened now. 'Come on, we both know the real reason you don't want to send the task force back into the field, and it's got nothing to do with strategic planning. It's her, isn't it? It was always her.'

Cain could feel the colour rising to his cheeks. 'What the hell are you talking about?'

'I know what you two have got going on. I've seen the proof. You've been a very naughty boy, Marcus. A case officer getting romantically involved with one of his assets.'

Cain felt like his stomach had just been twisted in a knot. Carpenter was perfectly right, of course. It had been going on for some time now, against countless rules and directives. They'd tried to be careful, tried to be discreet about it, but it hadn't been enough to escape this man's attention.

'Can't say I'm surprised,' Carpenter went on. 'After all, Anya's quite some piece of tail. And let me tell you, the surveillance footage makes for some pretty interesting watching—'

Launching himself off the counter, Cain grabbed the older man by the jacket of his uniform and angrily shoved him against the wall.

'Say another word,' Cain said through clenched teeth. 'I dare you.'

'Like I said, Marcus. You want to be careful, or you're going to hurt yourself.'

The implied threat wasn't lost on Cain. Carpenter was a trained killer, and they both knew it. He hadn't retaliated yet because he didn't need to. If it came down to a real fight between the two of them, the colonel could put Cain down as easily as a raw recruit in a drill hall.

Not only that, but Carpenter now had the ability to kill him professionally as well as physically. If it was revealed that Cain was personally involved with one of his operatives, it could sink his career.

'What do you want?' Cain demanded.

'You know what I want,' Carpenter said calmly. 'Let's finish what we started three years ago. And when we do, we'll all be heroes. Even Anya.'

'And if I don't?'

The colonel shrugged. 'Professionally, I'm obliged to report my findings to your immediate superior, so he can take appropriate disciplinary action. Be a shame to do it, but it is what it is.'

The son of a bitch wouldn't let this go, Cain knew. Carpenter: always the opportunist, always ready to take credit for other people's victories and trample anyone that stood on his path to glory.

'Come on, Marcus. Grow some balls, will you?' Carpenter taunted. 'Man up and authorize their redeployment, or you'll be relieved of command and someone else will. Either way, they're going back in. Like Simmons said, we're all at a crossroads. Think of it as my job to help you down the right path. So what's it going to be?'

There was no choice to make, Cain knew. If he called Carpenter's bluff, it would be the end of his career. And Anya's.

'Fine. You've got your war, but that's where it ends,' Cain said at last, releasing his grip and backing away. 'They finish this tour, and they're done. We're done, for good.'

'That's the spirit.' Carpenter smiled, stepping aside so that he was no longer blocking the doorway. 'They might be done after this, but I've got a feeling you and I are going to do great things together.'

Cain didn't trust himself to look at him as he brushed past, seething.

–

CIA headquarters, Langley – 30 March 2010

Removing his reading glasses, Cain closed his eyes and rubbed the sore spot on the bridge of his nose.

'Say that again,' he said, speaking quietly into his phone.

'Drake's tip-off was a trap,' Hawkins reported, sounding neither apologetic nor hesitant about the news he was delivering. 'The *Alamo* was rigged with concealed explosives that triggered when the assault team made entry.'

'Casualties?' Cain asked.

'Three men dead. We pulled out before local police units arrived.'

Cain knew he should have felt something at three men dying last night, largely because of him. He should have felt guilt, remorse, grief at more young lives sacrificed, yet nothing of the sort stirred. He felt only a vague disappointment and irritation, as if he'd run some arithmetic through and come up short of his target.

'What about Drake?'

A pause. 'He's gone. Escaped from the detention building while we were following his tip. He killed his guards, took their weapons and strung one of them up for us to find.'

Cain was taking a moment to digest everything. 'Sounds to me like his guards weren't up to much.'

'I work with what I'm given,' Hawkins said, in a none-too-subtle dig at the quality of the men Cain had supplied. 'Anyway, our assumption is that he'll get clear of the initial search area, then try to link up with Anya again.'

'And of course you'll find him before that happens, right?'

Another pause. 'We're working on it.'

Cain's grip on the phone tightened. 'You'd better do a lot more than just work on it, Jason. I trusted you to oversee this operation, and twice now you've let Anya slip through your fingers. I won't be so forgiving next time.'

Without waiting for Hawkins' response, he ended the call.

He was just replacing the encrypted cell phone in his desk drawer when the door to his office flew open. CIA Director Robert Wallace strode right in without troubling himself to knock, as was his habit – one of the little ways he liked to show his dominance.

'Please, make yourself at home, Bob,' Cain said, calling the director by his first name because he knew it irritated him. At the same time, he gently eased his drawer closed, keeping the encrypted cell out of sight. 'Can I get you a drink?'

Wallace shot Cain a scathing look as he paced the room, searching for some crushing remark.

'I'd settle for knowing why you made an unscheduled trip to Pakistan three days ago,' he fired, stopping at Cain's desk, hands on hips in what he probably thought was an intimidating pose. His suit jacket was unbuttoned – always a bad sign. Unfortunately all it did was expose a sagging gut and a narrow, weedy looking chest.

Cain shrugged. There was no sense denying it. As second in command of America's biggest intelligence agency, he couldn't travel halfway around the world without people eventually finding out. Including the man in charge.

'Like you said, we need results against al-Qaeda. I went to find some.'

Wallace's grey-blue eyes narrowed. 'I'm going to need more than that, Marcus. Because I'm hearing things coming out of Pakistan that are not making me happy. Like explosions and shootouts in Islamabad the night you happened to be there. Like the murder of Pakistani intelligence officers. Like black flights being dispatched all over Asia carrying unlisted prisoners!'

He inhaled sharply, his face tight and deeply flushed, and seemed to shrink slightly before Cain's eyes. A vein at his temple bulged, as if he was about to blow a gasket.

Cain watched in silence, enjoying his discomfort. When Wallace, a career politician more accustomed to committee meetings and legislative debate, had taken up the post of director a year ago, Cain had predicted he wouldn't last long with the constant stress, lack of sleep and heavy workload. Based on what he was seeing, he might soon be proven right.

Bad heart, high cholesterol, high blood pressure, a stroke, or simply age and declining stamina. Cain couldn't rightly say what was ultimately going to force the director's retirement, but he suspected it would happen before too long.

Wallace let out a slow breath and folded his arms. 'I want to know exactly what you were doing out there, and I want to know now.'

'No, you don't,' Cain replied evenly.

84

'Excuse me?'

Cain rose slowly from behind his desk. Drawn up to his full height, he was easily a couple of inches taller than the director, and still broad-shouldered and physically strong despite feeling distinctly middle-aged.

'You've been a politician most of your adult life, Bob. And I don't doubt you will be again after your assignment here is over,' he said, making his way around his expansive desk. 'You were brought in to clean up the Agency, improve its public image. So I'm sure you, more than anyone, appreciates the value of plausible deniability.'

For once, Wallace didn't look quite so cocky and sure of himself, especially with Cain standing mere feet away from him. 'What exactly are you saying?'

'I'm saying, being a CIA director is a lot like being president. You have a limited shelf life. And like presidents, most of them learn pretty quickly that the only thing more dangerous than knowing too little is knowing too much. Believe me, I've been around long enough to understand that.'

Wallace's weak jaw jutted defiantly, his eyes flaring with indignation. 'Think carefully about what you say next, because I don't take kindly to being threatened. Especially by one of my own employees,' he said, pointing a finger at Cain. 'You might have been around a long time, but I can change that.'

'You can,' Cain acknowledged. 'But you won't. Because unlike you, this job isn't just a stepping stone into public office for me. I've seen men in your position rise to some of the highest ranks in government, and I've seen others sink like a stone. It all comes down to how you're remembered, and what your name's attached to.' He let that sink in before going on. 'You asked earlier what exactly I was saying. Well, it's simply this – back off, be the knight in shining armour you were hired to be, take the credit when things go well, and let people like me get on with the real work of running this agency.'

Such was his shock, Wallace genuinely couldn't muster a response for the next couple of seconds. He simply stood, staring, as if Cain were a fortune teller who had just foretold the man's doom.

'If whatever the fuck you're cooking up… if it goes wrong—'

'Then it's on me,' Cain interrupted. 'If it all works out, then the director takes the credit, and his stock on the Hill goes way up.'

Wallace surveyed his deputy with undisguised anger. But mindful of his earlier outburst, he was careful to rein it in.

'And what the hell do you get out of it, Cain? A favour owed? Chips you can cash in later?'

Cain might have smiled. Wallace, still thinking like the politician he was, seeing everything in terms of leverage and capital.

'I get what we all want, Bob. Peace in our time.' Cain turned away and rounded his desk once more. 'Now if you don't mind, I have work to do.'

The director hesitated a few moments longer, no doubt trying to counter the feeling that he'd just been dismissed.

'All right, Marcus. I'll give a little latitude on this one. *Very little*,' he said, as if it were still his decision to make. 'But I promise you this. If your "deniable operation" goes south, I am going to come down on you so hard I'll make you wish I was a ton of bricks.'

With that, he strode out of the office, making sure to slam the door hard behind him.

Chapter 14

Compared to the soaking, freezing cold weather that he'd fought through, the warm and dry interior of the old Skoda was pure heaven, particularly after Drake had cranked the heating up to full power. Moisture from his slowly drying clothes quickly condensed against the windscreen, making it difficult to see outside, though Drake noticed the young woman maintained speed as if frightened of his reaction if she slowed.

'It's all right, you can slow down,' he said, speaking more calmly now that the situation was less desperate. Speeding might draw police attention that he certainly didn't need to deal with. 'Slow down.'

She glanced at him, uncertain, but gradually the speedometer began to drop.

With less chance of skidding off the road, Drake was afforded a brief opportunity to study the driver in more detail. What he saw was more baffling than enlightening.

She was young – early twenties at most. Her simple but revealing clothes emphasized a slender physique, narrow waist and breasts that were too big to be natural. Her hair was dyed blonde and cut to shoulder length, her face covered by heavy make-up that it didn't need. Who the hell was this girl? She resembled a glamour model, though her choice of ride was anything but glamorous.

'You speak English,' he said, thinking it best to be direct.

Again her eyes flicked to him, as if she were weighing up how much to reveal. Finally deciding to be honest, she acknowledged, 'Yes.'

'What's your name?'

He saw the muscles working in her throat as she swallowed. 'Lenka.'

Drake shifted position, trying to get more comfortable while keeping her covered. 'Where are we, Lenka?'

She gestured up ahead, where the lights of a small settlement were visible through the murky weather. 'That is Borinka up ahead.'

'I mean what country are we in?'

She peered at him in confusion, perhaps wondering whether this was a trick.

'Eyes on the road,' he instructed, wary of her losing control. 'And answer the question. What country is this?'

'Slovakia.'

Now he was getting somewhere. Eastern Europe was a logical choice for holding prisoners like himself and Frost without interference from local government. Many of the former Eastern Bloc countries had a cosy no-questions-asked relationship with the Agency when it came to hosting black sites on their territory, helped no doubt by large amounts of cash channelled their way.

However, to the best of Drake's knowledge, Slovakia wasn't one of them. Then again, the place he'd escaped from hadn't looked particularly well prepared or set up. Perhaps it had merely been a convenient location set up in haste to accommodate him.

'Are you going to kill me?' she asked. She seemed to have gotten over her earlier shock, her voice taking on a more blunt and practical tone as if they were discussing his dinner plans for that evening.

Drake blinked. 'What?'

'Are you going to kill me?' she repeated, speaking slower. He could see the tension in her body, as if she were preparing to act. She hardly struck him as a fighter, but that didn't mean she wouldn't try something if her life was on the line.

Drake knew the time had come to change tactics. He needed to reassure her that there was a way out – one that didn't involve dying.

'Lenka, listen to me. I've got no interest in harming you. I just need to get out of the area. If you cooperate, you'll walk away from this unharmed. Understand?'

The young woman nodded. He didn't know how much of it she believed, but some of the primal fear seemed to abate at least.

'What were you doing out here so early?'

'Going home,' Lenka replied, raising her chin a little. 'I work late.'

'Do you live with someone? Are there people expecting you?' He leaned closer, scrutinizing her reactions carefully. 'Tell the truth.'

She was quiet for a few moments. 'I live alone.'

'Where?'

'Stupava. The next town over,' she explained. 'Maybe four or five miles from here.'

It was closer than he would have liked, but it would have to do. With luck, a town like that would be big enough for two people to move around unnoticed, at least for a while. He needed somewhere to lay up for a few hours, to sort himself out and plan his next move.

'Take me there,' he said.

Lenka's eyes opened wide. Whatever she'd imagined coming of this unhappy encounter, having Drake take up residence in her home likely hadn't been part of it.

'But—'

'I said I don't want to hurt you, but don't push your luck,' he cut in impatiently, moving so the Glock was in her peripheral vision. 'Just drive the car.'

Lenka was wise enough not to protest further, but Drake saw her hands were firm on the wheel, and she pressed down on the gas a little harder than she needed to.

Whatever – he didn't care too much if she was pissed off with him. As long as she cooperated and didn't try to escape, that was good enough for now.

Chapter 15

Pontoise – Cormeilles aerodrome, France

The sleek Gulfstream G280 touched down at a small airfield north-west of Paris just after 9 a.m. local time, having ferried its two occupants from southern Poland. The journey had taken a little over 90 minutes.

'Well, that was… an experience,' said Alex as he and Anya disembarked.

Normally flying across Europe in his own luxury plane would be the stuff of dreams, but in this case it felt like the dreams had been influenced by a heavy dose of LSD. With an interior decked out in neon lights and purple leather, and a fully stocked bar and an entertainment centre that would put most hotels to shame, Alex felt more like he was in a strip club instead of an executive jet. The only thing missing was scantily clad women, though he suspected the jet's owner had them on hand when he flew.

He genuinely couldn't make up his mind who was more of a mad bastard: the mysterious – and presumably very wealthy – oligarch who travelled in such an aircraft, or the Russian pilot who flew it like it was a training simulator set up for his own personal amusement. Alex had never been so happy to set foot on solid ground.

'Who the hell installs a disco ball in a private jet anyway?' he asked, speaking so that only his companion could hear.

'Someone who makes a lot more money than you, little boy,' the heavily Russian-accented voice of the pilot reprimanded him. 'So don't be giving me shit. And you better not have been fucking around with the PlayStation, or I'll cut your balls off.'

Alex glanced up at the gangly figure leaning out of the open hatch. Lean and mean looking, with receding hair kept closely cropped, and a tanned, strong-featured face, the man Anya had introduced as Yevgeny had been about as unwelcoming as it was possible to be. He resented having to ferry them halfway across Europe, and he'd made no attempt to hide it.

'He didn't touch a thing, Yevgeny,' Anya promised him. 'I appreciate your help. We both do,' she added, elbowing Alex in the ribs.

'That's right,' Alex agreed, pasting on a fake smile. 'You're the man, Yevgeny.'

Yevgeny didn't look convinced. Reaching for the pack of cigarettes in his shirt pocket, he lit one and took a deep draw. He had the look of someone building up to a difficult question, his former bluster gone.

'We are even now, yes?' he asked, addressing his question to Anya. 'For Ignaty.'

'Yes,' the woman confirmed from the bottom of the jet's retractable stairs. 'We are even.'

He nodded, satisfied. 'Then I will drink to his memory. But first I must get to St Petersburg before my boss wonders where the fuck his plane is.'

Alex might have questioned how a man could fail to notice his private jet was missing, but he supposed anyone rich and insane enough to turn an aircraft into a flying nightclub probably wasn't too detail oriented.

'Good luck, Yevgeny. And thank you,' Anya said again. 'I mean that.'

That seemed to please him, and Alex saw the thin lips curl into what might have been called a smile.

'Take care of yourself, you crazy bitch. And don't count on this pussy to watch your back,' he added, flicking some ash casually at Alex.

'I won't.'

Bidding him farewell, they hurried away from the jet even as Yevgeny shouted to a passing maintenance worker about needing a refuelling truck. Alex waited until they were well and truly out of earshot before speaking.

'Real charmer, that one,' he said, resisting the urge to give their pilot the finger as they hurried across the tarmac to a cluster of office buildings. 'And what was all that stuff about Ignaty?'

'Ignaty was his brother. I killed him.'

Alex blinked in surprise. 'You mean he just forgave you for it?'

'No, he thanked me for it,' she explained, as if it should have been obvious. 'Yevgeny asked me to kill him. He has owed me a favour ever since.'

Alex was genuinely lost for words, and slowed down to process what he'd just heard.

'Come on,' Anya called over her shoulder. 'Our rental car should be waiting for us.'

Chapter 16

Stupava, Slovakia

Drake stood in the gloomy, piss-smelling hallway while his reluctant companion fumbled with her keys. Lenka had donned an oversized dark green parka for the short walk from the car to the three-storey apartment block she called home, and the bulky coat made her seem even smaller and more vulnerable than before.

The moment she managed to unlock her dented front door, Drake pushed the young woman roughly inside. Small and skinny, she put up no resistance, stumbling into the small corridor leading to the living room with a hiss of fear and anger.

Drake followed right behind, drawing the Glock pistol that he'd kept concealed in his jacket during the walk up from the parking lot. Closing and locking the door, he carefully surveyed his new environment.

The apartment was, he supposed, a good match for the car that had brought them here. Small, cheap, untidy and cluttered, it looked pretty much exactly as he'd expected. The TV in the far corner of the living room was an old-style unit with a stack of DVDs piled up next to it. The kitchen area was a chaotic mess of unwashed dishes, unopened mail, empty wine bottles, dirty cooking utensils and unsealed cereal boxes.

The furniture all looked like it had been bought at a thrift store, and seemed to date back to the 1970s. Then again, maybe that was cutting-edge fashion around these parts. He was, however, surprised by the number of thick, worn-looking textbooks scattered around. Written in Slovak, he had no idea what they related to, but the cover images of number formulas and calculations suggested they dealt with advanced mathematics.

The view through her grimy windows was hardly inspiring. A couple of decaying low-rise apartment blocks identical to this one, each festooned with satellite dishes and drying laundry. Beyond them, a maze of smaller private residences, interspersed with a few shops whose flashing neon signs were pretty much the only splashes of colour amidst the sombre grey buildings and dull, overcast sky. Drake was more than happy to draw the blinds and shut it out.

It wasn't much of a place to call home, but it was a hell of a lot better than his accommodation over the past couple of days, and offered a chance to sort himself out while he planned his next move.

After briefly checking the bedroom and bathroom, and finding no evidence of anyone but a cash-strapped young woman living here alone, he turned his attention back to the apartment's owner. Lenka was standing in the centre of the room, waiting to see what he did next.

'Phones,' Drake said. 'Any mobiles or landlines in here?'

She stretched out a slender arm and pointed to a landline unit on a sideboard near the TV. Drake started following the cable but, unable to find the phone socket and lacking the time or energy to keep searching, settled for ripping the line right out of the unit. He also powered down the woman's cell phone and removed the battery and SIM card.

Removing his sodden jacket, Drake eased himself down into a threadbare 1960s-era armchair, which reminded him of the kind of thing his grandparents kept in the Suffolk cottage he used to visit as a kid. Except here there were no servings of sponge cake and episodes of *Knightmare* to watch on TV.

'What do you want from me?' Lenka asked, intruding on his nostalgia.

Opening eyes he hadn't realized he'd closed, Drake looked at the young woman. 'A basin of hot water and a wash cloth for starters,' he said, trying to get back into work mode. 'After that, some hot food and as much strong coffee as you can make.'

As his brief reverie had just proven, he would have loved nothing more than to collapse on a bed and fall asleep. But caffeine and food would have to suffice. Once he'd cleaned himself and his clothes up, he'd be able to travel more easily.

Fortunately the early hour had meant few people out and about, allowing him to make his way upstairs through the run-down block without attracting attention. He couldn't count on that kind of luck a second time. Nor could he be sure his enemies wouldn't track him down if he lingered too long.

Hawkins was both persistent and smart, and he had the considerable resources of the Agency to draw upon. Every hour Drake stayed increased his chances of being caught. One way or another, he intended to be on his way to the border before long. His best bet was to cross over into the Czech Republic and make for Prague, where he and Anya had set up an emergency supply cache. It was a long drive, but it wouldn't be hard to blend in, with so many foreign tourists visiting.

The question remained of what to do with Lenka. The moment he was out of here, she would alert the police to her kidnapping. Taking her with him would be dangerous for both of them, and he felt unwilling to murder an innocent civilian just to make his own escape easier.

'Here,' she said, handing him a plastic basin filled with tepid water. A dirty-looking wash cloth floated near the bottom.

Fuck it, beggars couldn't be choosers. Briefly laying the Glock on the armrest of his chair, Drake reached down and slowly pulled the shirt over his head, exposing his torso for the first time. The young woman put a hand to her mouth when she caught sight of the torn and bloodied skin, heavily mottled with bruises from countless injuries and beatings.

'Don't get all emotional,' Drake advised. 'It looks worse than it is.'

'What happened to you?' she whispered.

'Been a rough couple of days,' he said vaguely, using the cloth to wash away the dried blood that had congealed around the deep lacerations to his wrists. The less she knew about him, the better.

Sensing her eyes still on him, he looked up at her. 'What about that coffee?'

Blinking, the young woman hurried into the small kitchen area to prepare a brew. Drake couldn't help noticing that she struggled to find the coffee jar, having to search several cupboards before she chanced upon it. Nerves getting the better of her, he supposed. Or maybe she wasn't a big caffeine drinker.

He was just turning his attention back to cleaning his injuries when he caught a glimpse of his reflection in a small portable mirror resting on the sideboard. Drake had never been a man terribly preoccupied by his appearance, but even he was shocked by the gaunt, unshaven, dirty and bloodied face that confronted him, the hollow and bloodshot eyes staring back. Dried blood stuck to his hair, and he couldn't tell if it belonged to him or one of the men he'd killed.

Reaching into the bowl, he cupped his hands and splashed lukewarm water on his face, then ran his fingers through his hair enough times to get the worst of the filth out. Really, he needed a shower to clean up properly, but he doubted his new friend was going to politely wait while he took care of it. A quick fix would have to suffice for now.

Lenka approached with a mug of steaming black liquid, and a bowl of what looked like instant noodles with a fork stuck in it.

'The milk has turned,' she explained, eyes darting to the coffee.

Drake could have howled with laughter. After everything he'd been through, and everything that lay ahead, sour milk was the least of his concerns.

'I'll survive,' he promised, taking both cup and bowl.

He wasted no time attacking the noodles, nearly burning his mouth in his haste to get them down. They were cooked in a thin sauce that tasted both salty and spicy, and probably had as much nutritional value as a block of wood, but he couldn't have cared less. They were food, and they were hot.

'What do you do?' he asked suddenly, laying the empty bowl down and taking an experimental sip of the coffee. It might have lacked milk, but she'd heaped in enough sugar to keep him wired for days. Good girl, he thought.

The young woman looked caught off guard. 'Do?' she repeated.

'You said you work late. Doing what, exactly?'

She didn't look like the average supermarket checkout girl or petrol station attendant.

He saw her cheeks colour red beneath the make-up. 'I dance. At club.'

Well that explained the life of austerity hiding behind a veneer of glamour, he thought, as well as her unusually good command of English. With Bratislava being a popular city for foreign men in search of fun, he imagined there were all kinds of opportunities for attractive young women with few inhibitions.

'I am not a whore, if that is what you think,' she added hastily, with more heat than he'd expected. 'I save the money. It pays for my study.'

To emphasize her point, she picked up one of the textbooks and held it up for him to see. Suddenly her modest living situation made a lot more sense, as did the shitty car that had brought them here.

Drake however merely shrugged and took another gulp of coffee. 'Trust me, I'm in no position to judge your career choices.'

In the past few hours alone he'd murdered three men, hijacked a car and kidnapped an innocent civilian.

Reaching for a pack of cigarettes resting on the kitchen counter, she tapped one out and held it to her lips before lighting up. 'You want one?'

Drake shook his head. Smoking was one vice he didn't indulge in.

Flicking the cheap plastic lighter until it produced a flame, she took a long drag and waited for the nicotine to take effect. He couldn't blame her for wanting some release, though he preferred a good malt whisky for such situations.

'I want to ask you a question,' she announced after taking a second draw.

'Go on, then.'

Lenka sat down on the edge of her couch with the cigarette smouldering away between her fingers, looking almost as tired and worn as the piece of furniture she was resting on. It had been a long night for both of them.

'What happened to you?' she asked, gesturing to his battered torso. 'Why have you been beaten? And who are you running from?'

'You don't want to know.'

'Yes, I do.'

Draining the last of the coffee, Drake laid it down on the threadbare carpet and rose to his feet. He was a good six inches taller than her, and even in his depleted condition probably weighed 60 pounds more. He needed her to appreciate both facts in that moment.

'I appreciate the food and the ride, but that's as far as this goes.'

Reaching for the shirt that he'd left drying atop the radiator, he threw it over his shoulders. It was still slightly damp, but at least now it was warm. And so was he.

'A word of advice once I'm gone – forget you ever met me, and don't even think about reporting this to the police. They won't find me, but the men who did this to me *will find you*. And it won't matter what you know or how much you tell them; they'll just keep going until there's nothing left to tell. And by the time they're finished, you'll be begging them to kill you.'

He felt shitty for aiming such threats at someone who had done nothing but help him, but he needed her to appreciate the danger she was in should she make herself known to the authorities.

Judging by her wide-eyed look, his message had hit home. She looked like she was about to throw up, but nodded her assent.

Satisfied that he'd done what he could, Drake fished the wad of euros he'd stolen from his dead captors out of his pocket, unrolled a few crumpled tens and laid them on the kitchen worktop. Not much in the way of compensation for what he'd put her through, but he'd need the rest for himself until he could get to the supply cache.

Lenka wandered over to the windows, absently nudging the blinds aside. As soon as her gaze turned to the parking area below, she backed away from the window as if she'd seen a ghost.

'The men who are after you,' she said, trembling. 'Do they drive a black 4 x 4?'

Drake reacted immediately. Rushing across the living room, he grabbed the young woman by the shoulders and pulled her to the floor just as something punched through the window, causing fragments of glass to explode inwards. A moment later, the high-velocity round slammed into the wall opposite, shattering the thin plasterboard. 'Shit, they've found us,' Drake hissed.

Chapter 17

Oblivious to the hustle and bustle of the lobby around her, Anya stood in silent contemplation, staring at the poignant memorial carved into the white marble wall in front of her. Fifty-eight stars were laid out in near rows, each representing a CIA operative killed in the line of duty since the organization's creation 41 years earlier. And written above it in gold lettering was the memorial's dedication.

IN HONOR OF THOSE MEMBERS OF THE CENTRAL INTELLIGENCE AGENCY WHO GAVE THEIR LIVES IN THE SERVICE OF THEIR COUNTRY

Beneath this, held within a steel frame and a protective glass case, was a simple leather-bound book on which were noted the names of those men and women whose sacrifice the Agency was allowed to acknowledge. Barely half the stars had a name; the rest might well be destined to remain unrecognized, their deeds known only to a select few.

On the rare occasions when she was required to visit the Agency's headquarters, Anya would pause by this sobering reminder and reflect on the true cost of their work. More than once she'd caught herself wondering if future generations might do the same thing, and how many stars would decorate the wall by then.

'Thought I'd find you here.'

Anya felt Cain standing close to her. She could smell his aftershave, feel the warmth radiating from his body. There was an undercurrent of unhappiness in his voice that she couldn't help but react to.

'It helps keep things in perspective,' she said quietly. 'Reminds me that all things end.'

Marcus Cain was dressed in an expensive suit and tie, his hair neatly combed, his shoes freshly polished, just like everyone else here. Even Anya had bowed to expectations, donning a skirt, blouse and jacket that felt entirely foreign, and uncomfortable shoes that clicked on the marble floor. A far cry from the worn boots and battledress uniform she'd become so accustomed to.

Both of them were playing a role, pretending to be something they didn't want to be.

She asked the question they both knew needed to be asked. 'How did it go?'

Cain didn't need to answer. She could tell by the way his back was held ramrod-straight, the heavy burden of responsibility settling on him once more.

'Walk with me,' he said.

Anya had read once that the designers of the CIA building had tried to evoke the atmosphere of a college campus. Taking in the extensive garden courtyard, with stressed-looking analysts taking walks across neatly manicured lawns, drinking coffee or smoking cigarettes, Anya wasn't quite sure if their vision had been realized.

The Agency was changing, and its home was changing with it. A massive new office complex was under construction on the other side of the courtyard, directly opposite the unassuming original headquarters building. A pair of shining glass towers framed by steel, still only partially completed, rose up into the clear blue sky, workmen swarming over them. That was the future. The college campus was making way for slick corporate professionalism.

Anya halted by a small fish pond near the centre of the courtyard, watching the sunlight-dappled surface and the occasional glint of golden movement in the depths. The peace of nature appealed more to her now than any grand building or shining tower ever had.

'They want to send you back,' Cain said flatly. 'Back to Afghanistan.'

Anya closed her eyes and imagined that she was living a different life, that she wasn't this person she'd chosen to become. That she wasn't being called upon again.

A passing glimpse of a life that would never be.

She'd known it was coming, of course. She could read most people with ease, and Cain most of all. She knew him as well as she knew herself, or so she believed.

But to hear him actually say it – that was harder than she'd expected.

'They seem to think we've got the Russians on the ropes, that a big defeat there will be enough to start more republics breaking away. Maybe even begin the collapse of the Soviet Union.' His words sounded hollow; just empty rhetoric spoken by someone else. 'They think we could end the Cold War.'

Grand sentiments, spoken by a thousand conquerors on a thousand bloody battlefields throughout history. Wage one war to end another. Kill one man to save ten.

'And what do you think?' Anya asked, staring at the surface of the water.

'Me?' He scoffed bitterly at the notion. 'What does it matter?'

'It matters to me, Marcus.'

She could sense him wrestling, struggling to make some inner decision. A man torn between duty and loyalty.

Duty to his country, loyalty to her.

'You don't have to go,' he said, straining. 'You don't owe them anything now. You've done everything that was asked of you and more. There's nothing more to prove, Anya – not to me, not to the Agency, not anyone. That's what I think.'

He was telling the truth; that much was plain. And if she chose, she imagined Cain possessed the ingenuity and the influence to have her exempted. She could walk away from this with honour, knowing she had done her duty to the Agency.

But the Agency wasn't the one who really depended on her.

'And the others?' she asked, knowing she had to. 'The men I fought beside?'

Cain glanced away, which told her everything. Task Force Black was going back to Afghanistan, with or without her.

'Then you know I can't abandon them,' she said, her voice measured. 'I can't let them go without me.'

When he looked at her again, she felt the breath catch in her throat. 'Would you, if I asked you to?'

She wished she could give him the answer he wanted, but it wouldn't have been fair. Not to him, or herself. 'No, Marcus. I wouldn't.'

She took a step towards him, raised a hand as if to touch his, but forced herself to pull back. They were in plain view, with dozens of employees able to see their every move.

'When I joined the Agency, I asked only for a chance to prove myself. And because of you, I was given that. You believed in me when no one else did, Marcus, and I will always be grateful to you,' she promised. 'But if I step back now, let my friends, my... family go into this fight without me, what have I done with that chance? All I have done is proven men like Carpenter right. I will not do that.' She sighed. 'If I have been asked to go in one more time, then I will. That is my duty to them. Let me do it, and let me finish this the right way.'

She saw him close his eyes, and was reminded of the same look that had been on her face moments earlier. That glimpse she had allowed herself of a different life. Perhaps he was seeing the same thing. She could almost feel the emotion boiling away inside him, could sense his need to embrace her, but knew he wouldn't. He couldn't. Not here.

But she knew something else. For better or worse, he accepted her decision.

Little did either of them know that it would alter the course of their lives for ever.

–

Paris, France – 30 March 2010

Seated at an outdoor café in the city's historic Latin Quarter, her eyes hidden behind oversized sunglasses, Anya took a sip of her latte. The long dark-haired wig she'd donned for this outing helped keep much of her face from passers-by.

According to Alex, this was where they would make contact with their target. She had run the operation in her head countless times on the way here, trying to anticipate everything that could go wrong, trying to devise a counter to every obstacle, but ultimately she knew there were far too many variables to accurately plan for. She would have to fall back on her wits, quick thinking and experience.

She shuffled uncomfortably as pain radiated from her injured ribs. She had changed the dressing around her wound, binding it as tight as she could without restricting her movement or breathing, but it was making life difficult all the same.

She was certainly in no shape for a physical confrontation, which was something that might be required of her if their target decided to resist. If she was anything like her father, Anya expected Lauren Cain wouldn't go down without a fight.

—

'Well, this place really puts York uni into perspective,' Alex said as he surveyed the vast open courtyard of Paris-Sorbonne University, surrounded by classically proportioned buildings, vaulted archways and magnificently carved stonework. Even the students looked as effortlessly stylish as their surroundings.

'How does it look?' Anya's tinny, electronic voice buzzed in his ear. She'd set him up with a concealed radio that fitted almost invisibly into his ear, allowing them to communicate while he went about snooping for their target. It did however leave the discomforting impression that Anya was with him at all times.

'I don't think I fit in here,' he said, watching as a pair of male students in designer jeans and sunglasses sauntered past, takeaway coffee cups in hand and satchels slung casually over their shoulders. Even their hair looked like it had just been professionally styled.

When he'd been that age, he'd had to make do with a can of energy drink and last night's cold takeaway before stumbling out of his student flat, looking like shit on legs. For some reason, these people looking better than he ever had stirred a sense of envy that was hard to ignore.

'You are young, scruffy and badly dressed,' Anya pointed out. 'You look exactly like a student should.'

'Aw, that's the nicest thing you've said to me all day,' he countered sarcastically. 'Also, fuck you. At least I've lived a life, unlike these metrosexual tossers.'

'Stay focussed, Alex. Remember why you're here.'

'Yes, Mum,' he said sullenly. 'No sign of her yet.'

According to the online snooping he'd done en route, Lauren was working up to a thesis on key figures in French neoclassicism, and would frequently consult the university library for its collection of historical documents and correspondence. It sounded boring as shit, but then he'd never had much appreciation for such things.

With the library entrance lying on the far side of the square, this seemed like a logical place to intercept her. He'd committed Lauren's face to memory, and was confident he'd spot her if she passed this way.

'By the way, it's just occurred to me that we're missing a vital element of this operation.'

'What?' She sounded concerned, even over the radio.

'Neither of us have codenames. I mean, come on – we're doing all this secret-agent stuff without codenames?' He tutted and shook his head. 'I want mine to be Broadsword. Yours can be Danny Boy.'

'Alex, we're on an encrypted radio net, and it is only the two of us speaking,' Anya said. She was using her exasperated schoolteacher tone again. 'We don't need codenames.'

'Bollocks, I'm using it anyway,' he said firmly, refusing to be robbed of his chance to reference *Where Eagles Dare*, his favourite war movie. 'Broadsword out.'

–

About a hundred yards away, at her table facing out onto the university, Anya had to bite her lip. Alex might have been useful as technical support, but he was an exasperating loose cannon in the field, either questioning every decision or simply refusing to take their situation seriously. Under normal circumstances she would have reprimanded and cut loose anyone displaying that kind of cavalier attitude. Unfortunately, Alex was all she had to work with.

She felt bad for not telling him the true purpose of his presence here, but knew that if he found out he'd likely have refused to participate. There was of course a danger, but hopefully most of it would fall on Anya herself rather than her reluctant companion.

'Broadsword calling Danny Boy. Target's in sight,' her earpiece announced, followed by, 'That sounded even cooler in real life than in my head.'

'I can hear every word you say… *Broadsword*,' Anya reminded him irritably. 'Are you sure it's her? I need you to be a hundred per cent.'

'Keep in mind who you're talking to,' he said. Alex was about as accurate a source of facial recognition as she was likely to find. 'She's approaching the library building from the west side.'

Rising from the table in a deceptively casual manner, Anya left enough money to cover her bill and started towards the university building at a brisk pace.

'Is she alone?' she asked, waiting for a break in traffic before hurrying across the road.

'No. She's got a bloke and two girls with her. I don't know if he's in the friend zone or what, but they're all heading for the library together.'

Anya felt her heart sink. There was no way they could secure Lauren if she was surrounded by friends, especially ones that might fight back. Anya didn't imagine any of them were capable of stopping her, but they'd likely raise the alarm before she could neutralize them all. They had to get her away from the others, create a distraction that would allow Anya to act.

'I want you to start a fight,' she said, unable to think of a better alternative.

Silence for a second or two. 'Say again?'

Jumping out of the way of a Citroën hatchback that seemed to have no intention of slowing down, Anya crossed the wide plaza to the Sorbonne building, where a big open archway led to the enclosed square.

'I need a distraction,' she explained. 'Pick a random student, a male, and find a reason to start a fight with him.'

She didn't expect this unorthodox instruction to be met with much enthusiasm, and she wasn't to be disappointed. 'Are you out of your mind? I'll get my fucking head kicked in.'

'You were just saying how much these students annoy you,' she pointed out, hoping to appeal to his male bravado. 'Here is your chance to get even.'

'Yeah, well, Hulk Hogan annoys me too, but you wouldn't catch me stepping into the ring with him,' Alex countered. He seemed poised to continue with his tirade, but events in the square prompted him to rein it in. 'Hold up, something's happening.'

–

Alex watched as the small knot of people stopped near the library entrance, their body language suggesting they were wrapping up whatever conversation they were involved in, and preparing to go their separate ways.

Sure enough, the man and one of the young women peeled off, heading towards the north side of the square which housed student support offices and admin areas. She had her arm around him, suggesting he wasn't in the friend zone after all.

'Right, the bloke and his girlfriend have just buggered off together,' he said, happy to report that their problems had just halved.

'What about Lauren?'

Alex turned back to their target. Lauren, dressed in casual jeans, a long coat and a fashionable loose scarf, was making her way slowly towards the library entrance, still chatting with her remaining friend. His hopes rose that her companion might go the way of the others, but it wasn't to be. Both young women disappeared inside.

'She and her mate are heading into the library together,' he reported. 'Must be joined at the hip or something. What do you want me to do?'

'Did you disable the surveillance cameras?' she asked.

Indeed he had. Compared to some of the top-tier encrypted databases he'd tackled in his time, hacking a university security system had been child's play. Once inside, it had been easy to reconfigure a few small but vital settings.

'I set the memory buffer to reformat every ten seconds. On the surface it'll look normal, but there'll be no record of anything that happens in there today. And I can kill the cameras completely from my phone if need be.'

'All right, follow them,' Anya instructed. 'Keep your distance, but try to maintain visual contact.'

He'd had a feeling she would ask him to do that. 'Roger that. Where are you?'

'Don't worry about me,' she said hastily. 'Just go. Don't lose them.'

'Broadsword's going in,' he said, quickening to catch up with his target. He couldn't shake the sense of foreboding as he passed through the arched entrance into the library building.

Chapter 18

Stupava, Slovakia

'Stay down!' Drake snarled, pinning Lenka to the floor as two more shots passed through the shattered window above, one of them blasting the toaster from the kitchen counter. The young woman let out a squeal, but made no attempt to get up.

Drake forced himself to stay rational and consider his situation logically. Clearly Hawkins and his men had caught up with them. How or why didn't matter at that moment. Trying to stand and fight would be suicidal. The only option was escape.

But how best to get out of here?

He hadn't heard a shot, which meant the sniper must be using a silencer. Based on the angle the rounds were coming in from, they were firing from an elevated position, most probably the roof of the nearest apartment block to the south.

That meant they couldn't hope to get to Lenka's car. Aside from the fact it was already compromised, such a journey would mean covering at least 50 yards of open killing ground. No, their best bet was to escape northwards, where their building would shield them from the sniper.

'They are trying to kill us,' the young woman whimpered, eyes wide in terror.

No shit, Drake thought. It was decision time. Cut her loose and make a break for it alone, or take her with him and risk her slowing him down.

'Lenka, listen to me,' Drake said, grabbing her head so they had eye contact. 'I'll get us out of this, but you have to trust me and do what I say. Understand?'

Leaving her here to be captured or killed wasn't an option, and only partly because she could give Hawkins information that would aid his search.

'Do you understand?' he repeated firmly.

Reluctantly she nodded.

'All right. We're going for the door. Stick close, stay low and follow me.'

With that, he turned and began to crawl towards the front door, keeping as flat to the ground as possible, broken glass crunching beneath him as he moved.

With the drapes still half-covering the broken window, the sniper had only a partial view of the apartment's interior, and had likely fired blind to slow them down while an assault team moved in. Drake could only hope they weren't waiting right outside the door.

He saw Lenka wince as she pinched a small, bloody piece of glass from the palm of her hand. There was nothing he could do for her. She'd just have to tough it out until they were away from here.

'Keep moving,' he hissed.

Reaching the door, Drake rose to his knees and undid the latch, drawing the Glock as he did so. The automatic was decent in a room-to-room fight, but like most pistols it lacked the stopping power to drop opponents in body armour. If it came to a firefight, he could do little more than hold his enemies at bay.

He pushed the door open and edged out just far enough to peer into the dingy corridor. No sign of movement. Maybe they were in luck and their enemies had been unusually sloppy.

'Hurry,' he said, beckoning Lenka.

The young woman jumped to her feet and rushed towards him. Drake grabbed her by the arm and pulled her after him as he sprinted for the stairwell. He hadn't made it halfway along before he pulled up short, straining to listen.

Sure enough, he could hear the hollow thump of boots on concrete. Multiple pairs, coming up fast, an assault team approaching.

'Shit,' he growled, reversing course. Left with little option but to follow, Lenka sprinted along beside him. At least her soft-soled shoes made no noise on the floor.

Rounding a corner, Drake found only a dead end.

'Is there another stairwell?' he asked, backing up against the wall.

Breathing hard, her face flushed from the short but intense run, Lenka shook her head and gestured back the way they had come. 'That is the only one.'

'Fire escape?'

She stared at him as if he were spouting gibberish. Maybe building regulations worked differently in this part of the world.

'Fuck.'

Hearing footsteps echoing down the corridor, Drake leaned back the way they had come. Sure enough, he counted three men in civilian clothes advancing towards Lenka's apartment. It wouldn't take them long to figure out their target had escaped.

'How many?' Lenka asked.

'More than I can deal with.'

There had to be another way out, he thought. If necessary he would break into one of the apartments overlooking the north side of the building and clamber down the outside. They were only on the second floor, so the climb might be possible.

Then again, it was equally possible he'd lose his grip and fall, killing or severely injuring himself in the process. And he was almost certain his fellow escapee lacked the upper body strength to make the climb.

Drake stopped, spotting something fixed into the cream-coloured wall opposite. A rectangular metal plate about two feet wide and nearly as tall, slightly battered and rusted in places, with a simple handle set into the centre.

'What's that?' he whispered, pointing to it.

'Chute,' she explained hurriedly. 'Where you put junk. I don't know word.'

Drake did, though. It was a garbage chute, allowing the block's residents to dispose of their household waste without having to descend flights of stairs. The vertical shaft probably led down to a dumpster below that could be removed and emptied when needed.

Hurrying over, Drake pulled it open. As he'd hoped, he found himself peering down a metal shaft about equal in size to the cover. A tight fit for him perhaps, but he was quite certain his female friend would fit easily. He could only hope the dumpster at the bottom hadn't been emptied recently, otherwise the landing was going to be far more unpleasant than being surrounded by rotting garbage.

'Get in,' he ordered.

Lenka stared at the opening in horror as his words sank in. 'In there?'

'Unless you want to take your chances with our mates back there. Get your arse in the chute.'

She hoisted her lower half inside but refused to let go, clinging onto the metal rim for dear life. Drake felt bad about what happened next, but he was pretty sure he'd feel worse if they both got gunned down because of her hesitation.

Squeezing her slender wrists, he wrenched her arms free. With nothing left to support her weight, Lenka suddenly disappeared into the darkness with a frightened scream.

Drake was right behind, knowing her cry would have alerted the assault team. He just hoped she had the presence of mind to move out of the way once she landed, otherwise she was about to get a 190-pound wake-up call.

Hoisting himself in, he was forced to twist sideways to accommodate his considerably larger mass. Straightaway he was hit by the unmistakable smell of decomposing garbage wafting up, which he took to be a good sign. At least there was something other than open pavement at the base of the shaft.

Pausing only to shove the Glock into the waistband of his jeans, Drake let go of his precarious handhold and allowed gravity to do the rest.

The descent was faster than he'd anticipated. He was able to brace his feet against the walls of the chute, slowing himself somewhat, but the sheet steel was too smooth for his boots to gain much purchase, and after 10 feet or so he lost all traction and fell.

He landed on something lumpy and yielding, and was immediately assailed by the powerful stench of the rubbish, which had clearly been lying there for some time. He found he was lying in a half-full steel dumpster, with another empty unit close by. The room was bare brick and unlit, save for weak shafts of grey sunlight filtering in through the open entrance.

Lenka was struggling to extricate herself from the piles of torn plastic bags, sodden cardboard boxes, leftover food and God only knew what else. Still, at least he hadn't landed on her.

'You okay?'

She muttered something in Slovak that he suspected was less than complimentary. Rolling over, Drake hooked his arm over the edge of the dumpster and pulled himself up and over.

Running over to her side, he caught the young woman just as she fell over the rim. Her coat and jeans were stained with a variety of unsavoury looking substances, and her expression reflected her disgust, but she was alive and apparently unhurt. Whether she stayed that way depended on what they did in the next 60 seconds.

Drake hauled the heavy trash receptacle aside until it was flush against the far wall of the room. It was unlikely to buy them much time, but anyone who tried to follow them down the chute was in for a far harder landing than they'd enjoyed.

'Come on,' he said, taking her by the hand and leading her outside.

The rain had abated at last, reduced to a sombre drizzle.

There wasn't much to see on this side of the apartment block. The main parking area was apparently on the opposite side of the building, leaving just a single-lane road, probably for use by garbage trucks emptying the dumpsters. Beyond this narrow strip lay about 50 yards of waste ground dotted with abandoned shopping trolleys and mounds of weed-choked rubble, where older buildings had been cleared to make way for the residential blocks.

Scattered woodland lay at the edge, rising up to a low ridge that seemed to run roughly west to east. Stripped of leaves by the lingering winter, the woods would provide little cover, but if they could get over the ridge then they might be in with a chance.

'We need to put some distance in,' he said quickly. 'You up for this?'

The young woman looked pale, but she managed a nod.

'Right, let's go. Stay low and close to me,' he instructed.

As countless soldiers on countless battlefields have discovered, sometimes when you have to cross a stretch of ground there's nothing for it but to get your head down and run. This he did, sprinting as fast as his body could carry him, leaping over half-buried bricks and wild bushes that threatened to catch at his feet, all the while aiming for the woods on the far side of the clearing.

Lenka followed as best she could, her gasps growing louder and more strained with each step. He had no idea how fit she was, but she was young and at least looked healthy. That had to count for something.

His course followed a zigzagging path towards the trees, partly because the obstacles that lay in their way forced them to detour, but mostly to throw off possible snipers. He didn't think the one on the opposite block's roof could get a line of sight, but there was no telling if there might be others. If there was one in the tree line ahead, their escape attempt was likely to come to an abrupt end.

They had just rounded a pool of oily water and were almost at the edge of the woods when Drake felt something whizz past his ear, followed an instant later by an explosion of rocks and wet earth off to his right.

'Oh, God!' Lenka cried out, trying to duck for cover.

'Keep moving!' Drake shouted, practically dragging her into the woods as more rounds thumped into the muddy ground.

Struggling up the leaf-covered ridge, Drake flinched as a round ricocheted off a tree bole just a couple of feet to his left, gouging a chunk of bark away. Clearly the weapons being fired at them were short-range, probably pistols or submachine guns positioned in one of the upper storey windows. No decent sniper could have failed to hit them from this range.

Losing her footing, Lenka pitched forward and landed face down in the mud, struggling to rise.

'Get up,' Drake said, hauling the young woman roughly to her feet. He didn't care that he might have hurt her. Staying alive was the priority.

The fire was slackening off now as it became clear they'd passed beyond the effective range of the assault team's weapons. No doubt the team's thoughts had turned to pursuit rather than engagement, which meant they needed to get the fuck clear of this area immediately. And they certainly weren't going to make it on foot. They needed a vehicle.

The other side of the ridge was steeper than the gentle slope that had led them up here, and both Drake and Lenka skidded down to the flat ground beyond, filthy and out of breath.

Still, Drake could make out the distinctive shapes of two-storey buildings through the tree trunks, and made straight for them.

As he'd hoped, another residential area lay on the other side of the narrow bit of woodland, which was likely too uneven to build on. The buildings were smaller than the apartment blocks, but seemed to belong to the same era and method of construction: flat roofs, square and functional structures that had clearly been designed for efficiency rather than aesthetic appeal.

A metal fence lay between them and the residential area beyond, consisting of spiked vertical stakes held together by a pair of cross beams. It looked like it had once been painted green, but this was mostly rusted away, and many of the stakes were hanging loose or missing altogether. Finding one makeshift entrance that had likely been used by locals as a shortcut, Drake squeezed through the gap, jumped down the low brick wall onto the pavement, then helped Lenka down.

On the opposite side of the road, the residential buildings towered over them, as foreboding as the sky against which they were silhouetted. But between them lay a small parking area, mostly empty save for two vehicles, one of which was propped up on bricks, all four wheels removed.

The other one looked sound, however. An old style Volkswagen Golf MK3 by the looks of it, sitting in one corner of the lot. The car was unlikely to win any style awards, but it would do. Assuming they could get it started.

Drake tried the driver's door just in case the owner had left it unlocked. Even in places like this, stranger things have happened. But he was out of luck, and had to settle for smashing the window with a good hard kick.

'What are you doing?' Lenka demanded as he unlocked the door from the inside, hauled it open and crouched down to get at the ignition system.

'Shut up. Just keep an eye out,' he said, teasing out the bundle of wires beneath the steering column. Modern cars had pretty sophisticated anti-theft systems, but relics from the mid-90s like this were a piece of piss to steal. Providing one had the skills.

Hotwiring had never been a favourite pastime of Drake's, but like all Shepherd operatives he'd been trained to do it if the need arose. It certainly had today.

He quickly spliced two wires together, which, he hoped, would control the engine fuel pumps and other components, then turned his attention to finding the ignition wire.

'Shit,' Lenka said under her breath.

An angry male voice shouted at them in Slovak from the other side of the parking lot.

'What's happening?' Drake said, unwilling to abandon his task. 'Talk to me.'

'Trouble,' Lenka replied, before shouting a reply.

'What kind of trouble?'

'The kind you get when you try to steal a man's car.'

Drake could hear another shout, closer this time. Whoever was out there was clearly not pleased at seeing his car window smashed and a mud-covered young woman loitering beside it.

Got it. Finding the ignition wire, he prised it free from the terminal.

'Fuck this,' Lenka decided. Reaching down, she grasped the Glock pistol shoved down the back of Drake's trousers, pulled it free and brandished it at the car owner, shouting a loud warning in Slovak for him to back away. She sounded frightened and angry in equal measure, but a gun was a gun at the end of the day. Drake certainly wouldn't have risked his life to protect a shitty car like this.

Touching the ignition wire against the crude circuit he'd created, Drake listened as the starter motor turned over, then caught into life as the engine fired up.

Standing up, he snatched the pistol from Lenka's shaking hands and pointed it at the car's owner – a short, fat bear of a man with close-cropped hair and a thick beard. He was backing away slowly with his hands up, chuntering in his native language. Probably telling Drake to go fuck himself.

'Get in,' he said to Lenka, keeping the man covered as the young woman jumped into the passenger seat.

'You, get lost,' he commanded, gesturing with the gun for the man to leave. He might not have spoken English, but he got the gist and turned away, still shouting abuse.

Lowering himself into the driver's seat, Drake threw the car into gear and reversed hard out of the parking lot onto the road beyond, before swinging the wheel over and accelerating away as fast as the engine could permit.

Chapter 19

Paris, France

The interior of the library building was, to Alex's surprise, sleek and modern, quite distinct from the classically styled outside. The floors were grey linoleum, the walls stark and white, and the furniture brightly coloured. It reminded him more of an office building than a centuries-old educational institution.

An information desk lay directly ahead, manned by a bored-looking staff member who looked him over momentarily and seemed to decide that he passed muster. Corridors branched off left and right either side of the desk. Sauntering in what he hoped was a nonchalant manner, Alex spotted the two young women heading down the left one. His French was far from fluent, but he did recognize signs for Reading Rooms 1, 2 and 3.

Keeping his pace slow and steady, he followed them.

'I've got them in sight,' he said quietly. 'They're heading for the reading rooms at the north end of the building.'

'Good. Stay with them,' came Anya's hushed reply. He still didn't know where she was lurking or what she planned to do, and neither fact made him feel good.

Passing through a set of double doors brought Alex into a different world entirely. Gone was the squeaky linoleum, the whitewashed walls and blandly economical furniture, and in their place were flawless marble tiled floors, high intricate ceilings, and an elegant staircase with a single graceful curve. Even the walls of this simple utility corridor were decorated with artworks that would likely have taken pride of place in many a collection.

The effect was like stepping out of a sterile twenty-first century into the opulence of an eighteenth-century palace, and Alex was taken aback by the disorienting change in his surroundings.

A pair of female voices filtering down from the staircase was enough to remind him of his purpose. He hurried up the steps behind Lauren and her companion as they reached the top, crossing a wide marble landing to a set of doors on the opposite side. The reading room lay ahead.

Alex watched as they disappeared, and raced to catch up with them. He'd done his best to familiarize himself with the layout of the building, but his knowledge was incomplete at best. All he could say for certain was that the reading room was the biggest of its kind in the entire complex. The sort of place it might be easy to lose sight of a person, if he didn't get a move on.

But big wasn't an appropriate word to describe the space. Over 200 feet in length, the massive room was not just long and wide, but high, with great stone and iron columns rising to a high domed ceiling far overhead. Light streamed in through great windows overlooking the courtyard below.

Most of the room's internal floor space was given over to row after row of wooden writing desks, reminding him of an exam hall from his university days, each station fitted with its own identical reading light and book rest. Given the relatively early hour however, barely a quarter of the reading stations were being used.

Five cross sections branched off from the main reading area, their shelves practically groaning under the weight of hundreds of leather-bound tomes. An impressive enough display by itself, but this was merely the tiniest fraction of the 2.5 million books housed in the library's collection. Most likely what he saw now were works specifically requested by students and faculty members in advance, and had been brought here out of storage for a limited time.

'Where are you now?' Anya asked.

'First-floor reading room,' he replied hastily.

Realizing he'd draw attention if he stood there gawping, Alex approached the nearest reference book section and picked a random text on human physiology that looked old, authoritative and extremely boring.

'Do you still have a visual on the target?'

Pretending to be studying the book, he glanced over the top at the two students. 'Her friend just sat down at one of the reading stations. Looks like she's settling down to study.'

In the middle of the room stood a large circular desk with computers laid out around it, manned by a couple of staff who looked about as excited as the receptionist he'd passed on the way in.

'Target's at the main information desk,' he said quietly.

'Good. I need you to do something for me.'

'If you want me to start a fight, the answer's still no.'

'I want you to start a conversation,' Anya corrected him. 'With Lauren.'

'Are you having a laugh?'

Suddenly conscious that he was being watched, Alex turned to see a short, plump woman staring at him from behind a pair of thick-framed glasses, having approached unseen from the other end of the aisle. She looked as if she couldn't make up her mind whether he was drunk, playing some kind of prank, or if he was the sort of man prone to holding conversations with himself.

'Sorry,' Alex said, holding his book up and offering what he hoped was a rueful smile. 'Sometimes I get a bit too involved, know what I mean?'

She didn't, and made it clear. Backing away, she turned and made a hasty exit back the way she'd come.

'Who are you talking to?' Anya demanded.

'Doesn't matter,' Alex said, making sure to keep his voice down this time. 'What the hell am I supposed to talk to her about?'

'Politics, the weather, pop culture… I don't care.'

'Did you just say "pop culture"?'

'Just keep her talking,' Anya said, irritation in her voice. 'Don't let her leave, and make sure people see you speaking with her.'

'Why?'

'Just do it, Alex.'

'Fuck,' he said under his breath, trying to think of some way of approaching her that wouldn't appear contrived.

Fortunately however, inspiration seemed to be on his side. As Lauren finished up her conversation with the desk clerk and began heading over to the books section, Alex was suddenly struck by an idea.

Having hacked into her private university directory, he was well versed in the subject of her dissertation, and had a feeling he knew where she was headed. Abandoning the book he'd been pretending to read, he quickly side-stepped behind his aisle, making for the section on French history.

He was moving fast, eager to reach his destination before she did while not drawing too much attention to himself. Fortunately she had more ground to cover, giving him a precious few seconds to scan the shelves in front of him. As he'd hoped, the books were arranged by author's name, mostly in alphabetical order.

'Come on, you fucker. Where are you?' he mumbled, eyes flitting down the rows of books until he found the section starting with V.

'Gotcha,' he said, grabbing the leather-bound edition as if it were an ancient treasure. He'd barely flipped open the cover when a voice spoke up to his left.

'*Excusez-moi, monsieur?*'

'Yeah?' Alex said innocently, turning to face her.

Though he'd seen pictures of Lauren Cain online, and even viewed her with his own eyes – albeit from a distance – it was quite different to be in her presence.

She was smaller than he'd expected, maybe five foot five, and lightly built. Having discarded her overcoat, he could make out the trim, compact physique of someone who clearly took regular exercise. Her wavy dark hair was worn loose, falling past her shoulders and framing a face that was at once delicate and feminine, but which hinted at the stronger will and intellect that lay behind it.

Her eyes, seeming to shift between green and brown, were regarding him with curiosity and a hint of interest. Her full lips were slightly parted with the beginnings of a friendly smile. She was a young woman for whom smiles came easily, he sensed. Someone who had no reason to see Alex as a threat.

That made him all too conscious of what he'd been sent here to do, and he felt an intense pang of guilt for being complicit in what was about to happen.

'I'm sorry, I assumed you were a French student,' she explained, her tone polite but warm. 'I take it you speak English?'

Alex opened his mouth to reply, but no words would come. It was as if someone had wiped his mind of all thoughts, and immediately he felt a blush rising to his cheeks. Seeing his difficulty, Lauren smiled a little in amusement, perhaps mistaking his embarrassment for something else.

'I think you've got something of mine,' she said, her tone one of mock severity.

'Make words come out your mouth, Alex,' Anya's tinny voice demanded, her tone hard and insistent in his ear. 'Anything will do.'

'Hmm?' Alex said, trying to focus his mind on two different conversations at once.

Lauren nodded to the book in his hands. *Lettres philosophiques sur les Anglais*, better known by its English title *Letters Concerning the English Nation*.

'I'd actually reserved that copy myself,' she said, a little more guarded this time. She was about to challenge him, and was testing to see how he'd react. 'I was just coming over to pick it up, but it… looks like you got there first.'

'Oh, I'm sorry,' Alex said, his brain finally starting to engage. 'I'm new around here.'

'I noticed,' she said, her smile broadening. 'England, right?'

'You've got me.' He launched into the story he'd concocted in the ten seconds or so it had taken her to get here. 'I'm only in Paris for a week or so, doing a bit of a research trip. I'd come to view some documents from just before the Revolution, but I happened to see this in passing. I'm such a big fan of Voltaire, I just had to take a look. Especially hearing his thoughts about my homeland.' He smiled, feigning rather than feeling embarrassment this time. 'Afraid I got rather absorbed in it. You caught me off guard.'

'Sorry about that. I promise, I'm not in the habit of sneaking up on people.' She was relaxing a little having discovered he shared her interest in French literature. 'I'm Lauren, by the way.'

The answer came out before he could stop himself. 'Alex.'

Lauren nodded to the book. 'Have you read many of Voltaire's works, Alex?'

He certainly hadn't, being about as familiar with classic literature as Anya was with crochet knitting, but he had memorized a good number of their titles during his research on Lauren. 'As many as I can find,' he assured her, with a tone of gushing enthusiasm. 'Especially *Candide*. That's one of my favourites.'

Her look of delight told him he'd hit the right mark with that one. 'Now you're talking. I must have read it five, six times. What did you think of the relationship between Candide and Cacambo?'

Fuck. Even his photographic memory couldn't help him with this one. Knowing the title of a book was one thing, but understanding the intricacies of its plot quite another.

'Well, I thought it was interesting how it changed over the course of the story,' he lied. 'But I felt like I was always waiting for Candide's friend to do something, like he was dragging his heels,' he added, hoping Anya was listening in and took the hint.

He could only bullshit his way through this conversation for so long before Lauren realized he wasn't what he claimed to be. He also couldn't communicate directly with Anya and tell her to hurry the hell up.

He just hoped that wherever she was, she got what she needed pretty damn fast.

Chapter 20

Anya was indeed hard at work, not that anyone would have known it to look at her. Having situated herself at a reading table in the far corner of the vast room, she was hawkishly scanning the students and the scattering of staff members around her for the one face that didn't belong.

She knew they were here somewhere. Despite the multitude of precautions taken to maintain her anonymity, a man like Cain wouldn't have left his daughter's security to chance. He would have a physical presence on site as backup, monitoring her movements constantly and ready to respond to any threats that presented themselves.

That meant at least one person in this room wasn't what they seemed. And Anya had to find and neutralize them before she could put the rest of her plan into action.

Her gaze shifted constantly from person to person, looking for anything that would clue her in. A suited field operative with a microphone wire trailing from his ear wasn't going to be the order of the day here. Any agent operating in a setting like this would be in deep cover, probably even based at the university to make their presence more believable. On the surface they would look, talk and act just like everyone else. She doubted even Lauren herself was aware that she was being watched 24/7.

Anya would have to go on gut instinct. She'd served as a field agent herself for years, and knew every trick of the trade.

Anyone taking an unusual interest in Lauren now that she was talking to a stranger would be a red flag. Casual glances or passing interest weren't enough. There had to be situational awareness, threat assessment, constant juggling of possible scenarios. All the things Agency operatives were trained to do without anyone seeing.

And Anya had mere seconds to find that person and act.

There. A young man standing at the end of a book aisle, his eyes on Lauren. He was tall and well built, and unusually clean-cut for a student, his hair cut short in a low-maintenance style. His clothes were practical, designed for movement and activity. A man with military training whose fresh-faced complexion allowed him to pass for someone several years younger, to serve as a deep-cover operative?

Possibly. She could feel herself preparing to move, only for her target to break into a beaming smile as a young woman approached him. Kissing her on the cheek, he headed for the exit at the far end, his arm around her waist. No go.

Alex's conversation was faltering. She could hear his vague responses and vain efforts to steer the chat towards a more comfortable topic. Like a typical British man, he had no idea how to talk to an attractive young woman. She could only hope he was able to keep Lauren in place for a little longer as her eyes continued to scan the room with increasing urgency.

That was when Anya saw her.

Lauren's friend. The one with the plain looks and the short red hair. She was sitting at a reading table not far from her companion, pretending to study, but Anya could see her eyes were on Alex almost the whole time. And her expression wasn't that of a friend intrigued by her companion's new acquaintance; it was the serious, focussed look of a trained agent.

Anya knew the thought process the young woman was going through, comparing Alex's face with known terrorists or wanted suspects, sizing him up for concealed weapons or malicious intent.

The Agency often employed women like this in the field, not because they were better at fighting and killing, but because they blended in. People were less inclined to see them as a threat, and dismissed them without even realizing it, often to their cost.

This one was a perfect example. Average height and build, neither beautiful nor ugly, and wearing little make-up. Her facial features and complexion gave little clue as to her age; she could have been anything from late teens to late twenties. Anya was betting she was closer to the latter, but pretending to be younger.

Her clothes were decent quality but understated, revealing nothing of the body beneath, designed specifically not to attract attention. All of these things helped make her the classic 'grey man', the kind of person you could pass in the street a dozen times a day without even noticing.

Well, Anya had certainly noticed her now. Rising from her seat, a stack of textbooks in her arms and a takeaway cup of coffee from the shop across the road balanced on top, she headed straight for the young woman, as if to pass by her reading desk.

It was so quick it would have been missed by all but the most diligent of observers. With a slight tilt of the books, she allowed the coffee to topple off its precarious resting place, and straight onto her target.

It landed on her left shoulder, the lid coming free and causing the frothy contents to spray across her jumper and reading table.

'Ow! What the hell?' the young woman cried out, jumping to her feet and wiping a hand across her stained top as she glared accusingly at Anya. The coffee had cooled sufficiently that it had caused no real harm, though it was clear her outfit was ruined.

All eyes in the library were now on them, including Alex and Lauren's.

'Oh, no! I'm so sorry,' Anya said, throwing on a fake look of concern, and affecting a thick Dutch accent. She'd chosen it on the basis that they were generally seen as a laid-back, genial people who weren't inclined to start fights. 'It just slipped out of my hand.'

The young woman looked as angry as Anya would be in her situation. 'You know you're not supposed to bring hot drinks in here, right?'

Anya feigned a look of surprise, moving forward to help wipe the coffee stains from her top. 'I'm sorry, I—'

'Back off, it's cool. We're good,' the young woman said hastily, putting up her hands and backing away a step to prevent further interference. 'Just chill.'

'You okay, Morgan?' Lauren asked, looking concerned for her friend. Around the room, quiet conversation was starting to resume as students went back to work.

Letting out an exasperated breath, Morgan nodded to Anya. 'Just a little accident,' she said, in a tone that was far less forgiving than her words. She pointed towards a sign for the restrooms. 'I'll be back in a minute, need to clean up a little.'

'Want some help?'

Morgan shook her head. 'Nah, I got this.'

'Cool. I'll be here, okay?'

Picking up her coat and bag, Morgan gave Anya a withering look. 'Try to be more careful next time, huh?'

Anya nodded, then reached down to pick up the coffee cup as the young woman scurried off to the restrooms. She gave it a few moments before disposing of the cup in the nearest waste bin, then quietly heading in the same direction.

'You're doing well, Alex,' she spoke into her radio as soon as she was in the corridor outside. She wasn't normally one for massaging egos, but Alex was a civilian and probably in need of some encouragement. 'Lauren will wait for her friend. You can stop talking to her now, but let me know if she tries to leave the library.'

He didn't reply directly, as she knew he couldn't, but she could hear his words as he commented on the minor scene she'd created. The phrase 'bloody idiot bringing a coffee cup in here' was used, as was 'no respect for a place like this'. She felt certain it was directed at her rather than Lauren.

Still, disrespect was the least of her concerns. There was only one place she was going now. It was time to take care of her Agency friend.

Chapter 21

'Goddamn it, what a fucking mess,' Morgan Brooks said into the mirror as she reviewed the dark splatters of coffee that marked her top. She was alone in the restroom, and felt perfectly comfortable voicing her frustration.

Of all the dumbass things to happen, some random bitch spilling coffee down her really took the biscuit. It had taken no small measure of restraint to keep herself from knocking the older woman on her ass in front of the whole library, finally putting all those rigorous months of Agency combat training to the test.

As if it wasn't bad enough being stuck on this detail for the past 18 months, babysitting the spoiled daughter of one of the Agency's big players, pretending to be interested in the bullshit she was studying, pretending to like her. Pretending she didn't resent her life of privilege, while Brooks herself was forced to act and dress like a bookish mouse. She'd be glad when the end of year rolled around and she could be relieved of this duty.

There was little she could do to salvage the top. A few dabs with a wet paper towel wasn't going to get the stain out, and it wasn't as if she could walk around in her underwear. There was nothing else for it – she'd have to go back to their dorm room and change.

'Fuck my life,' she said, tossing the wad of paper towels in the trash can.

The door creaked as someone entered. Perhaps Lauren had come to check up on her.

You've got to be kidding me, Brooks thought, taking in the sight of the older, dark-haired woman, the reason for her being here in the first place. She was standing by the doorway, looking right at her. What the hell did she want? If it was to offer another stammered apology, she'd find Brooks far less accommodating in private than she had been in public.

But she did no such thing. She didn't say a word, in fact. An icy feeling trickled down Brooks' spine. This situation was all wrong.

Something was on the ground by the woman's feet. Looking down, Brooks watched as she calmly used her boot to wedge the rubber door stop into place, preventing anyone from entering.

That was when the pieces finally came together. The unfamiliar young man who had struck up a conversation with Lauren, the coffee spillage that had forced her to come in here, the woman who had appeared so timid now standing yards away with a very different look in her eyes.

She couldn't believe she'd been complacent enough to fall for a ploy like this. Clearly 18 months of boredom and inactivity had eroded her situational awareness, made her slow to react.

Brooks thrust a hand into her bag, feeling for the concealed Glock 26 miniature pistol she always kept there.

The mysterious woman charged at her, covering the short distance from the door to the wash basins with frightening speed.

Closing her fingers around the weapon's handle, Brooks pulled the gun free, and flicked the safety catch off. She had no idea who this woman was or why she'd sought her out, but her adversary had made her intentions quite plain.

As soon as she was taken care of, Brooks would press the panic button on her key chain, engaging the emergency evacuation protocol for Lauren. There would be questions to answer, of course, and her time as an undercover operative in this city was certainly at an end, but those were concerns for later.

Sighting the target, she pulled the trigger, bracing herself for the weapon's formidable recoil. But her opponent's hand had simultaneously shot upwards, grasped the Glock's slide mechanism and yanked it backwards, almost tearing the gun from Brooks' grip.

Instead of the sharp crack of a subsonic round, there was nothing at all, not even a click. With the slide forced into its rear position, the weapon's mechanism was unable to engage, the firing pin stuck where it was no matter how hard she pulled the trigger.

Brooks reacted to this unexpected predicament with creditable speed. With the weapon neutralized, at least for now, she fell back on her unarmed combat training, lashing out with her free hand at the woman's throat. Striking at the face was a waste of time and a quick way to break knuckles, but a good hard blow to the trachea could drop a target like a sack of bricks.

–

In the library reading room, the grunts and snarls of Anya's fight were relayed to Alex's earpiece with frightening clarity. The only thing he couldn't tell was who was winning.

'You okay?' Lauren asked.

'Yeah,' he lied. 'Just my phone going off.' Thinking fast, he fished his phone out of his pocket and pretended to check his messages. 'Sorry to be rude, but I need to make a quick call. Do you mind?'

The young woman shrugged. 'Hey, don't mind me. Go for it.' She flashed a teasing smile, pointing to a sign that warned against the use of cell phones in the reading room. 'But I'd go outside first.'

'Thanks. Enough rule breakers already today, eh?' he said, turning away.

'Hey, Alex,' Lauren called after him.

Alex turned again, trying to look more relaxed than he felt, and the young woman held out a hand.

'You've still got something of mine.'

Alex glanced down at the book he was still holding, having quite forgotten about it. He handed the book over, hoping she didn't notice the slight tremor in his hand.

Lauren nodded in gratitude. 'Maybe I'll see you around.'

Alex said nothing further as she turned away and took one of the reading desks. Quickly retreating to a quieter corner of the room, he wasted no time speaking into his radio.

'Anya, what the fuck's going on? Where are you?'

–

Her opponent was trying to strike at her throat and incapacitate her. A sound tactic, especially when up against someone physically larger and stronger than yourself. Anya was ready for it, having been through much the same training. The difference was that Anya had a lifetime of experience to back it up.

Batting the attempted strike aside while maintaining an iron grip on the Glock, she drove a knee into Brooks' unprotected stomach, eliciting an instinctive change in posture to prevent another such blow. Capitalising on her opponent's momentary weakness, Anya jammed a boot into her left knee with merciless ferocity, buckling it.

Brooks dropped to her knees, her grip on the gun slackening. Injured and immobilized, she could manage only an uncoordinated punch that caught her enemy a fleeting blow to the ribs.

For Anya, it felt like she'd just been hit with a sledgehammer. White light impinged her vision as her ribs exploded with pain. It took great self-control not to cry out, to keep her mind on her enemy. Injuries could be sorted out later. Winning the fight was all that mattered now.

Twisting sideways to avoid another strike that would surely drop her, she tore the gun from her enemy's hand with a vicious kick, breaking Brooks' trigger finger in the process.

Anya saw a flash of defiance in the young woman's eyes even as she swept the gun around and caught her with a hard, solid blow to the base of her skull. There was no recovering from that. Brooks went down, landing hard on the tiled floor, a thin trickle of blood oozing from the cut at her neck.

Anya staggered for a moment, her breathing shallow, clutching at the countertop for support. She waited while she slowly regained her composure. She knelt down beside the young woman and felt the pulse at her neck. To her relief, it was fast and weak, but there.

The movies might show James Bond neatly incapacitating opponents with a deft blow to the back of the head, but the reality was far more dangerous and imprecise. Strike too hard and you risked a skull fracture and intracranial bleeding; strike too soft and you were left with an injured but very angry opponent. For that reason, Anya generally tried to avoid such tactics unless the victim's survival wasn't a priority. Still, needs must.

And in this case it seemed her gamble had paid off. Brooks would likely have a week or two in the hospital to look forward to when she woke up, but barring unexpected brain damage, she'd probably make a full recovery.

Anya didn't have the luxury of hospitals to fall back on. She glanced at her reflection and wasn't surprised to see a crimson stain spreading from the left side of her shirt. She closed her eyes and gently felt around the injury, searching for the telltale jagged lump that would tell her if she'd snapped a rib. Even this probing was painful indeed, but she could find no signs of more severe damage.

There was nothing to be done about the bleeding right now. The best she could manage was to pull her jacket closed and zip it up, though it was anyone's guess how long it would take the blood to seep through.

Her thoughts were disturbed by the sound of Alex's voice in her ear, hushed but filled with concern. 'Anya, if you're still alive, I'd really appreciate an update.'

'I'm fine,' she said, still having difficulty breathing properly. 'Stop yelling in my ear.'

'You sounded like you were murdering someone.'

Anya said nothing.

'Jesus, tell me you didn't—'

'She's alive,' Anya asserted, unwilling to waste more time on the matter. 'Do you have a visual on the target?'

'Yeah, she's in the reading room.'

'Good. Get ready to move,' Anya said, thrusting the compact Glock into her jacket pocket and pulling the dark wig off and running her fingers through her real hair.

'Where, exactly?'

'You'll see. Just stick close to her.'

With that, she reached into the satchel she'd brought in with her and fished out a grey, cylindrical device with a simple fuse, pin and priming lever attached to one end. Pulling the pin out and releasing her grip on the priming lever to allow it to detach, Anya rolled the smoke grenade into the furthest toilet stall.

A second or so later, a loud hissing sound told her the chemicals had gone to work, and white smoke began to billow out of the stall, quickly forming a dense wall of artificial fog. Snatching up her satchel, Anya removed the rubber wedge, opened the door and strode out into the corridor.

She'd spotted the fire alarm on her way in, surrounded by angry red text warning users to break only in case of an emergency. A sharp blow with her elbow broke the protective glass plate covering the alarm, allowing her to reach in and pull the lever.

Chapter 22

Lauren Cain was just starting to type up some notes when the peaceful air of the reading room was shattered by the harsh blare of a fire alarm.

For the next couple of seconds, nothing much happened. Whatever conversation had been going on fell silent as students looked for any obvious signs of fire. Most of them had been through dozens of drills and false alarms over the years, often by fellow students playing pranks, and were perhaps hoping that the alarm would shut off quickly.

It didn't, and when this fact became obvious, the senior staff member on duty at the information desk – a rotund little man with a red face and thinning, combed-over hair – began to address the room.

'Everybody, I must ask that you make your way calmly outside through the emergency exits,' he said in French, having to shout to be heard over the echoing electronic wail. 'Please walk, don't run!'

A collective groan passed through the room as students picked up bags and coats, and began to file out.

'Damn it,' Lauren said, closing down the laptop and replacing it in her bag, along with the notebooks she'd been working from.

She was reaching for her coat when Alex appeared, standing uncertainly over her as the evacuation unfolded.

'This sort of thing happen a lot around here?' he asked, looking unnerved. She didn't blame him, being in a strange place with no friends around.

Lauren made a face. 'You'd be surprised, especially around exam time.' Throwing her coat over her shoulders, she stood up and glanced over at the corridor leading to the restrooms. 'I'd better go get Morgan.'

'Won't she be outside already?' he asked.

Lauren frowned, torn about what to do. Alex was most likely right. Morgan wasn't stupid, and would probably have made her way outside with the rest of the students, but it went against her instincts to leave a friend unaccounted for at a time like this.

'I guess so,' she agreed reluctantly, unable to shake the feeling that something wasn't quite right. But realizing they couldn't linger here, she added, 'Come on. I'll show you the way out.'

Lauren dug out her phone and tried dialling Morgan's cell. To her dismay, the call rang out. Maybe the noise of the alarms had drowned out the ring tone, she tried to tell herself as they filed into the corridor outside the reading room.

That was when Lauren smelled it. Smoke. And as she turned right, she saw a grey haze drifting down the corridor, rolling along the ceiling in waves. This was no prank or scheduled drill, she realized. The building really was on fire.

Others had caught on too, and she heard a few frightened exclamations from her fellow students, their steps accelerating as they headed for the exits.

'Oh, shit,' Alex said, staring into the smoke.

Lauren punched in a rapid text message to Morgan and sent it off in record time.

Heading outside. Call me. L

She'd just shoved the phone into her back pocket when a woman came striding towards her. Tall, perhaps in her early forties, with short blonde hair and the authoritative stride of someone used to taking command of a situation.

'Lauren Cain?' the woman asked, her tone brisk and official.

Lauren blinked, shocked to hear that name spoken aloud. At her father's insistence, she'd been using her mother's name during her time here. No one knew who she really was.

'What did you call me?' she demanded, suddenly uncertain of what was happening. 'Who are you?'

The woman took a step closer and lowered her voice. 'Name's Erin Forsyth, ma'am. I'm a field agent with the Paris embassy. Your father assigned me to your security detail.'

'What security detail?'

'Your father takes your safety very seriously,' Forsyth assured her. 'And so do we. I'm afraid you may be in danger here.'

She couldn't believe what she was hearing. Her father had agents following her, spying on every aspect of her private life? How far had this gone?

Alex seemed equally taken aback by this revelation. 'Wait, what do you mean—'

'Sir, please back away,' the field operative warned him, one hand thrust into her jacket pocket as if she intended to draw a weapon on him. 'For your own safety, back away now.'

With little choice in the face of such a thinly veiled threat, Alex obeyed.

'Why am I in danger?' Lauren asked. 'Oh, shit. This fire was no accident, was it?'

'That's not a conversation to be had here,' Forsyth said, holding out a hand. 'Please come with me. We have a car waiting outside to take you to a secure location.'

Lauren was unwilling to trust her. In any case, if there was danger here, she couldn't leave knowing Morgan's life might be at risk. 'I have to find my friend—'

Forsyth grabbed her arm, preventing her from leaving.

'Let go of me!' she demanded, trying to get free.

'My job is to get you to safety by any means necessary, but it'd be easier for both of us if you cooperate,' Forsyth added with a meaningful look. 'Your call, ma'am.'

'I want to see some ID first,' Lauren said.

Forsyth's expression was one of long-suffering patience. 'Undercover agents don't carry ID. That's part of being in the Agency. Now let's go.'

Lauren finally acquiesced and allowed the older woman to lead her down the now empty corridor with fast, purposeful strides. She was hard pressed to keep up, and having one arm clutched deathly tight wasn't helping.

She watched as the operative reached up and pressed a finger against her right ear. 'We're en route to the evac vehicle,' she said. 'Meet us there, and be ready to move.'

'What sort of danger were you talking about?' Lauren asked as they rounded a corner. She'd always harboured an instinctive dislike of people who expected her to follow instructions without explanation. It was probably why her relationship with her father was strained at the best of times, but it had set a pattern for her life. She wanted answers from this woman.

'We believe a terrorist group may have learned your identity, and was preparing to abduct you,' Forsyth explained hurriedly. 'I was forced to put our evac plan into action.'

'You have plans for people trying to kidnap me?' Lauren asked, still refusing to believe someone would see her as so important.

The older woman glanced briefly over her shoulder at Lauren. 'We have plans for every scenario.'

Throwing open the fire exit, Forsyth led them out onto a side street running parallel to the Sorbonne, acting as if she expected masked gunmen to appear from the shadows and attack them. But aside from a few people looking inquisitively towards the blaring alarms, the place looked quiet.

'Let's go,' Forsyth said, leading her over to a black Ford Focus parked up on the kerb. A click of her key fob disengaged the alarm with a distinctive *whup, whup*, and she turned around to face Lauren. 'Get in, ma'am.'

She still possessed the same air of authority that had so struck Lauren at the outset, but there was a tautness in her face, as if she were uncomfortable or in pain. Lauren couldn't put her finger on it, but something wasn't right.

'We need to go, now,' Forsyth commanded, perhaps sensing her growing doubts.

Lauren noticed something staining the jacket that Forsyth wore zipped up tight. Something dark brown or reddish in colour, leaking through the fabric from underneath. It took her a second or so to realize what it was.

Blood.

She was running almost before she knew it, tearing off towards the fire exit she'd just come through at full pelt. Designed to open only from the inside, it would form an effective barrier to anyone trying to force their way in after her. At the very least, it would hold Forsyth, or whatever her name really was, at bay until Lauren could raise the alarm.

'Lauren! Stop!' she called out.

Lauren ignored her, gunning for the other side of that fire exit as fast as her legs would carry her. She hardly considered herself an athlete, but she did run and jog regularly, and could put on quite a burst of speed when necessary. Now was such a time. Forsyth by contrast was older, and apparently injured. With luck, it would slow her down just enough to give Lauren the edge.

She was just about to slip through the slowly closing door when another figure appeared in front of her. A young man with light brown hair, scruffy-looking clothes and several days' growth of stubble. The man who had introduced himself as Alex.

Lauren couldn't say for sure whether he was in on Forsyth's scheme, or whether he had followed her out of concern for her safety, but she was taking no chances.

Like many female students these days, she carried a small canister of pepper spray with her, particularly when going out alone. She'd never before had to use it, for which she was grateful, but that had just changed.

Whipping it out of her pocket while barely breaking stride, she pointed it at his face and pressed the button on top. A thin jet of clear liquid shot through the air, looking for all the world like she'd just fired a water pistol. Alex jerked his head to the side and raised an arm instinctively, but his sudden cry told her the pepper spray had got into his eyes all the same.

Lauren pressed forward, trying to shove her way past him to get inside. She was smaller and lighter than him, and now that he was blinded by the spray, he was only partially blocking the doorway.

'Out of my way!' she screamed, shoving and lashing out with her fists.

She was about to give him another dose of the spray when she felt something sharp press into her neck. She tried to reach up and pull out whatever had just jabbed her, but a sudden feeling of wooziness made her actions slow and leaden. The world seemed to be going into slow motion, all vague and indistinct.

She turned, trying to bring the pepper spray around, but could no longer control her limbs properly. She saw a fleeting glimpse of a woman's face as her legs buckled and the darkness closed around her.

Anya caught the young woman just as she collapsed. The last thing she needed was for Lauren to fracture her skull on the pavement. Her target's weight would normally have presented little difficulty for even an average person to support, but for Anya, every step felt like some immense boulder was resting on her, crushing her down. She managed to half-carry, half-drag the unconscious woman over to the waiting car, popped the trunk and bundled her inside.

She could hear distant sirens approaching. Hopefully fire engines, possibly police.

A set of plastic cable ties were already laid out in the trunk. Anya made sure to secure Lauren's wrists and ankles, then used a third loop to join them together. It was about as effective a way of keeping a target immobile as she could think of.

This done, she slammed the trunk closed and turned towards Alex, who was leaning against the wall, tears streaming from his eyes as he desperately tried to wipe the spray away. It was a wasted effort, she knew from experience. Rubbing them would only force the chemicals deeper into the skin, prolonging his discomfort.

'Alex, are you all right?' she called out.

He looked over in her general direction. 'No! I can't fucking see!'

Hurrying over, she led him to the passenger side of the car. As Alex fumbled with his seatbelt, Anya strode around to the driver's side, slid in, and started the engine.

Even as several pedestrians further up the street were starting to point at her car, she slammed into gear and accelerated away.

Chapter 23

Slovakia

The atmosphere in the car was tense. Drake was pushing the old Volkswagen as hard as he dared along the 1106 highway, following signs for the Czech border. He was eager to put as much distance between them and Stupava as possible, partly to avoid police follow-up, but mostly to get as far away from Hawkins and his men as he could. Every mile they travelled added dozens to the possible search area.

He still couldn't understand how Hawkins had caught up with them so fast, when they had spent just minutes in Lenka's apartment. Satellite tracking would have been too difficult and time consuming, even for a man of Cain's authority to harness without repercussions. It was possible the search chopper had spotted him, but if so why hadn't it followed and intercepted them in the woods, rather than waiting until they reached a populated area? Drones were another possibility, but operating them in Slovakian airspace without authorization, and in poor weather conditions, would be dangerous at best.

A lot of questions, for which he currently had no answers.

The terrain around them was dense woodland, towering pine and spruce trees crowding in close to the road, their thick canopy turning the already gloomy morning into near-total darkness. Rain continued to beat off the windshield, supplemented by spray kicked up by occasional trucks that rumbled past at high speed. With the driver's side window in pieces on the floor, Drake's journey was both loud and wet.

He and Lenka hadn't spoken a word to each other since their escape from Stupava, but a quick glance at the young woman made it plain what was going through her mind. Her life, such as it had been, had just fallen down around her. Everything she owned, all her plans for the future had just gone up in smoke. He couldn't blame her for being pissed off.

'Lenka, we—'

'Shut up, *chumaj!*' she snarled, thumping him in the arm, and following it up with a stream of what he presumed were more colourful Slovak invectives.

'All right, that's enough!' Drake shouted, having to fend off another blow with his free hand. Allowing her to vent her spleen was one thing, but he wasn't going to sit there and let her pummel him for the next couple of hours.

Finally the young woman seemed to simmer down and slumped back in her seat, still glaring at him like a feral cat waiting for another chance to strike out.

'I want to know who those men were,' she said at length.

'You don't—'

'Do not tell me it is for my own good!' she warned him, jabbing a finger in his direction. 'They tried to kill me. My home is gone. Everything I have is gone. I want to know who the fuck you are, who the fuck they are, and why the fuck they want you dead. Now speak, *chumaj*.'

Drake let out a breath, ducking his head aside as another blast of rainwater was kicked in his direction by a passing vehicle. He was starting to regret not trying to jimmy the door rather than break the window.

'All right, fine,' he conceded. 'The men who tried to kill us are CIA.'

Her eyes opened wider. 'Americans?'

Drake nodded.

'So what does that make you? Are you... terrorist?'

If only it were that simple, he thought bleakly. 'I used to work for them myself. Then I got caught up in something bad, found out the man in charge isn't what I thought. He's got his own agenda, and he's willing to kill anyone who stands in his way.'

'Including you.'

Drake said nothing to that. 'We tried to beat him to the punch, take him down first, but he was ready for us. Most of the people who helped me are either dead, missing or captured. Now it's just me.' He stared off into the murky distance, where the road was swallowed up by mist and gloom. 'Just me.'

The young woman mulled over everything he'd said. He didn't want or expect gushing sympathy from her, but it was clear his words had made an impact. 'How did you escape them?'

Drake doubted she'd feel comfortable around him if she knew the gory details of his escape. 'I got lucky,' was all he was prepared to say. 'I'm not counting on that again.'

'What will you do now?'

Drake shuffled his feet in the footwell. He and all his allies working together had failed against Marcus Cain, and some of them had paid for that with their lives. And yet, he still lived. Yesterday he'd been resigned to dying alone in the darkness of his cell. Now he was free. He was only one man, but he was free.

And he wasn't finished yet.

'Fight back,' he said. 'I don't expect to win, but maybe I can get even.'

'What about me?' Lenka asked, her voice quieter now.

Drake chanced a look at her. With her blonde hair now hanging in a damp mess around her shoulders, her face streaked with mud and make-up, her clothes filthy, she was a pathetic, bedraggled-looking figure.

Her anger had boiled away as she began to see the long-term implications of this morning's events, and a stark reality began to settle on her: she might well have been pulled into a dangerous, shadowy world. A world for which she was completely unprepared.

'First we get across the border into the Czech Republic, then head for Prague,' he said, thinking it best to keep her mind on more immediate matters.

His one cause for optimism was that the Czech Republic and Slovakia were both Schengen Area countries, with no physical borders and no passport controls. It was just as well, otherwise he'd have been shit out of luck with nothing but a stolen car and a few crumpled euros to his name.

'Why Prague?' the young woman asked.

'We need a place to hold up and sort ourselves out, and it's got the only supply cache within a thousand miles.' He offered Lenka an encouraging smile. 'I don't know about you, but I could use some fresh clothes.'

That at least prompted a laugh, which made him feel better than he had for some time. 'You mean this is not a good look for me?'

Drake couldn't help but laugh as well. When everything else is going to shit, sometimes humour is the only recourse. That was why soldiers took the piss out of each other on the eve of battle, he reflected.

'I still do not know your name,' she said, turning a little more serious now.

What the hell, he thought. She at least deserved to know that much.

'It's Ryan.'

'Ryan,' she repeated, trying it out for size. 'It suits you, I think.'

'Better than *chumaj*,' he mused, thinking about the word she'd applied to him several times already. 'What the hell does that mean anyway?'

'It is… a hard word to put in English,' she said, stalling. 'Closest I think is… stupid man. A moron.'

'Moron,' Drake repeated. 'Can't say it's the worst thing I've been called.'

'I do have other words for you,' Lenka assured him.

Drake didn't doubt it, but decided to let her keep them to herself for now.

Chapter 24

Alex's face was burning, and his eyes felt like they were cooking inside their sockets as the anti-personnel spray did its work. Never had he experienced pain quite like it, or endured the frightening sensation of near-total blindness. He could see nothing but weak light and blurry shapes.

All he could say with any certainty was that their car was moving at a rapid pace. He could hear the growl of the engine as Anya revved it hard, could feel the vibrations as the suspension fought against ancient cobbled roadways, and was occasionally pitched sideways by a sharp turn.

Reaching up, he tried to rub at his eyes, only for Anya to push his arm down. 'Don't,' she commanded. 'It will only make it worse.'

'Easy for you to say,' he said angrily. 'You didn't just get fucking maced.'

'Pepper spray,' the woman corrected him. 'Much less potent.'

'Do I look like I give a shit? My face feels like something from *Raiders of the Lost Ark*.' In frustration, he slammed his fist against the dashboard. 'Fucking hell!'

'I know what it feels like, Alex,' she assured him. 'Act like a man and take it.'

Alex opened his mouth to retort, but decided against it. Whether it was that her advice was sensible and pragmatic, or that her implied challenge had stirred a sense of masculine pride, he couldn't rightly say. He forced his hands down and did his best to endure the discomfort.

'I still can't see.'

'Your sight should return soon.'

'Where are we?' he asked.

'Heading south-west, out of the city.' An increase in speed suggested they'd just joined a larger road. 'With luck we can reach the safe house before dark.'

'Safe house?'

'We need a place to hold Lauren until I can organize an exchange.' She must have jerked the wheel left to avoid a vehicle, because Alex felt himself pressed against the passenger door. 'It's over the border in Switzerland. Unfortunately, the tranquilizer will wear off long before then.'

'What did you hit her with?' He knew Lauren had gone quiet pretty quickly after Anya got hold of her.

'Vecuronium bromide cut with sodium amytal.' Perhaps sensing those chemicals meant little to him, she elaborated. 'A combination we used back when I was an Agency field operative. It's strong enough to induce paralysis and unconsciousness within seconds. The only drawback is that it tends to wear off quickly. I'll have to dose her with a proper sedative when we stop.'

'Wait, shouldn't stopping be the last thing we want to do?'

Anya didn't respond.

—

Twenty minutes later, Alex was seated on the hood of their now stationary car, trying to look casual while watching traffic cruise past on the main road nearby. His eyes, still red from the pepper spray, were hidden behind a pair of dark sunglasses.

After leaving the bustling streets of central Paris and speeding along one of the main arteries leading out of the city for 15 minutes or so, Anya had decided it was time to deal with the unwilling passenger in the trunk. She had waited until they were in the midst of the Meudon national forest, just a couple of miles east of the palace of Versailles, before pulling over into a small car park.

Alex was relegated to lookout duty in case some random civilians pulled in looking for a morning stroll in the woods, and instead found themselves face to face with a pair of kidnappers.

Shafts of sunlight slanted down, showing the trees were just starting to sprout with spring growth, and birds sang as they flitted between the flowers. It rather reminded him of the half-hearted walking trips his parents used to drag him on as a kid, to 'get him away from those bloody computer screens'.

If they'd tried a little harder, maybe he wouldn't be where he was now.

'How much longer?' Alex asked, eager to get moving again.

'Not long.' Judging by the heavy breathing coming from the back of the car, Anya was hard at work. 'Just keep watch.'

Alex folded his arms. 'What do you think Cain will do when he finds out?'

Anya seemed to know him as well as anyone, and she wasn't inclined to sugar-coat things. If anyone could tell him the extent of the shitstorm they had just unleashed, it was her.

'What would you do, if it were your daughter?'

'Hard to say. Don't have any, at least as far as I know,' he added. 'Come on, give it to me straight. How deep are we?'

'Deep,' she admitted. 'Cain will mobilize every resource at the Agency's disposal to track us down. Our only chance is to stay ahead of him.'

'And you can do that, right?'

'No,' she admitted frankly. 'Not with the two of you slowing me down. Sooner or later he will catch up with us. All I can do for now is throw him off the scent, buy us time.'

'How, exactly?'

He felt something hit him in the shoulder, before banging off the hood of the car. Frowning, he picked up what looked like a little circular piece of plastic no bigger than a penny. The back was partially transparent, allowing him to make out the miniature circuitry within.

'Tracking device,' Anya explained. 'Sewn into the lining of her coat. There was another in her shoe.' She tossed a second device to him, which he caught this time. 'There is a toilet block on the other side of the parking lot. Take the trackers, and her clothes, and hide them in the trash can. Move.'

Sure enough, Lauren's clothes now lay in a pile on the ground by Anya's feet. Even the young woman's underwear was amongst it.

'Tell me you didn't just strip her naked,' he said in dismay.

'Believe me, I take no pleasure in it. But it's the only way to be sure Cain isn't tracking her, and us.' Anya slammed the tailgate closed. 'There are spare clothes for her at the safe house. Now move.'

Shaking his head, Alex snatched up the bundle of clothes and jogged over to the toilet block. Choosing the women's restroom, he found the trash can set flush into the wall beside the sink and stuffed the entire bundle into it.

As he did so, he wondered how many felonies his work today had added to what was already an extensive list, and how many more would be added before he was done.

Chapter 25

CIA Station Chief Hayden Quinn was no stranger to bad days. He'd had many of them lately, beginning with the appearance of a man named Hawkins, who had virtually taken over his position as director of operations in Pakistan. It was soon followed by the murder of a Pakistani intelligence officer, which had enflamed tensions with their ISI, and culminated in an armed confrontation in a residential neighbourhood that had left numerous men dead.

Questions were being asked at all levels, and Quinn found himself increasingly unable to answer them. Marcus Cain, who had appeared so suddenly to conduct a clandestine meeting with the Pakistanis, had vanished just as quickly, with barely a word of explanation. All he had told Quinn was that neither his meeting nor the confrontation in Islamabad were to be investigated.

His only source of consolation was that Cain seemed to have no knowledge of Quinn's involvement in the attempt on his life. It was he who had let it be known that Cain was coming to Pakistan, he who had allowed Ryan Drake and his group of rogue Shepherd operatives to know the location of Cain's meeting. He who had betrayed the deputy director of the fucking CIA.

But Cain was still alive. Whatever plot Drake had concocted, it had achieved nothing except to get a lot of people killed.

Quinn rubbed his sore neck. The office air conditioning was running at full capacity, yet his back and underarms were damp with perspiration. Events were spiralling out of control, and he was becoming increasingly paranoid.

'Fuck it,' he decided, reaching for the bottle of Wild Turkey in his desk drawer. Hardly luxury stuff, but difficult enough to get hold of out here. And it did the job well enough.

Pouring a glass, he held it up and stared at the amber liquid, before knocking it back with a grimace. He was just pondering a second glass when his desk phone rang. A glance at the caller ID told him it was the secure hotline from Langley.

Setting his glass down, Quinn reached for the phone, took a deep breath and picked it up. 'Station Chief.'

'Hayden, good to speak again,' Marcus Cain said, his tone upbeat, almost jovial. 'How are things there?'

'P-pretty good, sir,' Quinn managed to stammer, not sure what else to say. Doubtless Cain knew more about events here than Quinn did.

'That's good. Listen, I want you to do something for me – it's important,' Cain went on. 'Set up a meeting at the embassy with Husain Khalid, as soon as you can.'

'The director general?'

Husain Khalid was the leader of Pakistan's ISI. A vocal critic of US foreign policy, and a man with a track record for undermining CIA operations in this part of the world, he should be the last person Cain wanted to meet with.

'The very one,' Cain confirmed. 'Tell him he can bring as many of his senior advisors and security personnel as he likes.'

'Sir, he'll never go for it,' Quinn protested desperately. 'Stepping onto US soil, being searched, giving up his weapons...'

'Trust me, he'll go for this. Tell him we have information on who murdered his operative last week, that it's connected to the shootout in Islamabad,' Cain interjected. 'And tell him there will be no searches, no weapons confiscated, nothing. It's a gesture of trust on our part, and he'll be our honoured guest. Tell him we want to make things right.'

What the hell was Cain playing at? Kowtowing to the Pakistanis mere days after ordering the murder of one of their men? What did he hope to achieve?

'Sir, even if the Pakistanis did agree to your terms, you understand this would be a huge breach of station protocol—'

'I know the risks, Hayden,' Cain assured him. 'But considering what this meeting could achieve, it's a risk worth taking. And for what it's worth, this one's on me. Make it happen, and I promise I'll make things happen for you. Do you understand?'

Quinn wasn't sure that he did. But Cain hadn't ordered him brought back to Langley in chains, so that had to count for something. Could it be that there was actually a way out of this, despite everything he'd done?

'I'll do what I can, sir,' he promised.

'I know you will. Call me when you have an update.'

With that, the line went dead.

Chapter 26

New York, 24 June 1988

Anya let out a short breath as Cain entered her, pulling him close, her hands feeling the play of the taut muscles across his back. They moved in harmony as pleasure and desire mounted.

Anya rolled over so that she was on top. Her movements were slow and deliberate at first, trying to draw out the moment, but soon becoming faster and more urgent. His hands found her breasts as she continued to move.

Their breathing came faster and faster as they neared their peak. Finally, a moan of ecstasy escaped Anya's lips as pleasure overwhelmed her. Cain finished a moment later, his body tensing up and suddenly relaxing as he released.

She collapsed on top of him, completely spent. It was several moments before she was able to think clearly, but she reluctantly disengaged and lay next to him, her chest rising and falling as her heart pounded.

She had often thought that the times she felt most alive were when she was about to go into battle, when her own life was in her hands, but now she knew there was another time. It was at moments like this, with Marcus.

Tonight had been particularly intense because she knew there wouldn't be another like it for a long time. She was leaving tomorrow, rejoining Task Force Black for deployment to Afghanistan. There were preparations still to be made, work to be done, but for tonight neither she nor Cain cared.

They wanted, needed this night to themselves.

'Jesus, I feel sorry for the poor bastards in the room next door,' Cain said.

Anya giggled in amusement; neither of them had exactly been restrained, and the walls of this hotel weren't thick. Still, she didn't feel remotely self-conscious about it. The wine they'd had over dinner hadn't hurt either.

'Maybe they will be jealous of us,' she suggested.

'I'm going to miss this, you know.'

Smiling, Anya rolled over and pressed her naked body against his, still warm with the tingling afterglow. 'So will I. We'll have to make up for lost time when I come back.'

'That's not what I meant,' he said quietly. 'I worry every time you go out there, but this time it's different. I'm afraid they'll be putting another star on that wall at Langley. I'm afraid you won't come back.'

That admission hit her hard. Harder than she'd expected, because Cain wasn't a man to voice his fears. His words elicited a chill of foreboding, as if he were speaking of something already decided.

Anya sat up in the bed, looking down at him.

'Marcus, look at me,' she implored him. 'Look at me.'

Reluctantly, he did.

Leaning over to the bedside table, she picked up the set of dog tags she'd been issued with when she passed selection and officially joined Task Force Black. None of the team members were allowed them in the field in case they were captured, but Carpenter had insisted they were given all the same. Soldiers deserved dog tags, and that was what they were.

'Take these,' she said, pressing them into his hand. 'Take them, and keep them safe until I come back to claim them.'

Cain ran his fingers across the stamped metal surface, watching as they gleamed in the firelight. Slowly his fingers closed around them.

'I will come home,' Anya said, speaking with absolute conviction, banishing any thoughts of her fate being decided. 'No matter what it takes. No matter what I have to do, I will come back to you. I promise.'

Cain reached out, pulling her to him, holding her so tight it was as if he never wanted to be apart from her. Anya in return pressed herself against him, and her lips found his as she sought to give him what he so desperately needed, if only for a while.

—

Half a world away in his office at Langley, Cain hung up the phone. Quinn would do as ordered, he knew. The man might have proven himself disloyal after events in Islamabad, but he was frightened now that his scheme had unravelled, and frightened men were the most compliant of all.

There was still the question of whether the Pakistanis would go for his deal, but he suspected they could be persuaded. After all, Cain now had a man on the inside. A man they trusted implicitly after his decades of loyal service, and with a vested interest of his own in seeing this meeting go ahead.

He swung his chair and stared out of his window. Just beyond the Agency's campus lay the muddy curve of the Potomac river, flanked by dense woodland, and in the distance the soaring spire of the Washington Monument.

But Cain's eyes were focussed on something closer at hand. Below him stood the courtyard garden, a hundred yards of no man's land that lay between the Agency's old and new headquarters buildings. And in the middle of this landscaped greenery, the pool he'd stood beside with Anya a lifetime ago. The day he'd told her she was being sent back to Afghanistan.

He was almost startled by the buzz of his phone. Not his desk phone or his official work cell, but the burner he kept locked away in a drawer.

Fishing the phone out, he was surprised to see that the call was coming from Morgan Brooks, the operative he'd assigned to his daughter's protective detail.

'Cain,' he began, with a growing sense of unease.

'Sir, it's your daughter,' Brooks said. 'She's been taken.'

Part III

Provocation

'Provoke the enemy's power and force him to reveal himself.'

– Sun Tzu

Chapter 27

Grass, stretching away in front of her, the long stalks reaching past her waist, swaying and rippling like an undulating sea as the breeze sighed across it. Above, thin ribbons of cloud spanned a vast blue canvas of sky.

She crept forward, driven by the childish desire to explore. Ahead, near the crest of the gentle hill, lay a stand of trees.

Lauren Cain was floating in an endless sea of nothingness. A world without memory or feeling.

There!

A noise drifted in as if from a great distance. The noise was repeated, stronger and more forceful this time.

Not just a noise. A word, spoken to her. The flowing syllables seemed to grow more defined, resolving themselves into individual sounds.

Becoming a name.

Her name.

'Lauren.'

Her mind groped towards the source, trying to regain control.

'Lauren,' the voice repeated. 'Can you hear me?'

Lauren's eyes fluttered open, bright light flooding in. She blinked, squeezed them closed, then opened them a fraction and managed to tolerate it enough to take in her surroundings.

She was in a room. Sparsely furnished, very modern and clean, almost sterile in appearance. White walls, grey carpet, no decoration of any sort. But despite being spotlessly maintained, the air had the stale smell of a place that hadn't been lived in for a while.

The light was coming from a set of big full-length windows off to her right. She could see a lake, trees, blue sky and, to her surprise, snow-capped mountains. The treetops were swaying, the sun was high in the sky.

She was thirsty. How long had she been out?

'How do you feel?'

Lauren looked up as a figure moved into view. A woman, perhaps 40 years old. A woman she recognized.

A kaleidoscope of memories came rushing back. She heard the blare of fire alarms, saw a woman leading her outside, felt herself suddenly scared and running to escape, and then a pinprick in her neck.

That was enough to bring her fully awake. Seized by panic, Lauren tried to jump back, to flee, only to find herself unable to move. She looked down to see her wrists and ankles were bound by plastic cable ties to a metal chair. She also noticed that her clothes were gone, replaced by a plain white T-shirt and grey slacks.

She struggled even harder to break free. The cable ties bit painfully into her skin, but showed no signs of snapping.

'I wouldn't struggle, if I were you,' the woman advised. The Midwestern American accent was gone now, replaced by something that sounded Russian or eastern European. 'You will only hurt yourself.'

'Help!' she screamed, louder than she had ever cried out before. Her voice reverberated around the room. 'Someone help me! Please!'

The woman made no attempt to silence her. Instead she waited for a break in the shouting. 'You can scream as much as you want, Lauren. This house is soundproofed. No one will hear you, and no one is coming for you. Now, are you going to listen to me, or shall I leave you here until you've calmed down?'

Finally accepting the futility of her position, Lauren eased off, staring at the woman who had called herself Agent Forsyth.

The woman nodded, apparently satisfied that this represented some kind of cooperation. 'Good. Maybe now we can talk a little.'

Lauren squeezed her eyes shut and shook her head, trying to ignore a lingering headache, which was almost certainly a side effect of whatever she'd been injected with.

Noticing her difficulty, the woman offered an explanation. 'The headache and disorientation will pass.' She held up her right hand with three fingers extended, slowly moving it back and forth. 'Follow my hand. How many fingers am I holding up?'

'Go screw yourself,' Lauren yelled defiantly. 'You can use as many fingers as you want for that.'

Her captor gave her a look of mild disapproval, as if she were some unruly child refusing to come in for dinner.

Pulling up another chair, the woman eased herself down, seemingly with some discomfort. Lauren was reminded of the bloodstain on her jacket, and wondered how badly she was hurt.

Hopefully very badly, she thought.

'Before we go any further, there are some rules I want you to understand,' she said, still staring at Lauren. 'Rule one, you will not try to resist or escape. Failure to comply will be met with severe punishment. Rule two, you will answer any questions fully and truthfully. I will know if you lie to me,' she promised. 'Rule three, you will be released from your restraints to eat, wash and use the bathroom, but if you abuse this freedom it will be withdrawn permanently. And rule four, you will speak only when spoken to. Comply with these rules, and you'll be treated fairly and returned to your family unharmed. Understand?'

'Why should I trust you?'

'You shouldn't,' was the honest answer. 'But given that you are tied to a chair and I can think of a dozen ways to cause you unbearable pain with my bare hands, you should at least listen to me, Lauren.'

'Who are you?' Lauren asked, unable to keep a tremor from her voice. 'What do you want with me?'

There was something eerily familiar about this woman, who had torn her away from safety and security. It was a familiarity that went deeper than their encounter earlier in the day.

'Who I am is not important,' she said. 'But *you* are. You're going to help save lives.'

Lauren frowned. 'I… I don't understand.'

'I don't expect you to. But your father will.'

That sentence felt like a punch in the gut. 'What does my father have to do with this?'

Instead of answering her question, the woman stood up and walked towards the door.

'I will have food and water brought in soon,' she said. 'Until then, keep the rules in mind.'

'Wait,' Lauren implored her. 'You haven't—'

She was cut off as the door closed firmly.

Alex was waiting for Anya in the hallway, and for once it was his turn to offer withering disapproval. 'Very inspiring,' he remarked sarcastically. 'She must be scared out of her mind.'

'That's the idea, Alex,' Anya said tersely, brushing past him and striding through to the living room. Alex followed her.

Overlooking the placid waters of Lake Constance, and the fields and forests that slowly gave way to the towering snow-covered peaks at the northern end of the Alps, the view from the room's floor-to-ceiling windows was stunning. Even Alex, in a less than jubilant mood after the arduous six-hour journey here, was impressed.

'I have to admit, you know how to pick your safe houses,' he allowed, staring out across the vista. 'Took long enough to get here, though. Couldn't we have found somewhere closer to Paris?'

Anya was less interested in admiring the view, having seen it many times over the past couple of years. Instead she entered the open-plan kitchen unit that overlooked the living room, filled the kettle and set it over the gas cooker to start it heating.

'This isn't a safe house,' she said.

Although she only stayed here sporadically and had never troubled herself to personalize it to any great extent, this place had become, for lack of a better word, Anya's home. Bought with cash under a false identity, it was both secluded and about as secure as a civilian home could be. Two factors which appealed greatly to her.

'If you're making tea, I'll have a cup,' Alex chipped in hopefully as the kettle reached boiling point, steam billowing from the spout.

'Tea will have to wait,' Anya replied, removing her jacket and tossing it onto the kitchen counter. There were more pressing matters to attend to first.

Anya's close-fitting shirt was still stained with blood, her wound having reopened during the fight in Paris. The bleeding had slowed during the car journey, but it was clear the stitches would need replacing.

Reaching into one of the kitchen cupboards, she removed a first aid kit, unzipped it and selected a suture needle and thread. Threading the needle, she laid it in a shallow bowl and poured some boiling water in to sterilize it.

This done, she unbuttoned her shirt and dumped it in the sink, to be washed or disposed of later. Having spent much of her adult life in the field, where physical privacy was often impossible, Anya had no compunction about removing her clothes in front of Alex.

She was however less enthusiastic about the next part. Reaching down, she peeled away the dressing, dried blood tearing away from the skin.

'Jesus Christ,' Alex yelped, in shock at the ugly dark bruising that coloured one side of her ribcage, not to mention the wound in the midst of it. This was the first time he'd seen the extent of her injury. He'd had no idea how bad it was.

'Does it hurt?' he asked stupidly.

'I hope that's a joke,' Anya replied as she examined the injury, trying to determine how many stitches had torn. It was difficult to make out from her point of view, which was probably why she'd done such a poor job with the stitches in the first place. 'Pass me the saline solution.'

Approaching the first aid kit, Alex felt like a cave man in a supermarket, overwhelmed by things he didn't recognize. 'What am I looking for?'

'A plastic bottle,' she explained. 'Marked sodium chloride.'

Rifling through, Alex found the bottle and quickly handed it over. After pouring the solution over a cloth, Anya was able to clean most of the dried blood away, making the injury easier to examine.

'Alex, answer me a question,' she said, still looking down. 'Do your hands shake?'

He frowned. 'What?'

'Your hands. Are they steady?'

He was beginning to see where she was going with this. 'No way,' he protested, throwing up his hands. 'I'm not a trauma surgeon.'

'I need someone who can get a proper look at the wound, and you are the only one here. All I need you to do is put in a couple of stitches. Even you can't get that wrong.'

'Is that supposed to inspire me?'

Without offering a reply, she picked up the first aid kit and the bowl of steaming water, crossed into the living room and eased herself onto the couch, turning over so that the wound was facing upwards.

'I'll talk you through it,' she promised. 'Don't be afraid.'

Alex rolled his eyes and clenched his teeth. In typical Anya fashion, she wasn't going to take no for an answer.

'Fuck's sake,' he mumbled, striding over and kneeling down beside her.

'First clean your hands with the saline solution,' she instructed. Blood loss and flesh wounds she could deal with, but if the injury became infected she'd be in serious trouble.

Using the same bottle Anya had employed to clean the wound initially, Alex soaked his hands and washed them thoroughly.

Next she handed him a pair of surgical scissors and plastic tweezers from the kit.

'Some of the sutures have broken or ripped through the skin. You need to find them and pull them out. Use the scissors to cut them.'

Alex accepted the tools as if they could explode at any moment. 'This is going to hurt.'

'Yes,' she confirmed.

'Are you going to hit me?'

Her vivid blue eyes turned on him. 'Only if you get it wrong.'

'Very reassuring,' he said, bending over to begin his unpleasant task.

Sure enough, there had been four sutures holding the ragged wound closed. One was mostly intact, even if the skin around it had been partially ripped. The other three, however, had torn loose, allowing the injury to reopen. He decided not to look too closely, worried he'd see the white gleam of a rib bone beneath.

'Three of them are gone,' he said.

'Then you have three to replace.'

'Your maths is impeccable.'

Despite the gory task, he was also conscious of the fact that Anya was lying virtually naked right in front of him. Whatever experiences she had been through, they had clearly made a deep impression, both mentally and physically.

Her core was rock solid, her stomach flat and firm, her arms and shoulders endowed with the lean and sinewy musculature of real physical strength. Up close like this, he was also able to make out the old scars that crisscrossed her back, plus various other tracks of silvery-white scar tissue that stood as testimony to a long and violent career.

And yet, for all her obvious toughness and deadly capability, Anya remained unquestionably female. The swell of her hips was accentuated by the position she was obliged to lie in, and he couldn't help but glance at the full, rounded curve of her breasts, before forcing himself to look away.

'Stay in shape, don't you?' he said, coughing uncomfortably to fill the awkward silence. It was disconcerting in the extreme to see someone he generally thought of as a brooding menace, an unwelcome intruder or a ruthless killer in such an unexpectedly intimate and vulnerable light.

Anya seemed to have no sense of embarrassment when it came to being unclothed, but the look in her eyes made it clear she would happily break his arms if he entertained any thoughts of touching her inappropriately.

'Relax, you're not exactly my type. I prefer my women less... terrifying,' he assured her, knowing she wouldn't see such an observation as an insult. 'It's just... I find it helps to talk at times like this.'

'I don't,' she replied. 'Focus on your task.'

'Aye, aye, sir.' Clamping the suture in place with the tweezers, he brought the scissors in and carefully snipped them. Then, hesitating briefly, he pulled on the free end. Anya inhaled sharply as the suture thread slipped free, causing a trickle of blood to well up, but gave little outward sign of the pain she was in. It was the same with the other two.

'First part's over,' Alex said, as he dabbed at the wound with a sterile wipe.

'Good. Now get the suture needle,' she said.

Dropping the bloody suture into the bowl of steaming water, he reached in with the tweezers and pulled out the curved needle Anya had placed there.

'You only need to make one stitch at a time. Insert the needle about half a centimetre either side of the wound. Don't push it too deep. And make sure there is enough thread to tie it off.'

'Let me ask you something,' he said as he blew on the hot piece of metal to cool it a little. 'At moments like this, do you ever stop for a second and think, "I've made some really bad career decisions"?'

She snorted, which he took as a good sign. At least she hadn't told him to shut up. 'What would you have me do instead?'

He shrugged. 'I don't know. Tollbooth operator, personal trainer... No, wait. I tell you what – a librarian. Not one of the nice ones that wear oversized cardigans and remind me of my nan. I mean the really overbearing hard-arses that fine you if you return your book even a day late. I could see you settling into that role pretty well. There would be zero late returns on your watch.'

That was when Anya did something quite unexpected. She laughed. Not just a reluctant chuckle, but a proper, genuine laugh of amusement. It was so strange to see such an uninhibited expression of mirth that Alex was actually taken aback.

Then again, perhaps on some level it made sense to him. With everything that she was going through right now, and everything she seemed to have endured recently, perhaps even Anya needed to release some tension.

'It is good to know how you see me,' she said, once her laughter had subsided.

'Just helping people find themselves. Hold on to that good humour for the next few minutes,' he said, pushing the curved needle into her flesh.

She stiffened as he worked, having to apply more force than he'd expected. The curve of the metal made it easier to bring the needle out the other side of the wound, but his efforts had caused more blood to well up. Aware that he was causing her great discomfort, he hurriedly pushed it through all the way, drawing the suture thread with it.

With the hard part done, it was an easy enough process to tighten the thread, draw the two sides of the wound together, then secure it with a basic knot. The next two stitches were quicker as he became more adept at the process. He didn't imagine he'd get top marks from any medical examiner, but it looked like it would hold together.

'All done,' he said, feeling rather pleased with himself as he snipped away the excess thread. 'Just don't ask me to do anything like this again.'

'I hope I don't need to,' Anya replied as she sat up to inspect his handi-work. Apparently approving of what she found, she gave him a faint nod. 'Not bad.'

'That's glowing praise as far as you're concerned,' Alex remarked as she applied an adhesive dressing to the wound, then wrapped it with a bandage to help hold it in place. Watching as she rose from the couch, Alex turned more serious. 'Listen, bullshit aside for a minute. Are you sure you should be doing all this in your condition?'

'No,' she admitted. 'But there is no choice. I don't have time to rest and heal.'

Leaving the room and striding through to what he assumed was one of the bedrooms, she returned a few moments later wearing a black tank top. After packing up the first aid kit and returning it to its place in the kitchen, she opened another cupboard and, to his surprise, brought out a bottle of some kind of spirit he didn't recognize.

'What's that for? Disinfecting the wound?' he asked.

'Drinking,' Anya replied, laying a couple of shot glasses down on the breakfast bar that divided the kitchen from the living room.

As Alex approached warily, still convinced this was some kind of ploy, she cracked the seal on the bottle and poured a full measure into each. He caught the scent of alcohol, and reached for the bottle once she'd laid it down.

'Stumbras,' he read out, consulting the label.

'Vodka. From my...' She hesitated before finishing that sentence, hurriedly correcting herself. 'From where I was born.'

'Fair play, I'll bite,' Alex said, thinking it best not to push her. 'What's the occasion?'

For once Anya didn't seem guarded or closed off. 'You did a lot for me today that I had no business asking you to do, and you did it well,' she said, staring right at him. 'There are not many people in this world who have earned my gratitude, but if it means anything, you are one of them, Alex.'

Alex said nothing for a moment or two, sensing the significance of this moment but unsure how to respond. He was strangely touched, because he knew Anya wasn't someone to hand out empty praise and meaningless platitudes. If she said something, she meant it. And she meant this.

'Let's do this before I embarrass myself,' he said, holding up the glass.

'*Sveikata*,' the woman said, knocking it back in one gulp.

'Your health,' Alex replied, doing likewise. The potent spirit lit a path down into his stomach, and pretty quickly he began to feel the languid warmth spread through his body, helping to calm his racing mind.

'Not bloody bad,' he said. 'I could get used to this.'

Anya flashed a smile. 'Well, don't get too used to it,' she advised, screwing the lid on the bottle. 'I need you to keep watch for a while.'

'Where are you going?'

'To make a call.' Reaching into her jacket, she fished out the components of Lauren's cell phone, held together in a plastic ziplock bag. She'd removed the SIM card and battery during their journey to prevent tracking, but now reassembled the device and powered it up.

'Wouldn't do that. They can track it.'

Anya shook her head as she concentrated on the screen. 'The walls here are lead-lined,' she explained, scrolling through the phone's list of contacts.

'Wow. Is there anything you haven't planned for?'

'Too many things, unfortunately.'

Finding the contact listed simply as Dad, Anya made a mental note of the number before shutting the phone down and dismantling it again.

'I will make the call some distance from here, as a precaution,' she explained, fishing the car keys from her jacket pocket. 'In the meantime, give Lauren food and water, and make sure she is comfortable, but don't converse with her. The more she learns about us, the more dangerous she could be. Understand?'

'Zero talking. Got it.'

Nodding, she left the room and returned a short time later with a weapon in her hands. It was a Smith & Wesson 5900 series 9mm automatic, its stainless steel frame glinting in the early evening sunlight. Laying it down with a heavy thump, she glanced up at him, her expression deadly serious.

'Can I trust you with this?'

Now wasn't the time for flippant remarks. 'Yeah. You can.'

She inserted a magazine into the weapon's port and pulled back the slide to chamber the first round. 'The safety is engaged and a round is in the chamber. If you need to fire, flick this lever on the side here,' she explained, showing him how. 'Grip it with both hands and keep your arms fully extended when you fire. It will kick back hard, so be ready. And *don't ever* point it at someone unless you're prepared to kill them,' she warned him. 'Including me.'

Alex nodded, knowing that nothing less than complete agreement would work. Satisfied she'd made her point, Anya let go of the weapon, allowing him to take it.

'What about reloading?' he asked, testing the weight and feel of it.

She gave him a knowing look. 'If you need more than 15 rounds to get out of trouble, you are as good as dead anyway.'

As always, Anya was keeping it real. 'That's comforting.'

'Lock the door and don't open it for anyone who isn't me. If I don't return in an hour, I won't be coming back. Leave here and get as far away as you can,' she advised. 'There is money in a holdall in the hallway cupboard.'

'Anya,' he said just as she opened the front door. 'Just… come back, yeah?'

The woman remained silent, but nodded faintly before closing the door, leaving him alone with their hostage.

Chapter 28

Vizur Qalat let out a frustrated breath as he read an internal report. A pair of ISI operatives were attempting to reopen their investigation into the confrontation in Islamabad several nights ago, despite Qalat's best efforts to shut it down.

Explosions and gunfire on the streets of the nation's capital weren't the sort of thing that could be swept under the rug, even for a man of Qalat's influence. It had taken more than a few favours amongst Pakistan's police and intelligence agencies to minimize exposure of the incident and write it off as classified. These two jumped-up policemen could unravel everything he'd worked towards.

He might well have to employ more direct methods to silence them.

He was about to pack up for the night when his desk phone buzzed. It was the hotline from Executive Director Khalid's office.

Qalat wavered as he reached for the phone. If Khalid had gotten wind of the incident, and more importantly his efforts to cover it up, it could land him in an untenable position. Low-level intelligence officers he could handle, but the director of the ISI was another matter.

'Yes, sir,' he said, managing to keep his tone clipped and efficient.

'Qalat, I'd like to see you in my office,' the fleshy voice of the director announced. 'Something we need to discuss.'

There was no other answer to give to such a summons. 'On my way.'

A minute or so later, Qalat knocked politely on Khalid's door, receiving an immediate reply. 'Come!'

The office was, to Khalid's credit, remarkably austere, and devoid of the usual trappings of power that executive directors indulged in, perhaps reflecting his military background. The carpets were clean but not expensive, the desk and other furniture simple and practical, the pictures that adorned the walls mostly just photographs from Khalid's days in the Pakistani army, when he'd been noticeably younger and thinner.

'Vizur, thank you for coming,' Khalid said, slowly rising from his chair.

Some men in positions of power indulged in alcohol to curb their restless minds, others turned to women or drugs, but Khalid's weakness seemed to be food. His face was wide and deeply lined, his shoulders slumped, his legs thick with excess fat.

Only his short, swept-back hairstyle was the same as in the photos of his fitter and more youthful self, even if the hair was thinner and greying now.

'Of course, sir,' Qalat said, bracing himself for the worst. 'How can I serve?'

Khalid gestured to the centre of his office, where a pair of couches faced each other across a low coffee table. 'Please, take a seat.'

Qalat sensed the invitation was for Khalid's comfort rather than his own.

Qalat took the furthest couch, while Khalid heaved himself into the nearest, the springs and wooden frame creaking.

He stared across the coffee table at Qalat, his expression difficult to read. Whatever his faults and vices, Khalid was a man adept at playing his cards close to his chest. Qalat for his part managed to paint on a look of patient attentiveness – just a loyal subordinate waiting for his commanding officer to speak.

'We've received a message from the Americans,' Khalid said at last. 'An invitation.'

Qalat's fears vanished, replaced by a growing excitement for the opportunity that had just been created. Clever, Marcus, he thought. Very clever.

He cocked his head slightly, pretending to be intrigued. 'Invitation?'

'Two days from now,' the director went on. 'At the US embassy building. They claim to have found information about the murder of one of our intelligence officers a week ago. They say it's linked to the killing of two intelligence operatives, and a gun battle in this city three days ago. They want to meet with me personally and discuss intelligence-sharing across our two agencies.'

'I see,' Qalat said. 'And what can I do, sir?'

Khalid spread his hands. 'You can give your opinion, Vizur. You have worked with the Americans many times, and I'd venture you understand their mindset as well as anyone in this agency. So I'd like to hear whether you think this offer is genuine, whether you believe the Americans can be trusted, and if I should agree to meet with them.'

Qalat knew this was a crucial moment, and he had to answer carefully. To be too welcoming would invite suspicion and distrust from the conservative director, whereas being too lukewarm might confirm Khalid's inherent prejudices.

'If you're asking whether the Americans can be trusted, I would say no,' he replied cautiously. 'To believe they have Pakistan's best interests at heart would be foolish and naive, and I can't imagine you feel that way anyway.'

Khalid nodded at this, no doubt approving of Qalat's assessment so far.

'But whether or not their intentions are entirely good, they are not stupid,' Qalat said. 'They know all too well the cost of losing a war in Afghanistan, and that we're their only ally in this region. That means they need us, and they have to win our cooperation by giving us something real. So if you're asking whether I think this offer is genuine...' He paused, making it seem like he was still weighing up the matter in his mind. 'I think it is. At the very least, I think it's worth hearing them out. If you don't like what they have to say, then well… there's no need to take it any further.'

Khalid didn't say anything for some time. He was digesting everything Qalat had said, perhaps trying to find a flaw in his reasoning. Qalat held his tongue, knowing it was unwise to disturb the director in the midst of making a decision.

'All right, Vizur. Thank you,' he finally said, nodding towards the door. 'You've made your opinions clear on this.'

'If there's anything else you need, sir,' Qalat said, rising from the couch. 'You will be the first to know.'

Chapter 29

'What the hell happened?' Cain demanded, striding into the briefing room with no regard for protocol or the high-ranking personnel already assembled there. 'Somebody give me a sitrep right now.'

All he had so far were sketchy reports coming out of Afghanistan that Task Force Black had been intercepted by Soviet forces over the border, and that they had sustained casualties.

He wanted, needed, answers right now.

'Calm down, Marcus,' Simmons said, cool and aloof as always. A numbers man tallying up his accounts. 'Ranting and raving isn't going to help.'

Cain rounded on him. 'Sir, that's my team out there—'

'Our team,' Carpenter corrected him, his expression one of entirely false concern. 'Which is why we called you in.'

He glanced at Simmons, as if awaiting permission to elaborate. When it was given with a curt nod, he took a deep breath before beginning his briefing.

'What we know so far is that approximately 24 hours ago, Task Force Black was intercepted by Russian special forces units in the mountains north of Jalalabad, just as they were preparing to launch their operation. In an exchange lasting about 30 minutes, the task force was able to execute a fighting withdrawal to the east, before making a run for the border.'

'And we're only hearing about this now?' Cain asked incredulously.

Carpenter fixed him with a patronising look. 'They were hardly in a position to make a detailed report, with Soviet gunships trying to hunt them down. Anyway they were forced to destroy their comms gear in case it was compromised. It wasn't until the unit reached their forward operating base that they could call it in.'

Cain had no interest in the logistics of their escape. 'What about casualties?'

Simmons cleared his throat.

'They've reported two KIAs – Kurylenko and Melnik,' Carpenter said, his voice devoid of emotion. It wasn't the first time he'd read out casualty figures, and Cain doubted it would be the last.

Cain winced. Andriy Kurylenko and Panas Melnik, both Ukrainians by birth, both excellent soldiers. From what he'd learned of the unit, the two men had become fast friends, their shared homeland helping to form a bond that was cemented by battle. He even remembered Panas boasting once that his name meant 'immortal'.

It seemed, today, his mortality had caught up with him.

'They also report one missing in action,' Carpenter went on, and Cain's head snapped around to stare at him, his stomach twisting. 'It's Anya.'

Cain's world seemed to stop. The briefing room, the powerful men within it, the view of the new headquarters building under construction all faded as he struggled to process what he'd just heard.

It didn't make sense. Anya couldn't be gone. She was unstoppable, she had survived countless battles in one of the deadliest war zones on earth. She could take anything that was thrown at her.

She had promised to come back.

'What happened to her?' Cain heard himself ask.

Carpenter swallowed and glanced at the papers spread out before him. 'We're still collating our reports from—'

'What happened?' Cain repeated, slower, putting emphasis on both words.

The colonel looked him in the eye. 'When the rest of the team was falling back, she refused to break cover. They couldn't get to her, and she wouldn't come to them. Our best guess is that she panicked when the team came under air attack, froze up. There was nothing they could do.'

'No,' Cain said, shaking his head. 'No way. That's not Anya.'

'Marcus, I've seen it happen to even the best soldiers.' Carpenter was playing the part of the fatherly soldier now, the combat veteran who had seen it all and understood battle in a way that a desk jockey like Cain never would. 'There's no way to predict how people will—'

'I said no!' Cain shouted, rising to his feet and slamming his fist down on the table.

In the silence that followed, Cain could feel every eye in the room on him. He didn't care that they were doubting him, judging him. He didn't care that he'd just lost his cool publicly for the first time in his career.

His eyes were locked with Carpenter's, simmering with barely restrained fury. The man who had blackmailed him into sending Anya back out there. The man he wanted to reach across the table and throttle with his bare hands.

'All right, gentlemen. Obviously this is a difficult situation, but let's stay professional,' Simmons said, his tone making it clear that further outbursts would see Cain removed from the room – by force, if need be. 'We all knew the risks involved, and so did they. Frankly, we ought to be thankful the bulk of the team made it out alive. It could have been a lot worse. Marcus, I think you should take some time to process this.'

'I'm fine, sir,' Cain lied, staring straight ahead.

'You don't look fine.'

'It was a shock, that's all.' He raised his chin and looked at Simmons. 'Right now I'd rather discuss extraction options.'

He saw the look exchanged between Simmons and Carpenter.

'Excuse me?'

'If the Soviets have her, it's a safe bet they took her to the nearest military base for interrogation. There must be a way to get her back if we act quickly,' Cain said, latching onto the wild hope that somehow they could rescue Anya. 'Task Force Black have been staging extractions like this for years—'

'Marcus, maybe we didn't explain the situation clearly,' Simmons interrupted. 'There won't be an extraction.'

Cain stared at the man, unable to summon a response.

'The whole point of this task force was that it's a deniable operation,' Carpenter reminded him. 'In the event they're captured or killed, we disavow all knowledge of their existence. That's the plan – that was always the plan. We have full plausible deniability.'

Cain was aghast. On some level he knew Simmons wasn't telling him anything he didn't already know, but to hear it actually spoken about the woman he cared for, the woman he loved, was like a knife driven into his chest.

'Anya fought and killed for us.'

'And the United States government appreciates her sacrifice, even if its people will never learn of it,' Simmons said, his tone dry and official. It was clear that in his mind, Anya was already dead. A minor subtraction in the great equation that determined the balance of power. 'There's nothing more we can do for her.'

Cain zoned out as the briefing resumed. Already the talk had turned to bringing the remainder of the unit home, logistical arrangements that would be needed, mitigating actions for potential political fallout.

Cain stared into space as his future with Anya vanished.

–

CIA headquarters, Langley – 31 March 2010

'Give me a fucking update right now,' Cain demanded, pacing across his office like a caged animal. He was holding his cell phone so tight that he could practically hear the plastic creaking. 'I want to know what you've got.'

'Sir, we recovered your daughter's GPS tracking devices and her clothes at a rest stop ten miles south-west of the city,' reported Patrick Kavanagh, the officer now coordinating the hunt for Cain's daughter. 'Clearly her attackers knew what to look for.'

With Brooks hospitalized and in no condition to head up a search operation, it had fallen to the senior case officer in the region to take command.

'No *shit* they knew what to look for,' Cain shot back. 'We gave her the full Agency relocation package, removed everything that should have led to her, and still they were able to find her. How the fuck did this happen?'

'We're working on that as we speak, sir.' Kavanagh sounded nervous, as well he should. If Cain's daughter turned up dead because he didn't do his job, Cain would personally ensure it was the last mistake the man ever made.

'Great. While you're "working on it", my daughter's out there, someone's hostage.' Cain stopped pacing, forcing himself to calm down and think rationally. Now was not the time to let emotion cloud his judgement. 'Tell me what active protocols you've got in play.'

'We tried pulling surveillance footage of the attack, but everything from the university security system seems to be gone.'

'Gone?'

'Erased, sir. Someone recalibrated the video buffers so they overwrote themselves every—'

'All right, I don't need the details,' Cain interrupted. Clearly this attack had been orchestrated by people with a high level of technical, as well as physical, skill. 'What else?'

'External units seem unaffected, so we're reviewing all traffic cameras in the area,' Kavanagh explained, hoping to demonstrate that he was doing everything in his power to find her. 'According to eye witnesses, your daughter was forced into a car outside the library. Once we get a hit on the licence plate, we can track them.'

'Concentrate your search east of the city,' Cain instructed. 'Especially the border with Belgium, Germany and Austria.'

'East? But sir, we found the—'

'They're backtracking, trying to throw us off the scent,' he decided. 'What else do you have?'

'We've also got the NSA monitoring all the usual websites, message boards and social media, looking for any unusual chatter.'

Cain shook his head. 'There won't be any.'

'Sir?'

'This isn't some terrorist group or political extremists we're dealing with.' Cain clenched his jaw. 'It's *her*.'

Somehow Anya had gotten to her. He didn't understand how, but she'd done it all the same. Every precaution he'd taken, every safeguard he'd put in place, every layer of protection had all come to naught. Short on time and options, Anya had struck at the one person he'd worked so hard to protect for the past 20 years.

'Sir, I don't—'

Cain's phone bleeped then, signalling that another caller was trying to get through. An unrecognized number.

'Get to work, Kavanagh. I'll call you back soon,' he said, ending the call.

Cain rolled his neck and exhaled, trying to calm his emotions and focus his mind. Then he hit receive call.

'Cain.'

'You know who this is,' a female voice announced.

Cain's heart skipped a beat at the sound of Anya's voice. After so many years of hunting her, pitting himself against her, wondering where she was and what she was planning next, he was at last speaking directly to her.

'I had a feeling you'd call,' he acknowledged. 'Took longer than I'd expected.'

He made no attempt to initiate a call trace, because he knew it would be a waste of time. Anya was too well prepared for that. She was almost certainly using an encrypted satellite phone that would take more time to locate than he had.

And even if they could track her down, what then? The fact remained that Anya had his daughter, and was perhaps the most ruthless operative he'd ever come across. She could, and perhaps would, kill her before giving her up.

'Then you know what I want.'

'I can guess.' There was no anger in his voice – just cold, hard resolve. 'I have to hand it to you, Anya – you're good. Even I didn't think you'd stoop to this level.'

'You left me no choice. You take something of mine, I take something of yours.'

'You and your people came to Pakistan to *kill* me,' he reminded her. 'What was I supposed to do? Let you do it?'

His question was met with a couple of seconds of terse silence. He knew his words had made an impact.

'Be in Frankfurt, two days from now,' she instructed. 'I'll call you at 10 a.m. on the morning of the exchange to give you more instructions. Have Drake there ready to speak on the phone, so I can confirm he is alive and unharmed.'

Anya wanted him there in person for the exchange, and it wasn't hard to surmise what she had in mind. She wanted him exposed and vulnerable, so she could finish what Drake had started in Pakistan.

'You can't win this,' he warned her.

'Just be there, Marcus.'

'Even if you get Drake back, you'll still lose.'

He was expecting her to hang up abruptly without rising to the bait, but instead she offered a final parting remark. 'You still don't understand, do you?' Anya asked, her voice laced with sadness. 'We've both lost already.'

Chapter 30

'There's got to be a hundred reasons I don't blow you away right now,' Alex growled as he stared down the sights of his automatic. 'Right now I can't think of a single one.'

Holding the pose, he let out a sigh and laid the weapon down on the kitchen counter with an audible *thunk*, before regarding his reflection in the glass oven door. The face certainly didn't look like it belonged to a ruthless kidnapper, or the sort of person who stood against the most powerful intelligence agency in the world. It was the face of a man out of his depth.

A man charged with guarding a young woman who had no reason for being in her predicament, except the rotten luck of being born to the wrong father. A young woman he was going to have to speak to very soon.

'Hi, my name's Alex,' he said, adopting a friendly, conversational tone as he imagined the encounter playing out. 'I'm here to make your hostage experience as comfortable as possible, until we can figure out a way to give you back to your dad without getting murdered.'

What the hell are you doing, Alex? he asked himself for what felt like the tenth time in the past 24 hours. He was neither a soldier nor a mercenary, not a spy or an assassin, and definitely not whatever the hell Anya was. And yet here he was.

Leaving the gun where it was, he pushed himself away from the counter. The magnificent view outside gave him little comfort now, his thoughts dwelling on the dangerous and unpredictable future that lay ahead.

Anya had instructed him to give Lauren something to eat and drink, and while his cooking skills were hardly Michelin-star quality, he could prepare a simple meal without getting anyone killed.

A quick search of the fridge yielded little to work with. Clearly Anya hadn't visited for a while. Still, there was plenty of canned produce in the cupboards. Selecting a tin of tomato soup, he emptied it into a pan and set it on the hob. Even he couldn't fuck up soup.

As he waited for the soup to warm through, he glanced around the room once more, surveying it with a slightly more critical air now that he was alone.

His first observation was that there was no TV, and he was willing to bet it was the same story in the rest of the house. Neither was there a landline.

Anya seemed to regard modern technology as a necessary evil, to be endured when it was useful, and discarded when it wasn't.

Perhaps she felt the same way about him, he reflected.

Her lack of interest in modern entertainment media seemed in contrast to her appetite for literature. A wooden bookcase ran almost the full length of a wall, its shelves laden with thick volumes, many old and bound by leather covers.

Alex was intrigued. He doubted Anya was a fan of trashy romance novels or airport thrillers, and a closer inspection confirmed that her reading tastes were anything but superficial. There was a heavy emphasis on history and philosophy, with everything from ancient Egypt to the Napoleonic Wars, Socrates to Nietzsche represented. Hardly subjects that fired his imagination, but he wasn't surprised to find them on Anya's bookshelf.

He spotted some more familiar titles – *Moby Dick*, *The Count of Monte Cristo* and *A Tale of Two Cities* – mixed in amongst the stodgy, factual stuff. He presumed Anya had gotten more out of them than he had in secondary school English. All were cracked and worn at the spine, suggesting repeated use.

Leaving the bookcase for now, he glanced down the corridor, wondering what else he might find if he were inclined to go snooping. This was the first real glimpse he'd had into Anya's private life, and the chance to learn about her was too tempting to pass up, especially since she wasn't around to stop him.

Venturing from the living room, he advanced with the wariness of a man expecting some hidden enemy to leap out at any moment. Considering how most of his time with Anya had been spent, that fear wasn't entirely unjustified.

The first door led to the spare room where Lauren was being held. He'd avoided it thus far, reluctant to confront the woman he'd helped kidnap, though he'd have to do so soon. Part of him knew he was using this clandestine exploration as an excuse to put it off a little longer.

The second door opened into a bathroom that was as sleekly modern as the rest of the decor, while the third was the master bedroom. Alex opted to leave that undisturbed for now, partly because there was a certain level of snooping even he wasn't prepared to indulge in, and partly because he wouldn't be surprised if she'd rigged it with some kind of booby trap or alarm. Anya's trust in him might have been a little more than most, but not much more.

The last door at the end of the corridor was more interesting. Easing it open, he found a set of steps leading to the basement. He hesitated at this point, a little uneasy at what he'd find down there.

If horror films had taught him anything, it was that basements invariably provided a window into the darker aspects of a person's character. That being the case, he could only imagine how dark a person like Anya's must be. Still, curiosity won out over caution in the end, and he gently pushed open the door and descended the stairs.

His fears were soon allayed, however. The large, open and brightly lit room below seemed to serve as nothing more sinister than a workshop and exercise room, which was hardly surprising given the kind of physical condition Anya kept herself in. There was a heavy punchbag hanging from the ceiling, and various weights and pieces of exercise equipment set up around the room. All quite basic and low-tech – nothing that required power to operate.

The far corner had been given over to a workbench equipped with a mechanical vice, spanners, screwdrivers, wrenches, tins of oil and grease, and other more advanced instruments he didn't recognize. He imagined this work station was used for stripping and cleaning weapons rather than the kind of household maintenance tasks it had been designed for.

Alex was disappointed. He'd hoped for a dramatically lit room filled with rows of guns and explosives, high-tech security systems and computer screens monitoring every square inch of the house. That was the kind of thing spies were supposed to have in their basements.

He was about to take his leave when he happened to notice something stowed beneath the workbench. A metal tin about the size of a lunch box, battered and dented, its paintwork faded to the point its original colour was almost unrecognizable.

He knelt down and gently lifted it out, swinging the rusty lid open. To his surprise, the box contained what looked like military dog tags – easily a dozen or more, some old, others comparatively clean and new. One even had a ragged hole punched right through the thin metal, which had torn away the rubber edging at the same time. They all had one thing in common: there were no names printed on them.

Alex laid the box down, feeling both unnerved and strangely guilty for handling them. It was clear the owners of these tags were long since dead, but who had they been, and why was Anya now in possession of them?

It was then that he noticed something else hidden amongst the shining steel tags and chains. A photograph – one of the old fashioned Polaroids. Like the tin, it had clearly taken a beating over the years, its edges frayed and its image faded. Alex carefully lifted the picture to get a better look, and was startled by what he saw.

The image depicted a much younger Anya, probably in her early twenties at most, dressed in civilian clothes. She was sitting on a white sandy beach, with palm trees and buildings and blue sky in the background. He couldn't be sure, but it reminded him of the West Coast of the United States.

But it was her face that caught his attention most of all. She was smiling. Not the occasional flicker she'd shown him, but a proper smile of uninhibited joy and delight that seemed to light up her whole face. It was the smile and the vitality of youth, of optimism, of excitement about a life of adventure and glory waiting to be lived. And there was a sparkle in her eyes, a fire of attraction that even he could see.

What had inspired such a look?

The answer, he suspected, was visible near the edge of the shot. A man was sitting near Anya, apparently caught in the midst of conversation. Young, clean-cut and handsome, he seemed to be a good match for his beautiful companion. But Alex sensed that the connection between them went far deeper than mere physical attractiveness. There was an ease about their body language, a companionship, a closeness. *Whatever had become of the young couple in that picture?* he wondered.

Alex stopped then, alerted by a smell in the air. The scent of burning.

'Oh, shit!' he gasped, remembering the soup he'd left heating.

Quickly replacing the box under the workbench, he bounded back up the stairs and into the kitchen, where he found the pan of soup bubbling over, the spillage burning against the sides. Killing the gas, he grabbed a dish cloth and used it to lift the pan off the cooker, pouring its contents into a bowl and slopping some over the edge.

'Jesus. Nice one, Gordon Ramsay,' he said sarcastically, surveying the messy results of his work and shaking his head in dismay.

Apparently it *was* possible to fuck up soup.

Chapter 31

In the bedroom, still tied securely to the steel chair, Lauren had her eyes closed. She'd heard movement outside the room, but had no idea what was going on. All she knew with certainty was that she was both hungry and extremely thirsty.

She opened her eyes suddenly and frowned at the unexpected sound of someone knocking on the door. Who the hell would knock on the door of a hostage?

'Come in,' she said, not knowing how else to respond.

The door swung open to reveal a young man she recognized immediately from the Sorbonne.

'It's you,' she said with hostility. She'd still harboured a faint hope that Alex had been some innocent bystander in her abduction, but it was now abundantly clear he was in league with the woman behind it all.

'Evening,' he began uncertainly. 'Sorry to disturb you, I just…'

He trailed off, apparently not knowing what to say.

'Just came to gloat?' Lauren finished for him. 'You and your friend really did a number on me back in Paris. You must be feeling real good about yourself right now.'

'You'd be surprised, actually,' he said, having the good grace to look regretful. 'Kidnapping people isn't exactly a regular thing for me.'

If he was expecting empathy from her, he was looking in the wrong place. 'Do your eyes still hurt?'

'A little.' There was a certain redness to them still, she noted.

'Good,' she said. 'I actually felt bad about it before, but not now. Shame I didn't have something stronger and more permanent.'

He looked stung. 'Look, this isn't an ideal situation for either of us. There's no need to be a total dick about it.'

Lauren might have laughed. This man was actually chiding his hostage for being impolite.

'You and that… that *woman* attacked me,' Lauren said through gritted teeth. 'You drugged me and kidnapped me, and now you're holding me hostage. How exactly should I be about it?'

Alex let out a frustrated sigh. 'Trust me, I'd rather none of this was even happening. I don't know you and I've got no reason to see you hurt. But I'm stuck with you for now, so let's just make the best of it and act like civilized people, okay?'

'Says the man who's keeping me tied to a chair. What do you want anyway?' Lauren asked.

He edged his way into the room with a tray of food. 'I brought some food and water. If you want it?'

'It's a little tricky to eat when you're tied to a chair,' she observed, glancing down at her bound hands.

'I can help with that,' he replied, setting the tray down and fishing out a pair of wire cutters from his back pocket. 'Left or right?'

'Huh?'

'Are you left or right handed?' he explained patiently.

'Right.'

'Right, as in… you understand my question now? Or right, as in—'

'As in, I'm right-handed,' Lauren snapped. 'Jesus, tell me this is an act and you're not actually this dumb.'

Approaching cautiously with the cutters, he tried to discern her intentions. 'I really hope you don't take a swing at me when I do this.'

'Worried you'll get beat up by a girl?'

'Depends on the girl.' Reaching out, he snipped the plastic cable tie holding her right hand, then backed away out of reach.

Grateful to be able to move at least one limb again, Lauren flexed and tensed her hand, making a fist a couple of times. She could feel pins and needles creeping up her arm, and there was a red mark where the cable tie had been, but otherwise she was unharmed.

'Here,' he said, holding out a glass of water.

Caution held Lauren back. 'How do I know it's not drugged?'

Gulping down a mouthful himself, he held it out again. 'Happy now?'

'I'll be happy when you and your friend are arrested and put in prison where you belong,' she said, snatching the glass and greedily downing its contents, desperate to slake her thirst.

'If your dad catches up with us, it won't be prison we end up in,' he said, his expression darkening as he reached for the tray. 'He'll make sure of that.'

She stopped drinking. 'What would you know about my dad?'

'Enough to know people who mess with him end up dead. Like, in the ground dead.'

'That's ridiculous,' she countered. 'My dad is—'

'Your dad is *not* what you think he is,' Alex interrupted. 'You know the bad guys in spy films who meet in dark rooms and plot to take over the world? Well, that's pretty much your dad. Sorry if this is all new information, but it's time to wake up and smell reality. I mean, you *do* know he works for the CIA, right? What do you think he does for them? Runs bake sales? Delivers gift cards?'

'Shut up! I don't need to be lectured by someone like you,' Lauren shot back, keenly aware that Alex was the second person to have said such things. 'My father's a good man. Better than you'll ever be.'

In truth, her father had never talked much about his work, and eventually she'd learned to stop asking. She knew he worked for the government, that there were naturally many things he couldn't discuss, but he'd always assured her that his job involved nothing more exciting or dangerous than offices and meeting rooms. He dealt in information, research, facts.

He wasn't a killer. He couldn't be.

Alex said nothing, perhaps thinking it best not to antagonize her further. 'Fine, let's just get this over with, shall we?' he said instead. 'I've got tomato soup here, and a bowl of tinned peaches.'

Half of that meal wasn't going to work out well for her. 'I'm allergic to tomatoes.'

Trust him to pick the one thing in the world she couldn't eat.

Alex let out a breath, then calmly laid the bowl of soup aside. 'I've got a bowl of tinned peaches in that case. *Bon appetit.*' Laying the tray across her lap, he handed her a metal soup spoon. 'Now, I'm pretty sure nobody ever escaped captivity with a spoon, but please don't take that as a challenge.'

Lauren kept her head down as if focussed on her meal, while surreptitiously observing him. His shoulders were slumped, his face sallow, his eyes red from more than just the pepper spray earlier. He looked strung out.

'So what should I call you?' Lauren asked, slicing a peach segment in half with her spoon. 'Assuming you have a name? Your friend doesn't seem to.'

He shrugged. 'Just Alex.'

'That your real name, Just Alex?'

'I was telling the truth back at the library. Well, at least about my name.'

'Fair enough. So at least one thing about you isn't total BS,' she remarked. 'Doesn't mean I dislike you any less. But it helps to know who I'm dealing with.'

Lauren was feeling more confident and in control of the situation the more she conversed with Alex. The woman frightened and unnerved her, but she seemed to be gone for now at least, and Alex was different. He was soft, reluctant, unsure of himself.

'And who do you think you're dealing with?' he asked, running his hands through his hair.

Lauren laid her spoon down. 'Someone who doesn't want to be here.'

She knew she'd struck a nerve. There was little choice but to press the opportunity that might just have presented itself.

'Look, I don't pretend to know your history or where you came from, but I can tell this isn't who you are, Alex,' she said earnestly. 'Taking innocent people hostage, being on the run from the police... That doesn't seem like the life you want for yourself.'

He snorted. 'But it's the one I've got.'

'Maybe it doesn't have to be,' she said tentatively.

He frowned. 'What are you saying?'

'I'm saying, maybe we can help each other out,' Lauren pressed. 'If one of the people holding me had a change of heart and helped get me out of here... well, I'm pretty sure I could convince the police and everyone else that they were unfairly caught up in this thing just like I was.'

'What about your dad?' Alex asked. 'If he gets his hands on me, the police are the least of my worries.'

'I'll tell my dad you were forced to go along with this, and as soon as you saw your chance to help me, you did,' she promised. 'He'll believe me.'

'It's not that simple.'

'So let's make it simple,' she persisted, knowing she couldn't afford to let up now. 'I can tell you're not a bad guy. So for God's sake, stop this now before it gets out of hand. All you have to do is cut me free, and we can get out of here. Please, Alex. Help me.'

Alex rose to his feet and strode over to the window. She couldn't see his face, but could see his hands trembling slightly.

Lauren looked at the bowl in her lap. She could tell he was wrestling with the decision, that every word she'd spoken weighed heavily on his mind. All she could do now was pray he made the right choice.

'You might be telling the truth,' he said quietly. 'Maybe you'd do everything you just said. But it wouldn't work. He'd have me killed just for being part of this. He'd have me tortured to death if he thought it would help him get to Anya.'

Anya, Lauren repeated to herself, realizing Alex had just given away the name of his co-conspirator. That name meant something to her, and she was beginning to understand the connection the woman had to her father.

Alex swallowed hard, and she could see he believed every word he was saying. 'And if by some miracle I escaped your dad and disappeared, Anya would know I'd betrayed her. It wouldn't matter how far I ran, sooner or later she'd find me and kill me. So you see, I'm pretty much screwed either way. But if I had to choose a side, I know I'm on the right one. We're not the bad guys, Lauren. We're just trying to stay alive.'

With that, he turned away to leave the room.

'Wait,' Lauren said. 'I... I understand, Alex. I can't blame you for being afraid, even if I wish you'd trusted me. But it's your choice.' She sighed and looked away, her gaze resting on the empty water glass he'd set aside. 'Could I at least have some more water, please? I'm so thirsty.'

He nodded, picked up the glass and quietly left the room, apparently relieved to be out of there. The feeling was mutual.

Lauren immediately went to work. With the spoon in her right hand, she grasped the rounded head with her left and began to quickly bend it backwards and forward. The spoon looked fairly new, but it was made of soft steel like any other. After a few seconds, the steel began to give way at the narrow neck, until it separated altogether, leaving her with a narrow piece of steel ending in a ragged point.

In the kitchen, Alex leaned over the sink, Lauren's words swimming around inside his head.

The logical part of his mind knew that to betray someone like Anya was tantamount to suicide, and to trust his life to someone like Cain was little better. He couldn't make a friend of his enemies, and he didn't dare make an enemy of his friends.

Maybe there was no right decision in this whole mess. Maybe all roads ultimately led to death and failure for them. But he knew one thing – he'd rather stand with Anya than against her. Not because he was afraid of her, but because he believed in her.

He glanced over at the worktop, seeing the automatic handgun still lying where he'd left it, looking absurdly out of place in such domesticated surroundings.

'Shit,' he mumbled, picking up the weapon and stowing it in one of the drawers. He felt better with it out of the way. This done, he started the cold tap running and held the glass under it.

–

Lauren's friendship with her roommate Morgan had been born more out of necessity rather than shared interests. Still, Morgan had proven herself surprisingly practical, and one little trick she'd shared was how to release cable ties – a skill that had proven useful when they'd had to dismantle a six-foot sculpture held together with the damn things.

The tie around Lauren's left wrist was secured with a simple ratchet.

Finding the mechanism, Lauren jammed the broken end of the spoon into the small gap and pushed it upwards, forcing the tongue away from the plastic teeth inside. Then, wasting no time, she pushed her wrist upwards, away from the chair armrest, and the cable tie uncoiled and fell away.

With both arms now free, she went to work on the ties holding her ankles.

–

Switching off the tap, Alex turned back towards the hallway, glass of water in hand. Once Lauren had drunk her fill, he'd leave her alone for a while. He didn't imagine she'd want to spend any more time in his presence than necessary anyway.

And, with luck, Anya would return soon with some news. The sooner they got the exchange over with, the better he would feel...

His thoughts were interrupted as the bedroom door flew open in front of him and the young woman leapt out at him.

Alex saw something sharp and pointed in her hand as she brought it down against him like a dagger. The glass of water shattered on the wooden floor, and he threw up his arm to ward off the blow.

He let out a cry of shock as he backed away, the broken neck of the spoon deeply embedded in the flesh of his forearm.

Lauren paid him no heed, shoving her way past the injured young man and into the hallway, her eyes darting around, taking in as much as possible. She knew she had to make for an exit and get the hell out of here before he recovered. She had to choose the right direction.

Alex yanked the piece of metal from his arm, blood flowing freely from the wound.

'Lauren, wait!' he shouted as she tore towards the front door.

Alex sprinted into the kitchen, opened the drawer and drew out the automatic. He had no desire to use it, but if the young woman escaped, their only leverage against Cain would go with her.

Lauren fumbled to unlock the front door, which was held fast with both a security chain and a conventional lock. Her limbs were stiff and sore, but there was no choice except to move. This was her chance.

She could hear Alex's shouts from the kitchen, and knew he was doing something to stop her, perhaps going for a weapon.

'Lauren!' he shouted. 'Stop!'

Ignoring him, Lauren desperately pulled the chain free of its latch, grasped the door handle and tore it open. She caught a fleeting glimpse of a wide open driveway, an unpaved road, and beyond it, a dense belt of trees sloping uphill.

She went straight for them, without hesitation. She was a strong runner, and knew she could outpace Alex over open ground. What she couldn't outrun, however, were bullets, which meant she needed to get to the relative cover of the trees. She would figure the rest out later.

As she sprinted away, Alex rushed after her, the Smith & Wesson automatic clutched tight. The pain from his arm was unbelievable.

Skidding to a stop, he levelled his weapon at the retreating woman.

'Stop or I'll fire!' he shouted. 'I mean it! Don't make me shoot you.'

It was an empty threat. Alex had barely even used a gun before, and his chances of hitting a moving target from this distance were already questionable. He was bluffing, and the young woman was beginning to see through it. The fear was fading, replaced by a shrewd reassessment of the situation.

'You won't,' she said. 'You can't.'

She turned and sprinted the remaining distance to the tree line, ignoring Alex. Hope surged through her as she ran, mounting with every step. She was going to make it!

She was going to get herself out of this.

Lauren jumped in shock as something impacted her chest. She saw a figure, directly ahead, crouched low. An instant later, pain flooded her body as electricity surged through the conducting electrodes, robbing her of muscular control. She stumbled a few paces, propelled by her own momentum, before collapsing on the dirt road.

Nearby, Alex had watched the scene unfold with utter disbelief. Lauren, on the verge of escaping into the woodland, was now twitching on the road, trying feebly to move. What had happened to her?

His answer came a moment later.

'You were careless,' a voice remarked. A voice that was too high in pitch to belong to a man. 'She almost got away.'

Alex watched as the crouching figure moved forward into the light, giving Alex his first proper look at Lauren's mysterious assailant.

His eyes opened wider at what he saw.

'Who the hell are you?'

Chapter 32

The interior of the two-storey building was hot and dusty, the air heavy with the smell of tobacco and coffee and low-burning frustration. The grimy windows were shuttered, the thick wooden slats helping to dampen the drone of traffic outside.

Cain stared out through a narrow gap in the wood, squinting in the light. After travelling for the past 18 hours, and going far longer without sleep, he was already tired, but there was no question of resting now. Time was against him.

He turned away from the window, facing the men who were watching him in glowering, expectant silence. They were an intimidating group under any circumstances; each was as tough as iron, their bodies moulded by a training regime as gruelling and intense as any yet devised, their minds and spirits tempered in the heat of battle. Their faces were tanned and weathered by long exposure to wind and sun and snow, many sporting thick beards, and some still bearing the scars of recent action.

And all were now scrutinizing the man who had summoned them here.

They were the men of Task Force Black, the unit Cain had helped create to drive the Soviet army out of Afghanistan. Collectively they represented one of the most formidable paramilitary units on the face of the earth.

And they were angry.

They had lost their first battle, and two of their comrades had fallen. Another was missing. They wanted vengeance.

They wanted answers. But first he needed some from them. He had flown 7,000 miles from Langley, without permission, to speak to these men directly, before they were recalled to the US.

'All right,' he said, breaking the silence. 'Talk to me. What happened out there?'

'We lost,' one of them said, bluntly. Yunis Asadov, a tough little Azerbaijani who spoke little but always said what was on his mind. 'What more is there to say?'

'I need more than that.'

'The Russians were ready for us,' another said, speaking a little more calmly. Romek Karalius, an ethnic Lithuanian, like Anya. 'They ambushed us just as we were deploying. It was as if they knew where we would be, and when.'

Cain hadn't missed the implication. 'You're saying someone tipped them off?'

'The Russians have never been in that position before, and we were careful,' Romek said. 'I can think of no other explanation.'

If true, Romek's revelation was disturbing news indeed. Only a small cadre even knew about the existence of Task Force Black, never mind their deployment plans and operational details. Who would do such a thing? And why, after all this time? He could do little with unfounded opinions and rumours. He needed facts.

'Any suggestions?'

Romek spread his arms. 'You tell us. I am only saying what I saw.'

Cain said nothing. It would certainly bear further investigation, but he was here for a different reason.

'Talk to me about Anya,' he prompted. At this, the mood in the room seemed to grow even darker, if that were possible. 'Carpenter thinks she froze up during the battle, refused to follow orders. Is he right?'

Even Cain couldn't have predicted the uproar that followed. Immediately several of her comrades leapt to her defence, angry raised voices competing with one another, each drowning the other out.

The tumult was only silenced when Romek slammed his fist down on the table with such force that the impact reverberated down into the floorboards. All eyes turned to him – a huge, indomitable, menacing presence.

'Anya did not freeze up,' he said, choosing each word carefully. 'She is many things, but she is no coward. She fought as hard as any of us.'

Cain let out a breath. Romek's words had confirmed what he'd known all along. Carpenter, Simmons and the others were wrong about her.

'So tell me what really happened,' Cain pressed.

Romek was silent for a while, examining what was clearly a painful memory even for a man as resilient as him.

'We were outnumbered and taking fire from three sides,' he said at last. 'One of our comrades was already killed by Russian ground fire. We knew they had outflanked our position, and if we tried to hold our ground they would surround and destroy us. The only choice was to fall back. Anya and Panas agreed to stay behind and cover our retreat.'

'And you let her?' Cain asked, unable to keep the anger from his voice.

Though he had read the mission reports and was all too aware of Anya's reputation in combat, part of him couldn't ignore the fact she was still a woman. The idea that her comrades would willingly allow her to remain behind while they escaped was abhorrent to him.

The look Romek gave him was enough of a warning. Cain might have been their case officer, but he was a long way from Langley out here, and surrounded by men who could kill him as easily as squashing a bug underfoot.

'It was not our choice,' Romek said. 'She would not be moved, and Panas had command. They stayed, we pulled out.'

'And you reported that Panas was killed?'

Romek nodded. 'I saw him fall as we were retreating. I do not know where it came from, but he went down and stopped transmitting over the radio net.'

Cain could see the pall of grief that had descended on the group as he spoke. Panas had been well-liked and well-respected, a natural choice as leader when the group's former commander had been relieved of duty.

'What about Anya?'

'She was still returning fire the last I saw of her,' the big Lithuanian confirmed. 'She kept warning us over the radio net not to come back, that she was surrounded and there was no way to break out. We lost contact soon after.'

Cain was moved. Though Romek's dispassionate report of the battle conveyed none of the gut-wrenching danger the group had faced, he nonetheless could picture Anya's final moments with them.

'Tell me something, Romek,' he said. 'Could she be alive?'

The big operative didn't answer right away. He knew what Cain was asking, knew how much might depend on the answer he gave. 'If the Russians were looking for proof of American troops in Afghanistan, they would want prisoners. Whether she would let herself be taken alive...'

'Answer the question,' Cain demanded.

Romek's eyes glimmered. 'I can't say for sure. Anya is a survivor, but there are some things no one can live through.'

Cain looked down, feeling defeated.

'There is something else,' Romek added. 'Before we lost contact, Anya gave me a message to give you to.' The big man was studying him intently now. 'She said she would keep her promise.'

It took most of Cain's self-control to maintain his composure as those words sank in. Even in a dire situation like that, with destruction and death all around her, Anya's last thoughts had been of him.

It was then that he was struck by a sudden realization. Her message was more than just an acknowledgement of their relationship and his importance to her. She had foreseen this conversation, the doubts he would have about her survival, and she had chosen to confront them as only she could.

'She's alive,' Cain said suddenly, turning around to face the others, his heart beating faster. 'She promised me she would come home, and she will.'

Already he imagined the countless obstacles that lay before him, the difficulties and challenges, the layers of security and enmity, the perilous dangers that stood between him and Anya. He didn't care. He would tear down every one of them to get to her.

'We're going to get her out.'

—

Washington DC – 31 March 2010

It was a bright but chilly spring afternoon in the capital, the sun shining valiantly through breaks in the torn clouds overhead, bringing with it tantalising moments of warmth that were soon extinguished by the cool breeze.

The National Mall was busy with people heading home early from work, tourists snapping pictures of the various monuments and buildings, and college kids braving the cold to toss a few footballs around.

Marcus Cain watched one kid in particular sail through a couple of his buddies, easily fending off their half-hearted tackles, before throwing the ball to a teammate who immediately fumbled it, much to the amusement of the others.

Just for a moment, Cain's mind flashed back to a similar scene he'd witnessed two decades earlier. He'd been a young man sitting on a sandy beach beneath a cloudless sky, watching a game unfold, without a care in the world. And by his side, the woman who had given him that gift. The woman who had brought out the best in him.

Never could he have imagined the future that lay ahead for them both.

It was rare for him to venture away from the protection of Langley these days, but he needed to be away from it. He needed to breathe fresh air, to clear his head and be alone. Well, as close to alone as a man like him could be.

His Agency protective detail were hovering nearby, lost amidst the sea of suits emerging from nearby government offices. They were far enough away to give him some vestige of privacy, but close enough to intervene if any of the civilians passing by so much as looked at him wrong.

Reaching into his overcoat, Cain pulled out a photograph he'd brought with him from his office. He didn't have many pictures of Lauren, he'd realized earlier. Most parents filled entire albums with shots of their kids growing up, playing, celebrating little achievements and milestones, but not Cain. He'd been absent most of the time, and it had never occurred to him when he had been around. Another one of those things that came so naturally to other people, but which was missing from his life.

The picture in his hands had been taken ten years earlier on San Clemente beach in California. One of the rare occasions he'd taken some time away from work to be with his daughter. He'd taken her back to the place he'd grown up, the place he'd worked his first job, hoping in some way that this glimpse of his own childhood might help him connect with hers.

She was sitting cross-legged on the white sand, all skinny limbs and long hair whipped up by the breeze. Staring out to sea, lost in a daydream. The expression on her face was one of such serenity that it made his heart ache every time he looked at it. A perfect moment of peace in a life filled with so much disappointment.

He could feel his cell phone vibrating in his pocket. Blinking, he placed the picture carefully in his overcoat and reached for the phone. It was a call from the Agency's station in Pakistan.

'Yeah?'

'Sir, it's Quinn. Can you talk?'

'What you got for me, Hayden?'

'The Pakistanis came through, like you said. I just got the confirmation from their director's chief of staff. He's agreed to the meeting two days from now, on embassy soil.' Such was his excitement, he actually let out a laugh. 'I don't know how we turned it around, but they sound like they want to play ball.'

A cold breeze whipped across the Mall.

'That's good news. Well done,' Cain said, his voice hollow.

Quinn hesitated. 'It... would really help if I had an overview of what we're planning to present,' he ventured. 'So we know what to expect.'

In his pocket, Cain gently touched the photograph, his thoughts lingering on the young woman it depicted. 'Don't worry. You'll have everything you need.'

Lowering the phone, he ended the call and glanced back towards the grassy playing fields, where another game of improvised football was just starting.

Chapter 33

Drake pressed forward, passing rows of identical lockers, eager to recover what they needed and get out of there.

The storage facility was in a large industrial park in Prague's 4th district, near the outskirts of town. Drake had chosen this location specifically because it was unmanned, requiring only a security code to gain access.

This was fortunate, since everything he owned had been taken from him in Pakistan. Not to mention that the arrival of a man and woman in torn, mud-streaked clothes would certainly have aroused suspicion from even the most lax of security guards.

'What are we looking for?' Lenka asked, glancing fearfully over her shoulder.

'A security blanket,' he explained, his eyes on the unit numbers.

The young woman frowned. 'A what?'

'You'll see.'

Drake halted beside unit 561. It looked no different from the others – just a plain steel door with a reference number, painted blue and secured with a combination padlock.

'I need to pee,' Lenka whispered. It had been a three-hour car journey north from Slovakia, with no rest stops along the way.

'Hold it in,' he advised, indifferently.

Drake turned the padlock on its side to expose the four combination dials. Every cache he'd set up had its own unique code. He couldn't rely on notes or prompts – the only option was to commit each of the numbers to memory.

Turning the dials one after the other, he hesitated before twisting the final one into position. There was a click, and the shackle sprung free.

Drake opened the door a fraction and checked that the fragment of matchstick he'd wedged into the frame hadn't been disturbed. Satisfied that the tell was intact, he stepped inside.

'In,' he said, pulling Lenka after him and closing the door.

The storage locker itself was square, and small enough that Lenka could stand in the centre, stretch out her arms and touch the cinder block walls with ease. It was certainly not an expansive space, but it didn't need to be. The only contents were a pair of metal boxes pushed up against the wall.

'I do not understand,' Lenka said, frowning. 'There is no blanket here.'

'Look closer,' Drake replied as he knelt down in front of the first box, easing it open an inch or so.

The reason for his caution soon became obvious. The lid was rigged with a tripwire, attached to a simple hook inside. Anyone who tried to open it without disabling the concealed trap would trigger an incendiary grenade all but guaranteed to vaporize everything within the unit.

Disabling the tripwire, Drake swung the lid open. First and most obvious was the money: two thousand euros in various denominations, sealed in plastic ziplock bags. Certainly not a fortune – Drake couldn't afford to spread his resources too thinly – but enough to buy food and a place to stay, or secure travel to a safe location.

The next item was a gun: a Beretta M9 automatic with the magazine removed, and a box of 9mm shells. Since these caches were intended for Drake or his teammates, he'd chosen a weapon that all of them were comfortable using. The M9 was second nature to most.

Beside the weapon were four Canadian passports: one each for Drake, Frost, Mason and McKnight. Biometric security measures were making passports increasingly difficult to forge, but it was still possible if one knew the right people. An accompanying driver's licence was inserted into each.

He lingered for a moment on Samantha McKnight's passport photo. The woman who had betrayed them in Pakistan, facilitating their capture and the death of at least one of his colleagues. Drake knew he could never forgive her for such treachery, and caught himself wondering what he would do if their paths ever crossed again.

'You left this here?' Lenka asked.

'If we're ever in the shit, emergency caches like this contain everything we need – money, IDs and weapons. They're called security blankets,' Drake explained.

Lenka looked at him. 'There are others like this?'

He nodded.

'How many?'

'Enough,' he said as he lifted out what looked like a chunky, old-fashioned cell phone with a foldable antenna. It was powered down and had been sitting there for some time, but in favourable conditions the battery was supposedly able to retain its charge for up to 18 months.

Switching it on, he was rewarded with an electronic chime, and the screen lit up: 30 per cent charge remaining.

'Why keep that here?' Lenka asked. 'You can buy phones anywhere.'

'Not like this one,' he replied, powering the unit down again. 'It's a satellite phone, with customized GPS encryption. A good friend wrote the software. It's untraceable, in theory.'

She frowned. 'In theory?'

Drake said nothing, instead turning his attention to the second box. After disabling the anti-tamper device, he swung the lid open to reveal three sets of civilian clothes, neatly folded and ready to go. Like money and ID, you never knew when you might need a change of clothes.

'Here, these should fit you,' he said, tossing her the set intended for Frost. The two women were about the same height and build. Anyway, they had to be better than the filthy clothes she was wearing.

Drake gratefully peeled off his filthy jacket and the damp shirt underneath. He was happy to rid himself of every trace of his imprisonment.

'You want me to undress?' Lenka asked. 'Here?'

Drake looked at her.

'Wouldn't have picked you as the modest type,' he said as he pulled on a clean pair of jeans.

He realized he'd hit a raw nerve. 'That is different,' she said heatedly. 'I am not working now.'

Drake shrugged. 'Fine. Stay as you are, then.'

Glaring at him for a moment, Lenka finally resigned herself and removed her mud-covered parka, dumping it in the corner of the locker. It was soon followed by the rest of her clothes, leaving her standing in just her underwear, her skin dimpled with goosebumps.

Drake turned away, giving her some measure of privacy as she slipped on the unfamiliar clothing. As appealing as Lenka undoubtedly was, he had other matters on his mind now. He knelt beside the security blanket and removed the money and ID, quickly transferring them to his pockets.

He opted to leave the Beretta where it was. He still had the Glock 17, and the two weapons were roughly comparable in terms of accuracy and stopping power. There was little to be gained by lugging two of them around, and he certainly wasn't entrusting Lenka with a weapon.

Drake also took Frost's passport in case it might prove useful for his reluctant companion. The two women didn't look much alike, but they were at least in the same rough age group. With a change of hair colour and the right make-up, it was possible to bluff past most immigration controllers. Drake still remembered one of his regiment, who had travelled to three different countries on a friend's passport. It was simply a matter of bullshitting your way through.

The last item brought a faint, wistful smile to his face. A simple leather necklace, with three objects dangling from it – dice, a crucifix and a wedding ring. Once belonging to a member of Drake's team named Keegan, the lucky charm had symbolized his three big loves in life: gambling, religion and women. It had since passed on to Frost, who seemed to have inherited Keegan's penchant for charms and superstition.

'What is that?' Lenka asked, her voice quiet now.

'A good luck charm.' He sighed, thinking about Frost, about the torture she had endured, and the bloodstained dressings in the abandoned church. 'It belonged to a friend of mine. She was a big believer in stuff like this.'

'What happened to her?'

There was no telling where Frost might be, what condition she was in, or whether she was even still alive. But he chose to cling to that hope, however slender it might have been. He'd already lost two of his teammates. The thought of losing Frost as well was more than he could bear.

'I don't know,' he said. 'We got separated.'

To his surprise, he felt a hand on his shoulder. He turned to face the young woman. Seeing her standing there dressed in Frost's clothes was another painful reminder of the friends he had lost in the past few days.

'I am sorry,' Lenka said softly. He was suddenly very conscious of how close they were standing. 'For what happened to you.'

He understood, but he knew he couldn't afford to indulge such sentimental thoughts.

'Save it,' he said, slipping the necklace on. With luck, he'd be able to return it to its owner before too long. 'We have what we need here.'

Lenka withdrew her hand, looking crestfallen. 'What will you do now?'

Shoving the Glock down the back of his jeans, Drake looked her hard in the eye. 'I'm going to get her back.'

Chapter 34

Alex stared for several seconds, shocked by what he saw.

He couldn't have been more than 10 or 11 years old. His black, buzz-cut hair and dark complexion suggested Middle Eastern or Asian descent. His clothes were too big for his slender frame, which made him look even younger.

The chunky, plastic-covered weapon in the boy's hands looked almost like a toy – an impression heightened by the age of its wielder – though clearly it was anything but. Even Alex recognized a police-issue stun gun when he saw one.

'Who are you?' he repeated. 'Start talking or I start shooting.'

The boy's dark eyes flicked to Alex's handgun, which was now trained on him. 'Someone who does not like having guns pointed at him.'

He spoke perfectly serviceable English, but his accent suggested an Indian or Pakistani upbringing. It certainly fit with his appearance, but it still didn't explain what this kid was doing here.

'And I don't like uninvited guests,' Alex hit back, keeping his weapon raised. 'So that makes us even. Who are you?'

'You are Alex, yes?'

'That's right,' Alex confirmed, even more confused that this kid knew his name. 'Now answer my question.'

'My name is Yasin.'

'Lovely to meet you, Yasin,' he replied sarcastically. 'Now tell me what the hell you're doing here.'

Yasin hesitated, searching for the right words. 'I am... insurance.'

'Anya sent you?'

He nodded, then pointed at Lauren, who was beginning to stir. 'We must get her inside quickly. Pick her up.'

When Alex didn't move, Yasin frowned at him.

'Are you not listening, Alex?'

Alex blinked. Yasin's suggestion made perfect sense, but he couldn't reconcile the fact that a child was holding a gun and issuing orders, as if dealing with escaping hostages was routine for him. Anya's choice of allies was growing stranger by the day.

'I heard what you said. How do I know you won't use that thing on me next?'

Yasin shrugged. 'She told me not to shoot you unless I had to.'

'How reassuring,' Alex said, lowering his weapon. Removing his shirt, he angrily tore away one of the sleeves and wrapped it around his injured arm, swearing under his breath as he tightened the makeshift dressing.

Approaching the young woman, he gave Yasin and the taser a dubious look. 'Put that bloody thing away before someone gets hurt.'

'You are already hurt because you had *no* weapon,' Yasin observed. 'That was stupid. Anya will be angry with you.'

Of that, he had no doubt.

Lifting the semi-conscious woman onto his shoulder with difficulty, and doing his best not to get blood on her, Alex glared at the boy, who seemed to be watching his efforts with a combination of interest and amusement. He briefly considered his chances of using the taser against its owner, but decided against it.

He was in enough trouble already.

Chapter 35

Prague, Czech Republic

A short drive brought Drake and Lenka to a low hill overlooking the city's old town. Behind them rose the towering battlements, carved stonework and cathedral-like spires of Prague Castle. Below, the maze of red-tiled rooftops and tree-lined avenues was interrupted by the placid waters of the Vltava river bisecting the city. Pleasure boats and commercial craft of all shapes and sizes plied the wide, slow-moving waterway, while countless tourists and residents swarmed across the city's medieval bridges.

It was an impressive view, but Drake's mind was on other matters. He paced back and forth while he waited for the phone to acquire a signal. Satphones could be hit and miss, which was why he'd chosen high ground to make this call.

'How long will this take?' Lenka asked nervously, watching the tourists pose for selfies in front of the castle.

'You got somewhere else to be?'

'Yesterday,' she remarked pointedly. 'I was happy then. And safe.'

Drake ignored her barb as the phone finally locked onto a satellite signal. He dialled a number from memory.

It rang a couple of times before a crisp, efficient female voice answered. 'Access number, please?'

It was game time. Drake had just entered a highly secure and discreet switchboard, set up specifically for Agency field personnel when they had no other means of reporting in. Every call was carefully logged, every word recorded for later analysis.

Drake reeled off his old Agency access code from memory, knowing full well the reaction it would provoke once entered into the system. It didn't take long.

'Please identify yourself, sir,' the operator said, her voice a little less machine-like, a harder undertone emerging.

'My name's Ryan Drake,' he said. 'Connect me to Deputy Director Marcus Cain.'

'Sir, that's not possible.' All trace of pleasantries had vanished. 'I can't—'

'I know you're following protocol and running an automatic trace on this call. You're wasting time you don't have,' Drake interrupted. 'Put him on the phone right now, or I hang up and disappear. And you can explain to him why you allowed a blacklisted operative to slip away.'

He heard muffled voices in the background. She was consulting with a supervisor, trying to obtain the authority to transfer a disavowed rogue operative through to the second most powerful man in the Agency.

'One moment please, sir,' she said at last.

A series of clicks and low-level buzzes followed as the call was shunted through the Agency's complex internal communications system, each juncture bringing Drake one step closer to his enemy.

Then, finally, it was done. He heard the buzz as the call connected, the sounds of traffic and voices in the distance, the intake of breath.

'Ryan,' Cain began. 'I didn't think I'd be hearing from you again.'

'You thought wrong about a lot of things, Marcus,' Drake said, turning away from the tourists milling around lest they catch sight of his face. 'We both know people are listening in on this call, and your best men are trying to figure out where exactly I am right now. I left a few of them back at that church, as a reminder of what happens to people who come looking for me.'

He could imagine the frantic efforts to break his satellite phone's encryption and track down his location.

'Maybe they'll find me,' Drake conceded. 'Then again, maybe they won't. Maybe I'll disappear as soon as I hang up, drop right off the face of the earth, find a place even the Agency can't track me down. And every morning you wake up, every evening you leave the office, you'll have to wonder if today's the day I come for you. A man could go mad living that kind of life.'

He heard a chuckle on the other end. 'Son, I've been threatened by people far more dangerous and resourceful than you. If you were smart – and that's a big if – you'd be hiding in the deepest, darkest hole you could find. But since you're not, I assume you called to do more than throw idle threats my way.'

In that at least, he was right. 'You're holding Frost captive,' Drake said.

'I'm holding a disavowed former operative in connection with a terrorist attack,' Cain corrected, no doubt mindful that the call was being listened in on.

'Call it what you want. You're going to release her.'

'And why would I do that?'

'Because I have something you want.'

'Enlighten me.'

Drake looked out across the city. It was the kind of place a man like him could disappear in, leave his former life behind.

Last chance to back out.

'Anya,' he said. 'Give me Frost back, alive and unharmed, and I'll give you Anya. And we all go our separate ways. It's that simple.'

He knew nothing else would get Cain's interest, and Drake had no other cards left to play.

'What makes you think for one second you could just hand her over to me?' Cain asked. 'Better men have tried and failed.'

'They didn't have what I have,' Drake replied. 'Her trust. That's the only weapon I need.'

'And why the change of heart, Ryan?' Cain asked, clearly suspicious. 'I offered you this deal before, and you refused.'

Drake thought of all the people who had lost their lives over the past few years, the futures destroyed in a pointless, seemingly endless conflict. Where would it end?

Perhaps there was only one way it could end.

'I was your prisoner. I knew you'd kill us all the second you got your hands on Anya, no matter what you'd promised. Now I'm free, and we can make a proper deal. One we can both live with.' He glanced around at Lenka, who was sitting on a nearby bench smoking a cigarette, trying not to make it too obvious she was eavesdropping. 'I want out, Marcus. For good. I want this to be over.'

'Getting out isn't an easy thing to do. Especially for a man with as much blood on his hands as you.'

And you should know all about blood on your hands, Drake thought.

'But it *can* be done,' Drake insisted. 'I want full and total amnesty for myself, Keira, everyone associated with me. No pursuits, no surveillance, nothing. You're the deputy director of the CIA. You can pull the right strings.'

'Ryan, you surprise me,' Cain remarked with thinly veiled derision. 'So many people willing to fight and die for you, and here you are going behind their backs, cutting deals to save your own ass. What would Anya think of you if she could hear you now, so eager to bargain away her life for your own?'

Cain was trying to provoke him, trying to test his resolve, goad him into making an emotional admission. It took all of Drake's self-control not to rise to the bait.

'Anya chose this life, Keira didn't. I can't save them both.' He turned away once more, thinking of the woman who had changed the course of his life so profoundly, who he'd risked everything for, and who had done the same for him. 'Maybe one of them doesn't want to be saved.'

Cain weighed up Drake's offer. There were a hundred reasons he could reject it out of hand, and even more reasons for him to be distrustful. But none of those reasons mattered, Drake sensed. If his instincts were correct, Cain would accept his offer.

'All right, Ryan,' he said. 'Not many people get a second chance with me, but you might just have bought yourself one. If you come through.'

Drake knew he'd been right about Cain, right about this whole situation. But never had he so wanted to be wrong.

'You have 48 hours to deliver her to a location of my choosing. If you're not there *with* Anya, the deal's off. If you try to pull anything during the exchange, or if I even suspect something's not right, the deal's off. If you try to stall me or play for time, well, you can guess what happens. I hope for Keira's sake you don't disappoint me.'

'I won't.'

'We'll find out in 48 hours. Oh, and Ryan,' Cain added, seemingly as an afterthought. 'I'm looking forward to seeing you again.'

Drake ended the call. Powering down the satellite phone and stowing it in his jacket, he turned around to see Lenka still watching him, sitting cross-legged on a park bench.

'What was that all about?' the young woman asked, a cigarette dangling between her fingers.

'Confirmation,' Drake said, heading for their car nearby.

Chapter 36

Anya was in a pensive mood as she pulled into her driveway. There was a great deal of work to be done if she was to recover Drake and his team, and only 48 hours to do it in. She knew her mind should already have turned to the practical details: equipment, weapons, timings, logistics.

And yet her thoughts were on her brief conversation with Cain earlier. It was the first time she'd spoken to him in nearly a year. Despite everything, all the animosity that existed between them, the sound of his voice still stirred up intense, confused feelings that she wasn't sure how to handle.

She felt keyed up, in need of some kind of release. Perhaps she'd make use of the heavy punchbag in her basement later, she thought as she slipped out of the rental car and approached the house. Even if she was tired and hurting after a long day, a little physical aggression often helped calm her mind.

These thoughts vanished the instant she eased the front door open and spotted bloodstains on the carpet.

Straightaway she went into fighting mode, her senses heightened, keenly searching her surroundings for possible threats. Drawing the M1911 semi-automatic she kept in a shoulder holster, she advanced silently into the house.

Never let them come at you. Always try to take the initiative, make them fight your fight. That was the lesson that had been drilled into her a lifetime ago, and it had held true since then.

She could hear voices coming from the living room. Tense and angry. It was a male voice, speaking with an English accent. Alex.

Gripping the M1911 tight, she crept down the hallway until she was in position.

Alex was there, seated on the couch, his left forearm wrapped in a blood-stained bandage and her bottle of vodka resting on the table beside him. He started at her sudden appearance, clearly having failed to notice her arrival. Perhaps the vodka had something to do with his lack of awareness, she thought with a flash of anger.

Another person was in the room with him, standing in the kitchen and busy stuffing himself with a bag of potato chips. Yasin, the young boy she'd reluctantly brought with her from Pakistan after he helped her escape Cain's men.

Anya was hardly inclined to pick up waifs and strays during her travels, but had recognized his usefulness and, more importantly, the debt she owed him. With this in mind, she'd stationed him in the woods outside her house to keep an eye on the place, well aware of the boy's ability to blend into his surroundings and move quickly without being seen.

'Anya,' Alex said, jumping to his feet.

'What has happened here?' she demanded, lowering the weapon.

Clearly Alex was injured, though not severely. Was it possible he'd somehow encountered Yasin, and become the victim of friendly fire? If so, she doubted the two of them would now be sharing a house, never mind the same room.

That left only Lauren as a possible attacker.

Alex blushed, saying nothing. It was Yasin who offered an explanation.

'Your friend got careless,' he said between mouthfuls of potato chips. 'Almost let the prisoner get away.'

'Fuck off,' Alex snapped, giving him a hostile look. 'Like to see you do better.'

'I fucking did,' Yasin shot back. The taser unit Anya had given him as last resort self-defence was on the kitchen worktop, its conducting electrodes having been fired.

Alex jabbed a finger. 'Watch your language, you little arsehole.'

'You swore before I did,' Yasin pointed out, amused. 'And after.'

'It's different for me!'

'Why?'

'Be quiet, both of you!' Anya interjected, having no time for such petty bickering. 'Tell me about Lauren. Is she secure?'

'Relax,' Alex said, though he looked anything but relaxed now. 'She's in the holding room. I'm fine, by the way. Thanks for asking,' he added, holding up his bandaged arm.

Anya was less concerned about his well-being than she was about the condition of their hostage. Reluctant to take his word that everything was fine, she marched down the central corridor and threw open the bedroom door.

Sure enough, Lauren was securely tied to the chair, only this time there was a noticeable graze on one side of her head, and dirt on her T-shirt and trousers. A strip of duct tape had been placed over her mouth.

She looked up as Anya entered, glaring at her as she mumbled something into the tape. Anya was quite certain it was nothing positive. The young woman must have gotten free somehow and tried to escape, injuring Alex in the process.

Alex, the man she'd entrusted to guard their hostage. The very thought of it filled her with anger and disappointment.

Anya roughly tore the tape away.

'Are you hurt?' she asked before the young woman got a chance to speak.

'Screw you,' Lauren shot back. '*Anya.*'

The look of shock on Anya's face must have been obvious, because she saw Lauren flash a smile at her minor victory.

'Oh yeah, I know who you are,' she went on, in full flow now. 'My dad told me all about a woman named Anya. How he took her in, trained her, gave her a chance when nobody else would. And in return she betrayed his trust, tried to destroy his career. And now you're back, taking another shot at him. What the hell is wrong with you? Why can't you just let it go and move on?' She shook her head, looking at Anya with something akin to pity. 'Haven't you got anything else in your life apart from him?'

Anya didn't respond. She didn't trust herself to speak at that moment. Instead she replaced the duct tape over the young woman's mouth, despite Lauren's best attempts to avoid it. Lauren was mumbling more angry insults from behind the gag, but Anya ignored them as she backed out of the room, closing the door firmly behind her.

She found Alex where she had left him.

'You told her my name,' Anya said, burning with anger.

Alex stared at her blankly. 'I—'

Anya gripped Alex by his T-shirt and shoved him backwards against the wall with enough force to elicit a grunt of pain.

'You told her my name,' Anya hissed, her face just inches away from his. She wanted to lash out, vent her months and years of carefully repressed fury, let out everything she'd held in check since the disastrous operation in Pakistan. 'I warned you about talking to her and you did it anyway. I told you to be careful and you ignored me! I trusted you!'

'Trusted me?' he repeated incredulously. 'Really? That's why you had mini-Rambo over there hanging around outside with a fucking taser?'

'Yasin was there as insurance.'

'Against what?'

'Against you! And it was just as well, because clearly you weren't up to it. All you had to do was watch her and keep her under control. A woman, tied to a chair, Alex! And you couldn't even do that.' Her emotions were already fraught after the call with Cain. 'You did nothing but let me down again!'

Alex did something quite unexpected then. He reached up and slapped her arm away with every ounce of force and aggression he could, taking a step forward at the same time as if he wanted to fight her. Anya backed up and raised her hands, ready to defend herself.

'Fuck you!' Alex exploded, trembling with rage. He knew she could hurt him, could beat him to the ground with ease, and he didn't care one bit. 'I've done nothing but help you since the moment you showed up, Anya! You'd never have come close to finding that girl if it wasn't for me. I've been chased, pepper-sprayed, stabbed, let myself become a kidnapper – and that's just today – and it was all to help *you*! Because you asked for my help! You *needed* my help.'

Anya stared at him as he shouted, taken aback by the sheer vehemence of his argument.

'Yes, I fucked up. Is that what you want to hear?' he demanded. 'Well there it is. I fucked up and I let my guard down, and you know why? Because she's a fucking kid, Anya! She's a kid who is frightened and alone and surrounded by people who could kill her at any moment. And believe me, I know how that feels. So I tried to help, I tried to reassure her everything's going to be all right. *Because I'm not like you, and I don't want to be!*'

He turned away. Anya had expected him to wilt and crumble before her scathing tirade. She had seen Alex cowering, grieving and wracked with guilt. But never before had she witnessed him apoplectic with rage.

'Do you want to know something funny?' he said. 'Lauren said you didn't give a shit about me, that you were an evil person and that she could protect me if I helped her escape. And I defended you. I told her I'd rather stand with you and take my chances, because I knew you were right.' Alex shook his head. 'More fool me, eh?'

Anya felt as if she'd been punched in the stomach. His anger, though surprising when it came, was something she could understand and accept. She'd pushed him, and he'd pushed back. But the air of sad acceptance that had followed it was something altogether different.

Her pent-up anger dissipated, like a ship with the wind taken out of its sails. She began to see her actions for what they really were: asking an untrained civilian to act as a hostage taker. The fault lay with her, not him.

She glanced over at Yasin, who had stopped eating to watch the argument unfold. He was standing stock still, and wasn't smiling any more.

'Yasin, please go to the holding room and keep an eye on the prisoner,' Anya said.

The boy blinked. 'She is tied to a chair.'

'She was tied to a chair when I left, and look what happened.' Anya pointed towards the bedroom. 'Go now.'

'Can I take a gun?'

'No, you can't,' she replied firmly. She'd trusted him with a taser, where the worst he could do was accidentally shock himself, but a loaded gun was out of the question. 'And don't remove her gag.'

Yasin took his bag of chips and slouched through to the bedroom, closing the door behind him.

Alone now with Alex, she approached the young man carefully, almost tentatively, as if he were a bomb that might explode. Given his violent outburst earlier, that perhaps wasn't far from the truth.

She sensed an apology was in order, but had no idea how to phrase it, what to say, how to begin. She never really had. She wasn't used to dealing with people in this way, having to take others' feelings into account, having to admit she'd been wrong.

Reaching out, she laid a hand on his shoulder. 'Alex—'

'We've got nothing more to say,' he said, shrugging out of it and brushing past her. 'I'm going for some air. And I'm taking the vodka with me.'

Anya could have stopped him, could have pointed out that he'd already helped himself to her drink without permission, could have demanded that he stay and listen to what she had to say. But she didn't.

She stood there and watched him go, saying nothing, until she heard the front door close, leaving her alone in the middle of the room.

Chapter 37

Prague, Czech Republic

Drake stood with his hands braced against the wall, his head down as hot water sluiced down over him, tendrils of steam rising from his skin. This was his first proper shower in several days, and after everything he'd been through, this simple act of cleaning himself felt like absolute heaven.

One thing Prague didn't lack was places to stay. Exhausted after a long and difficult day, and with evening rapidly drawing in, Drake had booked himself and Lenka into a cheap hotel in the old town, on the east bank of the Vltava. The sort of place that accepted payment by cash and didn't ask too many questions.

He stepped out of the shower cubicle and stretched, his stiff joints protesting. He'd amassed quite a collection of injuries, and though the hot shower had eased some of the aches and pains, he knew he'd be feeling the effects for some time.

Moving over to the sink, he braced himself before wiping his arm across the steamed-up mirror. His face was grazed, cut and bruised in several places, with a particularly deep wound just above his left eye. His jaw was coated with several days' worth of growth, his cheeks gaunt and thin, his eyes hollow.

All things considered, he looked like shit, and that wasn't about to change any time soon.

'One thing at a time, Ryan,' he mumbled, then picked up the cheap disposable razor he'd bought on the way here, and went to work.

He emerged from the shower room a short while later, sporting a few extra razor nicks he'd picked up along the way, and a mostly clean-shaven face.

The room was surprisingly big for such a low-rent establishment. Then again, there was hardly anything in it – just a couple of lumpy single beds pushed together, a chair and wood veneer desk over in one corner, and a built-in wardrobe in another.

Lenka was sitting cross-legged on the bed, the room's old fashioned television switched on and a takeaway pizza box open in front of her. She was wearing a black vest and jeans, but her blonde hair was still damp from her own shower visit earlier. Clearly eating was a higher priority for her than personal grooming.

Drake was inclined to agree, and immediately scooped up a slice for himself

'Hard at work, I see,' he noted sarcastically, pointing at the TV.

The young woman gave him the finger. 'I was watching the news channels, in case they mentioned us.'

Smart enough, he supposed. Judging by the footage of angry-looking protesters brandishing handwritten signs, it seemed some sort of strike or industrial action was the top story.

Lenka glanced up. 'You shaved.'

'Well spotted,' he conceded as he sat down to lace up his boots.

She thought about it. 'I preferred the beard. It is better to think there is a handsome face underneath.'

Drake snorted. 'I'll assume there's a compliment in there somewhere.'

'There isn't.'

Drake reached for the bottle of alcohol he'd picked up on the way here, along with a few other essential supplies to see them through until they departed in the morning. It was slivovitz — a clear plum brandy that was easy to come by in this neck of the woods.

Unscrewing the cap, he poured two generous measures, held one to his lips and downed it in a single gulp. It was hardly wise to be drinking when they were still in danger, but he knew from experience that this stuff was as effective as any painkiller. And after everything he'd been through recently, he figured he'd earned a drink.

Refilling his glass, he held out the other to Lenka, who wrinkled her nose and shook her head.

'Seriously? You don't drink, you don't take your clothes off? What kind of stripper are you?' he taunted. 'Pardon me — erotic performer.'

The young woman looked to be seriously contemplating making him wear the pizza she'd been so eagerly devouring. Then, just like that, she snatched the glass out of his hand and swallowed the contents whole.

'That's more like it,' Drake said, taking a more conservative sip this time. 'I don't trust women who don't drink.'

'And I don't trust men who try to get me drunk.'

'I'm not that kind of man,' he said. 'But I prefer not to drink alone.'

Lenka held out her glass and he dutifully refilled it.

'Is that your plan?' she asked, looking down. 'Sit here and get drunk?'

Drake paused to consider the question. 'Well, let's see,' he said. 'Right now I've got every intelligence service from America to Pakistan out looking for me, plus enough black ops private military guys to invade a small African nation. One of my good friends is dead, and another betrayed my team to a man who wants to kill me. The only survivor is being held hostage, and the only way to get her back is to give up my last remaining ally. No matter which choice I make, my chances of living through this are slim at best. So yeah, I'm going to drink tonight.'

The young woman shuddered.

'Then maybe I should drink as well,' she said, giving a nervous little laugh that made her seem younger than she was.

Drake held up his glass in a mock toast, and together they took a gulp of slivovitz.

That was when it finally happened. Her shoulders started moving up and down and tears began to fall. He heard the muffled sound of a sob as she held a hand against her mouth.

Drake laid down his drink and crossed the room, sitting beside her as she clung to him, her warm tears soaking into his T-shirt. He held her, saying nothing, just letting her get it out.

In the past 24 hours she'd been the victim of an armed carjacking, shot at, thrown down a garbage chute, driven into a foreign country in a stolen car, forced to go on the run with a fugitive of dubious motives, and generally seen her entire life come crashing down around her.

'I'm afraid, Ryan,' she whispered when the tears had at last subsided. 'I am not brave like you. I think... I think I will die.'

'No you won't,' Drake said confidently. 'It's me they're after.'

She pulled away, shaking and vulnerable. She was far prettier without make-up, he realized.

'You will protect me?' she asked. Her slender arms were still wrapped around him, and he was very conscious of their closeness, the warmth of her body, the smell of soap that still lingered on her. 'You will keep me safe?'

'If you need me to.'

Lenka looked away for a moment, searching for the right words.

'You said there was a way to get your friend back,' she said, clearly hesitant to broach the delicate subject. 'By giving up someone else.'

Drake nodded.

'Her name is Anya, yes?'

'How do you know that?'

She took another drink to hide her embarrassment. 'I overheard you speaking when you made that phone call. I'm sorry, I didn't mean to...' She trailed off, knowing such apologies were futile. 'This Anya – she is the one they want?'

'That's right.'

'Who is she? Why is she so important?'

The full answer to that question required more time than either of them had. 'Anya used to work for the Agency herself, a long time ago. A man named Cain brought her in, used her to fight his battles for him. Eventually she turned against him, and ended up in a Russian prison for her trouble. But I helped her escape, she went rogue, and he's been looking for her ever since.'

'So she is like you?'

There was a time when Drake used to think of himself as very different from Anya, but he was starting to see how narrow the gulf between them had become. How long would it be before he ended up just like her?

Would he even live that long?

'She is who she is,' he answered. 'But she trusts me. Maybe I'm the only person left that she trusts.'

'She means something to you, yes?' she asked, noticing his change in expression when he spoke of Anya. 'She is... a friend?'

'Something like that,' he acknowledged.

'So what will you do?' Lenka asked. 'Will you give her up?'

Almost without him being aware of it, she had turned towards him, one leg draped over his, her face so close he could feel her breath on his skin. She was wearing nothing beneath her vest, her nipples standing out firm and erect against the thin fabric.

'Would you, if you were me?' Drake asked, trying to ignore it. 'Would you give up one life to save another?'

'I think it is more than just one life at stake. If you don't give them what they want, what will they do to your friend?'

'They'll kill her.' He was under no illusions about that. Frost was expendable to men like Cain, and especially men like Hawkins.

'Then they will come after you and me, and probably kill us both,' she finished for him. 'That means three lives for the loss of one.'

She made it seem so easy, as if simple arithmetic could determine the value of a human life. And yet, there was a certain merit in her suggestion, as cold as it might have seemed. By giving up Anya, he might save not just Frost's life, but also his own, Lenka's, even his sister's back in the UK.

'I'm sorry. Forgive me,' Lenka said, inching closer to him. 'I did not mean to be so... I do not know the word. Cold?'

'I asked for your opinion,' Drake reminded her. 'You gave it.'

'I did,' she said, nodding, her mouth parted, her breathing coming a little faster. 'I wanted to be honest with you, Ryan. Because I trust you. I think you are a good man.'

She tilted her head back and kissed him, tentative at first, but quickly growing stronger and more confident. She slid across, straddling him, her arms wrapped around his neck as she pressed her breasts against his chest. She let out a soft moan as she ground against him.

'We don't have to,' she whispered, looking unsure but hopeful at the same time. 'If you... don't want me.'

Drake didn't try to pull away from her. His voice was hushed when he spoke again. 'There's something I have to tell you, Lenka.'

She leaned forward, desperate to know. 'What?'

That was when he did it. Shoving her roughly away, Drake brought his arm around and backhanded her across the jaw, sending her tumbling to the floor. She landed hard, with an audible thump that would likely leave telling bruises tomorrow.

A trickle of blood was running from the corner of her mouth where he'd struck her. 'What... why did you do that?'

'Enough bullshit,' Drake said, rising to his feet and drawing the Glock from the back of his jeans. 'You're a good actress, but even you can't sell this one.'

'What are you talking about?' Lenka asked, staring at him in disbelief.

'You think it's coincidence that I ran into a car on that mountain road just when I needed it most? And who should be inside but a stripper, trying to pay her way through college? Very original.'

He hadn't figured it out right away, being too preoccupied and exhausted to properly examine his conveniently timed escape. Even now he was angry at himself for being so sloppy.

'But you know what gave you away? It was the coffee you made. You didn't know your way around your own kitchen. Do I even want to know what happened to the real owner of that place?' He trained the weapon on her forehead, taking a step towards her. 'Then the clumsy ambush, blind firing through your windows and sending up an assault team just slowly enough for us to escape. That was when I knew for sure. It was to make me trust you, want to protect you. Like I said, you were good. I wonder how far you would've gone to win me over?'

'I'd have gone as far as it takes. I always do,' she said, spitting bloody phlegm on the cheap carpet. Her Slovakian accent was disappearing, giving way to an American Midwestern lilt. 'Hell of a punch you've got there, by the way. That how you treat all the women in your life?'

'Depends if they're assigned to kill me.' Seeing her trying to sit up, he brandished the weapon. 'Stay the fuck down.'

'Nobody's assigned to kill you, for Christ's sake,' she hit back, wise enough not to push him. 'I'm a HUMINT specialist with the Agency, assigned to undercover work. I don't kill people. I was just brought in to get information out of you.'

Drake's eyes narrowed. 'By who?'

'I don't know his name, but his clearance level was way above mine. He was a big guy, with a scar on his face. He reported directly to the deputy director's office.'

Hawkins. That much made sense at least.

'What did he tell you?' Drake demanded.

The operative sighed and looked down. 'He said you were a former agent that went rogue, that you were working with a known terrorist and you'd tried to assassinate the deputy director. They knew they couldn't force you to give her up, so they gave you a window to escape instead.'

'Hoping I'd lead them right to her,' Drake finished for her, shaking his head. 'You know those bastards executed one of my team in cold blood, right? Tortured and threatened to rape another.'

She shrugged, unmoved by this revelation. 'They said you'd say that. Anyway, it's not my job to make moral judgements. All that matters is the mission.'

'The mission,' he echoed bitterly. 'Well, I've got a new mission for you. You're going to tell me where they're holding Keira.'

Her eyes opened wider. 'I don't know anything about that!' she protested, an edge of fear in her voice. 'I was just brought in to get information. The rest of this shit is above my pay grade.'

Drake looked her up and down, considering her words.

'Like I said, you're good, but I'm not buying it,' he decided. Grabbing a pillow from the bed, Drake jammed it against the barrel of the weapon to form a makeshift silencer, then took aim. 'First one goes in your kneecap. After that, we'll see where we end up.'

'Please! You're wasting your time, Drake. There's nothing I can tell you.'

Drake shrugged. 'Maybe not, but I've got 17 little friends in here that are just dying to find out.'

She had fallen near the armchair when he'd struck her. Her legs were near the base of the chair, and as he'd been interrogating her, he'd failed to notice her slow but deliberate change in posture as she positioned one foot carefully behind the piece of furniture.

With an explosive fling, she whipped her foot forward, sending the cheap, lightweight chair hurtling towards Drake. He reacted quickly, jumping aside to avoid being knocked off balance. However the sudden movement disrupted his aim, giving Lenka a small but precious window in which to act. A window she wasted no time exploiting.

Jumping to her feet, the young woman threw herself at him, going straight for the gun. Her hands clamped down on Drake's wrist and twisted it out of position, bending it backwards with vicious force, trying to snap the bone.

The room resounded with a muffled crack as a round discharged inside Drake's makeshift pillowcase silencer, impacting the ceiling in a spray of charred feathers. Drake felt her sharp nails gouge mercilessly into his skin, scratching and tearing, doing anything she could to disrupt his hold.

The gun was her only focus. She wasn't going to stop until that was in her hands or out of the equation. Unarmed, Drake's superior size and strength would give him an advantage she couldn't hope to counter. That being the case, the only course of action was to sacrifice the weapon she so desperately wanted.

A second unaimed round blasted outwards from the pillowcase, missing Lenka but obliterating the TV behind her. Sparks and broken glass exploded from the unit.

Drake could feel warm blood trickling across his hands. Lenka's nails were going to cause serious damage. He had to do something.

Lowering his shoulder, Drake shoved his way forward, practically lifting her off her feet, across the room and straight into the wall-mounted wardrobe. The mirrored sliding door immediately gave way as the pair slammed into it, knocked off its roller track, while shards of broken glass rained down on them. Ignoring this, Lenka lashed out with her foot, aiming for a groin kick that would take him out of the fight.

In response, Drake threw a hard strike at Lenka's neck with his free hand. His intention was to damage her larynx or windpipe, but instead she seemed to melt away, dodging to the left while deflecting the strike with her forearm. Her speed and agility were incredible.

She swiped at the weapon and finally knocked it from his hand. It landed a few feet away amongst the broken glass.

This was the chance she'd been waiting for, and she went for it. Even as she dived for the gun, Drake leapt up, tackling her around the waist and driving her into the thin plasterboard wall that divided the bedroom from the shower room. The young woman snarled, slamming a sharp elbow between his shoulder blades. Drake twisted aside to avoid another painful hit.

Making the most of the opening, the young woman jumped back and launched a high kick at the side of his head. As he'd done many times before, Drake fell back on his years of boxing training. His arms went up immediately, absorbing some of the considerable impact, and buying a precious instant to throw his weight to the side, away from the arc of her kick. It wasn't entirely effective, and the blow was nonetheless enough to knock him off balance, but at least he'd avoided blocking it with his head.

Even as he recovered, the young woman bent down, and used the shredded remains of the pillowcase to snatch up a foot-long shard of broken glass from the wardrobe doors.

She smiled at Drake, wielding the broken glass in a reverse grip as if it were a combat knife. 'The boss ordered me to keep you alive,' she said. 'You'll wish he hadn't by the time I'm done.'

Clearly the young woman had been thoroughly trained in unarmed combat. She might have been smaller than him, but a blade was more than enough to make up for such shortcomings.

She came at him, swiping left and right, aiming for anywhere she could make contact. Stabbing someone to death is no easy business at the best of times, and the idea of a single fatal puncture wound to the chest or back is pure fantasy. The ribcage makes for a formidable defensive armour that can easily catch and foul a blade. The harsh reality is that it often takes multiple penetrations of vulnerable areas like the stomach and neck to put someone down for good.

He knew this, and so did Lenka. She wasn't aiming to deal a lethal wound, but rather to slash and damage muscles and arteries, weakening him enough that she could subdue him.

She swiped wildly, backing him up into a corner. Fighting someone with a knife was always a tough day out. Your only chance was to accept you were going to get hurt to some extent, and try to take the blade out of play as quickly as possible.

She slashed again, aiming for his face, perhaps hoping to blind him. Drake was left with no choice but to throw up his arm to defend himself, and instantly felt a rush of white-hot pain as the shard cleaved its way through skin and muscle.

No sooner had the improvised blade done its work than she whirled around and reversed her grip on it, lashing out again. This time she aimed low, the glass slicing through his T-shirt on his right side, just below the ribs. He'd managed to throw himself backwards a little, but a flash of pain and a spreading warmth told him the shard had nonetheless hit home.

He bent lower to protect his injury, knowing even as he did so that it was a bad move, that it would only encourage her to come in from above, aiming for his face or neck.

A sudden kick to his side dropped him, and Lenka plunged the blade down again. Drake threw his hands up and caught her knife arm, managing to stop the sharp point impacting, only for Lenka to slam her fist down on the end of the blade like it was a nail to be pounded into a piece of wood.

Drake couldn't contain his scream of agony as the shard of glass penetrated his chest, grating on two ribs. He saw a look of triumph and eager malice in his enemy's eyes as she tried to force it in further.

His reaction was born from necessity. Swinging his hand sideways, he connected with the long tapering piece of glass hard enough to break it away, leaving the point still embedded in his chest.

He caught a glimpse of something lying on the floor beside him. A bedside lamp, knocked off its table during their struggle. It was a cheap and simple wooden item, with a flared base giving way to a narrow neck, and a simple paper shade on top. Not much of a weapon, but beggars couldn't be choosers.

Grasping it by the neck, Drake tore it from its power cord, which immediately shorted out the bulb, and swung the improvised club just as Lenka slashed at him with the remaining shard.

He was half a second ahead of her. That was all it took.

The impact of the solid wooden base meeting glass and bone was followed by a crash, then a musical tinkling as the shard broke apart in her hand. He saw bright red blood staining the empty pillowcase she'd used to protect herself, and heard her whimpering as she retreated, throwing herself at something on the floor.

The Glock.

Drake closed in, but knew he couldn't make it in time. He watched as she brought the weapon up to bear, took aim and pulled the trigger.

Click.

Nothing there. The weapon had been rendered useless even before Drake had allowed her to knock it out of his hand.

He saw her disbelief even as he raised the crude weapon and brought it around against the side of her head. That one was hard enough to break the lamp's wooden stem, but it didn't matter now.

As the young woman pitched sideways and landed in a limp heap on the glass-covered carpet, Drake dropped what remained of the lamp. The pain was kicking in big time, but he managed to reach up, grasp the fragment of glass still embedded in his chest and pull hard, stifling a groan as it slipped free of his flesh.

Tossing the fragment aside, he retrieved the gun from beside his enemy. It took him a few seconds to locate the magazine he'd ejected during the fight, unnoticed by Lenka in the general melee.

'Works better with this,' he said as he slapped it back into the magazine port and racked back the slide to chamber a round.

His heart was pounding as he looked around at the destroyed remnants of the room. People would be on their way soon, either concerned hotel staff alerted by the struggle, local police or, more likely, the black ops team that had deployed Lenka in the first place.

The first two he could handle. The third would be a real problem.

He peeled back his sticky, blood-soaked T-shirt to expose the stab wound on the right side of his chest. It was bleeding steadily, but his ribs seemed to have prevented the shard penetrating too deeply.

His injuries would need treatment, but right now that was less important than getting the fuck out of here.

No sooner had this crossed his mind than he heard footsteps in the hallway outside. Someone was coming.

Forcing himself to his feet, Drake grabbed the chair that his adversary had used as a makeshift missile. He rolled it across the room and jammed it against the door handle, barring the only way into the room, albeit temporarily.

The barricade wouldn't last long. Drake snatched up his jacket from the bed and threw it over his shoulders as he retreated to the far side of the room. He certainly didn't care about staying warm or dry, but the jacket contained the passports, satellite phone and money.

A sudden blast, accompanied by the splinter of disintegrating wood, told him his enemies were about to make entry, using a breaching shotgun to destroy the lock. The door resounded with the impact of a heavy kick, the chair legs screeching an inch or so across the floor but holding firm.

Turning and dropping to one knee, Drake levelled the Glock at the fist-sized hole in the door and opened fire, spraying a trio of rapid-fire shots.

The bark of the 9mm weapon discharging was enough to leave his ears ringing.

'Cover!' a voice yelled. Another shotgun blast punched a second massive hole through the wood.

Drake snapped off a couple more rounds before turning, seeking a way out. His desperate burst of gunfire might have bought him a little time, but seconds only. Now was the time to use them.

The room's only window lay directly ahead of him, about two feet wide and twice as high. It was fitted with a security latch preventing it being opened more than six inches, which he'd disabled not long after arriving. Still, he had no time to roll the window up and hold it in place while he clambered out.

Levelling the Glock at the centre of the window, he put two rounds through it. The glass pane shattered, adding to the general destruction of the room.

Drake paid it no heed, sprinting forward and launching himself through the gap, disappearing out into the night just as the door finally gave way under the relentless assault and armed men stormed in.

Chapter 38

Anya circled the heavy bag, bandaged fists raised and head down. Her vest was damp with sweat, but still she kept up the furious assault.

She laid into the bag with a burst of punches and kicks, letting out aggressive snarls as she connected with it again and again. The heavy leather swayed and lurched, its surface marked from previous blows.

She was hurting. Her hands were bruised, her arms aching from the effort, the injury at her side burning as stitches threatened to give way, but she didn't care. She wanted the pain. It helped focus the mind, sharpen her thoughts.

But this time it wasn't working. This time her thoughts drifted.

She saw herself seated with Alex in the Polish bar, heard his words of warning.

'This is the world we live in, Alex. He would do the same.'

'Then what does that say about the two of you?'

-

Drake was falling. The world turned into a blur as he tumbled through the air, bracing himself for the inevitable landing.

He had chosen this particular hotel for two reasons. The first and most obvious was that it was cheap and asked few questions of its guests.

The second reason only came into play when Drake made his seemingly suicidal leap through a second-floor window.

The hotel's main entrance, set slightly back from the street, featured an outdoor seating area, protected from inclement weather by a canvas awning extending about ten feet on either side of the building's main doors. Drake had made sure to secure a room directly above it.

The impact came about two seconds later. A sudden lurching deceleration, a violent pressure against his back as the canvas took his weight, then a loud crack as metal support roles ripped free of their mountings and the awning collapsed beneath him, accompanied by the screams of terrified passers-by.

He fell again. It was over faster this time, the drop barely more than ten feet, but the landing was far more painful with nothing to break his fall. Instinctively he drew in his arms and allowed his legs to relax just before he hit the pavement, just as his parachute training had taught him. Let your body and legs absorb the landing, slow yourself down, roll with it.

He did, but no amount of preparation could compete with a hard landing on concrete. Pain reverberated up through his skeleton as he came down with a violent crunch, surrounded by torn canvas, broken poles and collapsed tables.

Don't think about it, he told himself, just get up and move! Get up now!

–

Anya threw a final series of rapid hooks that hammered the bag like machine-gun fire. Every shot promised to short out the memories, yet none succeeded.

'My dad told me all about a woman named Anya. How he took her in, trained her, gave her a chance when nobody else would. And in return she lied to him, betrayed his trust, tried to destroy his career. And now you're back, taking another shot at him. What the hell is wrong with you? Why can't you just let it go and move on? Haven't you got anything else in your life apart from him?'

–

Drake managed to get his feet beneath him and forced himself up from the wreckage, ignoring the shocked stares from those nearby. One or two even had their camera phones out, eagerly recording the unfolding drama.

'Holy shit, bro. You okay?' a distinctively American voice asked. 'You just jumped through a fucking window.'

Drake found himself confronted by a man in faded jeans and crumpled linen shirt, and with a rucksack slung over one shoulder. Tall and gangly, with unruly blonde hair and a scruffy beard, he had the kind of deep perma-tan that suggested he should have been carrying a surfboard under his arm.

'Man, watch yourself,' a stocky kid of about the same age warned him. 'This guy's fucked up.'

An unfortunately accurate assessment, Drake thought. However, he had more pressing matters to contend with. The hotel faced out onto several busy streets, with crowded shops and bars, and cars backed up by red lights everywhere. The central location offered plenty of avenues for escape, and the heavy traffic would make blending in easier.

The space between the roads and buildings was crisscrossed by a confusing mess of phone cables and tram lines. Tempting as it was to simply run, he knew that would be suicidal. Such an open area would immediately become a killing ground both for himself and anyone caught in the crossfire, particularly with his enemies firing from an elevated position.

And that wasn't his only problem. Glancing past his new surfer bro, he spotted three men moving purposefully through the passing pedestrians, hands already inside their jackets, eyes locked on him. Every one of them looked like they lived in a gym, and they certainly weren't here to admire the scenery. An Agency field team, probably assigned to guard the hotel entrance in case backup was needed.

Drake reacted immediately, drawing the Glock and waving it in the air.

'Oh, shit,' the surfer gasped. 'Chill, man. It's okay, we're leaving.'

Drake pointed the Glock skywards and fired a couple of shots. As the gunshots echoed, the small crowd of onlookers scattered in panic.

Taking advantage of the confusion, Drake turned right and ran for it, limping slightly on an injured leg, and keeping as close as he could to the hotel wall without backing up against it. With luck, the building's projecting window sills would make it difficult for the men above to get a decent shot, while the fleeing bystanders would cover his retreat.

Either way, there was little choice but to go for it and hope for the best, pounding down the street as fast as his body would carry him.

–

Her strength waning, Anya swept her leg around in a powerful right kick, following it up with a pair of uppercuts as the bag swung back into position.

She wanted to focus on the sensations of the moment, but instead she saw herself outside a warehouse in Pakistan, up against a wall, in a fraught confrontation with Drake just hours before they went into battle. She was so close she could see a little scar above his left eye that she hadn't noticed before.

'Leaving you behind was one of the hardest things I ever did. But I did it to protect you… from me, from the same thing that happens to everyone who gets close to me. You don't deserve that, because you are a good man. Better than this… better than me.'

–

Drake was running for his life, ignoring the curious and frightened looks from locals as he shoved past them. He turned right down a narrow residential street, putting in as many angles between him and his pursuers as possible.

His only chance was to disappear amongst the city's complex network of side streets, alleyways and interconnected courtyards. Every block he covered would dramatically widen the search area, making it virtually impossible for them to seal him in unless they had serious manpower at their disposal.

His vision was weakening, his equilibrium disrupted as blood loss started to tell. He leaned against a wall to steady himself, leaving a bloody hand print on the stonework.

His stop gave him a moment to tune into his surroundings. He was vaguely aware of the wail of police sirens, and knew they were converging on this area. Reports of an armed man jumping from a hotel window then firing shots in the air tended to attract that kind of attention.

Being picked up by Czech police would be no better than having Hawkins' men catch him. Sooner or later the Agency would get to him, either through an extradition order or a simple snatch-and-grab operation.

Keep moving, he told himself. Don't stop until there's no more breath in your lungs.

Pushing himself off the wall, Drake dashed along the street, spotting a service alley running between two big apartment blocks off to his left.

Stumbling down the alleyway, dodging trash cans and bags of discarded refuse, he could see a road, then open ground and trees at the far end. A park, perhaps, or a playing field.

Encouraged by the hope of escape, he pressed on, digging deep into whatever reserves of energy he had left.

A screech of tyres announced the sudden arrival of a van or truck of some kind, practically blocking the entrance to the alleyway.

Drake skidded to a halt and raised his weapon, ready to open fire on anyone who tried to force their way in.

But no such thing happened. As the van's side door slid open, revealing a pair of shockingly familiar figures in the cargo area, Drake let out a gasp of horror.

'Drop the gun, Ryan,' Hawkins said, pressing his automatic against the side of Frost's head. The young woman, bound and gagged, was held in front of him as a human shield. 'Drop it now or things are about to get real messy.'

All hope of escape evaporated. Drake knew Hawkins would have left nothing to chance. He'd engineered this entire thing, and he was ready. He knew Drake would rather die than surrender, so he'd brought with him the only thing that would hold him back.

Drake considered opening fire on his enemy anyway, even if it meant sacrificing Frost's life. The two of them were almost certainly going to die after tonight's events, and perhaps he could spare her whatever agony Hawkins had in mind.

He saw the look of hope and expectation in her eyes as his grip tightened on the weapon. She understood what he was thinking, what it meant for her, and she wanted him to do it.

But as he stared at Hawkins down the sights, he knew he couldn't pull the trigger. In his condition, with shaking hands and failing vision, his chances of scoring a hit were fanciful at best, and his adversary was almost certainly wearing body armour. Frost was not.

'Don't make me ask twice, Ryan. Drop the gun.'

He couldn't do it. He couldn't kill her.

Tossing aside the weapon, Drake placed his hands behind his head as the three operatives from back at the hotel approached with weapons trained on him. He felt the cold steel of handcuffs being snapped around his wrists.

'I knew we'd see eye to eye.'

Drake looked up as the imposing form of Hawkins loomed over him, still wearing that malicious smile.

'You didn't think I'd kill you after all this, did you Ryan?' he asked. 'Today's your lucky day. We have other plans for you.'

A curt nod, and two operatives seized him by the arms, dragging him towards the waiting van. Drake was powerless to resist as he was hauled into the cargo compartment and the door rolled closed, slamming shut with a thunderous bang.

–

With an exhausted cry, Anya threw one last punch at the bag before falling to her knees. Her hands were shaking, and when she looked down she noticed bloodstains on the thin wrappings.

She wiped the perspiration from her eyes, knowing but not quite acknowledging that they were wet for a different reason.

At least now she had some measure of clarity. She knew what she had to do.

Clutching the bag for support, she pulled herself slowly to her feet and glanced up the stairs leading to the main floor of the house.

Chapter 39

Anya felt better when she emerged into the cool darkness outside. She'd needed to release some of her pent-up tension.

She inhaled, tasting the scent of grass and wild flowers and the sharp tang of pine needles from the woodland nearby. There was almost no noise apart from the gentle sway of the trees and the distant drone of a car skirting the lake below.

As she'd expected, Alex was sitting on the open ground by the side of the road, the bottle of vodka resting beside him as he stared out across the darkened mountains.

Anya approached and, without saying anything, sat down next to him. He didn't even acknowledge her presence.

For a time she said and did nothing, just sat there with him, watching as a thin ribbon of cloud drifted across the moon.

'When I was a child, there was a hill like this near my home,' she said. 'I would run there sometimes when I was angry, or frightened, or I just wanted to be alone. There was something about the movement of the grass stalks in the breeze that always seemed to calm me. I felt like I could picture the anger or the fear or anything else I didn't want being… carried off by that breeze, leaving just me. Of course, I usually didn't take a bottle of vodka with me,' she added with a rueful smile, hoping to add a little levity.

He wasn't biting, but neither had he asked her to leave.

'I was wrong to blame you earlier, Alex,' she said, deciding to cut to the heart of the matter. 'What happened with Lauren… it was not your fault. I asked you to be something you're not.' She sighed. 'You were right when you said you were nothing like me. You are a trusting man who sees the good in people. I can't imagine what that must be like.'

She saw him reach for the bottle, but not drink from it. He was waiting to hear what else she had to say.

'If you wanted to leave now, I wouldn't blame you,' Anya went on, speaking frankly. 'You have done your part. More than we agreed, in fact. If you decide to go, I can get you to the nearest train station, give you money and supplies. You can leave this behind, never see me again.' She allowed that thought to hang. 'If that's what you want.'

He turned to look at her, studying her as if she were some puzzle whose solution eluded him.

'What do *you* want?' he asked.

She shook her head. 'The choice is yours. I can't make it for you.'

'I don't mean about me,' Alex explained. 'I mean *you*. If this plan of yours somehow works and you get your friends back – and fuck me, it's looking like a long shot – what then? What do you actually want from all this, Anya?'

She leaned back a little on her grassy perch, her knees drawn up to her chest as she considered his words. She could have humoured him, could have told him what she thought he wanted to hear, but Anya had no interest in spinning lies. Now least of all.

'Answers,' was her reply. 'I did my best, gave everything I had to give. I want to know why that wasn't enough.'

She heard the glug of liquid in the vodka bottle, glanced over and saw him taking a swig. He grimaced as the alcohol went down, but looked at her with growing resolve.

'Then I'm still in,' Alex said, holding the bottle out to her. He shrugged. 'What the hell, right? A friend in need, and all that.'

Anya smiled as she accepted the bottle, surprised by how relieved she felt. For once it felt good not to be alone.

'I did not say we were friends, though,' she remarked, taking a sip.

Alex decided not to pursue that argument. It was enough to be there, to have put their disagreement aside. They stared out across the lake, each privately contemplating what lay ahead.

Chapter 40

Peshawar, Pakistan – 29 September 1988

Cain practically pounced on the phone the moment it started ringing.

'Don't speak to me unless you've got good news, Sully,' he began. Several days without sleep were taking their toll on both his concentration and his patience.

'I've got news, but I don't think you'll like it,' Tom Sullivan, one of his oldest comrades from Langley confirmed, though his tone was distinctly guarded. 'My guy at the National Reconnaissance Office came through.'

Since Cain's meeting with the remains of Task Force Black two days earlier, he had put out as many feelers as possible within the Agency, trying to pull together any intel that would help him understand what had happened during the ambush. And more importantly, what had come after.

The official line from Carpenter and Simmons was that the attempted ambush and the desperate battle that followed had ended when the task force slipped the Russian net, but Cain sensed otherwise. There was no way crack Soviet units like that would allow such a group to escape when they could easily have followed up their ground attack with air or artillery strikes.

No, something else had been at work, and Cain was determined to find out what. It seemed now that his covert snooping had yielded some results.

'He was able to backtrack footage from one of their KH-11s as it passed over the ambush site,' Sullivan went on. 'They missed the firefight itself, just like you were briefed, but as it happened they'd made an inclination adjustment to that bird a few days earlier. Because of that, they managed to capture Soviet troop movements in the hours afterwards.'

The KH-11 was one of most advanced satellites in the NRO's arsenal, orbiting a couple of hundred miles overhead. Their state-of-the-art imaging systems were able to take readings in infrared, display events in real time, and resolve details just a couple of inches across. Not enough to recognize human faces – yet – but about as close to it as technology would allow.

'And?' Cain prompted impatiently.

Sullivan was quiet.

'Jesus Christ, are you going to make me fly back to Langley and beat the answers out of you, or are you going to spit it out?'

Sullivan sighed. 'Fine, but it's your ass. The angle of inclination wasn't great, but it looks like the Soviet troop convoy diverted to Tajbeg Palace on the outskirts of Kabul before the rest of the ground forces returned to their dispersal areas.'

Cain's knew it well. That building had housed first the Afghan royal family, and latterly the country's president, before the Soviet invasion. These days it served a more militaristic function.

'That's the 40th Army's headquarters.'

'Like I said, I knew you wouldn't like it.'

On the contrary, Cain was elated. Anya was alive, and now he knew where she was being held. Regardless of how well defended the place might be, he would find a way in.

'Can you fax through a satellite overhead of the compound?'

'I guess so, but—'

'Great, you've got my number here. I need it as soon as you can.'

'Marcus, whatever you're thinking, you need to let this go,' Sullivan warned, clearly nervous. 'There's no way into a place like that, and there sure as hell isn't a way out.'

There would be. Cain would make sure of it.

'Just get that fax through. I'll be in touch, Sully.'

'Marcus, don't—'

Cain cut him off by jamming his hand down on the hook, then immediately dialling another number without bothering to replace the receiver. As he'd expected, it was answered straightaway. The recipient was just as eager for news as he'd been.

And for once, Cain had good news for them.

'Romek, call the group together,' he instructed, his voice tinged with excitement. 'I want a meeting within the hour, and make sure everyone's there. We've got a location.'

-

Andrews Air Force Base, Maryland

'Tell me you have Drake back in custody,' Cain said as he walked across the vast hangar towards the Gulfstream V jet that was waiting for him, flanked by a pair of armed agents.

He'd arranged this flight under conditions of extreme secrecy, making sure no details of it were officially logged and that its passenger's identity wasn't recorded. Andrews AFB was no stranger to hosting clandestine international flights. Even the Agency was largely unaware of his hastily organized trip to Europe, and with luck he'd be able to keep it that way until this situation was resolved.

'We've got him,' Hawkins confirmed. 'He put up a fight, but he's secure.'

Cain would have expected nothing less. 'Injuries?'

'A couple of our guys are—'

'I'm talking about Drake,' Cain interrupted. Casualties amongst the field team were Hawkins' domain. 'He's no good to us if he doesn't survive until the exchange.'

'He'll be alive,' Hawkins promised him. 'Can't say he'll look pretty, though.'

'Good enough. Did you get anything useful out of him?'

There was a pause, which told its own story. 'He blew our undercover agent.'

'Then your plan was a waste of time and resources, wasn't it, Jason?' Cain remarked as he ascended the stairs to the aircraft's hatch. 'Remind me again why I keep you around?'

'I captured Drake and his whole team for you in Pakistan.'

'But you didn't get Anya, which is the only thing that actually matters. The rest of them are no threat without her. And you lost half our field team in the process,' Cain snapped.

Individual casualties concerned him little, but collectively they became a problem that required more and more resources to contain. Hawkins undoubtedly had his uses, but he was overzealous and trigger happy. He was a sledgehammer in situations that called for a scalpel.

'You know your problem? You're messy, Jason. You don't clean up after yourself, and you leave too many loose ends untied. People like that don't stay in my good graces too long.'

Hawkins was hot-headed, but wise enough not to argue that particular point.

'Lucky for you I'm coming to handle this myself. You get a pass, for now,' Cain allowed, handing his overcoat to a crew member and ducking into the cabin.

'I'm ready, pilot. Take off now,' he called through to the cockpit as soon as he was in his seat.

'Yes, sir.'

The pilots were already going through their final pre-flight checks. Cain turned his attention back to Hawkins.

'My flight lands in Ramstein in eight hours. Be there to meet us, and have Drake and Frost prepped for transport.' As the engines began to spin up, Cain added, 'And mobilize every field asset you have. I want them all standing by.'

'I'm on it.'

'Oh, and Jason?' Cain added. 'Don't disappoint me again.'

Chapter 41

Lauren stared at the young boy who had apparently been sent to watch over her. He was as much of an enigma to her as everything else about this situation. No more than 12, he seemed to approach his duty with the nonchalant confidence of one who had been presiding over kidnappings his whole life, reclining in a chair with his long skinny legs stretched out before him, feet resting on the open drawer of a simple wooden dresser nearby. Making a show of it, demonstrating that he was in control and had nothing to fear from her.

Despite his laconic attitude, his attention remained focussed on her the whole time, a mixture of diligent alertness and mild curiosity, as if she were some unusual trinket. She sensed no hostility, but didn't doubt he would raise the alarm the moment he sensed trouble.

The silence was broken when the door opened and Anya entered, looking as if she'd just completed some strenuous physical task.

She spoke a few quiet words in a language Lauren didn't recognize, but presumably she was relieving the boy of guard duty, because he stretched and made to leave. Anya waited until he'd left the room before taking a step towards Lauren.

'I'm going to remove your gag now,' she said, reaching for the strip of duct tape. 'You can scream if you want, but I'd rather you didn't.'

Lauren braced herself, managing not to show discomfort as the tape was removed.

'How do you feel?' Anya asked. 'Are you hurt?'

'What do you care?'

'I don't. But my agreement with your father was to return you unharmed.'

'Well, we wouldn't want to disappoint him, would we?' Lauren said. 'Is Alex okay?'

Despite the fact he'd been complicit – albeit reluctantly – in her kidnapping, she did still feel a twinge of guilt for injuring him. It wasn't in her nature to wish harm on others.

Anya tilted her head slightly, curious. 'What do *you* care?' she asked, mirroring Lauren's earlier remark.

Lauren held her nerve. 'I stabbed a sharpened spoon through a man's arm. I'd like to know if he's seriously injured.'

'He won't die because of what you did, Lauren, but he has proven himself a poor guard. Luckily there was someone better prepared to back him up.'

'Yeah, interesting company you keep. Arming kids with tasers. What's next? Putting bombs in baby carriages?'

Of all the things to have derailed her escape attempt, the last thing Lauren would have expected was a kid with a stun gun. She still bristled at having come so close.

'We each use the tools at hand,' Anya said tersely.

Lauren was quick to seize on her choice of words. 'So that's what people are to you? Tools to be used?'

'I'm fighting a war, Lauren. I don't have the luxury of your moral judgements.'

'So you'd prefer to turn kids into soldiers?'

'I would prefer not to have to fight at all.'

Lauren tilted her head in mockery of Anya's gesture. 'Spoken like a true tyrant, pleading a love of peace while waging war. People like you have used that excuse for thousands of years.'

'People like me,' Anya repeated. 'Tell me, what do you really know about me?'

'I know enough,' Lauren contended. 'I know how much it hurt my dad when you betrayed him. And I know you're holding me against my will so you can hurt him again.'

Anya didn't respond to that one. Instead she reached behind her back.

Lauren heard the rasp of metal on metal. Anya slowly held a blade out towards her, so that she could see the keen edge gleaming in the stark electric lighting. She knelt beside Lauren's right foot and went to work with the knife.

Lauren felt tension and resistance around her ankle, and suddenly the cable tie fell away, quickly followed by the other. Anya repeated the process on her wrists, then backed away, giving her some room.

Lauren sprang to her feet, eager to escape the confines of the chair.

'What the hell are you doing?' she asked, watching in puzzlement as Anya gently laid the knife on the floor a few feet away, then eased herself into the chair that had been occupied by the boy earlier.

'You are no longer a prisoner,' Anya informed her.

Lauren stared at her. 'What?'

'I said, you are not a prisoner,' the woman repeated, speaking with deliberate patience. 'If you wish to leave, you can.' She paused, eyes flicking to the knife. 'All you have to do to win your freedom is kill me.'

Lauren's mouth gaped. She couldn't believe Anya was even remotely serious. And yet, one look at the woman was enough to persuade her otherwise.

'Go ahead, pick it up,' Anya prompted. 'I won't try to stop you.'

'Why are you doing this?'

Anya's eyes hardened. 'Pick up the knife, Lauren.'

Lauren couldn't believe what was happening. She took a small, hesitant step forward, waiting for a reaction, waiting for Anya to spring at her and snatch up the blade. But she just sat there, watching and waiting.

Another step, and another. Lauren felt her foot brush against the knife. Watching Anya with wide, fearful eyes, she inched slowly down, stretching out her hand, reaching, searching. She felt soft carpet beneath her fingertips, moved her hand left a little, then touched the solid haft.

Anya still had made no attempt to stop her. She was daring Lauren to do it.

Snatching up the blade, Lauren jumped to her feet, brandishing the weapon.

Only then did Anya rise from the chair. Her eyes were not on the blade, but rather on the young woman holding it.

'Stay back, I'm warning you!' Lauren said, holding the knife out in front of her.

'You don't need to warn me,' Anya replied, calmly. 'You had the courage to pick up that knife. Now let's see if you have the courage to use it.'

'You're sick! You're playing some twisted game.'

Anya shook her head. 'You wanted to know who I am, Lauren. This is who I am.' She spread her arms wide, as if inviting the blade now clutched in the young woman's hands. 'It's time to find out who you are. Will you use it on me? Will you kill me to save your own life?'

Lauren's throat was tightening, making it hard to breathe. Her hands were shaking as she raised the knife, pointing it clumsily at Anya's chest. The woman took a step forward so that the blade was almost touching her.

'You can do it,' Anya coaxed. 'Believe me, you can do almost anything when your own life is at stake. The only thing holding you back now is fear. But what are you really afraid of, Lauren Cain? That I'm lying to you, and I will kill you if you try to use that knife? Or that I'm telling the truth, and you really will kill me?'

Lauren tried to rally her body as she prepared to strike. She didn't even know what to do, where to aim, which was the proper way to hold the blade.

Guessing her thoughts, Anya helped her out. 'The best place for an amateur to strike is the stomach. It is vulnerable, unprotected, and if you angle the blade upwards there is a good chance you will penetrate the lungs or the heart. Either one will be fatal.'

She had to do it. She wouldn't end up as a helpless hostage, her fate to be decided by others. She couldn't let this woman get away with it. She had to act, had to strike now!

'This is your last chance, Lauren,' Anya said impatiently. 'What are you waiting for? If you won't fight even to save your own life, what right do you have to live? Do it, you coward!'

The blade fell from Lauren's hands as she let out a strangled, choking sob. She took an unsteady step back, felt herself bump up against the wall and slowly slid down it until she was on her knees, tears flowing down her cheeks.

Anya let out a breath – relief or disappointment, she couldn't say – and glanced away.

'Not so easy, is it? Taking a life,' she said, retreating to the chair. She was quiet, her expression pensive.

'I will tell you a secret, Lauren,' she said at last. 'The same thing happened to me, the first time. He was a Russian sentry, stationed in some outpost in Afghanistan, long before you were even born. I got close to him, so close I could smell him, see the hairs on his jaw where he hadn't shaved. I had my knife. I knew what I was supposed to do, what I had been trained to do, but something stopped me. It was as if my body refused to obey me. I couldn't take another man's life.'

She raised a sad, wistful smile.

'That hesitation almost got me killed, along with the rest of my team. But then a man named Romek stepped in and did what I could not. He protected me, you see? Not from the Russians, but from our own men, because he knew what they would do to me if the truth came out. He told no one what had really happened, said I did my duty perfectly, made sure they all believed it. I felt sick to my stomach. I didn't sleep that night. I lay awake replaying what happened, over and over. I had never felt so powerless and frightened in all my adult life. I hated myself for being so weak. So I made a decision never to feel that way again, never to hesitate, never to be weak.'

'You're saying that's what I am? Weak? Powerless?'

'I had to know what kind of person you were,' Anya answered. 'And you showed me.'

'No, I showed you what kind of person I'm not.' Lauren said. 'I'm not a killer like you. And I'm not ashamed of that.'

Anya shrugged, unwilling to engage in such an argument.

'You said you had an agreement with my father,' Lauren said, changing tack. 'What are you going to do?'

'I'm going to give you back to him, alive and unharmed as agreed. In return, he is going to give me three people he is holding hostage, hopefully in the same condition. Then we part ways.'

Lauren blinked, surprised by the matter-of-fact answer. 'Just like that?'

'Not quite,' Anya conceded unhappily. 'Your father has been hunting me a long time. He won't let a chance like this pass him by.'

Lauren shook her head, still not understanding the deep-seated enmity between them. 'Why?' she asked, her voice hushed. 'What could you have done that's so bad he'd want you dead?'

For a second, she thought Anya was going to tell her. She could see it
– the tension, as if she were a dam straining to hold back a great flood of
water on the verge of breaking through.

'We'll be leaving early tomorrow, and we have a long day ahead of us,'
she said. 'I suggest you get some rest tonight. The room is yours. I will not
keep you restrained unless you give me reason to. The windows are sealed
and there is no way out except through the door, which will be locked and
guarded at all times. I am showing faith in you, Lauren. Do not make me
regret it.'

Anya retrieved the knife from where Lauren had dropped it, and turned
away towards the door.

She was about to reach for the handle when suddenly she stopped. 'You
were right, by the way', she said over her shoulder. 'You should be proud.'

The young woman frowned. 'Of what?'

'I told you I wanted to see what kind of person you were, and I did,'
Anya explained, turning to face her again. 'I see a young woman who is
strong and intelligent, and resourceful enough to escape an armed guard
with no weapons. But I also see someone who is good-natured, kind and
compassionate. Someone who would rather sacrifice her own life than take
another.' She looked almost regretful. 'Those are things you should be proud
of. Hold on to them, because they are very easy to lose.'

She was just reaching for the door handle when Lauren spoke up.

'Would you have let me do it?' she asked, sniffing and wiping her forearm
across her eyes. 'If I had used that knife. Would you really have stopped me?'

Anya looked at her. 'Do you really want to know?'

Chapter 42

Drake grunted as a sharp shove sent him stumbling forward into the room. With his hands tied behind his back, the last thing he needed was to fall face-first onto a concrete floor.

The door slammed shut behind him. The room was wide and low-ceilinged, with various pipes and ducts snaking across the ceiling – almost certainly a basement or maintenance room of some kind. A temporary holding location before he was moved somewhere else, but where? And when?

The van ride here had lasted just over an hour; he'd counted out the minutes as he lay on the jolting, bumping floor, bound and hooded. That meant he was still in the Czech Republic, but the question was what Cain planned to do with him next.

'Ryan,' a voice exclaimed.

Turning suddenly, Drake was just in time to see a short, dark-haired woman emerge from the shadowy corner of the room and rush at him, her expression one of mingled relief, joy and sadness.

'Keira,' Drake managed to say as Frost threw her arms around him. He could feel her body shaking, heard the sound of muffled sobs as she pressed her face into his shoulder.

'Let me look at you,' he said when she seemed to have regained her composure. 'Let me see.'

Frost pulled away. Her face was bruised and cut down one side, her hair greasy and matted. Her clothes were ripped and covered in stains. It made his heart ache to see her like this.

He could barely bring himself to ask the next question, but he had to know. 'Keira, listen to me. Did they... do anything?'

Frost shook her head. 'It's okay, don't worry about it. Fucking pussies haven't come near me since you broke out.' She flashed the almost feral smile he'd come to know so well, but it was weaker now, strained. It was obvious she'd suffered a lot over the past few days. 'Must be losing my sex appeal.'

He managed to force a grin, which soon faded when he remembered the injury Hawkins had inflicted on her at the church.

'Your hand...'

Like Drake, her arms had been cuffed behind her back, but she'd managed to slip her hands beneath her feet to at least give her some use

214

of them. She held them up. Her right hand was still covered by grubby bandages, with spots of blood showing through the dressing.

'Won't be writing any books for a while, but I'm still in the fight.'

As if to prove it, she flexed her fingers. She managed to curl them into a loose fist, though it was painfully obvious how much effort it required.

'That's good,' Drake said, feigning relief.

'What happened to you?' she asked, eager for news. 'After we were separated...'

Drake related his escape from the church and subsequent flight to Prague, where everything had unravelled and he was recaptured.

'It was a set-up,' he finished bitterly. 'Hawkins faked the whole thing, even sacrificed his own men so I'd lead them to Anya.'

'And did you?'

He shook his head. 'There's some bad karma heading their way, I think,' he said, giving her a meaningful look. 'Around my neck. I brought you a little gift.'

As she lifted the lucky charm necklace Drake was wearing into view, Frost's grin returned, stronger and more heartfelt. 'No wonder the bastards are so pissed at you.'

Drake, however, was in no mood for smiling. This was the first chance he'd had to talk with her properly since the disastrous mission in Pakistan, and there were many things he wanted to say.

'Listen Keira, I'm sorry,' he began. 'What happened in Pakistan... I should have seen it coming. Cole's dead because of me.'

'Don't, Ryan,' she said, shaking her head forcefully. 'Don't go there, you hear me? You did your best; we all did. The only one responsible for what happened is Cain, and we're going to make that bastard pay for it.'

He knew she was saying it as much for herself as for him. She needed something to hold on to, to focus her grief on. It was easier to feel anger and hatred than grief and despair.

The moment was disturbed by the solid clunk of a steel bolt, and both Drake and Frost turned just as the door swung open to reveal a tall, heavily built man in silhouette.

'Well, isn't this a beautiful moment?' Hawkins said as he stepped across the threshold, accompanied by two armed guards who immediately trained their weapons on the two prisoners. 'You know, I could have held you in separate cells, but what's the point when it's such fun bringing people together?'

'Fuck you,' Frost said.

'Careful there, little firecracker. That mouth's already gotten you in trouble. Or do you need a *hand* remembering?'

Frost's eyes shone with fury, and Drake could sense her tensing up to attack him.

He moved in front of her. 'Save it,' he whispered. '*Save it.*'

Hawkins smiled. 'Got to admit, I underestimated you, Ryan,' he said, slowly circling Drake, forcing him to match his movements. 'I figured you'd make your move at the church, but I didn't know you'd get so... creative. Almost reminds me of the good old days. I especially liked the message you left for me.' He looked Drake up and down. 'Tell me, how do you feel about it now?'

'Take these cuffs off and maybe you'll find out,' Drake hit back.

'Believe me, I'd love nothing better than to party with you, Ryan. But wouldn't you know it, work's getting in the way. I've been asked to deliver you in one piece, and the boss is really riding me on this one.'

'Where are you taking us?' Drake asked, struck by Hawkins' choice of words.

Ignoring Drake, Hawkins carried on. 'There's just one thing I've got to know,' he added, resuming his pacing. 'When did you figure out Lenka was one of ours?'

'That little whore? Why do you care?' Drake taunted him. 'She's just another piece of shit you threw at a wall, hoping she'd stick.'

'That's no way to talk about a lady,' a voice said from over by the doorway.

Drake spun round see Lenka walk into the room, apparently recovered from the beating she'd taken at his hands earlier. She had changed clothes, now donning a black leather jacket and turtleneck sweater. Quite conservative compared to her previous attire.

The only evidence of their fight was some bruising around her jawline that was partially hidden by make-up, and a couple of cuts near her right temple, held together with surgical tape stitches.

'Show me one, and I'll rethink,' Drake said as she sauntered over.

She had the same maliciously gleeful look as Hawkins, of someone about to take great pleasure in what they did.

Drake felt nothing but contempt for her. 'Tell me, how does it feel having just one job, and fucking it up?'

Her right hand struck out at his unprotected midsection, and Drake immediately doubled over. He felt like he'd been hit with a hammer, the blow far stronger than she should have been capable of. Only when she turned her hand did he see the brass knuckles gleaming in the light.

'Damn, that felt even better than I expected,' she mused. 'Anything else to say, Drake?'

Drake tried not to show how badly he was hurting as he began to straighten up. 'Yeah, you hit like a girl. Do you even work out?'

Rather than being angry, she seemed excited. She wanted him to taunt her, to resist. Wanted an excuse to hurt him more.

She came in again, drawing back her leg and planting a vicious kick right in his stomach. This time there was no stopping it. Drake went down, coughing and struggling to draw breath.

Frost launched herself at Lenka, trying to knock her down, to claw at her face and eyes. She almost made it, before a brass knuckle stopped her in her tracks, and a sharp elbow to the head sent her staggering sideways. A final kick to the side dropped the former Shepherd operative as well.

Frost lay curled in a ball, bleeding and hurting, her burst of energy spent. Drake knew there was nothing he could do to help.

'I'd be careful, buddy,' Hawkins said almost sympathetically, having watched the violent display with satisfied approval. 'Riley here is one of my best operatives, and she has the worst temper. Even I wouldn't want to piss her off.'

Riley flashed a malevolent smile at her mentor, as she carefully removed her leather jacket and handed it to one of the guards. Giving herself more freedom of movement.

'Jason taught me everything I know,' she said, loosening up a little, as if the vicious beat-down of Frost had been nothing but a warm-up.

She turned her attention back to Drake, closing in on him as he struggled to get up. 'Especially how to do this.'

Another strike to Drake's back engulfed him in agony, like the metal implement had crushed his spine. He squeezed his eyes shut and clenched his teeth, trying to block it out, trying not to make a sound.

'It hurts, doesn't it?' she said, hunkering down beside him, relishing the torment that was etched into his features. 'A little harder, and I'll shatter a vertebrae. The bones will fragment into your spinal column, severing the nerve endings. You'll never walk, never run, never fuck again.' She smiled, before adding, 'Oh, and you'll probably shit yourself right here on the floor.'

Drake didn't respond, but Riley no longer cared. She'd spotted the lucky charm dangling around his neck.

'Well, look what we've got here,' she said, carefully removing it rather than snapping the leather necklace. With his hands bound, Drake was in no position to stop her.

Riley examined the objects hanging from it before glancing at Frost. 'This belonged to your little bitch here, right? But you know what? I think it'll look better on me,' she decided, slipping it over her neck and making sure he could see it. 'Now every time you look at me, you can think of her.'

Drake managed to push himself slowly and painfully up from the floor.

'You want me to stop?' Riley asked. 'I can. All you've got to say is please. You've got to beg me, Drake.'

Now on his knees, Drake opened his mouth to respond, but all he could manage was a strangled whisper, his voice stolen away.

'What's the matter?' Riley leaned closer, eager to hear his plea for mercy. 'Cat got your tongue?'

That was when Drake finally gave her an answer, but not the one she'd been waiting for. Throwing his head violently forward he felt it make contact, and saw her stumble backwards, clutching at her face. The two guards raised their weapons, ready to pull the triggers if he made another move.

But there was no need. Drake had done what he wanted to do.

'That clear enough for you?' he asked, his voice now strong and even, as if the repeated hits she'd laid on him had done nothing.

Riley rounded on him, blood seeping from a newly opened cut at the corner of her mouth. He saw her flare up inside as she advanced on him, saw her raise the brass knuckles to strike him again. There would be no restraint this time. She was out to break bones and deal the kind of damage you didn't recover from.

'Hold up,' Hawkins said, subtly placing himself between them. 'I think Ryan's done. Don't wear him out too soon.'

Riley looked up.

'He's not done until I say he's done,' the young operative said. 'I owe him.'

'And once we've finished our business, you can have your fun with him,' Hawkins said. He had moved a step closer, towering over her — a menacing and indomitable presence.

Cupping her chin, Hawkins gently examined the injury. 'Until then, we stick to the plan.'

Drake could see Riley was bent on revenge. But she also knew who really called the shots around here, and that Hawkins was not a man to tolerate insubordination — even from the most favoured of his students.

Riley touched the necklace, as if to emphasize to Drake that she could take what she wanted from him.

'I'll be seeing you real soon,' she promised, snatching her coat from the operative holding it for her.

'I'll be looking forward to it,' Drake called.

Hawkins watched her leave. 'You'll have to forgive my associate,' he said with mock regret. 'I don't know what it is, but you just don't seem to mix well with her.'

Drake looked over at Frost, who was only now starting to recover from the beatdown she'd suffered, then up at Hawkins. 'You can't kill us, can you?' he said, realizing that his captor's uncharacteristic restraint was down to more than a new-found sense of compassion. 'You've been ordered to keep us alive. That means Cain needs us.'

Drake knew then that he was on the right track, and he could already guess where it was leading.

'He's planning a trade, isn't he?'

The only person who could hold that kind of leverage was Anya. Drake had no idea what she was using to bring about this prisoner exchange, but it meant one thing — it meant Anya was still alive.

It looked like he'd gotten beneath his tormentor's armour and exposed a vulnerability.

'Oh, Ryan,' Hawkins said, shaking his head as his poise returned. 'You don't get it, do you? We only need you alive long enough to make the exchange happen. After that… well, I did make Riley a promise. And I'm a man of my word.'

He gestured for the guards to leave, following behind them at an unhurried pace, knowing that neither prisoner was a threat.

'Make yourselves comfortable tonight,' he advised. 'We've got a long day ahead of us tomorrow, and I want you guys fighting fit.'

–

Minsk, Belarus

Jonas Dietrich picked up the vodka bottle and turned it over to look at the label. Crystal Head – an expensive skull-shaped novelty from the United States that was starting to appear in Europe.

'I hope you don't mind me helping myself,' Dietrich said as he poured a measure into a shot glass, careful not to spill any on the mahogany sideboard. 'But I always wanted to try this stuff. Apparently they use no glycerol in the distilling process – gives it a cleaner taste. Sounds like bullshit to me, but there's only one way to find out.'

He raised the glass to his nose, then tipped it down his throat.

'Not bad. I must admit, you have good taste, my friend,' he decided, setting the glass down carefully. 'Now, where were we?'

There were three other men in the room, only one of whom was still alive. Konstantin Petrov was kneeling on the polished floorboards, his hands bound, trembling with fear. A man who had spent much of his life profiting from other people's misery, turning kids into drug dealers, young men into gangsters and women into prostitutes. A man who took great pleasure in throwing his weight around, and for whom no vice was unpalatable if it meant a healthy income.

Always with the protection of his enforcers, of course.

Not that they had served him well today, their blood and brain matter slowly pooling on the floor. Petrov must have had it waxed recently, Dietrich noted, because the gore wasn't soaking in like it usually did.

'Ah yes,' Dietrich went on, speaking in Russian. 'You were going to tell me everything you know about Bruno Muller, the young student you kidnapped in Estonia. His parents would very much like him back, and luckily they came to the right man.'

He saw a flicker of recognition, even as Petrov tried to hide it. 'Fuck you, German pig,' he spat, mustering some of his former bravado. 'My brother will make you eat your own balls when he finds out. You should leave now while you still can.'

Dietrich lifted his silenced USP .45 automatic from the sideboard, took aim and fired. Petrov's left leg exploded just below the knee.

Waiting until the man's screams had died down, Dietrich took aim at his other leg. 'Does this jog your memory, my friend?'

'I will bleed to death,' Petrov stammered. 'Then you will never know.'

'Yes, but it will take some time,' Dietrich acknowledged. 'And I can make this last all day.'

The man let out a choking sob and dropped his head. 'Tajoznaja,' he whispered. 'Number 57, apartment 12.'

Dietrich was about to reply, but was interrupted by the vibration of his cell phone. 'Hold that thought,' he said, holstering his weapon.

It was a US number.

'Yes?'

'Dietrich, it's Franklin.'

Dietrich's mindset changed. Dan Franklin was head of the CIA's Special Activities Division, and Dietrich's former boss. Back when he'd still been a Shepherd team leader, before Cain had shut the programme down, disbanding its members. Before Dietrich had been forced to take up a new profession chasing Russian gangsters and settling petty disputes.

'What do you want, Dan?' he asked, glancing at Petrov. 'I'm a little busy here.'

'Listen very carefully.'

It took Franklin less than 60 seconds to summarize what had happened, and what he needed from Dietrich.

'I need your help,' he finished. 'We won't get another shot at this. How soon can you be there?'

Dietrich hesitated, reaching instead for the vodka and pouring himself another glass. Franklin was asking him to return to a world that had almost killed him, to risk everything against a man with almost unlimited resources and not an ounce of mercy.

Bad odds by anyone's standards.

'I can't do it alone,' he said. 'I'd need help.'

'I have someone in mind.'

Of course you do, Dietrich thought. Franklin, always the man with an ace up his sleeve. He downed the second shot.

'I need an answer, Jonas,' Franklin pressed him.

'Give me a couple of hours to get organized,' Dietrich finally said as the vodka settled. 'I'll call you when I'm ready.'

Shutting down the phone, he turned towards Petrov.

'Thanks for your help, Konstantin,' he said, drawing the gun. It kicked back against his wrist, but this time there was no cry as the round hit home. Petrov let out a low grunt, and slumped backwards.

A couple of hours, Dietrich mused as he left the room. Enough time to reach the apartment where they were holding Bruno, and fulfil his contract before leaving Minsk.

Chapter 43

Grass stretched in front of her, the long stalks reaching past her waist, like an undulating sea as the breeze sighed across. Thin ribbons of cloud spanned the vast blue sky.

She crept forward, driven by curiosity and the childish desire to explore. Near the crest of the gentle hill lay a stand of trees, and she made towards it.

'Lauren!' a distant voice called out. Her father's voice. 'Don't stray too far!'

Lauren paid little attention as she moved beneath the shade of the leafy canopy. It was a warm day, and she was grateful to escape the hot sun.

She surveyed her little woodland haven, taking in the gnarled tree trunks, the tangled bushes and swaying branches. Then she spotted something on the ground ahead. Something that compelled the young girl to move closer.

A perfectly round hole in the ground, partially covered by old wooden planking, weeds and fallen leaves. Wanting to see how deep the well was, Lauren leaned over the edge.

The crack of rotten wood giving way was followed by a cry of fright as she pitched into the darkness.

Lauren sat bolt upright as Anya shouted. 'Get up.'

'What is it?' Lauren asked.

'Breakfast,' Anya replied. 'You have 60 seconds before I lock the door.'

Lauren couldn't recall falling asleep. She remembered exploring every nook and cranny of the room, looking for anything that might prove useful, some hidden object that could aid her escape. Lauren's only exposure to escape techniques had been the occasional kidnap movie and the fantastical adventure novels she'd read as an adolescent. Neither had served her well so far.

In any case, Anya's warning last night carried some weight. Even if she'd somehow broken out of her room, she didn't doubt that further measures would be waiting to thwart her. And if she somehow overcame them, she didn't rate her chances of evading a trained killer in unfamiliar woodland miles from civilization.

So she had finally given up, lying down on the bed and staring up at the ceiling as she brooded over everything. She'd thought about her enigmatic kidnapper, and the small, ragtag group that seemed to follow her. She'd replayed the frightening confrontation where Anya had given her a knife and dared Lauren to kill her, and the whirl of conflicting emotions that had followed. She'd thought about her friends back in Paris, whether they'd been told anything of what had happened to her. And most of all, she'd thought about her father.

He'd have to know that she was missing by now. What was he thinking? Was he looking for her? Was he frightened, inflamed or shocked by her abduction? She had found her mind drifting back to the words spoken by both Anya and Alex about him. The doubts she'd dismissed so vehemently had slowly crept back in, no matter how hard she'd tried to convince herself it was nothing but lies and false accusations.

She had told herself she wouldn't fall asleep, convinced that it would be impossible anyway. Exhaustion must have won out over fear.

Her stomach cramped, reminding her of how little she'd eaten over the past 24 hours. One bowl of tinned peaches wasn't going to cut it.

She'd slept in her clothes, so there was no need to get dressed. Taking a breath, she swung her legs over the edge of the bed, before cautiously crossing the room. Anya was waiting to escort her to the living room.

'We will be leaving soon,' Anya explained. 'I thought you would want to eat something first. Assuming you can be trusted to behave?'

Lauren ignored the feeling that she was a disobedient school child being lectured by a teacher.

'Yesterday you had me strapped to a chair under armed guard,' she said. 'Why the change of heart?'

'I prefer cooperation to coercion,' Anya said. 'It will make things easier for all of us. But if that is too much to ask of you…'

'Let's get it over with.'

Taking that for acquiescence, Anya gestured for her to go ahead.

Lauren found the other two occupants of the house already seated at the dining table. The boy was in the middle of devouring a slice of toast, while Alex was nursing a coffee. She noticed he now had a bandage wrapped around his forearm.

Lauren sat down, Alex moving his chair just a little further away from hers. She couldn't blame him. After all, there were plenty more spoons on the table.

Her eyes were on the plentiful breakfast options. Whatever else happened today, it made sense to keep her energy up. There was no telling whether she might need it.

Anya joined them at the table. She wasn't staring like the other two, but Lauren nonetheless sensed Anya was observing her in case she tried anything.

For her own part, Lauren was content to shovel heavily buttered toast and jam into her mouth, washing it down with gulps of orange juice. She was both hungry and thirsty, and eager to satisfy both needs as quickly as possible.

Alex seemed to have gotten over his surprise at her arrival, and gone back to his coffee. The boy, however, continued to gawp at her, making no attempt to hide it.

Finally it became too irritating to endure. 'What?' she demanded. 'What is it?'

Far from being embarrassed, he seemed relieved that she'd broached the subject.

'I want to say... apology,' he said. 'For shooting you. I did not want to hurt you.'

Lauren didn't quite know what to say. She wasn't ready to forgive him, but he did at least seem sincere.

'What's your name?' she asked.

His dark brows drew together in a frown, and he looked to Anya for permission, reassurance. She nodded.

'Yasin.'

'Yasin,' she repeated. 'Mind if I ask you a question, Yasin?'

'No.'

She took another bite of toast. 'What on earth are you doing here?'

Though he was young enough to be Anya's son, she didn't sense that kind of relationship between them. They were awkward around each other, as if they barely knew one another.

He seemed puzzled by her question. 'Why do you want to know?'

'Because I'm curious, Yasin. Normally 10-year-old boys aren't involved in kidnappings.'

'I am 12,' he corrected her, as if that made all the difference. 'And I am a man soon, not a boy.'

'My question still stands.'

'I make a deal with Fauji,' he said. Perhaps that was his nickname for her. 'I help her escape from battle in Pakistan.'

'Battle?' Lauren repeated. 'Battle against who?'

'Bad men,' the kid answered. 'She take me with her out of the country. I have saved her life, so now she owes me...' He trailed off, struggling with his English. 'I do not know the right word in your language. We call it *nanawatai*.'

She knew the concept he was trying to describe. It was quite familiar to her.

'Protection,' Lauren said. 'Or maybe asylum. You helped her, and in return that gives you the right to claim protection under her roof.'

The boy looked at her in surprise. 'How do you know this?'

'It's part of the Pashtunwali, right? The Pashtun tribal code. *Nanawatai* is one of the strongest-held beliefs. Even sworn enemies adhere to it.'

The Pashtunwali defined basic principles for how its followers should live their lives: from showing respect and loyalty to avoiding untruths, and in this case, providing food and shelter to those who requested it.

Yasin nodded, apparently warming to the conversation.

'I studied the history of Islamic cultures for a while. Didn't have time to get too deep into it, but I learned the basics,' she explained, then glanced at Anya. 'Never would have had you picked as a Muslim.'

'I am not. Nor am I subject to tribal law,' Anya fired back, though she looked faintly embarrassed by the turn in the conversation. Perhaps the revelation that she'd needed the help of a 12-year-old boy was more than she cared for Lauren to know.

She gave Yasin a meaningful look. 'We made a deal, nothing more.'

That seemed to take the wind out of the boy's sails a little, and he quietened down, returning to his breakfast. For a small, skinny kid, he was able to put away a startling quantity of food, and seemed to content to occupy himself with that for now.

'What about you?' Lauren asked, turning her attention to Alex. 'What's your story?'

'Maybe I don't have one.'

'Everybody has one.'

'Then maybe I'd rather you didn't know mine,' he said, wincing as he lifted his cup of coffee with his injured arm.

'Look, for what it's worth, I apologize for what I did,' she said. 'I was frightened and desperate, and for all I knew you were going to kill me. It was the only thing I could think of at the time.'

That last part was mostly true, even if the apology was far from genuine. Still, screaming and ranting was unlikely to accomplish much, and for all his dented pride, she sensed Alex remained the weak link. If she could win him over, there was still a chance he might help her later.

'Does it hurt?' she asked. 'Your arm?'

'It's fine. Just a scratch.'

'Well, like I say, I'm sorry for what I did, Alex.' She took a sip of her orange juice, trying to decide how to play this. 'I don't imagine any of us are going to come out of this as friends, but I was hoping we could at least be civilized.'

'If we all come out of this alive, that'll do for me,' Alex said

'Finish up, we'll be leaving soon,' Anya said. She rose from her seat and looked down at Lauren. 'If you want to shower and change clothes, now would be the time.'

Lauren nodded. 'Where are we going?'

'To return you to your father,' Anya replied, unwilling to be more specific.

Lauren was sensible enough not to push further on that. In any case, she had bigger concerns at that moment. 'Tell me I'm not going to spend the whole journey locked in the trunk.'

At this, Anya studied the young woman carefully. 'That depends on how you agree to behave. If you promise to cooperate, then as you say, we can be civilized. If I doubt your intentions for even a moment, I will have to be more… assertive with you. So, what will it be?'

Lauren had the unnerving feeling that Anya was somehow looking into her, as if she could see right through any deception to the hidden intent beneath. It would be unwise to lie to her at such a crucial moment.

'I'll cooperate,' she said.

Anya nodded, satisfied she'd made her point.

Chapter 44

Peshawar, Pakistan – 1 October 1988

Cain reached out to every contact he could think of, securing every piece of useful intel he could get his hands on, funnelling it all to Task Force Black. Galvanized by a new sense of purpose, they had immediately rallied behind him and what he'd quickly dubbed Operation Jurate.

He'd arranged air transportation that would get the team close to the border. From there, they would take vehicles from their local Mujahedeen allies and make their way to the objective, ideally being in place to launch the assault just after sunset.

Several rebel commanders who had fought alongside Task Force Black had pledged men in support. They would be standing by to launch a diversionary attack to tie down Soviet forces near the facility, hopefully buying the team enough time to get in, find Anya and get her out. There were no guarantees of success, but a unanimous vote had confirmed they were willing to take the risk to recover one of their own.

His pace of work had been feverish, broken only by brief snatches of sleep before launching himself into action once more. Anya was alive – he wouldn't allow himself to contemplate another possibility – and somehow he was going to get her out. Somehow he would find a way to bring her home.

He was just gulping down the tepid remnants of his cup of coffee, his desk strewn with printed documents and satellite images, when the door opened without warning. Cain looked up, startled by the imposing figure that had entered.

'Richard,' he said, rising to his feet.

'No need to stand on ceremony, Marcus,' Carpenter said, closing the door behind him. 'This won't take long.'

'What are you doing out here?'

Carpenter stopped in front of his desk. 'I could ask you the same question, only I know the answer already. Did you really think you could pull something like this without anyone finding out? Someone always finds out. You should know that better than anyone.'

Cain stood behind his desk, glaring hard.

'I came here out of respect, because this is the kind of conversation I'd rather have off the record. I'm here to talk some sense into you. Now, why don't you do yourself a favour, Marcus, and drop this thing before it gets out of control?'

'She's alive, Richard.'

Carpenter shook his head. 'We both know that's not true.'

'Bullshit.' Reaching for one of the printed images, he snatched it off the desk and held it up for Carpenter to see. 'I've seen the satellite images. This wasn't a search-and-destroy mission – it was a fucking snatch and grab. They captured her alive and took her to a KGB facility for interrogation. She's alive, and you're trying to cover it up!'

'And you want to go charging in like a knight in shining armour, huh?' Carpenter taunted. 'Wake up, Marcus. That's not the world we live in. You want to start a full-scale war over one woman?'

'We're already fighting a war!' Cain shouted back.

'That's where you're wrong. The Mujahedeen are fighting a civil war within the borders of Afghanistan. The US government has no official involvement.'

'Fuck you,' Cain snapped. 'Don't hide behind that shit. You know what we do here, you know what Task Force Black sacrificed for us. They helped change the course of this war. Now one of our own needs our help, and you want to abandon—'

'She's a deniable operator, Marcus. What do you think that means?' Carpenter said, raising his voice. 'Anya knew what she was signing up for, even if you didn't. Task Force Black was expendable; they were always expendable. That's why we created them in the first place.'

'She's not expendable to me.'

Carpenter smiled, both irritated and amused by his obstinacy. However, he had a trump card.

'You can see this any way that you want, but you're not hijacking Agency resources and endangering US foreign policy over one operative. I came here to tell you that face to face, out of respect for the work you've done.'

'What are you going to do? Fire me?'

The older man's smile had vanished. 'I already have, Marcus.'

'What?'

'Your judgement's become compromised. You've lost your objectivity. I'm afraid you're no longer a viable part of this operation. I'm shutting you down.'

'You're taking me off my own project. The task force I helped create, you son of a bitch!'

'I'm protecting you,' Carpenter corrected him.

'From what?'

'From yourself,' he explained. 'You're a good case officer, Marcus, but you don't have the balls for this kind of work. Better to end it now before more people get killed. I'll make sure you're quietly reassigned to other projects – somewhere your talents can be put to better use. There'll be no stain on your record, no adverse consequences for your career. Hell, you'll probably land a promotion before too long.' He leaned a little closer. 'It's a good deal, but it expires when I leave this room. You should take it.'

'Fuck this,' Cain said, reaching for his desk phone. 'I'm taking this to Simmons myself.'

He still believed he could win the director of Special Activities Division around, persuade him of the merits of his plan. Cain held more sway over him than the brash and ruthless Carpenter ever had. Then they'd see who was removed from command.

'You can't,' Carpenter said, sounding almost bored.

'Yeah? Why's that?' Cain asked as he started punching in the number.

'Because I spoke to him before I flew out of Langley.' That was enough to stop Cain in his tracks. 'He supports my recommendation, said you've become an unnecessary liability. He's prepared to terminate your employment with the Agency if I can't talk you round.' Carpenter took a step closer, his voice low and dangerous. 'Now put down the goddamn phone before you end what's left of your career.'

Cain's hand moved almost of its own volition, slowly lowering the phone back into its cradle.

'Now order Task Force Black to stand down,' Carpenter went on. 'I'll make the arrangements to have you flown back to DC. There'll be questions to answer, of course, but if you play it smart we can make most of this shitstorm disappear.'

Cain didn't look up. 'I need 24 hours.'

'Maybe you didn't hear me—'

'Twelve hours,' Cain said. 'They've dispersed, gone dark. I need to contact them, explain what's happening. They won't back down now unless I do this.'

Carpenter scrutinized him. 'All right, Marcus. Twelve hours. No more. If you don't report in by then… well, you might find yourself in the same boat as Anya.'

He turned to leave, pausing at the door to look back.

'It's been good working with you.'

Cain waited until he'd closed the door before swiping his arm across the desk. His phone, the documents and files and maps and everything else flew to the floor as Cain turned away in disgust.

He was being shut down, forced out of his own project. Carpenter held all the cards, could leverage what he had on Cain to destroy the younger man at any moment. It was over. He would go back to Langley in disgrace, his mad, desperate scheme to recover the woman he loved in tatters.

That was when it changed, when Carpenter's words were replaced by a very different pledge. Anya's last words before they lost contact with her, given to Romek to pass on to Cain.

I'll keep my promise.

This was a moment, he knew. One of those crucial moments in life that determined what kind of a man he was going to be, what path he would follow.

Cain's hands slowly clenched into fists as the idea took shape. It was foolish, self-defeating and would likely spell the end of his career, if not his life. But he no longer cared about any of that.

Fuck Carpenter. Fuck Simmons. Fuck the Agency. Anya meant more to him than all of them combined.

He had twelve hours before he was forced to leave the country.

Twelve hours to put his hastily planned operation into effect.

Twelve hours to get Anya back.

He would not fail her again.

–

It was a cloudy morning in southern Germany, with low-lying patches of mist hanging over the fields as Cain disembarked the Gulfstream jet. He stopped to take his first breath of fresh air since departing the US, then surveyed the cavernous aircraft hangar where the private jet had taxied to a halt.

As instructed, Hawkins was waiting to receive him, along with a pair of Agency security operatives and a silver Mercedes SUV. Not that they needed much protection here, of course. Ramstein AFB served as a major NATO command centre and was effectively a small city unto itself, with over 16,000 US military personnel alone serving there.

But he didn't intend to stay there long.

'Talk to me,' he said as soon as he'd descended the stairs. 'What's our situation?'

Hawkins fell into step beside him as he headed towards the SUV, two protective agents bringing up the rear. 'Frost and Drake are in custody, prepped and ready for transport.'

'Unharmed?' Cain prompted.

'Mostly,' said Hawkins.

Cain decided to let that one pass. He would get to Drake and his fellow conspirators in due course, but right now the priority was Anya.

'And our resources?'

'NSA intercepts have been alerted to look out for the usual keywords. If they get a hit on phone, email or radio, we should know within minutes,' Hawkins confirmed, raising his voice over the din of a C-130 cargo plane taking off from one of the distant runways. 'We've also mobilized every field asset available and vectored them into Frankfurt. They're still coming in, but as of this morning we have 18 reliable operatives in the city.'

Cain hadn't missed the emphasis on reliability. This wasn't some battle being conducted in caves in Afghanistan or a remote Iraqi desert, but a sensitive, clandestine operation in a major population centre. The goal was to apprehend Anya quickly and quietly, without causing a major incident either with the German government or for the Agency. For this they needed men they could trust not to talk.

'Forty more are on standby if we push the panic button,' Hawkins added. 'They're not part of our programme, but they'll follow orders if it comes to it.'

'What about the Germans?' Cain hoisted himself up into the big vehicle, Hawkins climbing in the opposite side.

The BND, the German intelligence service, was nominally a close partner – the two organizations were party to a complex agreement to spy on each other's citizens and share the resulting intel – but he didn't imagine they'd take kindly to a covert operation being mounted on their soil.

'The BND have been sniffing around. They suspect something's up in Frankfurt, but they don't have anything definitive yet. We should be able to stall them.'

'Doesn't matter. The exchange won't happen in Frankfurt,' Cain announced briskly.

'Excuse me?'

'You really think Anya would give us the name of the city 48 hours beforehand?' Cain asked rhetorically. 'She's playing us, Jason, making us waste time chasing ghosts. She'll give us the real location on the day.'

Hawkins said nothing.

'She wants us off balance and unprepared when the time comes,' Cain said as the SUV's engine started up. 'But we won't be. We'll be ready for her.'

The Mercedes pulled out of the hangar. Anya might have caught him off guard once, but it would be the last time he made that mistake. Tomorrow, she would find out just how wrong she'd been to make this personal.

Chapter 45

Lauren closed her eyes and leaned back in her seat, allowing the sunlight breaking through gaps in the clouds to play across her face. The steady drone of the car's engine, the faint vibration of wheels on tarmac, the rush of wind outside all seemed to blend together into a comforting, familiar feeling of movement.

They'd been on the road for close to three hours now, making steady progress northwards from Anya's home. Lauren had been blindfolded so she couldn't give away the location of the building later, but after the first hour or so Anya had finally consented to remove it.

Alex was the one doing the driving, with Yasin sitting in the passenger seat up front. That left Anya in the back to keep an eye on Lauren. Her rationale was obvious – she didn't trust anyone else to guard their prisoner.

Given her earlier escape attempt, that certainly made sense. But then again, what was Lauren going to do? Throw herself out of a car moving at high speed down a busy highway? If the fall didn't kill her, other vehicles would.

So she sat still and bided her time, taking in as much information as she could glean. The first conclusion she'd drawn was that they were in Germany. She'd seen signs for Stuttgart, Nuremberg and various other towns located in the south of the country.

With Anya hardly a spirited conversationalist, communication had been largely confined to the two males up front, particularly the young boy. Yasin seemed to have an immense interest in everything, staring in excitement at buildings, cars and advertising boards as they passed by, often pestering Alex with questions.

'What is that car?' he asked, pointing to a black sports car that had just zipped past them on the inside, taking full advantage of the lack of autobahn speed limits. They caught a fleeting glimpse of the driver, sporting designer sunglasses and grey hair pulled back into a ponytail.

Alex glanced at it without much interest.

'Porsche,' he replied, sounding like a weary parent trying to manage an overexcited child. 'Driven by a total arsehole, if I'm not mistaken.'

'Porsche,' the boy repeated, dreaming of fast cars, wealth and success. 'This is a cool car, yes?'

'Suppose so,' said Alex. 'Bit old school for me, but—'

'Then I will have one,' Yasin decided without waiting for him to finish. 'And I will wear sunglasses and drive it every day. And everyone will be jealous of me.'

'A little young to be having a mid-life crisis, aren't you?' Lauren said, smirking.

Yasin twisted around to look at her. 'Mid-life crisis. What is this?'

'When rich guys get to a certain age, they start feeling scared about getting old. So they buy expensive cars, grow their hair long, hook up with younger women.'

Yasin frowned. 'I do not understand. When you are rich, why worry?'

She shrugged. 'They say money can't buy happiness.'

Yasin laughed. 'Whoever said that has never gone hungry.'

It was Lauren's turn to frown. Earlier today Yasin had explained – albeit briefly – how he'd ended up here with Anya. But what she didn't understand was why he'd been willing to leave his home country with a virtual stranger, or what his family had to say about it. She'd considered the possibility that Anya had abducted him, but quickly discounted it. One way or another, he was here of his own volition.

'Tell me something,' she said. 'How did you meet Anya in the first place?'

'She catch me stealing from her,' he said, grinning conspiratorially. 'In a warehouse in Pakistan. I was fast, but Fauji is faster. I think she would make good thief, if she is not so old.'

Lauren checked to see if Anya was offended but she seemed to care little.

'Fauji want to kill me for this, but the others try to stop her,' he went on. 'There is big argument and they point guns at each other, but Ryan stops them. He gives me money and send me away, but I follow them instead. There is big fight in middle of city, explosions and shooting like in movies.'

Anya's expression was still carefully neutral, but Lauren sensed she was uncomfortable with the change in conversation.

'I find Fauji afterwards. She is hurt, and men are looking for her. I make deal with her then to help her escape, if she takes me with her. I know all the secret ways, how to move around city without being seen. She says yes, and now we are here.'

Lauren was beginning to understand the basis of their relationship a little better now, at least from his point of view. She also had a sense of why he'd been so willing to leave his old life behind.

'What about your family? Your parents. Won't they be worried about you?'

'They do not worry about anything now,' Yasin said. 'They are dead.'

It came out so easily, as if it were a matter of no consequence to him. Just some long-accepted fact that no longer had any meaning.

Lauren immediately regretted probing so deep. 'I'm sorry.'

The boy looked at her curiously. 'Why?'

'Enough storytelling,' Anya said, motioning at Yasin. Lauren appreciated her interruption.

Time passed and the miles crept slowly by, but Lauren could feel Anya's eyes on her. 'You keep looking at me,' she said. 'Something wrong?'

'You seem very interested in all of us. Why?'

'It's not like there's anyone else to talk to.'

Anya wasn't fooled.

'I told you before that I was willing to treat you fairly, provided you were honest with me. Do we need to revisit that arrangement?'

Lauren sighed. 'Fine. I was trying to understand what my chances are of making it out of this alive.' She turned to look at Anya again. 'I thought that if I got to know you all a little better—'

'We'd be less inclined to kill you?' Anya offered.

Lauren paled, and even Alex glanced at her in the rear-view mirror. 'Something like that, I guess.'

'If you believe that sentimentality will keep you safe, you are very wrong. I have killed people that I knew far better than you, Lauren. And I may have to do it again.'

The silence that followed was excruciating as Anya stared her down. 'Luckily, you are not one of them. I said I intend to hand you over to your father unharmed, and I will. Provided you give me no reason to rethink that decision,' she added ominously.

Lauren closed her eyes, trying to concentrate on the familiar comforting sounds of the car in motion.

'There's a police car behind us,' Alex intervened urgently. 'And he's got his lights on.'

Lauren's eyes flew open. She looked out of the back window, and sure enough spotted a BMW with the distinctive blue, green and silver colour scheme of the *Autobahnpolizei* tailing them about 30 yards back. Its siren hadn't engaged, but its flashing lights were on, giving them a polite but firm instruction to pull over.

There was no way they could outrun a high-powered highway patrol vehicle. And even if they could, the attempt would only invite a larger pursuit that they could never hope to evade.

If the German police were on to them, this could well mean her father had managed to track her down. This could mean the end of her captivity right here, right now. But then, how would her captors react? Yasin and Alex would likely capitulate without a fight, but Anya was cut from a different cloth. An attempted arrest could end in a bloodbath.

'I'd appreciate some input,' Alex said anxiously. 'What do you want me to do?'

Anya had seen it too, and seemed to be entertaining similar thoughts. It didn't take her long to weigh up the facts and come to the same conclusion Lauren had.

'Slow down and pull over, then kill the engine,' she said. 'Make no sudden moves.'

Alex stared at her in disbelief. 'If they pull us over, we—'

'Do it, Alex,' she said firmly.

The driver shook his head. 'Jesus, I hope you know what you're doing,' he said, flicking on his turn signal and easing them into the side of the highway.

The patrol car followed them, pulling to a stop about 20 yards behind and shutting down its blue lights. However, the occupants remained in their vehicle, making no move to approach.

'I don't like this,' Alex said, turning off the ignition. 'Why are they just sitting there?'

'Keep your nerve,' Anya advised. 'They will be running our licence plate through their database to check the car isn't stolen.'

'And is it?'

Anya gave him a reproachful look. 'The car is registered to me.'

'So what do we do?'

'We wait,' Anya said. Lauren noticed that she'd shifted position slightly, giving her easier access to the weapon she'd concealed behind the driver's seat. 'If they question us, you must do the talking, Alex. You are the driver.'

'What am I supposed to say?'

'Improvise. Think fast. And above all, stay calm.'

'Fucking Christ,' he said under his breath. 'Easy for you to say.'

'They are coming,' Yasin said, having spotted movement from the police car in the wing mirror.

Lauren's heart was racing as a uniformed officer steadily approached their car, his eyes hidden behind dark sunglasses.

'Lauren,' Anya said quietly, 'I will be watching you. If you try to signal for help, I will know.'

There was no need for her to say more. Lauren could guess what the consequences of disobedience would be. Her mind was racing as fast as her heart. She glanced left as the police officer's blue uniform passed by her window, halting beside the driver's door. A gentle tap on the window served as a prompt for Alex to open up.

As he lowered the electric window, the officer removed his sunglasses and bent down to speak with them. Lauren saw a youthful, clean-cut face with short dark hair and grey, impassive eyes that gave little away.

'Morning,' Alex said, forcing a weak smile.

'*Guten Morgen*,' the officer replied without emotion. '*Sprichst du Deutsch?*'

'Sorry, afraid not. English?' Alex offered, as if that were helpful.

Lauren saw momentary annoyance flash across the officer's face. 'Are you the owner of this car, sir?' he asked, speaking with only a mild accent.

Alex hesitated. 'Erm, no. My partner owns the car,' he said, gesturing to Anya in the back. 'I just took over to give her a break. She gets tired easily.'

Anya smiled and nodded acknowledgement to the officer.

'May I see identification for both of you? And the car's registration documents.'

'Sure, no problem,' Alex said. Going on what Lauren assumed to be pure instinct, he popped open the glove compartment and fished out a small plastic folder with the car's official documentation inside.

Next came his driver's licence, though Lauren noticed his hands were shaking slightly as he handed it over. Anya also passed her ID forward for inspection.

'Did I do something wrong, officer?' he asked. 'I didn't think there was a speed limit on the autobahn.'

'Just a moment, please,' the man said without looking up from the documents, his face set with concentration.

Silence prevailed as the seconds ticked by with agonising slowness. Lauren glanced over at Anya, who was now watching the officer's every move, her body held tense and ready.

'This car is registered in Switzerland,' he said, glancing up at last and fixing Alex with a hard look. 'May I ask your purpose in Germany?'

Alex cleared his throat. 'Family vacation. I haven't seen much of Germany, and neither has my sister here,' he added, motioning to Lauren in the back. 'I'm told people here are very friendly towards visitors.'

That last remark was slightly pointed given their current situation, Lauren thought. She was surprised he'd had the courage to challenge a police officer, even in an oblique way like that.

The officer's eyes had now swung towards Lauren, taking in her appearance, looking at her the way men often did when they saw an attractive young woman. He noticed the graze on her left cheek, where she'd hit the ground after Yasin had tasered her the previous day.

'Are you all right, miss?' he asked. Not on full alert yet, but doing his job, checking nothing was amiss.

Lauren didn't respond, frozen by indecision. This was her chance, she knew. If she was to do anything, if she was to get this man's attention and signal to him that something was wrong, then now was the time.

'Miss, can you hear me?' he asked. She saw his hand stray a little closer to the sidearm holstered at his hip.

At the same time, Anya's hand moved towards the concealed weapon behind the driver's seat. She couldn't force Lauren to respond, couldn't threaten her with the police officer watching their every move, but Lauren knew that if it came down to it, she would start shooting and take her chances.

She saw the officer reach towards his weapon, and knew he wouldn't get a chance to draw.

'Sorry, I was a little distracted,' she said, breaking the silence. 'I'm fine, thank you. I just fell when we were out skiing a couple of days ago.' She offered a rueful, faintly flirtatious smile that she knew helped smooth over difficult situations where men were involved. 'Believe me, it looks a lot better now than it did at the time.'

The officer seemed to relax, and his hand moved away from the weapon. He handed Alex back the car documents, along with his and Anya's IDs.

'I pulled you over because of the boy,' he said, nodding to Yasin. 'Under federal highway law, children under 12 must have booster seats. For safety.'

Even Lauren could see the surprise written all over Anya's face. Clearly she'd never had children of her own, because such a consideration had never even entered her head.

'Oh, I'm sorry about that,' Alex said, trying to hide the elation that this entire debacle had been nothing but a minor safety check. 'We'll get ourselves one at the first town we arrive in.'

'I am 12 already,' Yasin said, sounding faintly defiant at what he perceived as an insult.

The cop glanced at him, surprised by his outburst, then back to Alex as if looking for an explanation.

'He's small for his age,' Alex said, speaking quietly as if he didn't want Yasin to hear.

'I see,' the officer remarked, looking slightly dubious as he compared the two males in the front seats. 'He is your child?'

'He is mine,' Anya piped up. 'From a previous marriage. His father was from India.'

Smart, Lauren thought. Mentioning Pakistan would only invite more unwanted questions, and possibly snatch defeat from the jaws of victory.

The cop eyed Anya a moment longer. 'I will let you off with an advisory in this case,' he decided. 'See that you get the booster seat for the boy.'

'Will do,' Alex said, nodding emphatically. 'Have a good day.'

The man slipped his sunglasses back on as Alex wound up his window and started the engine. Within seconds, he'd pulled out into the traffic and they were on their way again, Alex furtively checking the rear-view mirror until the police car had faded from view.

'Christ, that was close,' he said. 'I don't know about you guys, but I could use a new pair of trousers.'

'You could have given us away, Lauren,' Anya said. 'I appreciate that you did not.'

'I didn't do it for you,' Lauren shot back. 'I did it for that cop, and for Yasin. I know you'd have started shooting before you'd ever let them take us in, and innocent people could have gotten killed. You might be willing to live with that, but I'm not.'

Chapter 46

It was late afternoon by the time they exited the autobahn, and by that point their final destination had become obvious.

Berlin had been the capital of a succession of Germanic nations, republics and empires for over 700 years, from Prussia to the divided East Germany of the Cold War. These days it was home to about six million residents.

Lauren had visited it the previous year during a summer break, and though she'd certainly been taken by the scale of the city, she considered it an impressive rather than a beautiful place. It was too stark, too modern, too uncompromising to be called beautiful.

Following the car's navigation system, Alex steered a course north-east through the city, passing the abandoned Tempelhof airport before following the busy traffic towards the city centre, heading roughly towards the massive spire of the Berlin TV Tower. An immense needle-like structure with a large spherical section near the top, the tower was visible from practically anywhere in the city – a prominent, if controversial, landmark.

Veering westwards after crossing the Landwehr Canal, they turned into the parking area of a large, semi-circular apartment block facing out onto Tiergartenstrasse. Pulling them into a space, Alex killed the engine, and seemed to relax slightly now that their journey was over.

'We're here,' he announced. 'Wherever "here" is.'

'This is where we need to be,' Anya said, stepping out of the car and beckoning Lauren to follow her. 'Come with me.'

The young woman was relieved to stretch her legs. She took in the evening air, tasting the fragrant scent of recently cut grass, the powerful smell of engine fumes from the main drag nearby, and the odours of cooking food from nearby restaurants. Alex and Yasin were already outside with her, looking equally pleased to no longer be travelling.

Retrieving the bag she'd brought, Anya slammed the trunk closed and hoisted it over her shoulder.

'Let's go,' she instructed, leading them towards the nearest apartment block.

Making their way inside, they ascended via an elevator to the fourth floor. Anya led them confidently down the corridor, stopping outside apartment 412.

The apartment key was held within a small, electronically controlled safe mounted on the wall. Anya punched in the six-digit combination.

The safe access light flashed green and the door popped open, allowing her to retrieve the key.

'Inside,' she said, unlocking the door and hustling them in.

The apartment was large but almost empty of furniture – clearly a safe house. What a waste, Lauren thought, surveying the impressive view out of the living room windows. From this height they could see all the way across the heavily wooded Tiergarten park, from the Victory Column in the centre to the Reichstag building on the north-east corner, rays from the evening sun glinting off the massive steel and glass dome cap. And beside it, the triumphal arch of the Brandenburg Gate.

'You own this place?' Alex asked, looking equally impressed.

Anya shook her head. 'No, but we can use it as long as we are in Berlin,' she said, dropping her bag on the polished floorboards and kneeling down to unzip it.

Lauren turned towards her. 'What happens now?'

Anya stood up, the taser in her hands. Lauren backed off instinctively, but instead Anya handed the weapon to Alex.

'I must go out for a while,' she explained, pressing the stun gun into his hands. 'The power pack is fully charged, and the safety is off. If she tries to escape, use it. Don't hesitate. Understand?'

'I suppose so,' Alex said, clearly reluctant.

Anya tightened her hold on the taser as he tried to pull it away. 'I'm trusting you, Alex. Don't fail me.'

His expression hardened as the gravity of the situation was at last impressed on him. 'That's not going to happen,' he said firmly.

Nodding, Anya relinquished the weapon and turned her attention to the young woman she was leaving him to guard.

'My trust extends to you as well, Lauren.'

'Clearly,' she replied, eyes flicking to the taser.

'It doesn't extend that far,' Anya reminded her. 'But I hope you have more sense than to try another escape. Cooperate, and you will be returned to your father tomorrow.'

'So you keep saying,' Lauren said, flopping onto the couch. 'Talk is cheap, Anya.'

Anya snatched up the car keys that Alex had left on the kitchen counter and turned to Yasin. 'I could use some company on my journey. Will you help me?'

Yasin didn't need to be asked twice, leaping from the kitchen stool he'd been sitting on. The request for help had stirred his youthful pride and chivalry, not to mention excitement at the prospect of exploring a foreign city.

'Of course. Where are we going?' he asked, hurrying to catch up with Anya as she made for the door.

'To see an old friend.'

Chapter 47

'Where does this old friend live?' Yasin asked, as Anya manoeuvred the vehicle down the thronging shop-lined streets of central Berlin.

'Not far from here,' Anya replied. She had an unusual look about her, Yasin thought.

As they threaded their way eastwards, crossing the Spree river into the Friedrichshain district, the character of the city and its architecture changed considerably. They were now in what was once East Berlin, a portion of the city occupied by the Soviets for over four decades.

For obvious reasons, much of Berlin had had to be rebuilt after the war. The British and Americans had pumped a great deal of money and resources into reconstruction work in the west, eventually building it into one of the most advanced and affluent cities in Europe. The same could not be said of the Soviet sector.

They were advancing eastwards along Karl-Marx-Allee, formerly known as Stalinallee after the Soviet dictator who commissioned it. A wide, tree-lined boulevard, it was flanked by monumental eight-storey buildings constructed in the elaborate wedding cake style of classical Soviet architecture, complete with marble and ceramic facades.

This was one of the Soviets' grand efforts to reshape Berlin into a socialist paradise, even if it was only for the newsreels. Still, it all looked very grand, clean and elegant.

Turning right about halfway along, Anya steered them into a quieter residential street. Apartment blocks loomed over both sides of the road, recently refurbished but probably dating back several decades.

The further they got from the central boulevard, the less clean and elegant their surroundings became. The quality of the buildings began to deteriorate, graffiti started to appear, and even the cars looked older and cheaper than in other parts of the city.

The stereotype of the former East Berlin was of crumbling 1960s-era apartment blocks, derelict pre-war buildings peppered with old bullet holes, and ramshackle market areas peddling shoddy counterfeit goods. Things had changed a lot since reunification, with vast investment still flowing east, but some vestiges of the Soviet occupation remained.

Pulling over, Anya pointed to an older apartment block opposite. Likely a survivor of the earlier nineteenth-century Prussian architecture that used to dominate the city.

'This way,' she said, locking the car and leading Yasin towards it.

Halting by the intercom panel, Anya pressed a button right at the bottom of the list.

'*Ja?*' a gruff, old-sounding voice asked.

'*Ich bin da, Felix,*' Anya replied. '*Mach auf.*'

There was a pause, followed by the buzz and click as the door's lock was disengaged. Holding it open, Anya waited until Yasin had passed her before swinging it closed.

The central stairwell beyond was pretty much standard for an apartment block of this age. High ceilings, stone floors, moulded steel railings that had been repainted so many times the details had long since been obscured, and the faintly stale, damp smell that often lingers around old buildings.

Rather than heading up, however, Anya took the stairs down to the basement. Yasin had an uneasy feeling as he descended the stairs beside her, their steps echoing off the cold stone walls. In his experience, basements were places where bad people lived, and worse things happened. Unconsciously he moved a little closer to Anya, hoping she wouldn't notice.

Only one door stood at the bottom, apparently a residential dwelling. Who would choose to live in a windowless basement, he wondered.

Approaching it, Anya knocked gently on the door. Seconds ticked by until they heard a muffled voice from within, the sound of footsteps approaching, slow and deliberate, then the click of chains and bolts being withdrawn.

The door swung open then, revealing a most unlikely figure.

Yasin had expected some sinister, thuggish beast of a man. What he saw instead was a small, gentle-looking old man with snowy white hair, dressed in faded brown corduroy trousers and a woollen cardigan. He must have seen 80 years at least, his body shrunken by age and his face deeply lined like a walnut. A pair of rounded spectacles perched atop his long nose.

He looked up at Anya and broke out into a beaming smile of affection.

'*Anya! Es ist schön dich wieder zu sehen!*' he said, warmly embracing the woman like a dear friend. '*Wie gehts?*'

Anya returned his gesture, and Yasin sensed her affection for him was genuine. Who was this man? Her father? Grandfather? He looked old enough to be either.

'I'm well, Felix. Thank you,' she replied, speaking English for Yasin's benefit. 'It is good to see you, too.'

She turned and gestured to her young companion. 'This is my… friend,' she began, hesitating slightly as if searching for a word that better described her relationship to him, and coming up short. 'His name is Yasin. Yasin, this is Felix. He lives here.'

The old man nodded and smiled. 'Pleased to meet you, young man. Any friend of Anya's is welcome in my home,' he said, his grasp of English almost as strong as Anya's. Then, as if remembering himself, he gestured inside. 'Where are my manners? Please, come in, come in.'

As the old man turned and shuffled off down the corridor, deeper into the apartment, Anya held the door open for Yasin. He gave her a questioning look as he passed, to which she answered in a whisper, 'Trust me.'

Yasin's sense of bewilderment only intensified the more he saw of Felix's living space. Basement apartments in rundown areas of town weren't exactly desirable spots, and given that an old man seemed to live here alone, it seemed inevitable that he'd be living in squalor and neglect, surrounded by a lifetime of hoarded junk.

What they found instead was a neat, tidy, well cared for and surprisingly spacious living area that seemed to occupy almost the entire footprint of the building, and complemented by tasteful-looking furniture. The polished oak floorboards were covered in places by thick, intricately decorated rugs. The faint smell of wood smoke directed the boy's attention to an open fire on the far side of the room, a couple of logs crackling and popping in the flames.

Even the lack of natural light didn't seem to be an issue, as a careful arrangement of lamps and overhead lights created instead a cosy atmosphere that made Yasin feel almost immediately at ease.

'I must say, I was pleased to hear you were coming, Anya,' Felix said as he made his way slowly into the room. 'It's not until you become old that you truly learn the value of good company.'

'You live here alone?' Yasin asked, unable to contain his curiosity. He still didn't understand what particular errand had brought Anya here. Surely now, with so much at stake tomorrow, she wouldn't waste time on social calls?

'Yes. For a long time, young man,' Felix said, then gestured to the selection of couches and armchairs positioned around the room. 'Please, make yourselves at home. Would you like some tea or coffee?'

Anya shook her head. 'I was hoping to talk business with you first, Felix. Did you manage to get everything I requested?'

The old man nodded. 'Of course. Come, see for yourself.'

Conducting them through to what seemed to serve as a small office or study, he gestured to a canvas holdall resting on a small, floral-patterned chair in the corner. Anya knelt down and unzipped it, pulling the bag open to expose the contents.

Yasin gasped in disbelief as his eyes alighted on the array of military-grade weaponry carefully packed away inside. The display of deadly technology stood in such marked contrast to the homely, peaceful study that he was having trouble processing what he was seeing.

Anya, however, immediately went to work. The first item to emerge was the distinctive frame of a UMP-45 submachine gun. Designed by Heckler &

Koch, it was essentially an updated and lightweight version of the venerable MP5 that had been in use since the 1960s. This one was fitted with an under-barrel laser sight and a forward hand grip to make it more versatile in confined spaces.

Racking back the charging handle to make sure the breech was empty, Anya shouldered the weapon, pointed it at the wall and pulled the trigger. There was a smooth, efficient click as the firing pin engaged. She also checked the laser sight to make sure it powered up.

Next out was a suit of Kevlar body armour, followed by several grenades. Rather than the pineapple-shaped devices depicted in the movies, these ones were cylindrical in appearance – smoke and stun grenades, designed to obscure and disorient rather than kill.

The last items were a trio of olive-green plastic boxes, rectangular and slightly concave in shape, with a pair of steel prongs mounted on their undersides. Their faces were printed with black Cyrillic lettering that Yasin couldn't decipher, but he knew enough to recognize them as anti-personnel mines.

'These are not Claymores,' Anya said.

Felix made an apologetic face. 'Claymores are not easy to come by these days, especially at short notice,' he explained. 'I had to use MON-50s instead. Russian, but still good. They have more explosive content and a bigger kill radius than the American mines, and they cost half as much.'

Yasin stared in awe. He'd taken Felix to be nothing but a doddering if good-natured old man, but now he realized there was something very different at play. Much like his basement apartment, his appearance was a carefully cultivated facade designed to hide his true purpose.

'This will work,' Anya decided, carefully packing the explosives and weapons away. Reaching into her jacket, she produced a roll of banknotes, easily several thousand euros, and handed it over to him. 'Thank you.'

'My pleasure,' Felix replied, pocketing the money in his cardigan.

'Where did all this come from?' Yasin asked in amazement.

'Felix is a fixer,' Anya explained. 'One of the best in Germany, as it happens. Whatever you need – weapons, equipment, passports – he can get.'

Felix shrugged as if uncomfortable under such praise. 'I'm retired now, mostly,' he added. 'Such adventures are for young men, and my contacts are not what they once were. But sometimes I do favours for old friends.'

'And they appreciate your help,' Anya said, zipping the holdall closed.

With the matter concluded, Felix clapped his hands together. 'Well, in that case, who's hungry?'

Ten minutes later, all three of them were seated around the apartment's big mahogany dining table as Felix served up dinner. Having been fore-warned of their arrival, he'd taken the liberty of preparing a meal of pot roast, sauerkraut, steamed vegetables and potato dumplings, accompanied by a bottle of red wine.

Anya took only a small measure of this herself and, much to his chagrin, refused to allow Yasin any. Had he been of a mood, he might have pointed out that he'd already tried a variety of alcohols, not to mention other substances, while living with other groups of displaced youths in Pakistan, but he'd already learned it was unwise to argue with her.

In any case, the quality of the food was enough to quell any dissent on his part. Pot roast and sauerkraut was a flavour combination unknown to him, but he recognized good food when he tasted it. If you'd spent much of your life fighting to find enough scraps to get through the day, the simple act of sitting down to eat a leisurely meal seemed like the height of luxury.

'I hope the meal is to your liking,' Felix said, amused by how quickly the boy was clearing his plate.

'It is good,' Yasin replied through a mouthful of bread, crumbs falling on the table.

'Don't speak with your mouth full, Yasin,' Anya said.

'Oh, it's all right,' Felix assured her. 'The boy is hungry. And by the looks of him, he could use a little feeding up.' He flashed Yasin a conspiratorial grin. 'You should have seen Anya when I first met her. She was rude, impatient, no manners whatsoever.'

'I was nothing like that,' Anya said gently.

'Tell me more,' Yasin implored, eager to learn more about his protector from someone who really knew her.

Felix took a sip of his wine, considering. 'Well, I first met her back in the old days, when the Wall still stood in Berlin,' he explained. 'You could only travel from one side to the other with special papers, you see. I was told that a contact would be coming to me, that they needed a full set of documents. I waited all afternoon, and nothing. Then, at midnight, I get a knock on my door, and there I find a young woman with messy blonde hair, bruised and bloody hands and torn clothes. I ask the poor girl what on earth has happened to her, and...' – he struggled to contain a laugh at this point – 'she pushes past me, sits down in my chair and says, "I have just beaten down two East German agents who tried to abduct me. I am tired, and hungry, and I want my documents, old man."' He was shaking with mirth now. 'And that was the first time I met Anya.'

Yasin couldn't help laughing too. And, much to his pleasure, even Anya smiled at the memory. 'You did not catch me at my best that night,' she remarked, which only encouraged more laughter.

The two guests remained there for another hour or so, listening to Felix tell stories of his long and apparently very eventful life, and laughing together. Yasin couldn't help but glance at Anya occasionally, surprised and perhaps a little taken aback by the change that had come over her.

It was perhaps the first time Yasin had ever seen her look happy and relaxed, and unconsciously he felt something he hadn't experienced in a very long time. A sense of belonging, of connection, of having people around him that he trusted and even cared about. It was a confusing, surprising realization.

It lasted a little while longer, before Anya finally announced that their time was running short and that they needed to be on their way.

Bidding farewell to the old fixer, they ascended the stairs back up to ground level, Anya with the holdall slung over her shoulder, Yasin with a full stomach and a sense of contentment unknown in his short life.

'I was thinking about Felix,' Yasin announced as they approached their parked car. 'He should be living in our apartment instead of that basement. It is not fair on him.'

It seemed like madness to him that such a bright, comfortable space should sit unused while a man like Felix spent his days in a windowless underground prison, no matter how well he'd arranged it.

'Not fair?' Anya repeated, opening the trunk.

'Yes,' the boy contended. 'I think he deserves better.'

Laying the holdall carefully inside, she closed the trunk and turned to look at him, regarding him as a teacher might look at a student who fails to see the point of a lesson. 'Who do you think owns our apartment, Yasin?'

His expression was one of astonishment. 'Then why live where he does?'

'Not all men need to surround themselves with luxury to feel rich. He has all he needs.'

Anya stepped past him, opened her door and slipped into the driver's seat. Only when the engine roared did Yasin stir from his thoughts, hurrying around to the passenger side in case she drove off without him.

Chapter 48

Cain once more found himself in the room where he'd met Task Force Black, only this time he was alone, pacing the makeshift ops room like a caged animal. The air around him felt hot and stagnant, trickles of sweat running down his face.

He was filled with nervous energy he couldn't expel. Every passing moment brought him closer to Carpenter's deadline, but also closer to being reunited with Anya.

He had triggered Operation Jurate shortly after his fiery confrontation with Carpenter, using the code word Austra on an encrypted radio frequency that he knew Task Force Black would pick up. For all his frantic work over the past couple of days, Cain's intel was still incomplete and the plan far from finished, but further delay was impossible. Either they went for it now or they abandoned the plan for good.

All he could do was trust that it was enough.

He knew the team must be getting close to their objective by now. He had received a message over the secure satellite comms unit several hours earlier as the task force crossed the Afghan border. He could almost imagine them closing in on the Soviet facility as the sun went down, weapons ready and senses alert.

Part of him wished he was with them. Another part knew he'd only slow them down.

A noise in the corridor outside returned his attention to the present. This building was vacant. Nobody else should be here.

Abandoning the communications console, Cain drew his M1911 sidearm and advanced towards the door, keeping the weapon in a tight grip. He'd never had to kill a man before, but he was prepared. Another noise – the creak of a floorboard.

Taking a breath, Cain gripped the door handle, flicked the weapon's safety off and quickly pulled the door open.

The man was immediately familiar. Medium height, slender and compact build, well dressed and with his dark hair neatly combed, there was no mistaking the Pakistani intelligence officer.

'Qalat,' Cain growled, keeping the weapon trained on him. 'What the hell are you doing here?'

Far from being intimidated by the semi-automatic, Qalat merely offered a smooth smile.

'Are you going to invite me in, Marcus? Or would you prefer to shoot me?'

Cain glanced out into the corridor. Qalat was alone and unarmed. All he seemed to have with him was a document folder, of the kind Cain was used to seeing back at Langley. This one, however, was unmarked.

'I'm not doing anything until you tell me why you're here. How did you find me?'

'I am an officer with the Pakistani intelligence service. Not much happens in Peshawar without us knowing, my friend.'

Qalat was many things, but the enigmatic intelligence operative was certainly not Cain's friend.

'As for why I'm here...' He held up the folder. 'I have something you should see.'

–

Walking eastwards through the Tiergarten park towards the Brandenburg Gate, Anya watched as the young boy gawped in excitement. He was particularly fascinated by the pair of T-34 tanks flanking the Soviet war memorial, speaking enthusiastically about how he'd once seen them rumbling down a highway in Pakistan.

Anya wouldn't have been surprised. The Soviets had built tens of thousands of the things, exporting them all over the world. No doubt some had made their way to Pakistan, and were possibly still in use.

'Have you ever driven a tank?' he asked with the kind of frank, childish curiosity that she'd found it so difficult to adjust to, but which she'd reluctantly found herself coming to appreciate.

'No, I haven't.' She'd almost been driven *over* by a tank during a tour in Afghanistan, but that was another story.

'What about helicopters? Have you flown them?'

'I've flown *in* them,' she confirmed.

'Was it fun?'

She thought about that for a moment. 'It is more fun when people aren't trying to shoot you down.'

'I would like to be a pilot,' he said. 'Flying in to save the day. And I would wear sunglasses.'

Anya was content to indulge him for now, to let him talk about whatever he wanted. It was a side to the boy she hadn't really seen before, but his enthusiasm wasn't annoying like she'd expected. In fact, it stirred a faint pang of sadness and longing in her.

Because she knew it was about to end.

'Yasin,' she said once they'd reached the end of the avenue.

He turned to look at her expectantly. He had changed a great deal from the scrawny, unkempt street urchin that she'd first encountered trying to steal the team's equipment in Pakistan.

Already she could see he was starting to put on weight as his body adjusted to an improved diet. His clothes were clean and new, his once greasy and unruly black hair now neatly cut, courtesy of a pair of electric clippers she'd forced upon him before leaving the country.

He was thriving, and might well grow up to be a handsome young man, but Anya knew she wouldn't be around to see it. That was the reason she'd taken him to visit Felix, why she'd suggested going for an evening walk even though there were more pressing matters to attend to.

'I told you there was something I needed you to do for me,' she said, speaking quietly in Pashto.

Yasin nodded, eager as always. 'Name it. I'm ready.'

Anya pointed towards the Brandenburg Gate, where a pair of uniformed federal police officers were standing watch.

'You see those policemen over there?'

'Yes.'

Anya let out a breath. 'I want you to walk over to them and turn yourself in.'

Yasin stared at her in confusion. 'I don't understand.'

'I want you to turn yourself in,' she repeated. 'You will tell them you are alone, say you fled your home country because people there were trying to kill you, and you request asylum in Germany. You will tell no one about me, or what you've seen or done since we met.'

Germany had a generous policy when it came to admitting refugees and asylum seekers, particularly children like Yasin. He might face a grilling at first, especially on how he'd reached Berlin, but she didn't doubt that a place would be found for him.

'You will have to answer lots of questions, but after that you will be given over to a social worker who will take care of the rest. They will help find a family for you to stay with, a school for you to go to. Everything you need.'

The boy shook his head vehemently. 'No,' he said, his tone flat and hard. 'No. I won't do that.'

'Yes, you will.' Anya reached out and laid a hand firmly on his shoulder. 'Because you have to. We both know you can't come any further with us, Yasin.'

The episode with highway patrol earlier in the day had simply confirmed what she already knew – she was no parent, and had no business trying to look after a child. She'd been unwise to bring him even this far. She should have handed him over to the authorities days ago.

'But we had a deal,' he protested.

'Our deal was to get you out of Pakistan, and I've honoured it.'

'No,' he snapped. 'If you make me go, I will tell them everything. I will tell them what you're planning, what you look like. I'll ruin all your plans.'

Anya sighed, knowing it was a bluff. He was lashing out simply because anger and aggression had served him far better in life than tears and self-pity. In that regard, she understood him all too well.

'Yasin, I can do no more for you,' she said. 'If you want to start a new life, then you need a home, education, people to look after you.'

'I don't need anyone to look after me,' Yasin argued.

That part was true, she acknowledged with grudging respect. Yasin's harsh upbringing had certainly matured him beyond his years, but he was still a child, and a child needed protection and stability.

She could offer him neither.

'Then you'll end up living on the streets again, and you'll be no better off than when I found you,' she said. 'If you want a chance at something better, this is how you must get it.'

Yasin seemed to deflate. 'I can still help you,' he said, though it was half-hearted at best.

'I know you can, Yasin,' she said, humouring him. 'But your work is done. I don't need anything more from you.'

Crestfallen, his anger melted away. 'What will you do now?'

Anya glanced back along the avenue, thinking about the young woman back at the safe house. An innocent life oblivious to the storm raging around her, but one that might hold the key to Drake's redemption. And Anya's.

'My work isn't finished yet, but I must do it alone. And you'll be better off without me anyway.'

'My father said the same thing.'

Anya stopped, taken aback not just by his words, but the tone of sad, bitter acceptance in his voice. 'What do you mean?'

Yasin looked away.

'When I was little, when they gave me away. I don't remember much, but I know why it happened. My mother died trying to give birth to her second child, and my father couldn't look after me. He took me to an orphanage in Rawalpindi and just left me there. I screamed and cried and begged him to take me back, but he wouldn't listen. He said the people there would care for me, that I was better off without him. That was the last time I saw him.' He shrugged, dismissing the memory. 'He said I was better off without him, but I think it was the other way around. He decided he was better off without me.' His eyes filled with accusation. 'I think grown-ups just say things like that to make it easier for them.'

Anya stared back at the child but she didn't see him. Her gaze was turned inwards, at an old memory which somehow always resurfaced. A memory of herself on a grassy hilltop overlooking her home, the sound of a car engine approaching, rising to her feet expecting her parents to return.

But it wasn't her parents' car. It was a police car. Sent to tell her that her parents were dead, that everything she knew had just evaporated. That she would never again know true happiness and contentment.

'I was trying to protect you,' she said.

'From what?'

'From me. From the things I do.'

'I know the things you do, Fauji.' Fauji: the nickname he'd taken to using for her. Anya knew it meant 'warrior' in Pashto. 'You don't have to protect me from that.'

Anya wished that were true. Whatever he'd seen and done, it could only pale in comparison to the death and suffering she'd visited on others. And what she might yet have to do.

'Let me come with you, let me help,' he implored. 'At least until the others are safe. I owe them a debt as well, and I must repay it.' His eyes glinted with a hint of humour. 'If it were not for them, I think you would have killed me in Pakistan.'

She wondered if he knew how close he was to the truth.

'All I ask is a chance to help,' he said, making one last effort to win her over. 'That is all. After this is over, I will leave. Will you not give me that much?'

For some reason, his plea reminded her of words she'd once spoken two decades ago, in a little cell-like interrogation room at Langley.

I do not want pity, just a chance to prove myself. So far my life has meant nothing to anyone. Let me do something with what I have left.

She had asked for the same chance Yasin was asking for now. A young woman, little more than a teenager, who knew nothing but fighting and clawing for her very survival.

'You will do exactly what I say,' she heard herself say.

'I will,' he promised.

'And when this is over, when Drake and the others are safe, you will turn yourself over to the authorities just like I said.'

'If that's what you want.'

Anya knew her judgement was being motivated by emotion rather than logic, which was dangerous for everyone involved, but she couldn't quite bring herself to send him away. Not until he could make peace with it.

She gestured back the way they had come.

'We should get back,' she finally said. 'We have work to do.'

Chapter 49

Despite its impressive view and expensive decor, the safe house lacked any form of entertainment – something both Alex and Lauren were becoming increasingly aware of.

'It's going to be a long night if we have to sit here in silence,' Lauren said, sighing and looking around. 'Jesus, this reminds me of detention with Mrs Templeman.'

Alex frowned. 'What?'

Lauren smiled faintly. 'The worst goddamned elementary school teacher you could ask for. Terrible Templeman, we used to call her. She once yelled at a kid for sneezing,' she recalled. 'One day I decided to teach her a lesson, so I hid a toy spider in her desk drawer, not knowing she had severe, hardcore arachnophobia. She opened it, and it was like she'd just been struck by lightning. I thought she'd never stop screaming.'

She couldn't help but chuckle.

'She hauled me into her office for detention, said I wasn't getting out until I admitted what I did. No way was I giving her the satisfaction, so I just sat there. I could see she was getting madder and madder, and that just encouraged me to stick with it. It was two hours before she finally gave up and told me to get the hell out.'

Alex found himself smiling at the thought.

'I had a PE teacher like that in secondary school,' he said. 'Henderson was his name. A lumpy, muscle-head arsehole, loved humiliating the weak kids in the class. His pride and joy was this big, stupid red BMW, so one day me and a couple of mates popped the bonnet and changed the fuses around, linked the horn in with his brakes. Every time he tried to slow down – honk!'

To his relief, Lauren laughed at that. A true, genuine laugh which he hadn't heard from her before. It was remarkable how it seemed to light up her entire face, and for a moment he caught himself wishing they'd met under different circumstances.

'I guess everyone's had an asshole teacher,' she conceded. 'You were more inventive than me anyway.'

For a time they amused themselves by swapping stories of their childhood exploits, recalling pranks, places they had visited, disastrous nights out. And for a little while, it was almost possible to forget everything else that had happened.

At last lapsing into silence, Alex glanced out of the window, where the dome of the Reichstag was visible in the distance, illuminated from within against the gathered darkness.

'I was a hacker,' he said suddenly.

Lauren glanced at him. 'Huh?'

'You asked me what I did before all this, how I came to know Anya,' he explained. 'I was a computer hacker. My job was to find out things that other people wanted to keep hidden. Your dad wanted to keep you hidden, so Anya brought me in.'

Lauren's smile faded. 'And you found me.'

He nodded. 'I've made mistakes in my life; I don't deny that. And I'm truly sorry that we had to do all this. I hope when it's all over you go on to live a long and happy life, but I don't regret being part of it. I'll take whatever comes my way tomorrow, good or bad, and I won't hide from it. Not this time.'

He couldn't rightly say why he'd felt the need to tell her that, whether he actually thought it might make any difference or whether she would dismiss it as self-justification from a man beyond redemption.

Lauren was still looking back at him, but he sensed a subtle change coming over her, like a dawning realization had been lurking beneath the surface this whole time, and had now begun to take form.

Before either of them could say anything further, the door swung open and Anya entered with a bulky holdall slung over one shoulder, followed closely by Yasin. Her eyes swept across the room, checking that nothing was out of place.

'Is everything all right here?' she asked, sensing she'd interrupted some-thing significant.

'Yeah,' Alex confirmed, casting a brief glance at Lauren. 'Yeah, every-thing's fine. Did you get what you needed?'

Anya nodded, laying the holdall carefully on the floor. 'If you want to take a break, feel free. I will watch Lauren.'

Something told him that Anya's offer had been a suggestion to take his leave. He wondered what Anya had in mind, but knew that any attempt at eavesdropping would be unwise.

In truth, he could do with getting out of the apartment and stretching his legs, not to mention grabbing some dinner. The apartment's cupboards were as bare as its decor, and he hadn't eaten anything since breakfast, which his stomach had been reminding him of increasingly loudly.

'Fine,' he conceded, laying down the taser and pulling on his jacket. 'I could use a walk anyway.'

Anya waited until he'd left before glancing at Yasin, who seemed to have lost some of his usual energy and was trying to stifle a yawn. 'Yasin, take yourself to bed and get some rest,' she commanded. 'You look like you could use it.'

Like any kid told to go to bed, the protests started right away. 'But I—'

Anya silenced him with a raised hand. 'Remember our agreement.'

He nodded sulkily and ventured deeper into the apartment, leaving the two women alone in the living room.

Lauren watched her captor settle herself into the seat Alex had recently vacated, feeling an odd longing for his return. At least his company was more agreeable than Anya's.

'Well, here we are, alone at last,' Lauren remarked, using sarcasm to hide her unease. 'Might as well come out with it.'

'With what, exactly?'

Lauren tilted her head, eyeing the older woman with disapproval. 'We both know you wanted to speak to me alone. So, are you going to get on with it or are you just going to keep staring at me? I hope not, because to be honest it's kind of creepy.'

She was expecting a reaction. Anya, though, seemed preoccupied and unsure of herself.

'I was thinking about what you said earlier,' she began at last. 'What your father told you about me.'

It was all Lauren could do not to roll her eyes. 'Let me guess. This is the part where you tell me it's all bullshit, that my dad's a monster who took advantage of you? You're going to list all his mistakes, every fault, every dirty little secret, so you can prove what a bastard he is.'

She couldn't have imagined what she was about to hear next.

'No, I'm going to do none of that,' Anya said in forlorn acceptance. 'Because your father spoke the truth.'

—

Peshawar, Pakistan – 1 October 1988

Cain said and did nothing for the next few seconds. He kept his weapon trained on the unexpected arrival, trying to decide whether this was some kind of ploy. Qalat simply stood there, waiting patiently.

'Who sent you here?' he demanded, taking a step closer so that the Colt .45's barrel was less than a foot from Qalat's face. 'Carpenter? Simmons?'

Qalat shook his head slowly, unconcerned by the weapon. 'No one sent me. No one from the CIA knows I am here,' he said. 'I came of my own free will.'

'Why?'

'To stop you making the biggest mistake of your life.' Again he waved the folder in front of him. 'You can choose to believe me, or not. It makes little difference to me. But I'd advise you to at least hear me out.'

Making his decision, Cain gripped Qalat by the arm and pulled him roughly inside, closing and barring the door behind him. Straightening his rumpled shirt sleeve, Qalat glanced at the satellite comms unit, the maps, the photographs spread over the table.

'They are getting close now, yes?' he remarked, making it plain he understood exactly what was going on. 'They could be in position any time.'

'And what would you know about that?'

'I know they are walking into a trap.'

An icy dagger of fear suddenly twisted in Cain's stomach. 'What are you talking about?'

'The young woman you are risking everything to rescue is not what she appears.'

'Bullshit,' Cain snapped back.

At this, Qalat laid the folder on the table, then stepped away, making way for Cain. 'Please, take a look. You will find your answers in here, though you may not like them.'

Cain took a step towards it, then another. With a leaden arm he reached out and flipped the folder open.

–

'He trusted me, he gave me a chance, showed faith in me when no one else would. And I betrayed his trust.' Anya turned her head slowly. 'I lied to him, Lauren. I lied about who I was, why I was there. And that lie almost destroyed us both.'

–

Cain's eyes darted across the pages, drinking in every terrible word, feeling his faith and trust crumble with every passing second. The documents were extracts from a KGB personnel dossier, written in Russian.

He almost wished he hadn't become fluent in the language, because the dossier dealt with only one subject – Anya, or at least the woman he'd come to know as Anya.

In the top right corner was a photograph, degraded slightly from having been photocopied but still clearly recognizable. She smiled back as if taunting him. The same full lips, high cheekbones and straight nose, the same vivid, intense eyes. Beautiful and terrible all at once.

A fantasy made real. A fantasy that he'd become caught up in.

As he forced himself to read, the true story of her life began to take shape. Recruited aged 18 from a young offenders' institution in Lithuania, her KGB handler's name was Viktor Surovsky. Studied advanced infiltration and intelligence gathering skills between 1983–84, rated highly proficient in all subjects, particularly at reading attempted deception. Deemed an ideal candidate due to age, gender and physical attractiveness. Approved for operational deployment, 1985.

Cain closed his eyes as the full magnitude of the dossier settled on him. Anya – his Anya – was a Soviet spy. She had been working against them the whole time. Working against him.

'It does not make for easy reading, does it?' Qalat remarked. 'Knowing that everything you built your life around is a lie.'

253

Cain whirled around, grabbed Qalat by the shirt and shoved him backwards until he slammed into the door. That was enough to shatter his air of patronising, infuriating self-control.

'It's not true!' Cain shouted. 'You forged this document to turn me against her, you son of a bitch!'

'It is no lie!' Qalat said. 'One of my sources in Soviet intelligence recovered it for us after we turned him in Afghanistan. It is the truth, Marcus! The ambush wasn't a search and destroy mission; it was a recovery operation! It gave Anya a pretext to leave the group without anyone realizing she'd been compromised.'

Cain released him, taking a step back as if struck.

'Do you not think it strange that she alone volunteered to stay behind, and she alone survived to be captured?'

Cain didn't say anything. Thoughts and memories were cascading through his head faster than he could process them.

'She's fought for us, killed for us, helped us win this war,' he said, struggling to understand what he was hearing. 'What spy would do that?'

'Acceptable losses,' Qalat said coldly. 'More than worth it for the greater prize – proof that America has been fighting a covert war against the Soviet Union in Afghanistan. Detailed information on the CIA's plans, key personnel, ongoing operations in this part of the world… everything the KGB needs to cripple you for decades. It all rests with Anya.'

--

'Your father saw everything,' Anya went on with the same look of bitter regret. 'All the secrets I had been trying to keep from him since I arrived in America. My recruitment into the KGB, my mission to infiltrate the CIA, my handler's name. All of it.

'I should have known it would happen,' she went on. 'But I was young, and stupid, and I thought I was smart and fast enough to outrun my past.' She shook her head. 'I was wrong.'

--

It was at this moment that the satellite comms unit on the table crackled into life, as a transmission filtered down from the orbiting sat relay.

'Come in, Vector. Repeat, come in.' Even through the garbled mush of static, Cain recognized the voice as Romek's. 'Jurate is in position. All elements ready to move. We're awaiting go command.'

Cain stared at the radio, not moving, torn between it and the man who had just brought such devastating news with him.

'If you send them in, you will be sending those men to their deaths,' Qalat said, taking a step towards him.

'Get the fuck away from me!' Cain barked, drawing the gun on him once more.

Qalat, always playing the odds, was smart enough not to push him. 'Your team is walking into a trap, Marcus. The Soviets will be ready for them, and they will never find Anya.'

'Repeat, Jurate is awaiting go command, Vector,' Romek pressed, his voice more urgent. 'Acknowledge this message.'

Cain ached to do it. Every fibre was telling him to order the strike anyway, to disregard Qalat's warnings, throw aside his doubts and trust the young woman he remembered. Because the Anya he knew would do the same for him.

The Anya he knew.

But had he ever truly known her?

'You may be willing to sacrifice your own life, Marcus Cain, but are you willing to sacrifice theirs?' Qalat asked. 'How many more people will you give up for a woman who never even existed?'

'Vector, we are exposed here. We must attack now,' Romek warned him over the radio. 'If we don't hear from you now, we will deploy ourselves.'

Cain saw it happening. He saw himself stepping towards the table, saw himself reaching for the radio unit, saw himself raise it to his mouth.

But it was a different man who spoke the next command.

'This is Vector. Fall back. Abort mission right away.'

Seconds of incredulous silence followed.

'Say again your last, Vector?'

'I repeat, abort the mission,' he said. 'Acknowledge abort code Giltine now.'

'We are in position,' Romek repeated, speaking slowly and clearly as he struggled to hold his emotions in check. 'We can do this, Vector. Why are we aborting?'

Cain felt hot tears stinging his eyes. 'It's a trick. Maras is not on site. I say again, Maras is not on site. We blew it, the mission's over.' He steadied himself. 'I'm sorry.'

'Not as sorry as we are, Vector,' Romek replied, voice darkened with anger. 'Abort code acknowledged. Jurate is falling back.'

Cain dropped the radio unit and leaned against the table as the full weight of betrayal and grief settled on him.

–

'I spent two months in that Soviet prison,' Anya reflected. 'Two months. I was a very different person when I managed to escape.'

Lauren frowned, confused by what she'd just heard. 'Escape? But you said—'

'Pakistani intelligence were right that I came to America as a KGB agent,' Anya explained. 'But they drew all the wrong conclusions about me. What they didn't know – what none of them could know at the time – was that I had turned against my Russian handlers long before I was sent to Afghanistan. From the moment the KGB recruited me, I did nothing but play along, tell them what they wanted to hear, learn everything they had to teach me so that one day I could use those skills against them.'

'Why?' Lauren asked, fascinated by what she was hearing. It was the most Anya had ever spoken about herself, and the more she learned, the more caught up she became. It was obvious that even after all these years a fire still burned deeply in her.

'They killed my parents,' Anya said. 'They had identified them as a threat to the State, and they did what they always do to such people – made them disappear. I was a loose end to be tied up, but apparently they thought they could use me first.

'That was why I volunteered to go to Afghanistan with Task Force Black. I wanted to fight back, take revenge, make them suffer as I had. I was young, and stupid, and angry. And I thought my old handler Viktor would never catch up with me.' She shrugged. 'I was wrong. That ambush was done for one reason – so Viktor could get his hands on me. He was willing to sacrifice anything to make me suffer, and he did make me suffer, Lauren. More even than I could endure.'

Lauren tried to hide a shudder. Given the kind of woman Anya was, she could barely imagine the torments that must have been inflicted.

'I don't blame your father for what happened,' Anya concluded. 'Not really. He did what he had to do, and in his place I might have done the same. But it didn't make it any easier to accept at the time.' Her expression was deep and abiding, that of someone who has spent a lifetime reflecting on what might have been. 'Neither of us knew it, but that was both a beginning and an end. It was the end of what we once had, and the beginning of the path that led us here.'

Lauren stared back at her, stunned into silence. Never could she have imagined the scale and tragedy of the events that had torn this woman apart from her father.

'Why?' she finally managed to say. 'Why tell me this now?'

'I am a killer, Lauren. I have killed more people than I can remember. Some deserved it, some didn't. Some were just unlucky enough to get in my way. There was a time when I used to feel guilty about that, but now I feel nothing. That is who I am now, and I have made peace with it. But I wanted you to know that it wasn't always like this. The things your father and I have done since that day, the choices we made… I wanted you to know where it began. We imagined a better future than the one we created. We imagined peace in our time.' She almost laughed. 'That was supposed to be our gift to the next generation. To people like you. But we failed.' She shook her head, her final words coming out as barely a whisper. 'The things we could have done together.'

Silence descended on the room then.

Anya rose slowly from her chair, looking suddenly weary and pained, as if the years sat more heavily on her.

'Wait,' Lauren implored, snapping out of her awed silence and jumping to her feet. 'Don't do this, Anya. Whatever you're planning tomorrow, don't go through with it. Taking revenge against my father, it's not going to turn the clock back 20 years. Make this right.'

'I can't.'

'Yes, you can,' the young woman said, with desperate hope.

Anya shook her head. 'It's too late for that. Too late for me.'

'It's never too late! If what you said is true, if…' She bit her lip, struggling with what she was about to say. 'If you and my father really did care about each other, then please *stop this*. Whatever you might think of him, he's not an evil man, and… I know you're not either. I know that now.'

'You know nothing,' Anya retorted, her voice strained and taut.

'Either I'm wrong, and my dad's the monster you've convinced yourself he is, or I'm right, and this war you're fighting is all for nothing. Maybe you both made mistakes, but whatever happened between you two, let it go,' she begged, putting her all into this final, impassioned effort. 'You've wasted so much of your life regretting your past when you could have changed your future. You said you're a killer, but you don't have to be what they made you. Not any more. Don't you understand? You can *choose* to be something else, something *better*. Isn't that worth fighting for?'

For the first time since she'd met her, Anya looked at Lauren not with contempt, not with simmering dislike or cold professionalism, but with fear. She backed away a step, staring as if she were a ghost risen up to haunt her.

Lauren could tell her words were making an impact, that she was close to breaking through Anya's layers of armour, finally reaching the person within. The proud, vulnerable, brilliant and flawed woman who had once dreamed of carving out a better future.

Just a glimmer, a glimpse, and then that young woman was lost again. Despite everything, Lauren felt a great upwelling of sadness and pity for Anya.

'Rest now,' Anya said, her defences restored. 'Tomorrow this will be over, and you can go on with your life. I hope for your sake you make more of it than I did.'

Lauren knew her chance had passed. That Anya was set on her course, and that nothing she could do would divert her.

Part IV

Conflagration

'Peace has its place, as does war. Mercy has its place, as do cruelty and revenge.'

– Meir Kahane

Chapter 50

It was a chilly spring morning in Berlin, with only light traffic on the roads and the early-morning joggers just visible through the fog.

It was Anya's favourite time, having risen early while others slept. A time to contemplate the day ahead, to focus on the challenges and dangers that stood in her path.

The long journey that had brought them here was almost over. By the end of the day, she would either be reunited with Drake and what was left of his team, or they might all be dead. It all depended on whether she could make the exchange work.

Kneeling on the damp, springy grass, she leaned forward until her face was almost touching the ground, and she could smell the rich loamy soil. Brushing her fingers lightly across damp stalks, she then drew them across her face, leaving drops of cold water on her skin.

Sitting up with her eyes closed, she could feel the steady beat of her heart, the damp mist on her skin, the faintest breeze stirring her hair.

When she opened her eyes, she became aware of a new presence nearby.

'What is it, Alex?' she asked.

Alex was standing a short distance away, leaning against the trunk of a big oak tree with his arms folded. She had heard the rustle of his footsteps through last season's fallen leaves, but hadn't acknowledged him until she was finished with her ritual.

'I didn't want to disturb you,' he said quietly. 'I can leave if you like.'

Anya shook her head. 'I'm finished here.'

'That was...' He trailed off, not sure what he'd witnessed. 'What were you doing?'

'An old habit, nothing more,' she said, rising to her feet with the ease and grace of long practice. 'Do you need something?'

'A few minutes of your time.'

Anya glanced at her watch. They would have to get moving soon; there was much work to be done before the exchange could take place. But she could spare him a little time if necessary.

'All right,' Anya agreed. 'Walk with me.'

They steered a path through the man-made forest, heading generally northwards towards a long ribbon-like lake that occupied the central section of the park.

'Today's the day, then,' Alex remarked as they walked along the shore.

'It is.'

'Are you afraid?'

She thought about it. 'No.' She had worries and concerns aplenty, but it had been a long time since Anya had felt genuine fear. Maybe she no longer had it in her. 'Why do you ask?'

'Just trying to figure out if I'm the only sane person around here,' he said frankly. 'Don't you even care that you might be dead by the end of the day?'

Anya stopped walking and turned to look at him. 'How would that be different from any other day?' she asked. 'Everyone dies, Alex. I am no different.'

He opened his mouth to question her, to push harder for answers, but he knew her enough to know that none would be forthcoming.

'You can still back out, if you want to,' she said. This was no time for doubts. If he wasn't committed, he had no part to play. 'There is no shame in it. But be honest and tell me now.'

Alex took his time before replying, genuinely thinking over what she'd said. Good – she wanted him to understand what he was committing to if he said yes. And for once, she really didn't know what he was going to say.

'As fucked up as this might sound, you're probably the closest thing I've got to a friend these days,' he finally said. 'And that's saying a lot, considering you once had a gun to my head.' He flashed a weak smile, but there was a determination behind it that she'd been looking for. 'That being the case, I can't let you do this alone. I'm in, all the way.'

Anya felt herself relax a little. She could improvise and make this work without his help if necessary, but despite everything, she was glad he'd chosen to see it through.

She stared out across the water, feeling no need to say anything further.

'I went down into your basement,' Alex said. 'And I opened the box you keep hidden down there.'

Anya nodded slowly. 'I know.'

She'd noticed it when she'd been down there working out her frustrations on the heavy bag, and soon guessed the cause.

She knew that was the real reason he'd sought her out this morning.

'Why didn't you say anything?'

'Why didn't *you*?' she replied.

He looked a little embarrassed. 'I didn't know how you'd react.'

'But you're telling me now,' Anya observed coolly. 'You might as well ask me.'

'Ask what?'

'Who those dog tags belonged to. Why there are no names on them. Why I keep them down there.'

'Will you tell me?'

'I will make a deal with you,' she decided. 'Ask me once this is all over. Then I will tell you the truth. How does that sound?'

'What if we don't live that long?'

Anya laid a hand on his shoulder. 'Then it won't matter.' Letting go, she gestured back to the path they'd taken through the quiet parkland. 'Come, we have work to do.'

Chapter 51

The bars and taverns on Capitol Hill were regular hangouts for reporters in search of scoops, government employees and politicians looking to blow off steam, and anyone looking to trade information and political gossip. Tonight, however, Marcus Cain was here to do one thing only – drown his sorrows.

Helped by a plentiful supply of whisky, he'd been doing a creditable job of it so far. Waiting until the bartender had poured him a double measure, Cain lifted the glass to his lips, inhaling the heady fumes rising from the potent alcohol. No need for ice or soda; he was taking it neat.

The drink went down like liquid fire, settling hard in his stomach. Nonetheless, he went right ahead and ordered another. He needed it.

It had finally happened. His impetuous adventure in Pakistan had been discovered, despite being called off at the last minute. Simmons, the head of the Agency's Special Activities Division, had called Cain into his office that very afternoon.

Unsurprisingly, the conversation had been brief and unequivocal.

'You're insubordinate, unstable, lacking in judgement and objectivity. You launched an operation into foreign territory without authorization, endangered Agency resources and personnel, and came minutes away from starting a war. You're a liability, Marcus. A liability I'm not prepared to tolerate any longer,' Simmons had informed him. 'I want your resignation on my desk tomorrow. I can't put it any plainer than that. You've done great things for the Agency, which is why I'd prefer you to go on your own terms, leave with some sense of dignity. If not, I'll have no option but to call an official hearing. You'll be destroyed and humiliated. That's not what you want, is it?'

What he wanted was irrelevant. Cain's career was over.

How quickly he had fallen from grace. Everything he'd worked towards had come crashing down. Because he'd trusted the wrong person.

He should have hated Anya for what she'd done to him – for lying to him, for playing him, for pulling him down with her, yet he couldn't quite bring himself to forget what they'd once had. None of that had seemed to matter. Together he'd felt like they could change the world.

How vain and naive he'd been.

'Rough day?' a voice remarked.

A woman had settled into the seat beside Cain – someone he'd never seen before. She was about his age, well-dressed, dark-haired and attractive, with a slender and graceful physique accentuated by a close-cut dress.

'You have no idea,' he said, taking another sip of whisky.

'I can take a guess.' Her voice was soft, smooth, her accent unmistakably British. 'It's a woman, then. Only a woman can leave a man with that kind of look.'

Cain had heard enough. Innocent flirtation it might have been, but he was in no mood to revisit everything that had brought him here.

'I'm not the kind of company you're looking for, honey,' he said, hoping she'd take the hint and seek out a more willing companion. With a body like that, it wouldn't be hard.

She gave a fake pout. 'Oh, that's a shame. But to be honest, that's not the reason I'm here tonight, Marcus.'

Straightaway he tensed up, alert despite his drinking. 'How do you know my name?'

'I know a lot about you, Mr Cain,' she said, keeping her voice low so that their conversation would be lost amid the hubbub of the bar. 'I know you work for the CIA. I know your career's taken a turn for the worse recently, and that's why you're here drowning your sorrows.' She leaned forward slightly, taking in the scent of his drink. 'Laphroaig. Not a bad choice for that kind of thing, I suppose.'

'You know your whiskey.'

'I know it smells like paint stripper. More of a gin drinker myself.'

'Then knock yourself out. But do it alone,' he said, making to leave. Clearly this woman was foreign intelligence of some kind – hopefully MI6 given how much she seemed to know about him.

'Don't go,' she said, reaching out.

Cain looked down at her. 'Take your hand off my arm now,' he said, cold and menacing. Woman or not, he would happily knock her on her ass if she screwed with him any further. 'Wouldn't want to make a scene.'

'Nor would I,' she affirmed, showing a hint of steel beneath her refined appearance. Still, she let go. 'I'm simply asking you to sit down, finish your drink and listen to what I have to say. If you want to leave after that, I won't try to stop you.'

He sensed that staying would be a bad move. There was no telling who this woman really was, who she worked for or what she hoped to get out of him. Nonetheless, his instincts told him to hear her out.

After all, what the hell did he have left to lose?

'Fine,' he said, lowering himself back into the seat. 'But I should warn you, if you're hoping to recruit me to MI6, you're wasting your time. I'll be out of a job soon anyway.'

The woman smiled. The smile of a poker player about to reveal a winning hand. 'Wrong on both counts, Marcus. The group I represent is a little more... international. And as for your job, well, I might just be able to help you out with that.'

'Why?'

'Because I think you have potential, Marcus. And so do my employers. You've had some rotten luck recently, and I don't blame you for drowning your sorrows,' she said. 'But this doesn't have to be how your story ends. You can still do remarkable things, make the difference you always wanted to.'

'What's your name?' he asked.

'My name's Freya.' She smiled then, knowing she had him. 'And I'm about to make your life a great deal better.'

—

It was ten o'clock in the morning when Cain's phone buzzed, just as he'd known it would. He was ready for it, standing by the window of his hotel suite overlooking Frankfurt's bustling financial district.

'Had a feeling you'd be calling.'

'Put Drake on the phone.'

Knowing Anya would call off the exchange if she couldn't verify Drake was still alive, Cain had brought him up to his suite via the freight elevator, making sure to avoid the hotel's security cameras.

Cain studied his prisoner for a moment or two. Battered and bloodied, worn down by fatigue and injury, he should have been a pathetic, diminished sight. But Drake was still standing unbowed, refusing to be beaten down.

'It's for you,' Cain mocked, as he held out the phone and enabled hands-free mode.

Flanked by a pair of operatives who were watching his every move, ready to stun him if he so much as laid a finger on Cain, Drake shuffled forward, limping slightly. His eyes were on Cain the whole time, burning with hatred.

With his hands still cuffed, he took the handset, although it was a good couple of seconds before he finally spoke.

'I'm here, Anya,' he whispered.

'Ryan, I...' Cain could have sworn he heard her voice start to break, though she quickly recovered. 'What's your situation?'

'I'm hanging in there.'

'And the others?'

Drake's eyes flicked to Cain. Never had he seen a human as desperate to murder another.

'Cole's dead,' he said. 'Samantha's gone too. She was working for Cain the whole time.'

Cain could see now how deeply that loss had hurt Drake. Samantha McKnight had been his mole, his informant and at times his saboteur. Even if she'd ultimately proven unreliable and forced Cain to dispose of her, he would never let Drake know that. Better to let his pain and hatred fester.

'I understand,' Anya said. 'I'm... sorry things didn't work out as we planned, Ryan.'

'They never do,' Drake acknowledged. 'We must have bad karma.'

'How long do you think you can hold out?'

Drake swallowed, raising his chin a little. 'As long as I have to.'

Cain had heard enough. Snatching the phone back, he gestured to his two operatives to remove Drake from the room. He wanted to be alone for this.

'You've got your proof,' he hissed, 'now give me mine.'

He heard some muffled noises as the phone was passed over, then suddenly another voice came on the line. Young, frightened, hushed.

'Dad?'

It wasn't often in life that something could punch through the layers of armour, the endless plans and schemes, all the contingencies Cain surrounded himself with, penetrating through to the very core of his being. But Lauren was one of those things.

'I'm here, Lauren. It's okay,' he assured her, speaking fast, lest Anya snatch the phone away. 'I'm going to get you back soon, I promise. Are you all right? Have they hurt you?'

'No, Dad. I'm okay. They've treated me well.'

Relief rushed through Cain. A tiny victory in the battle that still raged around him.

'I'm…' He hesitated, knowing he didn't have long. Anya wouldn't give him much time, just as he'd given her little with Drake. But he had to somehow express what he'd ached to say for so long. 'I'm sorry, for not being there.'

'You couldn't have stopped this—'

'I don't mean that,' he interjected. 'I was never there for you, Lauren. Not when I should have been. Even when I *was* around, I wasn't there for you. I wasn't the father you deserved.'

'They're listening in. They can hear what you're saying.'

'I don't care,' he said. 'You are the only good thing that has come out of my life, Lauren. The only thing I somehow managed not to screw up. I only wish I'd seen that sooner.'

He heard a sharp intake of breath – shuddering, strained. A young woman trying to hold her emotions in check.

He had to say it. He couldn't hold it back any longer. 'Lauren, I lo—'

A sudden noise on the line accompanied by Lauren's protests told him Anya had just wrested back control of the phone.

'As you put it, you have your proof, Marcus,' Anya said. 'Now it's just you and me. Be in Berlin by 1 p.m. I'll give you the final exchange point shortly afterwards.'

Anya hung up, leaving Cain alone with his thoughts.

Slipping the phone into his pocket, he closed his eyes and took a slow, measured breath, forcing calm and focus into his mind. Anya had chosen where to make her last stand. A few hours from now, they would be face to face for the first time in eight years, and he was ready for it.

He'd been ready for a long time.

Turning away from the bustling metropolis, Cain swept out of the room.

Hawkins was waiting for him in the anteroom, expensively suited and booted, his hair neatly combed and his face clean-shaven. A monster in the guise of a civilized man. A monster Cain was soon to unleash.

'What's the word, sir?' he asked, watching Cain carefully as he approached.

Cain stopped in front of him. 'We're going to Berlin.'

A smile twitched at the corner of his mouth, the scar tissue twisting it into a cruel sneer. 'I'll have the boys saddled up in five minutes.'

'Good. And Hawkins?' Cain pulled the bigger man close so that he was speaking just inches from Hawkins' ear. 'No one touches Anya but me. She's mine.' His grip tightened as he allowed some of his boiling emotions to show through. 'Understand?'

He saw a flicker of something dark and dangerous as Hawkins began to sense weakness, but nonetheless the operative nodded. 'Perfectly.'

Chapter 52

Anya had gathered Yasin and Alex around the apartment's dining table, taking this opportunity to go over her plan one final time. After this, any last-minute changes or unexpected developments would have to be handled on the fly.

'You both know what you have to do,' she said, looking at each of them in turn once she'd finished summarizing the chain of events she imagined unfolding. 'Yasin, you are our eyes on the ground. You will stay out of sight, watch Cain's men and report what you see.'

Yasin's advantage was that he was completely unknown to Cain and his subordinates. His presence would arouse no suspicion. Also, he had already proven adept at moving stealthily in urban environments, and Anya intended to get him to the meeting point well ahead of time so that he could familiarize himself with the area.

'No one will see me. You have my word,' he promised.

'When the shooting starts, you will leave the area of engagement and get yourself to the rendezvous point,' she added. 'You will not try to interfere, and no matter what happens you will not wait for me. Understand?'

He nodded slightly.

'I want to hear you say it, Yasin,' she insisted. If she had any doubts about his intention to stay clear of trouble, she would leave him behind.

'I understand,' he said impatiently. 'It will be done as you say.'

Satisfied, Anya moved on to the next phase of her plan.

–

A dozen operatives lined the crew compartment of the Sikorsky S-70 transport helicopter, the civilian version of the Black Hawk, as it thundered towards Berlin at its maximum cruising speed of 160 knots. Several thousand feet below them, small villages rolled by, tiny cars dotting roads that snaked across the green fields.

In the centre of the group sat Hawkins, even the most hardened field operatives seeming to shrink away from him.

'All right, I'm only going to say this once, so listen up,' he said, speaking over his radio headset. 'We're waiting for a final location, but we know it's going down in Berlin. We're vectoring in additional manpower to secure a perimeter, but we're the tip of the sword on this one. That means it's on us to get it done.'

He glanced over at Riley, his young protégé, who had so very nearly worked her magic on Drake. He could see her eagerness, her excitement at the prospect of the fight, her burning desire to wreak bloody vengeance. She'd pitted herself against Drake once and come up short; pride demanded that she even the score.

'We have one hostage to be secured,' he went on. 'Until I say otherwise, her safety is our first, last and only priority, so we *do not* move in until we've confirmed she's in the clear. I'll be real disappointed if any of you get itchy trigger fingers.'

Lauren Cain was an annoying distraction. Riley wasn't the only one with scores to settle today – Hawkins was eager to get his hands on Anya, but he knew Cain would show no mercy towards anyone who got his daughter killed. This situation required finesse and restraint. Rewards could come later, once he'd fulfilled his duty.

'On first contact, we establish a perimeter. I want it airtight – no one and nothing gets in or out without our knowledge. Is anyone unclear about what I've just said?'

He was met with a dozen voices responding as one. 'No, sir!'

—

With Yasin briefed, Anya turned her attention to Alex.

'You will control electronic surveillance at the site of the exchange,' she said, pointing to a mark on the Berlin street map laid out on the table. 'This residential parking area is two blocks away, and that should be far enough back to be outside their perimeter.'

'How can you be so sure?' Alex asked.

'Cain will have limited manpower. He will be using trusted men, not Agency field teams who might talk or ask questions. Anyway, he wants me, and his attention will be focussed on that goal. For both reasons, his perimeter will be tight.'

'Doesn't leave a lot of room for you to get out, in that case,' he remarked, searching for an explanation that would allay his fears.

'Let me worry about that,' she said dismissively. 'With luck I can cause enough confusion to help us get away, but the longer we delay the more chance we have of being intercepted. So if I tell you to go, leave with or without me. *Don't wait.*'

'I thought soldiers never left a man behind?'

'You are not a soldier, and I am not a man,' Anya pointed out.

Alex folded his arms, clearly unhappy. 'Fine. But for the record, I don't like this.'

'Neither do I. But it's the best we have.'

Hawkins glanced at his team. A dozen trained killers, well armed and well prepared, all of them forged in the heat of war, about to pit themselves against an enemy the likes of which they'd never encountered before. He had no doubt that some of them would be dead before the day was out. The only question was how many lives Anya would take with her when she fell.

'Everything you've just heard is the official line,' he said, bringing the first part of his briefing to a close. 'But this next part's for me.'

Their eyes were fixed on him, keen to hear what he'd say next. Most of them held Hawkins in the highest regard, a few were openly intimidated by him, but all were watching their leader in rapt attention.

'The enemy we will face today is one of the most highly trained operatives the Agency ever fielded,' he began. 'She is resourceful, experienced, ruthless and utterly without mercy. Make no mistake, the second you underestimate this woman, you're as good as dead. So believe me when I say we have a difficult day ahead, and not all of you are going to see the end of it.'

A few nervous glances were exchanged as his words sank in. Good, he wanted them on edge. He wanted them to respect their enemy.

Only then would they be able to help him kill her.

–

Leaning on the table with her head down, Anya sighed, gathering her thoughts before speaking again. When she looked up, her expression was different. Softer, less sure of herself, almost vulnerable. This wasn't something she was used to doing, and it showed.

'Neither of you are soldiers,' she said. 'I have asked you to do things that I have no right to ask of anyone. I want you to understand that neither of you owe me anything, so if you are here only out of guilt or obligation, I release you from it. You can walk away now and I will think no worse of you.'

She was watching them closely, waiting for a response, needing to hear it from them. Neither Alex nor Yasin said a word.

–

'If any of you still expect this exchange to pass smoothly and peacefully, then you're going to have a real bad day,' Hawkins barked. 'Anya will do everything in her considerable power to fuck this up for us. She will try to play games with us, lure us in, catch us off guard, and wait until we're at our weakest and most vulnerable. Then she will strike, and she will show no mercy.

'But she will not succeed,' he continued, his voice rising with growing power and conviction. 'She will fail in her mission, because *we* are stronger than her. We hold all the advantages: we have the only two people she's willing to risk her life for, and that *will* be her downfall. We will overcome every obstacle she throws in our path, we will counter every strategy, we will defeat every plan. We will exhaust her options, shut down every means of escape until we have the bitch backed into a corner. Then she'll be ours.'

Hawkins could feel the fire rising with every word he spoke, the growing confidence in their victory. They were ready. He knew it.

'God willing, she will not live to see another sunrise,' he finished, scanning their determined faces. 'Anyone got a problem with that?'

For the second time, the dozen warriors spoke as one. 'No, sir!'

–

'There are not many people in this world I can call friends,' Anya said. 'But the two of you are amongst them. Knowing the risks, I must ask whether you're prepared to go through with this.'

'You know I'm in,' Alex said. 'If nothing else, I deserve to meet the guys I got pepper-sprayed for.'

Yasin drew himself up to his full if modest height. 'I said before that you owed me a debt for saving your life in Pakistan,' he said, then shook his head slowly. 'I was wrong. *You* saved me from something worse – a life with no meaning, slowly dying every day. For that, I am yours. I will do whatever you ask, for as long as you ask it.'

Silence descended on the room. Alex suspected Anya didn't trust herself to speak. She was human after all.

'Shit, did you rehearse that one?' he asked Yasin, surprised and a little jealous of his eloquence. 'Kind of puts mine to shame.'

Yasin beamed with confidence. 'Your words were simple, Alex. Just like your mind.'

Even Anya smiled a little, the tension suddenly broken. She rolled up the map. 'Then we go,' she said, the matter settled. 'Get your things. We leave in five minutes.'

'Wait a second,' Alex said as Anya knelt beside the holdall full of weapons. 'Did you really call me a friend? I need to write this down.'

'That can change very easily, Alex,' she replied, with mock seriousness. 'Come on, let's finish this.'

Chapter 53

Islamabad, Pakistan

It was early evening when the three-car convoy rolled out of the ISI's headquarters, bound for the US embassy compound across town. On board were Executive Director Khalid, a cadre of his closest advisors, a heavy security contingent, and Vizur Qalat.

Khalid had insisted that Qalat accompany them, partly because his sage advice had been instrumental in Khalid's decision, and partly because he had come to trust Qalat implicitly when it came to dealing with the CIA.

Qalat sat upright as he watched the busy roadways of central Islamabad slide by outside his window. The sun was already close to the horizon, casting long shadows across the ground, but the sultry heat of the afternoon persisted. Only the car's powerful air conditioning kept the temperature down, though Qalat could nonetheless feel tiny beads of sweat trickling down his back.

'Something on your mind, Vizur?'

Blinking, he noticed Director Khalid watching him with interest. 'Many things,' Qalat answered vaguely.

Reaching into his jacket pocket, Khalid produced a pack of cigarettes. 'I'd feel better hearing you thoughts,' he said, lighting up and taking a draw.

He was nervous, Qalat knew, even if he was trying to hide it. Khalid had largely given up cigarettes, only bringing them out during times of stress or difficulty. He disliked the Americans already, and sensed there was more to this meeting than a simple exchange of information.

He was looking for reassurance.

'I feel like this could be a historic day for our country,' Qalat said, mustering an appropriate level of gravitas for his lie. 'My gut tells me the Americans have learned they can't push us around and work behind our backs. If this is our chance to make them treat us as equals, I hope we prove worthy of the task.'

Khalid stifled a cough as he pondered Qalat's words.

'If it is indeed as you say, history may remember both our names,' he remarked. 'There will be many opportunities for men like us.'

Qalat forced a knowing smile. Amid the doubts and fears, Khalid's mind was alive with thoughts of the prestige and influence a diplomatic victory could buy him. Already director of the ISI, it wouldn't be hard to see him parlaying that influence into a career in the higher echelons of government.

'We will hear what the Americans have to offer,' Khalid went on, blowing acrid tobacco smoke into the car's interior. 'Then I will decide if it is good enough.'

Chapter 54

Not only had Felix provided Anya with weapons and equipment, he'd also been able to secure a Volkswagen Transporter van. It was waiting for them in the parking area outside their apartment, the keys secured to the underside of the driver's wheel arch.

In short order they had loaded their gear, secured Lauren in the back, with Alex covering her, and were on their way. Barely 30 minutes stood between them and their meeting with Cain.

'What are their names?' Lauren asked suddenly.

Anya glanced at her in the rear mirror. 'What do you mean?'

'The people you're doing this for,' the young woman explained. 'You said my father was holding your friends prisoner. I wanted to know their names.'

'Why?'

'You're risking your life – and mine – to get them back. I think I at least deserve to know who they are.'

Anya didn't say anything for a few seconds, and Lauren began to wonder if she was refusing to answer. 'The first is called Keira Frost.'

'What's she like?'

'She used to be a technical specialist with the CIA, then she went rogue like myself.'

Lauren chuckled then shook her head. 'You've told me what she does. I asked what she's like – as a person.'

Anya gave her an annoyed look, but nonetheless conceded. 'She is young, stubborn, quick to anger and slow to forgive. She acts first and thinks later, and never backs down – even when she should. She tried to kill me once.'

Lauren raised an eyebrow. 'Sounds charming.'

'I was not so different when I was young,' Anya said.

'Hard to imagine you ever being young,' Lauren fired back. 'What about the second one?'

Anya seemed to tense up at this question. 'His name is Drake.'

It was clear she had no desire to say more, and Lauren was quick to pick up on it. 'I get it. This Drake… he means something to you, right? He must be something pretty special if you're willing to risk four lives for him.'

'That's enough,' Anya snapped.

Lauren glared back at her fearlessly. 'What are you going to do? Kill me?'

'I won't kill you, Lauren. But I will have you gagged and blindfolded. Is that what you want?'

It was clear that this was no idle threat. Lauren leaned back against the side of the compartment. 'What I want is for this to be over.'

'It will be soon,' Anya said.

-

US embassy – Islamabad, Pakistan

Station Chief Hayden Quinn was in his office when his desk phone rang. He pounced on it immediately. 'Quinn.'

'Gate security, sir,' one of the guards outside reported. 'They're here.'

Quinn could feel his throat growing dry. The time had come. The meeting he'd never imagined possible was about to begin. The Pakistani ISI delegation was waiting for him.

'Good, let them through.'

'We haven't processed them through security, sir,' the man replied.

'No security checks,' Quinn said firmly. 'They're here under a diplomatic banner. That's how they'll be treated.'

'Sir, this is against protocol—'

'It's on my authority, son,' Quinn cut in. 'I'm station chief, and I'm telling you to let them through. I'll be down to meet them right now.'

A pause, then a reluctant, 'Yes, sir.'

Quinn grabbed his jacket and shrugged into it, taking a couple of deep breaths.

Hurrying downstairs, he was just in time to meet the Pakistani delegation as they emerged from their silver Mercedes SUVs. A cursory glance was enough to tell him most of the major players in the ISI were here, including Director Khalid himself, flanked by heavy-set security men.

'Director Khalid,' Quinn began, approaching him with his hand outstretched. 'I'm Hayden Quinn, the station chief here.'

His first impression of Khalid was that he was both shorter and fatter than expected, his belt and shirt struggling to contain a protruding stomach. He also looked older than his intelligence dossier photos had suggested, his wide face deeply lined, his scalp showing through thinning hair.

'Mr Quinn,' Khalid said, gripping his hand like a vice rather than shaking it.

'I'm pleased you accepted our invitation,' Quinn went on, undeterred. 'It's my hope this represents the first step towards better cooperation between our agencies.'

Khalid's face was giving nothing away. 'That depends on what you have to show us,' he said, releasing Quinn's hand. 'I hope for both our sakes this was not a wasted trip.'

Quinn took a step back, hoping he looked more confident than he felt. 'Of course. We have a conference room waiting for us inside.' He gestured towards the embassy building. 'This way please, gentlemen.'

–

Berlin, Germany

They were here. Pulling into a parking area, Anya shut down the engine, stepped out and surveyed their surroundings carefully. They were in an open space flanked by multistorey buildings facing onto the main road nearby. On the south side was a modern high-rise shopping and office complex, while to the north stood an older government building – according to Alex's research, an urban planning office for the German government.

To the west, their parking lot gave way to a grassy, tree-covered recreation area for the apartment blocks facing it. A small island of greenery in a sea of concrete.

Satisfied their arrival hadn't drawn undue attention, Anya moved around to the van's rear door. Taking her holdall, she gestured for Lauren to come outside. Reluctantly the young woman complied, refusing Anya's offer of assistance and jumping down lightly onto the uneven tarmac.

Yasin jogged over to confer with Anya and Alex.

'This is where we split up,' Anya announced. 'You each know what you have to do.'

Neither of them was in any doubt now.

'Check your radios.'

Much like during the mission in Paris, they were wearing covert radio earpieces that allowed the team to communicate unobtrusively. Their effective range was limited to a hundred metres or so, but with luck that would be enough.

Flicking the switch that powered up her unit, Anya turned away from them and spoke quietly. 'Radio test. Check.'

'Got it,' Alex's voice crackled in her ear.

'I hear you too,' Yasin said.

Turning back to face them, she paused, trying to think of some parting words for them. She wasn't used to doing such things, and struggled to find the right way to begin.

'I trust you both to do this,' she finally said. 'Keep your wits about you, think slow and stay calm. I will take care of the rest.'

Without warning, Yasin threw his arms around her. He said nothing, just held Anya tight. It was the only physical affection he'd shown in the entire time she'd known him, and it caught her so off guard that she dropped her holdall.

At first Anya didn't know how to react, but then she reached down and laid her hand on his head, running her fingers through his short, bristly hair. She vaguely remembered her mother doing something similar when she was frightened or upset, but it was quite alien to her, as were the feelings it evoked.

At last Yasin stepped away, though he avoided her gaze. 'I must go now,' he announced as if nothing had happened. 'I need time to look around, find a good vantage point.'

Anya nodded. 'Go. Stay in contact over the radio.'

'I'll be seeing you soon, yeah?' Alex said, watching her closely.

'With luck,' Anya replied, still refusing to commit.

He seemed poised to say something more, but thought better of it, perhaps realizing that any further debate was futile. Instead he held out his hand, which Anya clasped tight for a few moments.

He looked at Lauren. 'However things play out today, I hope you come out of this all right, Lauren.'

'And you,' she said as she stared into his eyes, surprising both of them.

The moment was broken when Anya spoke up. 'Time to go,' she said, picking up the holdall and gesturing for the young woman to head towards the main road. 'Follow me, Lauren.'

Glancing back over her shoulder at Alex, who seemed to be watching them with an expression of sadness and regret, Lauren did as instructed.

'Where are we going?'

'For a cup of coffee.'

Chapter 55

Cain's advance teams had already established their command and control centre in a hotel room overlooking Potsdamer Platz in central Berlin. Walking into the room, the deputy director found himself confronted by a menagerie of laptops, secure radio comms units, satellite uplinks and surveillance equipment, with technicians bent over their hastily constructed work stations. It was just as well he'd mobilized assets all across the country the day before, otherwise they'd never have been ready in time.

As soon as Cain's arrival was noted the activity ceased.

'Who's in charge here?' Cain asked.

A man in the centre of the room raised his hand. 'I am, sir,' he said, a little hesitantly. 'Senior operative Javadi.'

'What's your sitrep?'

'I'm tied into the Berlin traffic cam network,' Javadi reported. 'As soon as we have a confirmed location, I can access every camera in a five-block radius. Berlin police frequencies are locked in, so we'll know exactly what they're up to. We're also monitoring microwave and radio transmissions, but as you can imagine there's a lot of data to sift through. It'll be easier once we can narrow the search area.'

Cain didn't doubt it. Anya had chosen well, hiding in the midst of six million people.

'Good work, Javadi,' Cain said. 'Call out as soon as you have something.'

'Will do, sir.'

Turning to Hawkins, Cain lowered his voice. 'Are our field teams ready to deploy?'

'Say the word, we're good to go.'

'And the prisoners?'

Hawkins' scarred face twisted. 'Riley's got it under control.'

–

Drake grunted in pain as a strike to the back of his legs dropped him. A moment later, his hood was ripped off, allowing him to see properly for the first time in several hours. He'd expected to find himself blinking and screwing up his eyes as bright light flooded in, but the reality was quite different.

He was in an extremely large room which was lit only by a haphazard collection of portable work lights.

He had to assume it was underground and, it seemed, still under construction – little more than a bare concrete floor with thick stone columns supporting the roof. Portable cement mixers, steel girders and various tools were scattered around.

There was a muted thump and a muffled curse to his right, where Frost had also been forced to kneel. One of their captors yanked her hood off, revealing a bloodied and very angry face. She glared up at the man who had struck her, an inch away from leaping up to attack him, but with her hands bound even Frost knew it would be a wasted effort.

'Try that without these cuffs next time, you fucking pussy,' she taunted him. 'We'll see how it works out for you.'

'You all right, Keira?' Drake asked, his tone upbeat, almost conversational. He wasn't going to let them know how much it hurt to see her like this.

At the same time he was trying to take in as much information about their captors as possible. There were two that he could see, both of whom were dressed in civilian clothes but almost certainly wearing concealed body armour.

The closest was keeping them covered with an FN P90 – a Belgian submachine gun notable for its small size and 50-round magazine that fitted flush with the frame itself. It was a serious piece of kit that was more than capable of killing the two of them with a single burst of 5.70mm gunfire.

The other operative was busy with a holdall laid out on the ground, containing technical equipment rather than weapons. Perhaps they intended to set up a communications point here.

Two guards – not much considering what they were up against – but a fuck-load more than Drake and Frost could contend with as long as they were bound and unarmed.

Frost turned to him, giving him a wink. 'Doing great. I was just hoping these pussies would grow a pair and get on with things.'

'We'll get to that soon enough,' a female voice responded.

Riley emerged from the darkness, smiling maliciously as she walked around in front of them. Drake could feel his muscles tightening as she approached, noticing that she was still wearing the lucky charm necklace she'd stolen from him in Prague.

Hawkins was a sadistic piece of shit, but even he knew when to respect Cain's orders not to harm their captives, their only leverage. Riley, however, was another sort.

However, he was momentarily distracted as the operative beside her placed a camera mounted on a tripod facing them. It was clear the camera was intended to broadcast images of them, and there could only be one reason for that.

Riley followed his gaze. 'What? You really thought we were going to just hand you two over?' she asked. 'We've got something else in mind. But hey, at least you get to be on TV, right?'

Drake had suspected something like this. Cain had no intention of bringing them to the exchange. Not physically, at least. But he would beam a live feed to Anya so she could watch Riley go to town on them.

'Not long now,' Riley remarked. 'I was hoping we'd have a little more foreplay before we got down to it.' She reached out and laid a hand on Drake's chest, right at the point where she'd hammered the glass shard into him. 'Oh well, I'll just have to make the most of it.'

With that, she pressed her thumb into the wound. Drake clenched his teeth as white-hot pain exploded, and warm blood tricked down his chest. He could feel his breathing coming faster, his heart leaping into overdrive as his body pleaded with him to pull away from her, to stop the agony that seemed to intensify with every passing second.

But somehow, through some immense effort of will, he remained silent.

'It's okay,' Riley whispered in his ear, her voice as tender and intimate as if they were lovers. 'You can scream, Drake. Nobody's going to hear us down here.'

When he finally opened his mouth, it wasn't a scream that reverberated around the room. It was a laugh.

So taken aback was Riley that she actually slackened her grip on his shoulder, pulling back at little to look at him. 'I'd love to know what you've got to laugh about.'

'I was just thinking back to that hotel room in Prague,' he said, still chuckling. 'I really should have fucked you before I beat the shit out of you. At least then Cain would have gotten his money's worth.'

He was expecting to see her pretty face contort in anger like it had last time, but it didn't.

'I'm a girl of many skills. You'll find that out soon enough,' she said, looking at the operative powering up the digital camera. 'We ready to go live yet?'

'Almost,' he said. 'Just setting up the connection.'

'Good.' Riley folded her arms. 'Wouldn't want to miss the big show.'

–

Cain's phone was ringing, and he knew who was calling.

'We're ready. Where are we doing this?'

Anya gave him the location, and straightaway he knew what she had in mind. He had to admire her flair for drama, if nothing else.

'Be here in 20 minutes,' Anya instructed. 'If you're late, the deal is off.'

'I want to speak to Lauren.'

'Time is ticking, Marcus.'

'I don't care. I want proof she's with you.'

There was a pause. Cain waited until another voice came on the line.

'Dad, I'm here,' Lauren said. 'Anya says not to try anything. Please just give her what she wants.'

'Don't worry, I'll make sure she gets what she deserves,' Cain promised. 'I'm coming for you now, Lauren. Hang in there just a little longer, okay?'

'Dad, I—'

She was cut off, Anya's voice returning. 'You have 19 minutes and 12 seconds. I suggest you hurry.'

As the line cut out, Cain turned to address the room. 'All right, listen up. We have a location,' he said, reeling off the address. 'Vector our field teams there now. Javadi, get a hold of every traffic and security camera you can, and scan for radio transmissions. They'll be using encrypted transmitters, so I want them locked in and decrypted ASAP. Anyone not clear on what I just said?'

Not a word was spoken.

'Good. Now move!'

As the tempo suddenly ramped up, Hawkins gripped Cain by the arm. He was holding a Kevlar vest — the kind designed to be worn discreetly beneath regular clothes — which he offered to the deputy director.

Cain shook his head. 'I don't need it.'

'I really think you do,' Hawkins said, his tone almost condescending. A veteran operative trying to instruct an overeager desk jockey in the harsh realities of life.

Cain fixed him with a sharp, knowing look. He'd been doing things like this when Hawkins was still in school.

'If Anya really wants to kill me, a fucking vest isn't going to stop her.'

Hawkins seemed to concede this. Laying the vest down, he instead reached for his sidearm and held it out to Cain. It was a silver Colt Delta Elite, a 10mm variant of the old M1911 handgun that had been around since the First World War. Cain knew from experience that it was both accurate and powerful, but with only eight rounds in the magazine it demanded careful use.

'Then maybe you ought to take this?' he suggested pointedly.

Cain reached out for the weapon. It had been a long time since he'd been in the field, and even longer since he'd fired a weapon in anger. The gun was heavier than he'd expected, the metal frame cold to the touch.

And today he might well have to use it.

Chapter 56

US embassy – Islamabad, Pakistan

As the Pakistani delegation filed into the conference room on the embassy's second floor, they were accompanied by Quinn and his key staffers. They looked stiff and uncomfortable, face to face with men who had been actively working against them for years.

It was also clear they were less than pleased by Director Khalid's security team.

Qalat's mind, however, was on what was about to play out. Taking a seat, he pulled out the burner phone, keeping it low and out of sight, and quickly punched out a text message.

In position. What now?

Barely 30 seconds passed before the answer came.

Be ready to move.

Qalat resisted the urge to loosen his uncomfortably tight collar. He could feel beads of sweat on his brow, and hoped fervently that nobody would notice his discomfort.

On the other side of the room, Quinn was drawn aside by Barrett, one of his most senior analysts and a man very familiar with the ISI.

'They're here, so what the hell are we supposed to do now?' the older man demanded, annoyed by Quinn's failure to give orders. 'The longer we sit on our hands, the more chance they're going to walk out on us.'

'Stay cool, I'm handling it,' he whispered, dialling the number for Cain's cell phone.

–

Berlin, Germany

En route to the meeting point, Cain felt his phone vibrating in his pocket. It was Quinn, calling from the embassy in Pakistan.

'Sir, the ISI delegation is here,' Quinn announced, voices audible in the background. 'Now's the time. We're all set up to conference you in if you're ready to speak with them?'

'Well done, Hayden,' he said, watching a father walk by with two small children in tow. Not a care in the world.

Reaching for his burner phone, he began to punch in a text message. 'I wanted to thank you for everything you've done to bring us to this point. I really am grateful that you've played your part.'

Even as he said this, he sent his message to Qalat.

Go now.

—

The time had come.

Qalat glanced around. Director Khalid had already lit up a cigarette, despite smoking being banned in the conference room, and was leaning in close to one of his advisors, who was speaking quietly in his ear.

Nearby, Quinn was on his phone, listening intently, concern etched on his face.

Qalat approached one of the American delegates and gently steered him aside. 'I am feeling unwell,' he said quietly, now glad that he was visibly perspiring. 'Where is the restroom?'

The man, white-haired and clearly well past retirement age, regarded him curiously before noticing his obvious discomfort. 'It's just outside. I'll show you the way,' he said, leading Qalat out of the room.

Khalid watched him go, suspicious of his sudden disappearance. He took another drag on his cigarette, making a mental note to discuss the matter with Qalat later.

Distracted by these thoughts, he failed to notice the briefcase positioned under the table. A briefcase that belonged to no one in the room.

—

'We need to get started now, sir,' Quinn said, a little unnerved.

Cain sighed. Despite everything, despite the fact Quinn had betrayed him to Drake, he did feel a measure of regret for what he was about to do. Quinn wasn't a bad man, but he was weak and disloyal. Two traits that Cain couldn't tolerate in a subordinate.

'Just one thing before you go, Hayden.'

Selecting another number from the burner phone's directory, his finger hovered over the call button.

'I'm sorry for the way things worked out.'

Then he hit the button.

—

Qalat was standing at the furthest end of the restroom when it happened. A thunderous blast rumbled through the building, the pressure wave blowing the door off its hinges and knocking him flat on the floor. Shattered glass and brickwork fell all around him as part of the wall collapsed, taking a portion of the ceiling with it. An instant later, the lights flickered and went out.

Opening his eyes and shaking his head at the ringing in his ears, Qalat groped around in the darkness. He could feel blood trickling from his head, and was vaguely aware of the distant sounds of car alarms, voices and screams.

Rising on unsteady legs, he scrambled through the rubble and out the now empty doorway. The white-haired man who had accompanied him outside was lying on the ground, unconscious or dead, he couldn't tell. But that mattered nothing to Qalat now.

He stumbled towards the conference room, coughing as dust and smoke seared his throat. He almost bumped into a figure in bloodied clothes who looked dazed and confused.

It was Naqvi, one of Director Khalid's security operatives.

'Vizur,' he said, with the kind of mild surprise one might expect when bumping into an acquaintance in the street. 'What has happened?'

Qalat almost backed away in shock. 'Your arm, Naqvi.'

Frowning, Naqvi looked down at what remained of his right arm, which now ended just below the shoulder in a stump of ragged flesh, snapped bone and shredded clothing. When he glanced up at Qalat again, he opened his mouth to speak but couldn't seem to find the words.

Qalat supported him as the big man's legs gave way and he slid down the wall, already going into shock.

'Rest, my friend,' he said. 'I must help the others.'

Pushing past the dying bodyguard, he emerged into what had once been the conference room. One look was enough to confirm the bomb had done its work, reducing the plush meeting space to a horrific charnel house of smoke, fire, destroyed furniture and human remains. Anyone lucky enough to survive the blast would soon be killed by fire and smoke inhalation. The smell of burning wood and plastic was underpinned by something far worse – the scent of scorched flesh.

Throwing the phone used to contact Cain into a pile of flaming debris, Qalat turned away from the gruesome sight, already making to join the other surviving embassy staff who were evacuating outside.

–

Cain slipped the phone back into his pocket, satisfied that at least one problem had been handled. He hoped for Qalat's sake that once he was appointed interim ISI director the man made good on their agreement, otherwise their working relationship would prove to be short-lived indeed.

'This is close enough,' Cain decided, recognizing their location. 'Pull over here.'

As the car pulled over, Cain took a deep breath. One problem resolved, one more to take care of.

Chapter 57

The junction of Friedrichstrasse and Zimmerstrasse in central Berlin wouldn't have meant much to anyone born outside the city, and in truth it had no inherent geographical or strategic significance. It commanded no high ground, controlled no vital road or rail links and faced no important buildings.

It was much like any other busy thoroughfare in that thriving European city – the air filled with the sounds of car engines, music, ringing cell phones and excited conversation, the nearby cafés and restaurants still in the tail end of the lunchtime rush.

In most respects there was little to differentiate it from any other street in the Freidrichstadt district.

Apart from one thing. It was standing in the centre of the street: a little wooden hut, painted off-white, barely big enough for two men to sit comfortably inside. The kind of modest, unassuming structure one might find in the corner of a suburban garden. And above it, in stark black lettering, was a sign:

US ARMY CHECKPOINT

The location might have held no real significance, but 50 years of Cold War history had endowed this place with an almost legendary status: one of the focal points of that great, terrible, inspiring, wasteful and ultimately pointless struggle.

It was here that visitors to East and West Berlin were able to cross between the Soviet and American occupation sectors – from one world into another. It was here that US and Soviet tanks faced off in October 1961, the world holding its breath as the two superpowers came within a hair's breadth of going to war. It was here that dozens of desperate civilians tried to flee from the east, many losing their lives in the process. And it was here, in November 1989, that the Soviets finally bowed to overwhelming pressure and opened the gates for good, ending five decades of division and ultimately the Cold War itself. The USSR would dissolve barely two years later.

Crossing the street, Cain glanced over at the group of students posing in front of Checkpoint Charlie, flanked by a pair of military policemen – one in American fatigues, the other scowling behind a Russian uniform.

They weren't real, of course. Just actors hired to play the part, soaking up money from tourists who wanted a cool Facebook update. The checkpoint hut wasn't real either. The original structures had long since been demolished or transferred to museums. All that was left were fading memories and tacky souvenir shops.

The coffee shop he was approaching had once been named Café Adler – a legendary haunt for hard-bitten journalists, unscrupulous diplomats, and even the odd spy, if the rumours were to be believed. A dangerous place, an exciting place; a place that made one feel alive just by visiting it. Back in the days when Checkpoint Charlie had been more than just a replica guard house and a couple of lousy actors in ill-fitting uniforms.

Now the café and its colourful history were gone, replaced by yet another bland chain serving generic coffee and cakes that had been made in a factory days earlier. How things changed, he thought.

'Alpha team is Oscar Mike on left flank,' a voice said in his ear. 'We'll cover you.'

'Negative,' Cain replied. 'All teams hold the perimeter and stay back until I say otherwise.'

'You'll be going in unprotected. We can't cover you from out here,' Hawkins warned.

'It's my call,' he said. 'Stand by.'

With that, he reached up and switched off his concealed radio transmitter. What he had to say next was for Anya only. Nobody else was going to listen in.

Opening the door, he was greeted by the usual smell of roasted coffee beans, elderly tourists in unfashionable clothes and pompous-looking idiots tapping away at their laptops.

None of these interested Cain, however. He'd already found the two people he was looking for, seated at a table near the far corner of the room. He angled towards them, feeling like he was in a dream, his steps slow and deliberate.

Anya and Lauren watched as he approached, their expressions mirroring their very different reactions to seeing him.

In Lauren he saw a mixture of relief and trepidation. She was frightened, but holding it together. Good girl, he thought. She'd always been strong and level-headed, just like her mother, never one to lose it in a moment of crisis.

He looked her up and down, quickly checking for signs of injury or mistreatment. Aside from a minor graze by her right temple, there was no outward sign that she'd been harmed. In that regard, at least, Anya had kept her word.

Satisfied that Lauren was safe and well, Cain finally turned to the woman herself, taking his first proper look at Anya in eight years. There had been a time when he'd known every curve, every line, every angle and feature of her face, which he'd truly believed the most strikingly beautiful he'd ever seen. She embodied both strength and vulnerability, wisdom and innocence, joy and sorrow.

He had ached to see her again.

Outwardly, the woman was not so different from the Anya he'd met all those years ago. Her features were a little harder and more definite, with fine lines around the eyes and mouth that hadn't been there before, but physically she had changed little. It was what lay behind her face that was different. A lifetime of fighting and sacrifices had wrought their changes upon Anya's soul. And Cain was acutely aware how much of that was down to him.

She was sitting with one hand on the table, the other hidden from view. It almost certainly held a weapon of some kind. She tensed a little as he drew near, readying herself.

Cain pulled up a chair and sat down. Two enemies opposite one another, with just a couple of feet of worn, coffee-stained tabletop between them.

–

Hawkins stood on the other side of the road, watching the scene unfold through the window. He could see Anya with such clarity that he felt he was sitting right beside her.

He dearly wanted to be in Cain's position. Had he been, he was quite certain the entire situation would have been resolved already, and he felt a surge of frustration and resentment that Cain was the one to face her. A bureaucrat who had never fired a weapon in anger, never killed, never looked into a person's eyes as the life faded from them.

What a waste.

Anya deserved to be killed by a fellow soldier. She deserved to be killed by him. Whatever their rivalries, Hawkins and Anya were bound by their professional mastery of killing, and he'd have loved the chance to go head to head with her. He'd had that chance in Istanbul last year, and the few minutes when they'd faced off had been glorious, but they'd been interrupted before either could prevail.

'Bravo team, make sure all exits to that building are covered,' he said. 'I want this perimeter airtight.'

'Copy that, we're in position. All entrances and exits secured,' the team leader responded. 'Nobody's getting out of there without us seeing.'

Hawkins didn't share his confidence. Anya was planning something – of that he was sure. And since he'd been prevented from taking offensive action, the only choice was to dig in and wait.

Feeling a pair of eyes on him, he glanced around to find a young boy. Asian, by the looks of him, no more than 10 years old. A scrawny little shit whose clothes looked too big for him.

'Fuck off, kid,' Hawkins advised. 'You don't want to be around for this.'

Suddenly fearful of the big, intimidating figure, the boy backed away and fled.

'Delta, where are we on surveillance?' Hawkins asked, resuming his work.

'Traffic cams are up. We've got full coverage of all roads in and out of that area,' Javadi reported, his voice slightly distorted by range. 'We're backtracking now, trying to find how and when they arrived.'

That would take time, he knew. Time they might not have.

'What about cameras in the coffee shop? Can you get us an internal view?'

'Afraid not. If they have them, they're not accessible online.'

Hawkins clenched his teeth. 'Keep looking. Call out when you have something.'

–

For the first few seconds, neither of them said a word or moved a muscle, as if fearful that the slightest action would provoke a violent response.

In the end, it was Lauren who made the first move, reaching out and touching her father's hand. It had been a long time since she'd done something like that, and for a brief moment the simple gesture took Cain out of their dangerous situation.

'It's going to be okay, honey,' he said, watching Anya as if she were a cobra that might strike at any instant. 'I told you I'd come get you. You've been so brave, but it's almost over now.'

'Dad, I'm sorry,' Lauren said. 'I had no idea, about any of this. The work you did, the people you were involved with...'

'It's all right,' Cain promised her. 'None of that matters now. What matters is I'm here, and I'm going to take care of this.'

'Anya told me some things, Dad.' Lauren's voice was stronger now, more assertive. 'About what happened between the two of you.'

'Did she really?' Cain asked, eyeing Anya as he imagined the kind of lies she might have tried to spin.

Anya remained silent, just as she'd done since his arrival.

Lauren shook her head vehemently. 'It's not like that. I understand why you're angry now, why you're set against each other. It doesn't have to be like that. You can stop this.'

'We'll talk about this later, Lauren,' Cain said firmly. 'Once this is over.' His attention switched to Anya. 'I'm going to ask my daughter to stand up and walk out of here now. And I'm asking you not to stop her.'

Anya shifted position. 'And what do I get in return, Marcus?'

'You get me,' he said simply. 'That's what you wanted, isn't it? That's why you came after me in Pakistan, why you've gone through all this. Well, here

I am. You don't need Lauren any more.' He leaned a little closer. 'She's an innocent kid. Let her go.'

Anya said nothing for a while. Whether she was trying to decide or whether she was just enjoying making him wait, he couldn't be sure.

But finally, mercifully, she nodded.

'Go on outside, Lauren,' he said, turning to his daughter. 'There will be some men there waiting for you. Go with them, they'll get you to safety.'

But Lauren could see the look on his face, and on Anya's. 'Dad, please don't do anything—'

'It's okay. Nobody's going to do anything stupid.' His eyes flicked to his adversary across the table. 'Anya and I are just going to talk. Now go on. Please.'

The young woman hesitated a moment longer. Then, giving his hand a final squeeze, she stood up and ran outside, leaving Anya and Cain alone.

—

Not far away, Alex sat hunched over his laptop, staring intently at the screen as he clicked through the various surveillance cameras overlooking the coffee shop. After figuring out the security protocols of the system firewall, he'd been able to hack into Berlin's traffic camera network.

His digital vantage point allowed him to observe their enemies far better than he could with his naked eyes.

'Anya, heads-up. I count at least five men on the street near the coffee shop,' he said quietly.

It hadn't taken him long to spot familiar figures amongst the hustle and bustle of passing pedestrians. Men who were loitering for no good reason other than waiting for an order to storm the coffee shop and kill Anya.

'I count six,' Yasin chimed in over the radio net.

'You're sure?'

'I have been watching passers-by, and I am close,' Yasin assured him, his voice hushed. 'Six men do not belong here.'

Alex switched feeds, finding one that looked into the access road and courtyard behind the coffee shop.

'I've got another four at the rear. I guess they've been sent to cover the exits.'

He was no tactical expert, but Alex understood the basics of their plan – box Anya in, close off all avenues of escape until the time was right to strike. If she tried to flee, she'd run straight into a wall of guns. If she stood her ground, she'd be condemned to a battle she couldn't win.

Either way, she lost and Cain won.

Alex inhaled, his breathing tight and constricted, his heart racing. He could only imagine what was going through Anya's mind as she sat face to face with her bitterest enemy.

'Hope you know what you're doing,' he whispered, then watched as Lauren emerged onto the sidewalk, feeling relief mingled with sadness.

He would probably never see her again.

–

Just as her father had promised, a man was waiting for Lauren outside the coffee shop. A big man, dressed in casual clothes. But his manner was anything but casual. He advanced across towards her purposefully, elbowing his way past a couple of pedestrians moving in the opposite direction. As he drew close, she noticed an ugly scar marring one side of his face.

'Lauren, my name's Jason. I'm here to get you out of here,' he said, throwing an entirely unconvincing smile as he took her firmly by the arm.

'I'm not leaving my dad,' she protested, trying to turn around. 'Not until he's out of there. Not until he's safe.'

The pressure on her arm increased.

'That's not your choice,' he said as he led her over to a parked car. 'Don't make me ask you again.'

Chapter 58

They had come to it at last. The moment was upon them. Cain had played this meeting in his mind a thousand times, pondering what they would say, what they would do, which direction their encounter would ultimately take.

And now that they were finally here, he felt at a loss. How could one sum up their history of regrets, mistakes, accusations, misunderstandings in just a few sentences? Where to begin?

'I have to commend you on your choice of venue,' he said finally. 'Always a student of history. I guess you'll appreciate a place like this.'

A waitress, spotting the new arrival, had come over to take Cain's order. Recognizing the need to keep up appearances, he'd ordered a cappuccino.

'You know, back in the old days I actually made a point of visiting the Berlin station just to come to this café. Can you believe that? They did the best cappuccinos and apple strudel I've ever tasted.' He took a sip of his coffee; it was bitter and burnt. He set it down again. 'But it wasn't really the food that brought me back. It was the feeling you got when you walked in through that door. Being right here, on the front line, knowing you were just yards from the Soviet sector. It was like… electricity in the air. You knew history was being written all around you. Every word being spoken, every movement, every glance at a passer-by; it all meant something. Now…' He drew his eyes up from the unpalatable beverage to the fake checkpoint outside. 'Now it's a different story.

'I guess a lot of things have changed since then,' he continued. 'We played a different game, but at least we understood the rules. At least we knew what we were fighting for. Hard to believe now, right? Like those World War One soldiers who put down their guns and came up out of the trenches on Christmas Day, just because it seemed like the decent thing to do. Some dumb relic of a different age.'

He looked at the woman seated opposite him, who had been watching his entire monologue in silence, her icy-blue eyes never leaving his.

'Is that what we are, Anya?' he asked. 'Relics?'

She didn't answer right away. At moments like this, she always allowed the silence to hang in the air for just a little too long, knowing her adversary would feel compelled to fill it – and might just end up saying more than they'd intended. He knew this because he'd trained her to do it.

A lifetime ago. When the street behind him had still been divided by a grim concrete wall topped with barbed wire. When he'd still believed in what he was fighting for.

So he waited patiently for her response. He'd been waiting a long time for this moment; a few more seconds wasn't going to hurt.

'I didn't come here to reminisce about the "good old days", Marcus,' she informed him coldly. 'Neither of us were ever that young, or that idealistic. And those days you miss so much? They weren't so good for me.'

Her tone remained firm and even, but Cain had seen what she'd tried so hard to hide. The emotions behind her mask of self-control. The glimpse of the young woman he'd once known. The pain of the betrayal she still felt.

'So why are you here?' he asked. 'Did you come to kill me, finish what you started in Pakistan?'

Anya surveyed him across the table. Giving nothing away, as always. To casual observers, Anya no doubt appeared a model of cool, focussed attention, but Cain knew her better than that. Perhaps more than any other person on this earth, he could see through her facade to the soul that lurked inside, and what he saw would have given the bravest man pause for thought. He could practically feel the years of repressed anger radiating from her like the heat of a furnace.

But he could also see something else. Sadness, grief for what had been lost, mourning for what might have been.

'I am not here to kill you,' she said.

'Then what do you want, Anya?' Cain pressed. 'Ever since you got out of that Russian prison three years ago, you knew this moment was coming. You've killed everyone else who stood in your way. Every dead body you left behind was just another step in the road leading to me, and now here we are. So I'll say it again. What do you want?'

He saw the pain in her eyes, the fury at his betrayal, the agony of a life robbed of meaning.

'Why, Marcus?' she asked in a voice close to breaking. The voice of the young woman he'd sat with on that beach, staring out across the shining waters of the Pacific and imagining a future together. 'Why did you turn against everything we believed in? Why did you turn against me?'

Cain felt like their surroundings had faded away. Seeing Anya like this, seeing the damage he'd caused revealed to him at last, he felt a sudden upwelling of pity. And something else – he felt ashamed. Ashamed that he'd allowed it to happen, that he hadn't fought harder to get her back. That he hadn't been there to save her.

But no sooner had these emotions formed than darker, more powerful thoughts rose up to overwhelm them. Anger that she had lied to him. Rage that he'd had to give up so much to undo the damage she'd caused.

Long-suffering frustration that he was the only one who truly understood what it had taken to keep her alive.

'Betray you? Is that what you think I did?' he asked, shaking with the effort of keeping his anger under control. 'I *protected* you, Anya. All those years, I kept your past a secret, I covered up your lies. The Agency would have *killed* you if they'd found out who and what you really were, but *I* stopped them. I ruined careers and destroyed lives for you. You never saw it, you were never aware of it, but I fought for you.'

Anya didn't say a word, just sat there listening as the flood of words and emotions came pouring out.

'Even after everything that happened in Afghanistan, even when I realized the Anya I once knew never really existed, I still cleaned up your mess, and I got myself so dirty in the process that no matter what I do, I'll never be clean again. So hate me if you want, but don't *ever* accuse me of turning against what we both believed in, because at least I was honest about it. At least I really did believe in it once. What did *you* ever believe in?'

He saw Anya's right hand clench into a fist. Her left was hidden from view, still gripping a concealed weapon, but it didn't matter. What mattered was the reaction his words had provoked.

'You're lying,' she said, still filled with that same self-righteousness.

Cain did something even she hadn't expected. He leaned forward in his chair, staring hard into the eyes of the woman he'd once known so well.

'Am I?' he challenged her. 'You're the one who knows the truth about people. You're the one who can read them like an open book. Tell me now, am I really lying to you?'

Anya stared back at him, and once again he saw a chink in her armour exposed. She hadn't expected this. She'd become so used to seeing him as an enemy, she'd never imagined dealing with him any other way.

'Why?' she asked then. 'Why would you do all that for me?'

Cain let out a breath, some of his fury dissipating as he thought back to that hospital ward in Pakistan 20 years ago. The image of that wretched, emaciated, scarred and broken young woman would be etched into his mind until his dying day. Even now, the thought of his Anya lying there like that was enough to break his heart.

'Because I saw what you'd gone through,' he said, his voice quieter now. 'What they did to you in Afghanistan... it should have killed you, Anya. It would have killed anyone else, but somehow you made it back. I knew how hard you'd fought, how much you'd sacrificed, and I couldn't bear to see them kill you for it.'

With a slow, deliberate movement he reached into his jacket pocket, seeing her ready herself in case it was a weapon.

'Remember when you gave me these?' Cain asked, laying Anya's dog tags on the table. The old chain rattled as it hit the wooden surface.

Anya stared at the tags with haunted eyes, slowly reaching out and lifting them, turning them over in her hand. The metal was faded and dulled with age, but the marks stamped into them were still legible.

'It never got better than that night,' he said sadly. 'The whole rest of my life. It's been empty without the woman who gave me those tags. Even if she was a lie, she was real to me. And I would have died to protect her.'

Anya let out a ragged, painful breath.

'She was real to me too,' she said softly. 'And I believed as she did.'

Just for a moment, Cain sensed the scales starting to tip, that his words were making their way through the layers of anger and hatred and bitterness, and he felt his heart quicken in the knowledge that he was close to reaching her.

Just for a moment.

'But that young woman is gone now,' Anya said, regaining her self-control. Shutting him out. 'She died in Afghanistan, and so did the things she believed in. Now I'm all that's left.' She looked up at him, her eyes hardening. 'I made mistakes back then. I don't deny it, but I paid for those mistakes. What did you do? You say you protected me, but you protected yourself first. Everything you did was to serve your own interests. You released me from prison in Russia so I could kill the enemies you couldn't reach, settle old scores with old rivals. You let me fight your battles for you, while you clawed your way into power. Well, your enemies are gone now – all except one.'

Her left hand had moved just a little, perhaps getting ready to draw the weapon she had hidden beneath the table. Perhaps ready to kill him at that very moment.

He should have felt afraid, but he didn't. All he felt was disappointment.

'Careful what you do. Enough wars almost started at this spot,' Cain urged her, indicating over his shoulder, where two of his men were stationed on the sidewalk. Their weapons were hidden, but both were keeping a wary eye on every movement Anya made.

He was quite certain a soldier of Anya's calibre would have spied them already, but it didn't hurt to remind her of her situation. Four more agents armed with concealed submachine guns were stationed on the other side of the street, ready to intervene, not to mention electronic surveillance and covert operatives covering the building from every conceivable angle, from snipers and spotters in neighbouring buildings to ground and mobile units standing by.

For all his forlorn hopes of reaching a peaceful resolution, Cain had come expecting war, and wars demanded an army.

'Wouldn't want all these innocent people to get hurt in the crossfire,' he added. The café was busy with civilians, easily 20 or more, from old couples enjoying a quiet coffee to a group of young tourists, to a tired-looking family with a pair of kids squabbling over a slice of cake.

None of them aware that a battle could erupt around them at any moment.

–

In the makeshift command centre at Potsdamer Platz barely half a mile away, Javadi was poring over security camera footage from around the café, frantically searching for evidence of their enemy's arrival.

He found what he was looking for. Anya and her hostage Lauren emerging from a parked van, along with a very unlikely pair of accomplices. One was a young boy no more than 10 years old, the other a soft-looking civilian.

The boy quickly darted off, and Anya and Lauren left for the café shortly after, but the man climbed back into the van. Javadi scrolled rapidly through the footage, waiting for the van to depart or the man to leave, but neither happened.

And as playback caught up with real time, he realized that Anya's accomplice was still in the van.

'All teams,' he said into his radio. 'Be advised, we have possible suspect and getaway vehicle on site.' He quickly reeled off the location and a description of the van.

It didn't take long for Hawkins to seize on it. 'Copy that. Delta team, move in and take him down. Everyone else, stand by.'

Chapter 59

Alex had been listening in on the exchange with Cain in shocked, awestruck silence, stunned by the raw emotion and deeply buried grudges that had been unearthed. He couldn't say whether Anya had intended for him to hear all of this, whether he should have cut the feed, but either way he'd listened, spellbound.

However, it was clear that their verbal sparring was nearing its end. The tension was becoming unbearable.

'He's telling the truth, Anya,' Alex whispered into his radio mic. 'The place is sealed up tight as a drum. If you start shooting, it's going to be a fucking slaughter.'

Yasin concurred with his assessment. 'The men outside are ready to move.'

She didn't reply. Alex knew she wouldn't, but he had to warn her anyway. It was the only thing he could do.

'Whatever you're going to do, do it now.'

–

Anya's expression changed then, her smile cold and merciless. Reaching up, she unzipped her jacket to reveal what Cain immediately recognized as a Kevlar vest. Hardly surprising considering the odds she was facing, but the vest itself wasn't what he was looking at – it was what she'd strapped to it.

A pair of anti-personnel mines were fixed to the front of her vest, their distinctive curved plastic cases painted a drab olive green. Russian in origin, he'd have guessed MON-50s or some derivative. He knew them well enough – the Soviets had scattered tens of thousands across Afghanistan two decades earlier, many of which had been recovered by Anya and her comrades for use against the very troops who'd planted them.

He knew a lot about these weapons – enough to be certain that the two strapped to her were more than capable of killing every living thing in the room.

The hand that Anya had kept hidden beneath the table now moved into view, but it wasn't holding a blade or gun. It was an electronic detonator, the conducting wire hidden inside the sleeve of her jacket.

'Recognize this?' she asked Cain. 'It's a negative pressure trigger, just like the Agency taught us to build, and it's armed. The second my finger slips off it, the device detonates.'

Rising calmly to her feet, Anya held her arms out wide, allowing everyone a full view of the makeshift suicide vest she was wearing.

'*Allahu Akbar!*' she called out loudly. '*Allahu Akbar!*'

The screaming started within seconds as the café's patrons recognised the words that had been plastered across internet forums, news broadcasts and magazines for years, and panic set in. People scrambled for the exit, desperate to escape.

–

'Oh, shit!' Hawkins heard over the radio net as the rooftop spotters reacted to the scene unfolding in the café. 'She's wearing a suicide vest!'

He was moving in seconds, drawing his weapon as panicked civilians spilled out of the café.

'Talk to me,' he said into his radio. 'Anyone got a shot?'

'There's too many people in the way,' his sniper leader replied. 'Can't get a clean shot without killing civilians.'

It took Hawkins about half a second to make his decision. 'Fuck them.' He'd long since stopped thinking of civilian casualties in terms of the grieving families he'd be creating. 'Sniper teams, you are weapons free. Drop the hammer on that bitch.'

No sooner had he issued this instruction than Cain's angry voice came over the radio. 'Belay that order!' he snarled. 'All units hold back! Nobody moves an inch unless I say so.'

Hawkins' pace slowed, until he had come to a stop facing the café. From this range he could see Anya quite clearly through the windows. A single well-placed shot would be enough to take her out.

'What are we doing, boss?' the operative beside him hissed, torn between the conflicting orders and trying to decide which man he feared most.

Hawkins gritted his teeth. 'Hold your position.'

Javadi's voice crackled in his ear. 'Got emergency calls going out all over the place,' he said, urgent voices calling out in the background. 'Everyone with a cell phone is trying to get the police on the line.'

'Can you shut them down?' Hawkins asked.

'Not for long.' Hawkins could hear him working manically at his keyboard. 'You've got three or four minutes, tops, before the Berlin police start to mobilize.'

–

Several blocks away, in a car fighting its way through busy Berlin traffic, Lauren Cain reacted in horror as reports from field operatives played out through the encrypted radio unit mounted on the dash.

'*She's wearing a suicide vest!*'

She heard the voice of the man who had bundled her into the car. '*Talk to me. Anyone got a shot?*'

'*There's too many people in the way. Can't get a clean shot without killing civilians.*'

'*Fuck them. Sniper teams, you are weapons free. Drop the hammer on that bitch.*'

'Oh my God,' she breathed, realizing that not only was her father in mortal danger, but that the men he'd employed were cold-blooded murderers, happy to kill innocent people to take down their target.

Everything she believed in seemed to be unravelling. Her father knew who they were, what they were, and he'd sent them anyway. Because those were the kind of men he used. Those were the things he did.

Alex had been right.

'Take us back,' she pleaded.

'No way, ma'am,' the driver said. 'I've got orders to get you out of here.'

'Screw your orders!' Lauren shouted. 'That's my father back there!'

'I don't give a shit, kid,' he replied, his polite veneer slipping. 'You're coming with me.'

Lauren's next move was one of desperation. Waiting until they were obliged to slow by congestion, she suddenly threw open her door and bolted from the vehicle.

'Help!' she screamed, sprinting away even as the driver jumped out in pursuit. 'Someone help me! That man's trying to kidnap me!'

She didn't know if anyone would believe her, much less have the nerve to challenge the intimidating-looking operative, but it might just give her the edge as she ran, darting between the startled pedestrians and heading back the way she had come.

Back to her father. Back to Anya. Back to Alex.

–

'We're live,' the technician said, checking the video footage being streamed via his laptop. 'The boss isn't streaming the feed yet, but we're broadcasting.'

Riley smiled. 'Good. Let me know when he tunes in,' she instructed, then paused as another idea occurred to her. 'Oh, and Sharpe?'

The man glanced up from his screen.

'Record the whole thing. I'll want to watch it back later.'

Drake heard the rasp of a knife being drawn, and watched as Riley revealed a blade that was hooked so that it appeared bent almost at right angles. Clearly this was no conventional weapon, but rather a tool intended to inflict a specific trauma and suffering.

'You like it?' she asked, turning it slowly so that its edge gleamed in the glow of the work lights. 'It's a gelding knife – a little gift from Jason. He said I'd know what to do with it.'

Drake imagined a woman with her penchant for torture would figure it out pretty fast.

'Now I've got to admit, I've never used one of these bad boys before, so my work might be a little rough. But we've all got to start somewhere, right? How else are we supposed to learn?'

She was taunting him, making him sweat, trying to accomplish psychologically what she couldn't do physically. Drake held her gaze even as she lowered the blade towards his groin.

'Do us both a favour and use it on yourself first,' Frost said in disgust. 'And spare us the "little girl acting tough" bullshit.'

Riley approached Frost. 'You've got balls, I'll give you that,' she decided. 'Not the kind I can use this knife on, obviously, but balls all the same.'

Reaching out, she ran her hand gently down Frost's cheek as if she were caressing a lover, while the knife strayed lower, tracing the contours of her breasts and snagging occasionally on her T-shirt. Frost glared at her, forcing herself not to move, not to show fear or revulsion.

'You know, that's something I really like in a girl,' Riley whispered, leaning closer as if to kiss her.

Then, suddenly, she seized a fistful of Frost's hair and yanked her head back, bringing the blade up to her face.

'Another thing Jason told me about this knife,' she hissed as Frost started to struggle. 'It's real good for removing eyes. The trick is to get the angle just right, then you can sever the optic nerve and scoop the eyeball out in one piece.'

'No!' Drake shouted, trying to rise, only to be kicked back down by the man behind him.

'He tries that again, put one through his kneecap,' Riley ordered the operative.

'Count on it,' the man replied, disengaging the P90's safety.

Riley allowed the blade to stray closer to Frost's left eye, the tip just touching her cheek. 'Tell me, how are those big brave balls of yours now?'

Frost was forcing herself to stay quiet, knowing how badly the young operative wanted to do it. Drake could see her trembling as the blade crept closer, millimetre by millimetre, knowing at any moment it would start slicing and gouging soft and vulnerable flesh.

Chapter 60

The last of the terrified customers were shoving their way out the door and spilling into the street, where their panic was rapidly spreading to others. Like frightened sheep flocking together, people began retreating in both directions, most having no idea what they were running from.

Only one of the café's serving staff remained. A gangly kid of no more than 18 with greasy skin and a wispy goatee, he was cowering behind the counter, stupidly pressed against the wall. He'd been paralysed by fear when the others fled.

'If you value your life, I would leave now,' Anya said to him, gesturing towards the exit.

Finally that seemed to push him into action. Vaulting clumsily over the counter, scattering a plastic cabinet full of cookies, he tore across the room and out the door.

Only Cain remained, still seated at the table, watching Anya with shrewd contemplation. 'Clever,' he acknowledged. 'I thought you'd have something up your sleeve.'

'We have nothing more to say to each other, Marcus,' Anya said, taking her seat once more. 'We came to make an exchange. You have your daughter, I want Drake and Frost.' She held the detonator up a little higher. 'Now.'

Cain looked at her.

'Of course,' he said, taking out his cell phone.

Rather than making a call, however, he accessed a live stream from a web camera. It showed two people kneeling side by side in a poorly lit construction site, their heads lowered, hands bound behind their backs, their clothes ragged and bloodstained. A man and woman.

Even on the slightly grainy digital image, Anya recognized Drake and Frost.

'Where are they?' she demanded.

'Not far. And they're safe, for now.' Cain was clearly not going to give her more than that. 'But one word from me, and you get to watch them executed live over the internet. If you blow the bomb, same deal. You're not the only one who can rig a dead man's trigger.' He paused for a moment, allowing the threat to sink in. 'On the other hand, if you give yourself up peacefully, I promise you they'll both be allowed to go free. That's my offer – take it or leave it. It's that simple.'

Anya burned with fury, the realization dawning that he still held the upper hand. Cain was holding the only people she still cared about, and anything except her total compliance would mean their immediate deaths.

'There's no sense in prolonging this. You've shown me your hand, and I've shown you mine. You've got no more cards to play. Fold.'

She didn't make a move, didn't take her finger off the trigger.

'Tell me, how did you imagine this playing out?' he asked. 'Did you really expect me to let you just walk away? Come on, Anya. We both know how this has to end. The place is surrounded. You're outgunned, outnumbered and out of options. This is one game you're not going to win.'

He was expecting her to capitulate. Even if it went against her nature, even if she would rather die than surrender, she had to know that here, at last, she was beaten. Out of time and out of choices, the only thing left was to admit defeat.

But she didn't. Instead, Anya's lips parted in a faint, ironic smile. She was about to reveal her winning hand.

'That's what you still don't understand, Marcus,' she said quietly. 'I didn't come here to win. I came to get even.'

Chapter 61

For an agonising couple of seconds, Riley held the blade beside Frost's eye, not moving or blinking. Just listening to Frost's rapid breathing, watching the fear course through her.

'What do you think, Drake?' She called out. 'Jason was big on giving you choices, so I'll let you decide. Left eye or right? If you won't choose, I'll just go ahead and take both of them.'

But Drake didn't try to bargain or plead for his comrade's life. His reply, when it came, was measured.

'I don't need to decide,' Drake said. 'You've already lost, you're just too stupid to know it.'

Riley looked at Drake, realizing he was no longer glaring at her in impotent rage, no longer cowed and fearful for his comrade's safety.

The dumb bastard was either bluffing, or he'd just lost it and no longer appreciated the reality of his situation.

'You know what? I've changed my mind,' she said, glancing at the gunman covering both prisoners. 'You can go ahead and take out his knees. But leave his balls intact – I'll take care of them myself.'

The man brought the silenced submachine gun up to his shoulder, the laser sight colouring the back of Drake's knee as he squeezed the trigger.

The muted thump of the silenced round was followed by the soft crunch of tearing flesh and splintering bone. Yet Drake didn't scream in agony. Instead, the man covering him jerked suddenly, as if struck by lightning, then suddenly went limp and collapsed to the ground with blood and brain matter painting the floor in a wide spray to his right.

At almost the same instant, a second silenced round took down the technician, spinning him around so that he fell onto his side, with what was left of his brains seeping out onto the dusty concrete.

Riley reacted immediately, grabbing Frost and yanking her to her feet while hooking the knife around her throat. Her eyes swept her surroundings, desperately trying to locate the source of the deadly gunfire.

'Hold your fire!' she called out, her voice now sounding empty and frightened as it echoed around the vast space. 'I'll fucking kill her, I swear!'

'Bad move, little girl,' a German-accented voice replied. 'Then I'll have no reason not to kill you.'

Drake watched as a figure emerged from his cover in the shadows behind a support pillar. Tall and rangy, with dark hair and a grim, severe face that seemed quite at home in their gloomy surroundings. Grey-blue eyes stared down the sights of his silenced MP5-K submachine gun, which was now trained on Riley, the red dot of its laser sight illuminating her forehead. Smoke still trailed from the barrel.

Riley bared her teeth, tightening her grip on the knife. 'Who the fuck are you?'

'We're the cavalry. And you're fucked.' A second aggressor appeared to Riley's right, similarly armed. A younger man, with buzz-cut blonde hair and a short beard, wearing black tactical gear and a Kevlar vest.

Riley held her ground, constantly turning and moving to disrupt their aim, her eyes briefly flicking to the camera that was still recording her actions. Maybe she could hold out until her plight became obvious and backup was dispatched. The younger of the Germans quickly put paid to that notion, moving over to the camera and powering it down.

'I won't tell you again,' the dark-haired man threatened. 'Put it down. Maybe you'll live through this.'

Riley however had no intention of surrendering, and brought the knife in to slit Frost's throat, fully intending to take her hostage down with her.

A single silenced gunshot rang out. Riley screamed and staggered backwards, blood flowing from her injured arm. The blade clattered to the floor as she rounded on her enemies again, only to find a pair of automatic weapons staring back at her.

'Secure her,' the dark-haired man growled. 'And take her comms unit.'

As the younger operative roughly shoved Riley to her knees, his comrade drew a knife. 'Saving your ass is becoming a full time job, Ryan,' he said, sawing through Drake's restraints. 'I'd say I'm due some *good karma* after this.'

In better circumstances, Drake might have laughed. 'Karma' was their code word for the emergency rescue operation to recover Drake and Frost. During their brief phone conversation the previous day, Drake and Anya had communicated their plan using a carefully agreed system of words and coded phrases, starting with karma, all of it designed to coordinate his rescue with Anya's endeavours.

'Never thought I'd be glad to see your ugly face, Dietrich,' Frost remarked.

Jonas Dietrich had been a necessary member of their team when they'd first been sent to recover Anya from a Russian prison. With a long-standing grudge against Drake and a bad attitude to match, he'd done little to endear himself to the others, even if his knowledge of Russian jails had been vital to their success. He'd since proven to be a useful ally, if a reluctant one, and today had been no exception.

'The feeling's mutual, Keira,' he said. 'Maybe you'd prefer I left you here.'

'Shut up and cut me loose.'

The second member of their rescue team called over from the laptop. 'Our jamming signal worked,' he reported. 'I don't think they saw what happened.'

'Who's the kid?' Frost asked, rubbing her neck where Riley's knife had nicked the skin.

The blonde-haired operative glanced at her. 'The "kid" has a name,' he said. 'It's Schaeffer. You can call me Mr Neumann.'

'I still have some friends in the BND,' Dietrich explained, referring to the German intelligence service he'd served with before joining the Agency. 'Schaeffer here is young and stupid and eager for action. In short, he was perfect for this mission.'

Schaeffer gave Dietrich the finger as he finished up his work. 'I've looped the webcam footage. It won't fool them for long, but it should buy us some time. Luckily your friend here decided to record the whole thing.'

He cast a disparaging glance at Riley, now on her knees with her hands cuffed behind her back, blood flowing freely from her upper arm.

She looked up at them and spat contemptuously on the ground. 'How did you—'

'How did we find you?' Dietrich finished for her. 'Luck.'

Stepping forward, Frost reached for the lucky charm necklace Riley was still wearing. 'You won't be needing this now,' she said, holding it in front of Riley's face for a few seconds.

Riley had never thought to look for it, but a miniature tracking device had been implanted into the necklace, which Drake had activated the moment he'd slipped it on. The signal it broadcast had immediately been relayed to Dan Franklin in Washington, allowing him to track Drake's movements. Dietrich had been tailing him ever since, waiting for the right time to make their move. Waiting for Cain to expose himself.

'Couldn't have done it without you,' Drake added, relishing her look of crushing disbelief as the full weight of her mistake settled on her.

'Doesn't make any difference,' she decided, regaining her nerve. 'That bitch of yours is still going to die.'

'Only one bitch is going to die today,' Frost snarled, snatching up a sidearm from one of the dead operatives.

'No! We need her alive,' Drake said, stepping in front of Riley.

Frost looked ready to hit him. 'Bullshit. I want her.'

'We need her alive, for now,' Drake said, before turning to Dietrich. 'Where the hell are we? How far is Checkpoint Charlie from here?'

Dietrich stared back at him. 'That's not the plan, Ryan—'

'How far!' Drake demanded.

The German operative chewed his lip. 'Three blocks south-west. But this is crazy, you're in no shape to go—'

Drake ignored him, picking up the P90 that had belonged to his former captor, as well as Riley's gelding knife. 'Get to the rendezvous point. I'll meet you there.'

'Hold on one goddamned second,' Frost protested. 'If you think I'm letting you do this alone—'

'I have to finish it. Now get the hell out of here!' he ordered her.

'Just kill that bastard, Ryan,' Frost pleaded. 'End this.'

Chapter 62

Three of Hawkins' operatives closed in on the van, still parked at the edge of a grassy play area where Anya had left it. The few civilians in the area quickly scattered at the sight of the guns.

Checking the driver's cab and finding it empty, they closed in on the rear doors. With one hanging back to provide cover, the other two moved quickly, knowing they could be spotted by the occupant at any moment.

Utterly focussed on the confrontation in the café, Alex didn't even see them coming. Not until a soldier gripped the handle, paused to glance at his comrade, then yanked the door open.

The two men stopped in their tracks, staring at the webcam in the middle of the van's cargo area, pointing straight at them.

On a rooftop a hundred yards away, Alex was alerted by a bleep from his laptop, and a new window opened on his desktop. He was almost amused by the confusion and disbelief on their faces.

Cain's men weren't the only ones capable of hacking Berlin's security camera network – Alex had just got there first, looping the footage from the camera covering his van. His exit from the vehicle had passed unnoticed by Javadi, who believed he'd found his man. It was soon to prove a fatal mistake.

'Sorry, lads,' he said, reaching for the remote detonator Anya had given him. 'Missed me.'

Anya had taken two of the Russian anti-personnel mines with her, but the third was sitting in the back of the van, pointed towards the doors.

A flick of the switch resulted in a brilliant flash, followed by a thunderous boom and a pall of white smoke that enveloped the entire vehicle. The men closest to the blast were killed instantly, their bodies shredded by hundreds of steel ball bearings, while the third died moments later as the vehicle's fuel tank ignited, further adding to the destruction.

The assault team was gone.

–

Cain tensed, startled by the explosive boom that rattled the café's windows. It had come from no more than a couple of hundred yards away, the noise of the blast echoing and reverberating off nearby buildings.

He looked at Anya, caught off balance. Something had changed. He hadn't expected this, hadn't planned for it. Her body language told him that whatever moment she'd been waiting for had finally arrived.

'Remember what I told you once, Marcus?' she said. 'I'd rather die for something than live for nothing.'

With that, she held up the detonator.

'No!' Cain shouted as she released the trigger.

–

Hawkins was thrown to the ground as the front of the café disintegrated in a maelstrom of smoke and dust and flying debris. The men around him dived for cover behind parked cars and kiosks, some struck down before they could get to safety.

The roar of the explosion was loud enough to trigger car alarms and shatter windows a hundred yards in every direction, raining broken glass down on the assault team. Seconds later, the cloud from the destroyed café engulfed everything.

Coughing the smoke and dust from his lungs, Hawkins strained to see through the murk, knowing as he did so that it was a futile effort. Anya had triggered her suicide vest.

She was dead, and she'd almost certainly taken Cain with her, sacrificing her life in a final, bitter act of vengeance.

–

'Oh, God,' Alex gasped, staring at the expanding cloud of smoke that had engulfed the street below, accompanied by frightened screams and the blare of car alarms. Most civilians had been clear of the blast radius, but there was no telling who might have been hit by falling glass and other debris.

He shook his head, his ears ringing.

'Anya, come in,' he said into his radio.

Nothing but static.

'Anya, do you hear me?' he repeated, slamming his laptop closed and hastily packing away his gear.

There was no response.

'Yasin, can you see anything?'

'Nothing,' the boy replied, coughing as the dust cloud reached him. 'The café is gone. What do we do now?'

Anya's instructions had been clear, as much as he hated to obey them. 'We stick to the plan,' Alex said. 'Get to the rendezvous point. Go now!'

Chapter 63

'Come on, princess,' Dietrich said, shoving Riley roughly ahead of him as the group rushed to the ground floor of the building, where a van was waiting for them. 'Don't give me an excuse to hurt you.'

Riley winced as her injured arm took most of the impact, her hands now cuffed behind her back. 'You know you're wasting your time, right?' she hit back at him. 'Drake's probably been killed already, and the three of you won't be far behind. They'll find you. They always do.'

'No, we found *you*,' Schaeffer corrected her. 'And you're going to tell us everything you know about your asshole employers.'

'I'm not giving you jack shit. Might as well kill me now and save us all some time.'

'You're not afraid?' Schaeffer asked. 'You should be. The little one looks like she has all kinds of hurt in mind for you.'

Riley raised her chin defiantly and pulled hard against the handcuffs. Her hands were narrow and slender, but the cuffs had been ratcheted up tight. Getting out was going to mean dislocating her thumb and causing a fair bit of damage to the skin and muscle around it. These things could be put right later, but that wouldn't make the experience any more pleasurable.

'After the shit I've seen and done?' she said truthfully, managing not to cry out as she felt the joint finally yield to the relentless pressure and pop out, the cuffs slipping free. 'You people are pussies by comparison.'

The group halted as a distant, thunderous explosion echoed across the city.

Frost glanced at Dietrich. The blast had come from where Ryan was headed.

The distraction was just what Riley had been waiting for. She lunged towards Schaeffer, her hands now free, even as Frost cried out a warning and turned her gun towards the prisoner.

Schaeffer brought his weapon up to defend himself, but he was too late. Riley's hand shot out, with the steel cuffs wrapped around it, landing a blow to his windpipe that immediately collapsed his trachea. He opened his mouth wide to scream, but no sound emerged.

Even as the German began to fall, Riley yanked something from his Kevlar vest and tossed it to the ground.

'Grenade!' Dietrich shouted, throwing himself clear of the weapon's blast radius.

Frost twisted aside and closed her eyes just as the flashbang detonated, the concussive boom echoing around the enclosed space like the pealing of thunder.

When she opened her eyes, spots of light pulsed across her vision. Her ears were ringing, leaving her temporarily deafened and disoriented.

She glanced down at Schaeffer, saw him lying unmoving on the ground and knew he was dead. She had to find Riley and kill her before she escaped.

Raising the weapon, she stumbled past Dietrich, who was only now starting to recover from the grenade blast. She didn't bother speaking, since neither was capable of hearing the other.

Instead, she made for the far end of the room, where scaffolding and plastic masked the empty windows. Silhouetted against the bright daylight filtering through the plastic sheeting was the blurred outline of a figure sprinting away.

Raising her weapon, Frost paused briefly to take aim and fired. She barely heard the bark of the weapon in her hands, but she certainly felt the recoil that jarred up her arm. Adjusting her aim slightly, she fired again, and again.

Her target fell forward and disappeared from view.

Frost ran towards the window ready to empty the remainder of the Glock's magazine into her target. But she found only a gaping hole ripped in the protective sheeting.

And 10 feet below the billowing strips of torn plastic lay a Berlin street.

'Goddamn it,' she whispered.

Chapter 64

Opening her eyes slowly, Anya coughed and shook the dust and glass out of her hair, taking a look at her surroundings. The world was one of smoke and fire and dust, the café devastated by the blast.

Yet she lived, and her survival was no miracle.

The two anti-personnel mines strapped to her chest were nothing more than empty casings, intended to create the impression of a suicide vest. She had removed the plastic explosive the night before, fixing it to key points on the café's outer walls so the majority of the explosive force was directed outwards.

To an observer, it would appear she had annihilated herself and the building, while in reality she had emerged almost unscathed. She'd been thrown to the ground by the force of the explosion, hit and cut by flying debris, and her injured ribs blazed with renewed pain. But she was alive.

She had bought a few precious seconds to escape. Now was the time to use them.

The heavy wooden table had protected her from the worst of the flying shrapnel, but it had been upended by the force of the detonation and its collapsed remains were now blocking her exit. Anya reached up to push it away, straining to shift the considerable weight.

Even as Anya fought to free herself from the wreckage, something emerged from the smoke and flying sparks, like a demon come to claim her. His clothes were torn and darkened with soot, his face bloodied.

'You planned all of this,' Cain said. 'Everything you did, every person you killed, all of it brought you to this moment.'

Anya turned away, looking desperately around for her carry bag, seeking the compact UMP-45 submachine gun.

There!

The bag had shifted in the blast, but lay just feet away now, partly ripped open to reveal the weapon's stock. She stretched out towards the weapon.

Cain watched her as he approached, knowing he had the advantage now. Knowing he could take his time.

'You said you would rather die for something than live for nothing,' he said, drawing an automatic from inside his jacket. 'Is this what you're ready to die for, Anya?'

She was almost there. Her fingers brushed against the canvas bag; she could almost pull it towards her, so close but infuriatingly far.

'You were right,' Cain said as she kicked frantically at the table, gaining a few meagre inches. Straining towards the weapon. 'In the end, it did come to the two of us.'

He raised the gun, taking aim with deliberate precision. Anya's eyes turned on him, knowing she had lost. The eyes of a cornered animal, hunted down and awaiting its fate.

'It was always between us,' Cain said, staring down the sights. 'The things we could have done together,' he whispered.

Cain held her gaze, the automatic pointed right at her, his finger resting against the trigger. Then he did something even Anya had never expected. He lowered his gun and tossed it aside, as if it were a toy that no longer held his interest.

Anya let out a shocked gasp. Finally heaving the ruined table aside, she scrambled for the submachine gun, tugging it from the canvas bag and turning it on her enemy.

'What are you doing?' she demanded, pressing the safety catch off.

'You came here to kill me,' Cain said, taking a step towards her, all anger and animosity gone. 'Well, here I am. Take your shot. Finish your mission.'

Anya watched in disbelief, her heart pounding, the air searing her throat. 'Why, Marcus?'

It would have been easy to kill him if he'd been a threat. She could justify that. But why had he thrown his weapon away?

He took another step towards her across the rubble-strewn floor. 'Because I'm through fighting you. I'm through hunting you.' He opened his hands, giving her a clear shot. 'You asked me to prove what kind of man I am. This is who I am. The question is, who are you?'

'Stay back!' Anya shouted.

'What are you afraid of? Afraid you don't have what it takes to pull that trigger?'

She knew she should do it. She knew she *had* to do it, not just to avenge the countless innocent lives Cain had sacrificed, but also to protect those he might yet claim. She knew this, yet she couldn't pull the trigger.

The gun began to shake in her hand.

Standing so close the barrel of the weapon was almost touching his chest, Cain looked sadly at the woman he'd once been willing to give his life for.

'There are still things we could do together, Anya,' he said. She saw hope rise within him as he whispered, 'It's not too late.'

She could feel it then. The person she'd once been: the idealistic, impulsive, vibrant and passionate young woman who had died in Afghanistan. Anya felt her stirring once more, felt the same longing, the same desire to be part of something larger than herself.

To share that future with someone who truly understood her.

Anya lowered the weapon slowly, and for an instant she saw Cain relax, knowing what it meant.

Just for an instant.

Sweeping the weapon around, she struck a glancing blow to the side of Cain's head, sending him off balance.

She retreated to the doorway leading to the kitchen, and halted there just as he looked up, his face just discernible amidst the swirling smoke and the glow of flames.

'Don't come looking for me, Marcus,' she said. 'Let this go. Please.'

She slammed the door shut behind her, reached for the nearest shelf laden with food and equipment, and toppled it over, blocking the entrance. It wouldn't hold for long, but it might give her enough time to escape.

–

Riley darted along the sidewalk, bloodied and furious, shoving angrily past anyone barring her way. Unarmed, there was little she could do but withdraw, much as she would have liked to go back and settle the score.

In any case, she had bigger issues to attend to now. She could make out a pillar of smoke several blocks away. The situation was spiralling out of control, and she was too far away to influence it.

Spotting a young man trying to record the aftermath of the bomb blast on his cell phone, she changed direction and took the phone from his hand.

'*Hey! Was ist das?*' he demanded, even as she sprinted away.

'Fuck you!' she snarled at him, struggling to hold the device in her injured hand while jabbing in a number with the other.

It was answered before the second ring.

'It's me,' she said. 'They found us. My team's down, and Drake's on the move. I repeat, he's coming for you!'

–

Several blocks away, Hawkins ignored the groans of injured operatives around him, listening intently as Riley's report was relayed to him over the secure radio net.

'Copy that,' he said, relieved at least that Riley had escaped the ambush. He'd protect her from any recriminations. 'All units, be advised that Drake is no longer secure. Repeat, he's loose and he's inbound. If you value your lives, watch your backs.'

Hawkins returned to the battered shell of their SUV and seized the M4 assault rifle hidden in the passenger footwell.

He would have loved to find and kill those responsible for Drake's escape, but that would have to wait. Let Drake come, he thought.

'Christ, the boss is gone,' he heard someone say over the radio. 'She killed herself to take him out.'

The smoke was starting to clear, revealing the shattered building.

'Hold up,' Hawkins said, stopping in his tracks. 'All units, be advised target is still active.'

'Say again? She was wearing a suicide vest.'

'The blast damage is on the *outside* of the building,' he said, staring at the blast holes. 'She set the explosive charges there to make it look like a suicide. It was a distraction to keep us occupied while Drake escaped.'

He began to run, his weapon up and ready. 'All units, converge on the building now! Spotters, you got anything?'

'Nothing from up here. Too much fucking smoke.'

'Switch to thermal imaging, concentrate on the rear exit. She'll try to break that way.'

'Copy that. What are our rules of engagement?'

He leapt through the shattered shell of a window. 'I want her alive. She's mine.'

Chapter 65

Stumbling through the storeroom at the rear of the building, Anya pushed her way into a corridor, heading for the rear delivery door. Beyond it lay a service alley that, with luck, would be lightly guarded after her apparent death.

She was hurting as her various injuries took their toll, but she forced herself on with the iron will that had carried her through so many battles before.

Kicking open the door, she drew out a flashbang grenade from inside her jacket and tossed it into the alleyway, ducking behind the wall and covering her ears as it detonated. She followed this with a smoke grenade, hoping it might help obscure her escape.

As the grenade began to spew clouds of chemical haze into the narrow alleyway, Anya raised the UMP-45 to her shoulder and advanced, sweeping the weapon left to right in search of targets.

No hostiles. Move!

She'd covered about 10 yards before something slammed into her right side, followed almost immediately by a second impact. It felt like a pair of iron fists had just pounded into her body.

Straightaway she knew they were rubber bullets. Non-lethal, intended to subdue her. She'd been ambushed!

Gritting her teeth, she swung her weapon around and sighted the first target advancing on her with a shotgun up and ready. She saw his arm move as he worked the pump action, chambering the next round.

Anya opened fire, barely taking the time to aim. The powerful .45 calibre submachine gun chattered in her hand, the recoil jarring her arm as he went down, blood flying from several critical wounds.

She was about to rise again when something stung her upper arm. An instant later the electrodes discharged, paralysing nerve endings and robbing her of muscular control.

Anya fought desperately to swipe the twin prongs away and end the torment. Her finger tightened involuntarily on the trigger, sending a long burst of automatic fire thumping into the walls and ground around her as she went down.

'Tango down! We've got her!' she heard a voice call out. 'Keep hitting the bitch. Don't take any chances.'

She saw dark-clad soldiers coming from both sides, at least five or six of them, and knew then that there was nothing more she could do. Cain's men must have anticipated her move, must have realized how she planned to escape.

She had failed in her final effort.

Gloved hands hauled her up, dragging her towards the far end of the alley. Anya tried to resist, but could manage nothing more than feeble flailing as her body refused to obey her instructions.

That was when she heard it. The thump of silenced automatic gunfire, followed by the soft, wet crunch of bullets impacting flesh. The man carrying her suddenly cried out and stumbled backwards, blood pumping from half a dozen gunshot wounds.

Chaos erupted then. Anya's captors shouted in urgent, panicked voices, punctuated by bursts of gunfire and chilling screams.

Through blurred vision, Anya saw a man she recognized, who had thrown himself right into the midst of her captors, taking advantage of the smoke and confusion by getting in close so that their superior firepower meant nothing.

Even after witnessing acts both heroic and terrible on countless battle-fields over two decades, Anya had never before seen such a spectacle. He was everywhere and nowhere at once, a whirl of knife strikes and gunshots that no weapon seemed to touch and no man could stand against. The one-sided struggle lasted only seconds, but it was perhaps the most gruesome and frenzied assault she had ever witnessed.

Only when the last operative fell to the ground, his neck sliced open by a distinctive curved knife, did her saviour finally relent.

In shock, Anya stared at Drake, breathing hard, splattered with both his own and others' blood, seemingly unconcerned by his injuries. He was surveying the dead men lying at his feet, as if viewing the grisly results of his work through the eyes of another.

Only when his attention rested on the woman lying in their midst did he snap out of it.

'Anya,' he said, rushing forward to help her.

Anya threw her arms around Drake and pulled him tight, so tight that her ribs burned with pain, but she didn't care. Drake was alive. And he was with her.

'What... why are you... here?' she managed to say, still recovering from the taser burst. Why had he come? And what dark part of his psyche had awoken to inflict such carnage?

'Cain,' Drake demanded, pulling her to her feet. 'Where is he?'

'He's gone,' Anya said evasively.

Drake gripped her arm. Hard enough to hurt.

'We're not leaving until he's dead. Where is he?'

Anya twisted out of his grip. 'It's over. The police are on their way,' she said, the wail of distant sirens already reaching them. 'We have to leave now, Ryan! Please! This is not worth dying for.'

He tossed aside the blood-covered knife, the reality of their precarious situation breaking through the red haze of his fury at last.

'Stay close to me,' he urged, leading the way.

Chapter 66

Yasin was sprinting down the sidewalk, dodging between civilians trying to flee the scene and a few foolhardy souls trying to press forward for a better view of the deadly spectacle. He ignored all of them, intent on reaching the rendezvous point, where Alex would be waiting for him.

And perhaps, just perhaps, Anya.

He had no idea whether she'd been captured or killed in the blast, but he hoped she'd made it out. She was tough – tougher than any woman he'd ever encountered – and resourceful enough to evade her enemies. He refused to believe she'd been killed.

A hand grabbed him violently by his shoulder and spun him around. He twisted out of his opponent's grip, crouching low and preparing to lash out with fists and feet if he had to. Had one of Cain's men spotted him? Was some police officer who had connected him with the explosion trying to arrest him?

'Yasin! It's me!' Lauren cried out, holding up a hand.

'What are you doing here? You are supposed to be safe!'

'I heard the blast. I had to see it. My father… he was in the café.'

'Your father was not killed by the bomb. It must have been a fake, to cover Anya's escape.'

Lauren stared back at him. 'She's alive too?'

'Yasin, what the hell's going on?' Alex's voice crackled in his radio earpiece. 'Who are you talking to?'

Yasin ignored him.

'As far as I know she still lives,' he said stoutly. 'But I must leave this place.'

It took Lauren all of two seconds to make up her mind. 'I'm coming with you.'

'But—'

'No arguments,' she said firmly. 'Those men were going to kill all of you. If I'm with you, maybe it'll stop them.'

Yasin didn't like it, but he knew Lauren could likely keep pace with him even if he tried to escape. And he had to admit there was merit to her suggestion. If her presence afforded some form of protection, then it might be worth the risk.

'All right,' he decided at last. 'But do not slow me down.'

'Yasin, will you tell me what the bloody hell is happening?' Alex demanded again, his voice loud and urgent in Yasin's ear.

'Stop shouting at me! I have Lauren here with me,' Yasin replied.

'Lauren? What the hell is she—'

'Be quiet and listen,' the boy snapped. 'She wants to come with us. She thinks it will protect us.' He dropped his voice before adding, 'She will not be turned away, Alex.'

'Jesus Christ,' Alex breathed, clearly stunned. 'Okay, get to the rendezvous point now. *Don't* let anything happen to her, Yasin.'

Yasin concentrated on getting out of the area as fast as possible, but the sirens were getting louder and louder.

–

Hawkins surveyed the carnage littering the alley. Spotting something lying amongst the dead, he reached down and picked up a bloody knife. The gelding knife he had given to Riley.

'Son of a bitch,' Hawkins said. This was the kind of gruesome handiwork that had once been Drake's hallmark. His grip tightened on the weapon as his rage slowly rose.

Turning to the far end of the alley, he hesitated as he spotted movement on the far side of the street. It took him a second or so to process what he saw. Lauren Cain, barging and slipping through the confused mass of pedestrians, accompanied by a young boy.

The same boy he'd seen earlier, outside the café.

'Hawkins, what's your sitrep?' Cain demanded over the radio. 'Have you found Anya?'

Cain had sustained only minor injuries in the blast. His men had already shepherded the deputy director into an undamaged vehicle, to evacuate him before the police arrived, but he still had operational command.

'Hawkins, acknowledge!' Cain snapped impatiently.

Hawkins calmly pulled his radio earpiece out and stamped on it with his boot. He didn't want Cain or anyone else witnessing what came next.

–

'Goddamn it!' Dietrich swore as he forced their van between two cars, accelerating through a red light and ignoring the angry horn blasts.

'Can't this fucking thing go any faster?' Frost demanded from the passenger seat, burning with impatience. 'Why the hell didn't you bring a proper car?'

Dietrich shot her an angry look. 'Show me a Porsche that six people can fit into, and I'll start giving a shit what you think.'

Frost ground her teeth. 'Just get us there, Jonas!'

Chapter 67

Alex was sweating and short of breath as he turned off Anhalter Strasse, several blocks west of the café, staggering into a small courtyard behind a hotel. Most of the parking spaces were taken, but there was no activity as everyone crowded around windows, anxious to learn more about the explosion just a few blocks away.

This was their rendezvous point. Close enough to the café that each team member could make it there on foot, but far enough to avoid the quickly descending police cordon.

His heart pounding, Alex glanced around the courtyard, anxiously waiting for the others to arrive. There was no sign of Anya or Yasin – or Lauren.

He couldn't believe the young woman had opted to join them, turning against her own father, trusting them over the man who had raised her. What had swayed her? Why had she risked everything to join them?

'Yasin, come in,' he said, hearing only the wail of sirens. 'Yasin, are you there?'

'He's here, and so is his friend,' a voice replied, but it wasn't Yasin's. The voice that spoke was American, heavy with derision and malice.

Alex's head snapped around, and he stared in horror as Yasin and Lauren emerged from an archway. They had their hands up, their faces etched with fear as they edged forward, prodded by the armed man using them as human shields.

He was big; tall and broad-shouldered, his considerable mass bulked out further by a Kevlar vest. He was crouched slightly behind his prisoners to better protect himself, but Alex could see enough to recognize him.

It was the same man he'd encountered in Istanbul last year. The man who had tried to kill Anya, and come perilously close to succeeding.

'Alex Yates,' Hawkins said. 'Goddamn if you aren't the world's most persistent cockroach. First London, then Istanbul, now Berlin. You just can't get enough of this shit, can you?'

'Neither can you, it seems,' Alex said, trying not to show how frightened he was – not just for himself, but for his companions.

Hawkins smiled. 'It's my job. Not that I don't enjoy it at times,' he added. 'But you – you really are an enigma to me, Alex. At first I took you for some gutless keyboard warrior living in his mom's basement, then I figured you were just out to save your own ass. But I was wrong – I think there's something more to you. Be a shame to kill a man like you.'

Alex's mind had gone into overdrive even as Hawkins gloated. He still had the semi-automatic Anya had given him, but it was tucked down the back of his trousers. Hawkins was a trained killer, armed with a far more powerful weapon.

'I'm sorry, Alex,' Lauren whispered as Hawkins prodded her forward.

'Now Alex, you're lucky that I'm not here for you. Tell me where Drake and Anya are, and we can all go our separate ways without this having to get messy.' When Alex hesitated, Hawkins' smile faded a little. 'Don't make me ask twice, son.'

'You won't kill us,' Lauren said, rounding on Hawkins. 'You can't. My father ordered you to protect me.'

'Your father isn't here,' Hawkins reminded her. 'Nobody's going to save that pretty little ass of yours. Besides, you're not my only playing card.'

With that, he turned the gun on Yasin, who stood his ground, resolutely refusing to show fear.

'You scared, kid?' Hawkins taunted him.

'Leave him alone,' Lauren hissed.

Yasin raised his chin. 'This isn't the first time I've had a gun pointed at me.'

'Could be the last, though,' Hawkins remarked. 'I don't know who you really are and I don't much care. Right now you're the wrong guy in the wrong place at the wrong time. How wrong depends on what Alex does next.'

'Really?' another voice asked. 'I'd say Alex is the *least* of your worries now.'

Hawkins glanced over at the woman who had suddenly risen up from behind a parked station wagon, and who now had a weapon levelled at his head. Standing barely 10 yards away, there was little chance she would miss.

'Mitchell,' he said, recognizing her immediately. He was almost amused by the timing of her arrival. 'Now why would you get involved in this again?'

'I guess I'm just a glutton for punishment.'

Olivia Mitchell, a former Agency operative who had fallen foul of Hawkins' team in Istanbul the previous year, suffering near-fatal injuries in the process. Drake and his Shepherd team had rescued her from a hospital, barely managing to evade the field agents sent to recover her, before spiriting her away. Against the odds, she must have survived the ordeal – and now she'd come looking for payback.

'Put your fucking gun down,' she said as she thumbed back the hammer.

But, far from capitulating, Hawkins kept his weapon trained on Yasin. 'You kill me, I kill the boy,' he reminded her. 'Sound like a fair trade to you?'

'You really want to find out?' she challenged him.

It was all the delay he needed. In covering Hawkins, Mitchell had failed to notice another figure creeping up on her from behind, moving silently between the parked cars. Only when they leapt out did Alex scream a warning.

'Mitchell! Look out!'

Riley was on her in an instant, throwing a blur of kicks and punches that immediately overwhelmed Mitchell, making it impossible for her to bring her weapon into the fight. Unarmed and injured she might have been, but Riley was a formidable combatant at close quarters, and her assault was ferocious and unrelenting.

Hawkins, too, had turned towards the scuffle, ready to open fire on Mitchell while she was defending herself against Riley.

That was when Yasin, sensing his opportunity, charged at the man without hesitation, without even a thought for his own life.

'No!' Lauren cried out.

Hawkins saw the movement in his peripheral vision. He flicked the M4's fire selector to full automatic, braced the assault rifle against his shoulder and pulled the trigger.

A shape moved in front of him just as the rifle spat a thunderous burst.

Lauren stiffened suddenly, and looked down in surprise at the red stains spreading across her chest. She remained standing for a moment, as if her wounds had made no impact on her. Then slowly her legs crumpled beneath her and she fell, Yasin throwing himself forward to try to shield her.

Hawkins watched as she went down, the weapon still at his shoulder and empty shell cases smoking at his feet.

'Lauren!' Alex cried in horror.

Turning to her assailant, he drew the pistol from the back of his jeans and, face twisting in fury, opened fire.

The weapon kicked back harder against his wrist with every round, but he didn't care. He fired again and again, tears blurring his eyes, heedless of the danger. All he cared about now was killing Hawkins.

Rounds tore into the masonry around Hawkins, showering him with pieces of stonework, while another flattened itself against his body armour. Retreating into the archway as the frantic flurry of gunfire ran its course, Hawkins called out to his comrade.

'Riley, cover!'

Abandoning her furious assault on Mitchell, Riley ducked between a pair of parked cars.

The firing stopped, and Hawkins smiled to himself. The stupid bastard had wasted his ammunition without scoring any vital hits, and that rookie mistake was about to cost him his life.

Leaning out, Hawkins took aim as Alex tried to reach the woman lying sprawled on the ground. He would never make it. One burst in his torso would be enough to put him down. Maybe he'd even survive long enough for Hawkins to stand over him and watch his life fade away.

But no sooner had Alex crept into Hawkins' sights than a van tore into the courtyard, screeching to a halt between Hawkins and his target. A moment later, a door slid open to reveal Drake, Anya and a third man he didn't recognize.

He did, however, recognize the submachine guns in their hands, and immediately took cover behind the solid stone of the archway. The crackle of several weapons firing on automatic roared around the courtyard, deafening in its intensity.

'Alex, get in!' Anya screamed, struggling to be heard over the roar of the engine and the thunder of gunfire. 'Get in now!'

Alex, however, was making for Lauren, who was on her back, her blood staining the cobbles. Yasin was cradling her head in his lap, talking to her, trying to rouse her. But one look was enough to convince Alex she wouldn't be getting up.

She was gone. She was dead.

But still he tried to get to her.

Only when Mitchell sprinted over, grabbed him by the shoulder and hauled him into the vehicle did Alex finally abandon the effort. Anya, forced to leave the safety of the van to reach Yasin, paused only for a moment to look down at the young woman.

Within moments they were all aboard.

'We have to get to her!' Alex protested as Drake slammed the door shut. 'We have to help her.'

'You can't,' Anya said, shaking her head.

'We can't leave her here.'

'She's gone, Alex!' Anya shouted, even as the engine revved and the van lurched forward. She spoke forcefully, but he could see her eyes glistening with tears. 'You can't do anything for her. She's gone.'

Alex slumped against the van's side, ignoring the painful jarring as it rumbled over cobbles, ignoring the holes punched through the rear doors by automatic gunfire, forcing the others to flatten themselves against the deck. He glanced at Yasin, noting with a vague sense of detachment that the boy was crying too. He didn't even notice the tears running down his own cheeks.

A moment later they swung hard right out of the courtyard, merging into traffic heading south. Away from Berlin, away from the destruction and death they'd left behind.

They had made it, but at a terrible cost.

Part V

Conclusion

'Next to a battle lost, there is nothing so terrible as a battle won.'
– Duke of Wellington

Chapter 68

Cain took a deep breath as he opened the door. His daughter was lying on a table, covered up to her chest with a white sheet, her long dark hair flowing around her head.

His team had recovered her before the Berlin police could seal off the scene, spiriting her body away to a safe house outside the city. The news had reached Cain not long after, and he'd immediately diverted there, ignoring the danger, ignoring his own untreated injuries. None of that mattered now.

All that mattered was Lauren.

She looked so peaceful, as if she were only sleeping, he thought. Her skin was still warm to the touch. He half-expected her long lashes to part and her beautiful hazel eyes to look into his. But they wouldn't, he knew. Lauren would never smile, never laugh or cry again.

She was gone.

'Tell me what happened,' he said quietly.

Hawkins was lingering behind him. He still smelled of burned cordite. 'We were fanning out to search the surrounding areas when we heard shooting. I moved in to check it out, and that's when I found her lying there, with Anya and the others mounting an escape vehicle.'

'You're saying one of them killed her.'

'I can't think of any other explanation,' Hawkins said. 'They opened fire on me when I tried to intervene, and I returned fire as best I could. They were gone before I could stop them.' Cain heard a faint sigh of disappointment. 'I'm so sorry, sir. I—'

'You're dismissed, Hawkins,' Cain said, unable to listen to more. 'Give me the room.'

'Sir, are you sure you shouldn't—'

'Leave,' Cain said, without taking his eyes off Lauren.

He heard footsteps retreating, heard a door open and close behind him.

She had always been pretty, with a delicate face that still recalled the soft curves of youth. But looking at her now, lying silent and peaceful, Cain could see a hint of the woman she might one day have become.

She isn't gone, he thought, as if by sheer force of will he could undo what had happened. She isn't gone. Even if it was just for a moment, he needed to believe she was still alive.

Closing his eyes, he bent down and kissed her forehead. She isn't gone, he kept thinking, as he remembered the way she'd looked in that photograph on the beach. The look of joy and wonder and excitement on her face, and her radiant smile that made his heart ache. She was the most beautiful thing he had ever seen.

–

Grass, stretching away in front of her, the stalks reaching past her waist, swaying and rippling like an undulating sea in the breeze. Thin ribbons of cloud stretched across the vast blue canvas of the sky.

She crept forward through the sea of grass, driven by curiosity and the childish desire to explore. Ahead, near the crest of the gentle hill, lay a stand of trees, and instinctively she made towards it.

'Lauren!' a distant voice called out. Her father's voice. 'Don't stray too far!'

Lauren paid little attention to his warning as she walked beneath the gentle shade of the leafy canopy. It was a warm day, and she was grateful to escape the sun for a while.

She glanced around her little woodland haven, taking in the gnarled tree trunks, the tangled bushes and the swaying branches overhead. Then she spotted something on the ground ahead. Something that compelled the young girl to move closer.

A perfectly round hole in the ground yawned below her, partially covered by old wooden planking, tangled weeds and fallen leaves. Curious to see how deep the well went, Lauren leaned over the edge to get a better view.

The crack of rotten wood snapping was followed by a cry of fright as she pitched forward into the darkness.

Then suddenly she felt a firm hand around her arm, jerking her to a stop, pulling her back from the abyss.

Lauren looked up to see a pretty young woman with bright blonde hair, and eyes that were so blue that she couldn't help staring at them.

'You should be more careful,' the woman told her. 'It's dangerous to go off by yourself.'

'I'm sorry. I just… wanted to look.' She blinked, feeling embarrassed, and tried to change the subject. 'I'm Lauren. What's your name?'

The blonde woman hesitated before replying. 'No one important.'

'Lauren!' she heard her father call out. 'You okay up there?'

A strange look passed over the blonde woman's face.

'That's my dad,' Lauren explained. 'He always worries about me.'

'I can tell,' she said gently. 'You should go to him, let him know you are safe.'

She turned to go, then hesitated. 'What about you?'

Lauren saw a strange look of sadness and longing in the woman's eyes. 'I think I'll stay here a while.'

'Alone?'

'Some people are better off that way. Now go, be with your father.'

Lauren nodded, and was just turning away when the young woman spoke up once more. 'Lauren?'

She turned to look back.

'I think you will bring out the best in him.'

'Lauren!' the voice called again, closer now. 'Can you hear me?'

'I'm okay, Dad!' she replied, shouting back down the hill. 'I was just...'

When she glanced back towards the blonde woman, she saw nothing. She'd disappeared into the woods again. As if she had never been.

–

Only when he was alone did it finally hit Cain.

Grief and shock and anger and utter desolation swept through him, pushing away all rational thought as he broke down and wept. This young woman, this child of his, who had been so wonderfully, vibrantly alive only moments before, was lying dead in front of him. Her life had ended so abruptly that he almost couldn't make sense of it. It didn't feel real.

But it *was* real. And the woman responsible for Lauren's death was out there somewhere. The woman who had taken away the only thing left in his life that mattered.

When at last Cain had given into his grief, he raised his head, his tear-reddened eyes hardening with absolute resolve.

He would find Anya. No matter how long it took or how many lives it cost, he would find those responsible, and he would kill them.

He wouldn't stop until every one of them was dead.

Chapter 69

The group was exhausted by the time they reached Anya's home in Switzerland. Trailing slowly out of the van beneath a bright red and orange sunset, they were oblivious to the magnificent view before them.

Drake, numb and worn out, drifted from room to room, checking on each member of the unlikely team that had now assembled here. Even now he couldn't bring himself to let go of his responsibility.

Mitchell was in the living room, saying little while she tended to Frost's wounds. The young operative had protested that she was fine throughout the journey, but exhaustion and pain had finally caught up with her, and she'd fallen asleep on the couch. For once, Drake thought, she actually looked at peace.

Mitchell gave him a nod. 'Been a long time, Ryan,' she said, offering a weak smile.

'It is good to see you, Mitchell,' Drake said, genuinely meaning it. From what he'd been told, Olivia Mitchell had risked her life to help Anya escape from an ambush in Istanbul a year before, very nearly getting killed in the process.

Mitchell shrugged. 'I have you to thank for that. If you hadn't sprung me from that hospital, I'd be dead or in prison by now.'

It was a mission he hadn't thought much about in quite a while, just a favour he had done at Anya's request. Risking his team to save a woman he'd never met. And yet, he'd never once regretted it.

'You deserved a second chance, I think.'

Mitchell gave him a knowing look. 'Maybe we both do.'

Dietrich was standing nearby, staring out at the view. Drake felt the need to say something to him.

'Quite a view,' he remarked when Drake stood beside him.

'It is,' he agreed. Exhaling, he turned to face the big German. 'Keira and I would both be dead if it wasn't for you, Dietrich. You did well.'

'Not well enough,' he said grimly. 'Schaeffer's dead, thanks to me. A kid looking for a little action.' He shook his head. 'I wonder why they keep dying, and the old bastards like us linger on?'

Drake had pondered the same question many times, yet he still had no answer. Maybe it wasn't needed.

'For what it's worth, I'm sorry about Mason too,' Dietrich went on. 'He was a good man. I know that means nothing, but there it is anyway.'

He was wrong about that. It did mean something, but Drake didn't trust himself to respond.

'What will you do now?' he asked instead.

Dietrich sighed and looked around the room. 'Maybe I'll stick around a while, see if I can keep you and the others out of trouble.' He shrugged. 'If they'll have me.'

Drake nodded. He and Dietrich had a far from glowing history, though he respected the man for his actions today. And he sensed they would need every ally they could get in the battles that still lay ahead.

But those were concerns for another day. For now, he was simply too drained to think about it.

Yasin was sitting on a chair nearby, his knees drawn up to his chest. Drake recalled him putting on a facade of relaxed confidence, trying to seem older than his years, but that was gone now. He looked like what he was: a child, scared and shaken.

How and why this kid had ended up in Anya's care after Drake parted company with him in Islamabad, he had no idea. Anya would doubtless explain it later, but the fact remained he was here now.

Drake didn't know quite what to say to him, but he approached anyway, feeling a strange responsibility towards the boy.

'All right, mate?' he asked, kneeling down beside him.

He turned his big, liquid brown eyes on Drake. The look in them was heartbreaking. 'She died for me,' he said.

'What do you mean?'

'Lauren. I tried to charge at that man with the gun. He was going to kill me, but she stepped in his way. She died to protect me.' He swallowed. 'Why would she do that?'

Drake felt like a hand had reached inside his chest and closed around his heart. He knew who was really responsible for Lauren's death, and it wasn't Yasin.

'She must have been a good person,' Drake managed to say. 'She wanted to help.'

'And now she is dead.'

'But you're alive. Be thankful for that.' It was all he could think to say. 'Make the most of it, for her sake.'

He nodded slowly, and Drake stood up to give the boy some time alone. In truth, he needed to be by himself too.

–

Anya was outside. She'd found Alex sitting on the same patch of grass where they had spoken two days earlier. He had barely said a word during the journey, but she could tell Lauren's death had hit him hard.

'It will be dark soon,' Anya said, looking towards the setting sun. Already the temperature was starting to drop.

'I don't care.'

Anya sat down beside him. 'Do you want to talk to me about it?'

'She was never supposed to be there, Anya,' he said, his voice heavy with guilt and grief. 'Why did she come back?'

'I don't know. Maybe she thought she could help us. We will never know.'

'People keep dying around me,' he said, as if pleading with her to make sense of it. 'Most of them don't deserve it, but people like Cain and Hawkins are still here. Where's the fucking fairness in that?'

Anya felt a deep sense of grief and longing at the mention of Cain's name, which she struggled to contain. Instead she reached into her pocket and held something out to him. It was a set of dog tags.

Her dog tags.

'I promised you once this was all over that I would tell you where these came from,' she said. 'They belonged to my unit. We were deniable, expendable if we were caught, so we did not wear them in battle as most soldiers do. Instead we left them behind, with people we trusted and cared about. Those people would keep them if anything ever happened to us. And one by one, each set ended up with me. I'm all that's left now, Alex.' She sighed and looked up at the darkening sky. 'There is no luck, no right or wrong, no justice in who lives and who dies. The life we live isn't fair. All we can do is keep going.'

Alex said nothing. She knew he understood, and that was enough for her now.

There was one person she had yet to speak to.

—

Unable to be around the others any longer, Drake was in the basement. He was weary and hurting, but couldn't bring himself to rest. There was a fire of rage still burning that needed to be quenched.

He slowly circled the heavy bag, waiting for a moment before throwing a succession of left and right hooks, laying into it harder and harder until finally he backed away, breathing hard. He was sweating profusely, his injuries burning and stinging as it soaked in.

He didn't care. He wanted that pain. He needed it.

—

There could be no denying it now. Samantha had been working against them the whole time.

'No...' Drake said, looking at the floor to avoid Hawkins' triumphant smile.

'Women, huh? Never can trust them,' Hawkins said. 'Anyway, now we've got that out of the way, you and I have other business to attend to.'

He went in again, swinging hard, thudding his gloved fists into the bag over and over.

—

Hawkins pressed the gun against Mason's head. Drake's eyes met them in that final instant, seeing not fear but acceptance. And gratitude.

'No!' Frost screamed as Hawkins pulled the trigger.

The shot echoed around the room, drowning out Drake's cry of grief and agony as his friend slumped to the floor.

—

Drake's breathing was erratic, his punches growing weaker as he hammered at the bag with increasing futility. It swayed and lurched but remained upright as the broken, furious man vented his anger.

'Your punches are sloppy,' a voice chastised. 'I expected better from you.'

Drake felt his body stiffen as Anya descended the stairs. They had said little since their reunion in Berlin, the tension between them gradually intensifying as the day wore on.

Now that they were alone, it was magnified tenfold.

'I don't need company,' he announced.

She stared searchingly. 'You have been avoiding me, Ryan. Why?'

'You don't want to know,' he said, turning away and laying into the bag again.

She laid a hand on his shoulder and he whirled around, fists clenched. His look of wild anger simmered down quickly, but she'd seen it all the same.

Anya took a step back, as if resigning herself to some unpleasant fact. She turned away, and for a moment Drake thought she was going to leave.

Only when she slipped on a pair of lightly padded gloves did he see what she had in mind. 'What the hell do you think you're doing?' he demanded.

'If you won't talk to me, fine,' Anya said, tightening the Velcro straps. 'But you *will* listen. We have unfinished business, you and I.'

'Anya, you don't want to—'

He didn't get a chance to finish. Anya's left fist lashed out and landed a stinging blow on the point of his chin, snapping Drake's head back and almost causing him to lose balance. It was intended to get his attention rather than cause real damage, but the effect was the same.

Anya was hunched over slightly with her gloves up, muscles taut and ready for fighting.

'You owe me a round, Ryan,' she said, moving a step closer. 'Well, I want it. Now!'

'Don't try it,' he warned, though it took every ounce of his willpower to hold his anger in check.

Ignoring his warning, she swung again with a left hook that reopened a cut over his right eye. 'Fight me, you coward!' she snarled, laying into his midsection with a series of sharp body shots. 'Or are you afraid? Afraid of hurting me, or afraid I'll beat you – like I always have?'

That was it for Drake. Something snapped inside him. As Anya moved to attack again, he leapt in, batted her punch aside like he was swatting a fly, drew back his fist and slammed it into her face. He was wearing padded gloves that softened the blow to a degree, but it was delivered with such ferocity that Anya was knocked to the ground.

'Is this what you wanted?' he yelled, standing over her, shaking with fury. 'Is this enough for you?'

Anya looked at him, blood dripping from her nose.

'Don't get up. Stay down. I won't hold back next time.'

She was skilled in most forms of unarmed combat, but when it came to boxing there could be only one victor. They both knew that, but still Anya rose to her feet.

'You still don't understand,' she said, raising her gloves. 'I don't *want* you to hold back.'

Drake came at her again, drawing back his fist for another haymaker. Ducking aside, Anya lashed out with a right cross that sailed over his guard and caught him with a glancing blow across the cheek. She followed with a pair of hard strikes to the ribs that nearly doubled him over.

–

Yasin turned his big, liquid brown eyes towards him. The look in them was heart-breaking. 'She died for me,' he said quietly.

'What do you mean?'

'Lauren. I tried to charge at that man with the gun, tried to distract him. He was going to kill me, but she stepped in his way. She died to protect me.' He swallowed hard, his voice close to breaking. 'Why would she do that?'

–

'Is that all you've got?' she demanded. 'Get up, Ryan! Get up and finish this!'

Ignoring the pain and fatigue, Drake straightened up. They each lashed out with wild, brutal strikes, no longer giving any thought to protection. This was no longer about attack and defence, strategy and counter-strategy: it was a slugging match, pure and simple.

It was just a question of who could take more punishment.

'The things we could have done together, Anya,' he said, his tone one of profound regret. *'The things we could still do.'* She saw hope rise within him suddenly as he whispered, *'It's not too late.'*

She could feel it then. The young woman she'd once been: the idealistic, impulsive, vibrant and passionate young woman who had died in that prison in Afghanistan. Anya felt that young woman stirring deep within her once more, felt the same longing, the same desire to be part of something bigger than herself.

To share that future with someone who truly understood her.

–

They were both still swinging, but their blows were having less and less effect as fatigue set in.

Drake swung again, landing a clumsy punch to Anya's shoulder that almost knocked her off her feet. However, slowed by exhaustion and accumulated damage, he was unable to block the counterblow, and white light exploded across his vision as his legs threatened to give way.

But Drake still had a little left, and he laid into her with punch after punch. He could barely raise his arms to throw them, but his pent-up emotions drove him on, and Drake held nothing back.

–

Smoke and haze. Silent, faceless men with drawn weapons. Drake was running, stinging smoke and heat rasping his throat. A blood-red sun casting its glow on everything.

A blood red sun, growing stronger and darker. Growing black, absorbing everything, until the world was swallowed up around him.

Screams in the darkness.

–

Weakened and hurting and no longer capable of defending herself, Anya finally succumbed and fell to her knees. The fury and adrenaline that had driven Drake this far was leaving him now, and he collapsed beside her as he was swinging his last punch.

Bruised and bloodied, exhausted and broken, the barriers between them were finally gone. Anya clung to him, her head resting against his shoulders, and she did something she hadn't done for a long time. She cried.

She cried for the young woman who had died because of her, and for the old man who was alive because she couldn't bring herself to pull the trigger. She cried for the teammates Drake had lost. She cried for everything they had sacrificed, and for everything that might have been.

'I'm sorry,' she whispered. 'I'm sorry.'

Drake held her tightly, his eyes shining with tears. They sat there clutching each other, their bodies bruised and aching, their emotions spent. There was no need to speak now. It was enough to know that whatever awaited them, they would face it together.

Chapter 70

It was a sunny spring day in the capital, only a few white clouds drifting across the clear blue sky. The sun glinted on the Tidal Basin, looking out towards the great white columns of the Lincoln Memorial. A pleasant day to be out walking.

The weather was lost on Cain as he listened to the young woman, forcing himself to hear every word, no matter how difficult it was to accept.

'I wanted to tell you,' Anya said once she'd finished. She'd confessed everything: all of it, from the loss of her parents to her recruitment into the KGB, her eventual arrival in America and her induction into Task Force Black. It had all come pouring out. 'I wanted to, but I was afraid. I knew you would never trust me again.'

Trust, Cain thought bleakly. It seemed that neither of them had lived up to the trust they'd placed in each other. Everything that had seemed so certain and immutable had proven all too easy to destroy.

But if his personal life was in ruins, at least his career had gone from strength to strength. Freya, the mysterious woman he'd encountered just a few months earlier, had made good on her promise to turn his fortunes around. Mere days after Cain accepted her offer, Simmons had announced his resignation as director of Special Activities Division, citing a desire to spend more time with his family.

His regular visits to escorts had had nothing to do with it, apparently. But with the position vacant, Simmons had been good enough to recommend Cain for the role, resulting in his immediate promotion. From a minor case officer on the brink of resigning, Cain became a major player in the Agency.

But as with all good things, his rapid rise came at a cost.

Using a potent mix of bribes and promises, Cain had convinced Vizur Qalat not to reveal the devastating information about Anya's past, though Cain was motivated as much by protecting his own career as hers. If it ever emerged that he'd allowed a Soviet spy to infiltrate the CIA, everything he'd worked for would be lost.

Cain turned to look at her, standing in the midst of the cherry blossom trees overlooking the Potomac near the Jefferson Memorial. They were in full bloom as the world slowly returned to life after a long winter. Anya, too, had fought her way back from the brink of death after they brought her to a hospital in Pakistan – sick, terribly injured and malnourished.

Over the past few months she had regained weight, recovered most of her once robust health, and even started training again with her former zeal. But she was different now — older, more reserved, more distant. Some wounds never fully healed, some experiences could never be forgotten.

'And what would you have me do now?' he asked. 'Where are we supposed to go from here?'

Anya opened her mouth to reply, but the look of lingering sorrow and accusation in Cain's eyes stopped her. He didn't forgive her. Even after everything she'd said, everything she'd told him, he couldn't move past it. Whatever she'd intended to say, whatever vision of the future she'd still held on to vanished in that moment.

It was over.

She lowered her head, as if acknowledging that their chance had come and gone. 'I'm sorry,' she said, looking out across the bay as a breeze stirred the trees and cherry blossoms began to fall. 'I should have had more faith in you, Marcus. Maybe then you would have shown more in me.'

Cain wanted to respond, but a different voice spoke up. A woman's voice, with a British accent.

'But we do have faith in you, Anya,' Freya said, approaching from the Jefferson Memorial building, where she had been observing the exchange. 'That's why I'm here today.'

Anya regarded this new arrival as if she were a deadly enemy. Freya merely smiled that same dazzling, disarming smile that she'd offered Cain several months before.

The smile of a chess player about to take another piece.

'Who are you?' Anya demanded, her eyes flicking accusingly to Cain.

'My name is Freya,' she said. 'And I'm the reason you're not rotting in a prison cell right now. I came because Marcus spoke up on your behalf, said you were someone with great potential, and I'm inclined to agree with him.'

Anya's eyes narrowed. 'What do you want from me?'

'Want? I want to give you a chance the Agency never did. A chance to live up to your potential. We're going to do great things together, Anya.'

–

George Washington and Jefferson National Forests — 7 April 2010

Marcus Cain felt like he'd been living in a daze, still coming to terms with everything. Yesterday he'd buried his daughter, and today here he was, sitting by the banks of a river near a small cabin he maintained about a hundred miles west of DC. No guards, no protection, no intrusions.

Langley was still in crisis mode after the bomb blast in Islamabad. A memorial service had already been held for those lost, even before the inquests began.

Naturally, Cain had made sure that his own involvement was untraceable, so the current theory was that Quinn had overstepped his authority by neglecting to search the Pakistani delegation, allowing one rogue ISI agent to smuggle in a bomb.

Still, the loss had played right into the CIA's hands. Already there were murmurings of a crackdown on dissident elements within the ISI, and a new regime spearheaded by the only senior leader to survive: Vizur Qalat.

Cain heard his private cell phone ping. A message from none other than Qalat himself.

Congratulations, everything going to plan. You will have the information you sought within the week.

Cain felt nothing. No elation, no excitement at the victory that would soon be his. No victory could be worth the price he'd paid.

He heard a car pull up. It wasn't the kind of big 4 x 4 suitable for the difficult forest roads in the area, but a luxury Lexus sedan, its silver paintwork splattered with mud.

The door opened and Director Wallace emerged, glancing around at the trees and water as if the environment were alien to him. His demeanour lacked its usual brisk aggression, and for once he appeared almost sympathetic.

'Director,' Cain said. 'What brings you out here?'

'You turned off your work cell, not that I blame you. I came to offer my condolences for your loss,' he explained. 'I can't imagine what it must be like, losing a daughter.'

'I appreciate the sentiment, but I'll be back at the office next week,' Cain said, waving it off. Such platitudes meant nothing, and he sensed there was another reason Wallace had driven all the way out here. 'What can I do for you?'

Wallace looked at the ground before speaking. 'I was hoping to deal with this discreetly. That's why I came, to speak alone.' He paused. 'We are alone, right?'

'Nearest hunting cabin is five or six miles that way,' Cain said, pointing north. 'What exactly do we need to deal with?'

Wallace wasted no time sugar-coating it for him.

'I'm afraid I'm going to have to ask you to step down as deputy director, Marcus,' he said. 'There's no need to make a big deal of it. You can step down quietly, citing personal issues. Nobody would question it after what happened to your daughter. You can leave with full honour, but leave you must.'

Cain mounted the river bank, his hands trembling. 'May I ask why you're firing me, Director?'

Wallace flinched. 'Please,' he said. 'The truth is, I'm hearing rumours about Islamabad, Marcus. Rumours that you ordered Quinn to set up that meeting. Nothing definitive, but enough to start alarm bells ringing.'

'What are you saying?'

Wallace's face was growing redder. 'I'm saying you're too close to this whole goddamn mess, Marcus. Bombings in Islamabad, terrorist attacks in Berlin, and you at the centre of it. I don't know what you're involved in, but I can't have you in this agency any longer. I want your resignation letter on my desk by the end of the week.'

'And what if I refuse?' Cain asked.

'Come on, Marcus. You really want a war you can't win?' Wallace asked. His blood pressure was high; Cain could see the man straining to keep his cool. 'You're finished. At least go with some dignity.'

Dignity. Did the man really think that mattered now?

Cain sighed, then laid a hand on Wallace's shoulder. 'You could be right, Robert,' he conceded. 'I've been in this game a long time. Maybe too long, and maybe I've fought too many wars. But you know something I learned along the way?'

Wallace frowned, looking uncomfortable.

'Every war demands sacrifices.'

Grabbing Wallace by his shirt, Cain shoved him onto the damp, rocky ground. The director cried out in shock, but Cain's hand was over his mouth before he could make another sound.

Sitting astride him, Cain kept both hands over Wallace's face, preventing him from drawing breath. And as he held Wallace, watching the life slowly drain out of him, images of Anya, of Drake, of his daughter lying dead on a table, flashed through his mind. Cain's tears flowed as Wallace's frantic struggles eased, then stopped altogether.

His work finally done, Cain stood up, breathing hard, heart pounding, adrenaline surging. He took several deep breaths, felt his pulse begin to slow, then reached into his jacket and dialled a number from memory.

As always, it was answered promptly. A good soldier, eager to serve.

'Hawkins.'

'I need a clean-up crew. Reliable men,' Cain said, then gave his address and directions to the isolated cabin. 'And they have to move fast. The subject is time-sensitive.'

He believed what Wallace had said about having coming out here alone, but he was still the director of the CIA. His movements would be monitored, and any absence noted. Wallace's car and body had to be found far from here.

'I know someone, but men like that don't come cheap,' Hawkins cautioned. 'Neither does their silence.'

'I leave that in your hands. Just get them here,' Cain ordered. As if money was of any concern now. 'It has to look like an accident.'

That wouldn't be difficult. A highly stressed man in questionable health, driving a suburban car down muddy, winding forest roads at an unsafe speed... Cain could almost picture him suffering chest pains at the wheel, losing control on a tight bend and plunging down a steep hillside to his death.

There would certainly be questions to answer, and Cain didn't doubt that the spotlight would fall on him as the last man to encounter Wallace alive. But he knew such enquiries would ultimately lead nowhere. A good clean-up crew would erase all evidence of foul play, and when it came to answering questions he was well versed in the art of deception.

He had made a career out of distorting the truth.

'Copy that. I'm on it.'

Replacing the phone in his jacket, Cain walked slowly back to his spot by the river, and resumed his silent vigil while waiting for the cleaners to arrive. He paid Wallace's prone body not the slightest bit of attention, his thoughts having already turned inwards.

He had lost everything. All that remained was the war – and it was nearing its end.

One way or another, Cain would be the one to finish it.